Classic Sword & Sorcery

In the Tradition of Conan the Barbarian

NIALL

of the

Far

TRAVELS

Collection

D1715947

by Gardner Francis Fox

Originally printed in Dragon Magazine 1976 - 1981

digitally transcribed by Kurt Brugel 2017
for the Gardner Francis Fox Library LLC

Gardner Francis Fox (1911 to 1986) was a wordsmith. He originally was schooled as a lawyer. Rerouted by the depression, he joined the comic book industry in 1937. Writing and creating for the soon to be *DC comics*, Mr. Fox set out to create such iconic characters as the *Flash* and *Hawkman*. He is also know for inventing *Batman's* utility belt and the multi-verse concept.

At the same time he was writing for comic books, he also contributed heavily to the paperback novel industry. Writing in all of the genres; westerns, historical romance, sword and sorcery, intergalactic adventures, even erotica.

The Gardner Francis Fox library is proud to be digitally transferring over 150 of Mr. Fox's paperback novels. We are proud to present - - -

Table of Contents:

SHADOW OF A DEMON

Chapter One

He came into Angalore from the eastern deserts, a big man wearing a kaunake of spotted fur over his link-mail, his legs bare above war-boots trimmed with miniver, with a sense of his own doom riding him. Niall of the Far Travels had not wanted to come to Angalore, for an old seeress had prophesied that he would be taken from this world by demons, should those war-boots carry him into that ancient, brooding city.

Yet he had come here because his fate had so decreed.

He was a mercenary, a sell-sword, a barbarian out of the forested mountains of Norumbria. A wanderer by nature, he earned his keep wherever he went by the might of his sword-arm, by his skill with weapons. He feared no living thing, man or animal, though the thought of demons put a coldness down his spine.

Now he paused on the crest of a hill and stared at the city. Massive it was, and old, so old that some men said it had been here since men had first learned to walk upright. It lay between the river and the desert over which the caravans came from Sensanall to the south and Urgrik to the north. Ships lay in the little harbor that was formed by the river, riding easily to the lift and fall of its tides.

Angalore was the city of Maylok the magician.

An evil man, Maylok. Niall had heard tales about him, over campfires and in the taverns where men drank wine and watched dancing girls perform. Rumor had it that he used demons as men used pawns when they played their games of chance. Gossips also said that in the dungeons and stone labyrinths below his palace, Maylok had stored the treasures of his world, gold and silver, diamonds and rubies and emeralds, and golden vessels carved and fashioned by famous sculptors.

Niall moved his heavily muscled shoulders, uneasy as a wild animal might be, walking into strange country where it knew nothing of the dangers to be faced. Yet he had to go to Angalore. There was no way

4

out, if he wanted to eat and drink. The desert had offered no oasis, no plant from which to pull the roots to allay his hunger. He had been offered employment by a captain of mercenaries, and was on his way to join up with the black eagle banner of Lurlyr Manakor of Urgrik when he had been attacked by a huge mountain lion out of the Styrethian Hills. He had killed the lion but not before it had broken the neck of his horse.

On foot, he could never reach Urgrik. He had known that, and so he had set his feet to the westward, to reach the river that ran through these lands. On the river he might find a boat to carry him to Urgrik.

His wandering had brought him to Angalore, instead.

Niall hitched at his sword-belt and gave the city a hard grin. There would be food in Angalore, and cold wine. Niall had a need for both, maybe even a wench if he could find an agreeable one.

His feet carried him down the slope toward the landward gate. Niall was not a fearful man, nothing frightened him; still, that threat of demons made him wary. He was not one to put overmuch confidence in the babblings of soothsayers, but old Thallia was not your usual prophetess.

He had stumbled onto Thallia in Cassamunda, where he had met that mercenary captain. She was an old woman, clad in rags, but she carried a small bag that clinked as she moved, and two ruffians had tried to take it from her. Niall had been passing, had leaped to her protection, had buffeted the ruffians with his big fist and knocked them senseless.

Old Thallia had been grateful. Her bag held her wealth, such as it was, a few coins and some jewels which she kept by her to sell when she needed food. He had escorted her to the cheap little room above the tavern where she lived, and she had insisted on giving him some wine and a barley-cake.

She had read his fortune, too.

'Beware of Angalore,' she had whispered, her rheumy eyes wide and fear-filled. 'There are demons there, who serve Maylok the wizard. They will snatch you away with them when they come. And — there is no return from a demon world.'

The landward gate was closed, at this time of day, with the late afternoon shadows black and ominous. No caravans were expected in before the morrow, and guards stood their watch on the walls, half drowsing in the sunset. Niall stopped before the wall and shouted upward that he was a stranger in need of food and drink, and desired also a cot on which to lay his body.

After a time, a small door inset in a larger one creaked open. Two warriors wearing the griffin insignia of Angalore scowled at him suspiciously. Niall grinned and moved forward.

"There is a fee to be paid," one of them said, "It is after the hour when we admit travelers."

Niall shrugged. He had no wish to remain outside these high stone walls, knowing that inside them he would find what his belly told him he so desperately needed. His big hand fumbled at his worn leather belt-pouch, extracted a few coins, and dribbled them into the outstretched palms. The stink of bribery was strong in his nostrils, but beggars had little choice.

He moved off along a cobbled street, his eyes hunting a sign that might tell him where a tavern waited with its warmth and merriment. These buildings past which he walked were warehouses where were stored the goods that came by caravan, with no hint of roasting meat nor smell of chilling wine.

Niall had never been in Angalore before and so he lost his way, moving down narrow little alleys and into cul-de-sacs, always aware that his hunger and his thirst were growing with the darkness. And then in a narrow passageway between buildings which seemed to lean their walls together, he saw the girl.

She was clad in leather rags that fluttered in the wind moving off the river. Her long legs were brown and shapely, and the hair that fell almost to her haunches was black as Corassian ebony. She was turning her head to stare back at him, shrinking against the wall behind her.

Niall grinned. "You seem as lost as I am."

Green eyes studied him. "I am not lost. I know my way." She added, almost ominously, "To where I want to go."

"There's no need for hurry." His gaze took her in, seeing the tatterings of her worn leather tunic, its stains and spottings, the manner in which it failed to hide the curve of her breasts and revealed almost

6

the complete length of a bare leg. "Come eat with me, I'll pay the fare. And I'll give you as much wine as you might care to drink."

The green eyes softened, but her voice was cold. "Go your way, barbarian. Let me go mine..."

Niall shrugged. It mattered little to him whether she went with him or not, but she was pretty enough, with full lips and a tilted nose. She would have made a good bed-companion for the night. He might even have taken her to Urgrik with him and — if he could afford it — buy her some decent clothes.

He walked away, putting her from his mind.

And then he heard the clank of metal.

The Far-traveler turned his head. Behind him four men were moving out of a little alley toward the girl. She had seen them and was shrinking back, away from them. The men were grinning at her.

"Come along now," one said, putting out a hand to grasp her arm.

The barbarian turned and waited.

"No," she whispered. "I know you men. You serve Maylok."

"And Maylok needs female blood for his incantations."

They leaped, all four of them, and the girl disappeared behind their big bodies. Niall snarled and went on the run, not bothering to draw his sword. His big fist should be able to handle these carrion.

He caught a man, swung him about, drove knuckles against his face, pulping his nose. A second one he caught and rammed his head against the stone wall so that he went limp and crumpled.

The other two yanked out their blades, swung them at him. Niall laughed softly, put his own hand to sword-hilt and drew out Blood-drinker. The barbarian had little wealth, except for his sword, that had been forged long ago and far away and that Niall had found in a tomb which he had looted, early in his youth. He had been offered fortunes for that blade, he had always refused to part with it.

He fought swiftly and terribly, did Niall of the Far Travels. With parry and thrust and overhead blows he drove the two ruffians before him until their backs were to the building wall, and there he ran them through.

The girl had never moved, but stood erect and as coldly disdainful as ever. Niall felt surprise at sight of her, he was certain she would have run away when given the opportunity. He growled as he wiped his steel clean, "What are you waiting for? Why didn't you run?"

"You fool," she breathed. "You fool!"

She stamped her sandaled foot. Her cold anger beat out at him like a living entity, and the sell-sword stared. "Has Emelkartha the Evil stolen your wits? Or did you want to go with those men to be sucked dry of blood for Maylok's wizardries?"

Her eyes lidded over and she drew a deep breath. "You would not understand. You are only a common warrior. Besides, what do you know of Emelkartha?"

"She is the mother of demons, that one. I've heard it said that all demons regard her wishes as commands."

The girl shrugged. "I pray to her for vengeance."

"She ought to hear your prayers, then. She's malevolent, that one."

The green eyes glowed. "Is she, warrior? I hope so. Perhaps she will grant me my revenge on Maylok then."

He caught her bare arm, drew her with him. "Tell me about it. Mayhap I can help a little, though I've no fancy for wizards myself, and usually I stay clear of them."

She went with him readily enough, but cast a look behind her where two men were stirring and two others lay in pools of then-own blood. Was it only fancy, or did that face of hers mirror a faint regret?

"What's your name? Where are you from?" he asked.

The green eyes slid sideways at him from under long black lashes. "Call me — Lylthia. And — does it matter where I come from?"

"Not to me," he chuckled. "Are you hungry? Thirsty?"

His eyes ran over the cheap leather tunic that barely hid her body. She carried no money pouch, the only thing on her besides the tunic and her tattered sandals was a rope belt about her slim middle. As the river-wind grew cooler, she began to shiver.

"We'll get you into a warm tavern and put some meat in you," he said. "Also some Kallarian wine."

"Little good it will do you," she muttered.

Niall grinned. He had a way with wenches like this. Yet as he walked with her along the torch-lit streets, he failed to notice that while those torch flames cast his shadow, there was no shadow for the girl.

Chapter Two

The tavern was warm and noisy, filled with seafarers of the Aztallic Sea, with wanderers from the western lands, with mercenary warriors and with women who plied their ancient trade between the tables, to sit where they were welcomed and join in the feasting and the drinking. A great hearth held a huge log that blazed with a sullen roar and threw a scarlet hue across those nearest it.

Niall pushed Lylthia onto a bench and waved an arm at a serving-maid.

"Thort steaks and Kallarian," he ordered, then turned his attention to the girl. She was staring around her with wide eyes, almost as though she had never been in such a hospice before.

"So you seek vengeance on Maylok," he murmured. "But why? What has Maylok done to you?"

The green eyes regarded him. "He has taken that which was mine. He has not offered to pay for it, nor will he."

"What could you own that's so valuable?"

Her leather tunic was stained and discolored, it hardly hid the swells of her breasts nor the lengths of her supple thighs. She was a poor girl, that much Niall would swear on the War-god's sword.

She shrugged. "You would not understand."

Something about those green eyes made him murmur, "If I can help you, I shall. Though I don't fancy warlocks."

She smiled suddenly, and those eyes lost their coldness. "I need no help. Though I thank you."

Niall was not so sure that she could not use a blade like Blood-drinker to side her when she went hunting Maylok in his palace, and said so. "No man can take him by surprise, it's rumored. He has set spells and cantraips on all the doors and windows so nothing can catch him unawares. At least, so I've been told. Only by his will can a man or a woman enter his stronghold."

"That is true enough."

"Yet you think you can gain revenge on him? Unarmed and — well, practically naked? Without coins with which to bribe a way in?"

"I need neither sword nor gold. Here's your food. Eat it."

Niall glanced at her in surprise. There had been an imperiousness in the way she had spoken that indicated she expected to be obeyed. It was almost as if she were a princess in disguise. Niall felt uneasy at that, he had no experience with people of royal blood. Serving maids and tavern wenches were more his familiars.

Still, he ate the savory meat, slicing it with his knife, using his fingers to wolf down the blood-dripping meat. He loaned his knife to Lylthia, watched how daintily she ate. He filled her leathern jack with wine, drank his own empty and then refilled it.

Lylthia drank sparingly, as if not quite trusting the Kallarian. There was suspicion in her, he knew; she expected him to take her into a bed and enjoy her body. Well, that was what he meant to do, all right; he didn't blame her for eyeing him so watchfully.

By the War-god! She was a pretty thing. He liked her. And she had a body on her, he could tell that easily enough because of that scanty leather tunic. She would be fun when he got his arms around her. If she was enough fun, he would carry her to Urgrik.

An almost naked woman came into a cleared space and danced. Niall was torn between the dancer and watching the disdain that was so easy to read in Lylthia's pretty face. As applause rang out and the girl sniffed, Niall leaned close to her.

"You can do better, I suppose?"

"I would drive you mad were I to dance for you."

She said it calmly, but there was a ring of truth in her voice. Niall shifted uneasily on the bench. There was a mystery about this girl, he knew that much; she was not as other women he had met in his far travelings, willing to offer smiles and a soft body for a good meal and some glasses of wine, and a part of him regretted that. He thought of Lylthia in a warm bed with himself beside her, and stirred restlessly.

He asked, "Will you stay the night with me? It grows late, and Maylok may have other men searching the streets."

She nodded. "I will stay with you."

He paid for the meal with the last of his gold coins, accepting silver in change. Then he walked behind Lylthia's swinging hips along the narrow stairway to the upper rooms.

There was a bed and a washstand in the room he selected, and a single window that looked out on the stars and the glittering ring of matter which wise men said was the remains of the moon which had circled this world once, and had been shattered many eons ago, to be caught and held by gravity in the sky. Niall unbuckled his sword-belt and hung it over the back of a chair, slipped out of his link-mail shirt and kicked off his war-boots

He lay down on the bed and beckoned to the girl. "Come here, Lylthia. I want to taste the sweetness of your mouth."

To his surprise she walked toward him and sat on the edge of the bed. She leaned closer as if to kiss him, but his gaze was caught and held by her green eyes that seemed to swell and swell until they were all that existed in the room.

"Sleep, Niall of the Far Travels," those eyes commanded. "Sleep!"

And Niall slept, and Niall dreamed.

He sat on a stone throne in his dream in a great hall, dark except where tall torches glowed in sconces, forming a pool of light in which Lylthia danced. Naked she danced, and her body was a pallid white and disturbingly sensual. She was all the lusts, all the sensuous dreams of man, every need he had for that which would satisfy his animal nature.

In that dream, Niall hungered for her flesh but he could not leave the stone throne which seemed almost to hold him back. His arms stretched out, he called to her to come to him. She was a dainty promise whispered in the ear, a shapely seduction with her white legs

11

and quivering haunches. She turned and dipped, pranced and swirled, and always the need in him for her flesh grew more sharp.

Niall woke to the first pink rays of dawn, sitting up in bed and gasping. His dream was still strong upon him, his eyes went around the room hunting for the girl. She was not here, he was alone.

He shook himself as might a shaggy mountain bear roused from its winter sleep, Under his breath he muttered curses as he stumbled to the washbasin and poured cold water from the pitcher over his head. The water shocked him to full wakefulness and he lifted his head and stared out the window.

She was out there, in this city. He knew that. He thought he also knew where she had gone. He could not see Maylok's palace but he would find her there. He reached for his sword-belt and buckled it about his middle. A flash of light from the corners of his eyes caught his attention and he stared into a cracked minor, seeing his face.

His skin was bronzed and his black hair hung uncut almost to his shoulders. A scar was white against the dark sun-darkened skin of his chin. A swordsman in the hire of the Great Kham had bloodied his face, and had paid with his life for scarring him. His shoulders were so wide they could scarcely fit between the lintels of a wide door, ridged with muscles standing out like ropes beneath his sun-burnt skin.

Niall was a mercenary, a sell-sword, but he had a code of sorts. Lylthia had made him a promise last night, or as good as. He would go find her and bring her back to this tavern and throw her down on that rumpled bed. The barbarian chuckled. But he must not gaze into her eyes. No. It might be best to blindfold that one.

Well, he was going after her. Now. No matter where his war-boots took him.

He ate sausages and eggs in the common room, making plans in his head. She wanted vengeance on Maylok. The only place she could get that would be in his palace. He, Niall, would go also to that palace and find her and bring Lylthia out of it on a shoulder.

Uneasily, he remembered old Thallia and her prophecy. Demons would carry him off in Angalore, she had said. No matter. Maylok would have to cast a spell on him before he could summon up demons to take him away, and by that time, Maylok would be dead.

He went out into the sunlight and walked the streets of this ancient city, angling his feet always toward the huge pile of masonry standing close to the river's edge, that was the wizard's palace. It was built against the outer wall, and had a wall of its own, but smaller than the city wall, surrounding it and its gardens. Niall stood a long time studying that wall.

He could go over it easily enough. But what would he find when he dropped down onto the other side? He was no fool to go rushing into danger when there was a safe way out of it. Maylok would have guards posted. And, probably, big Commopore hounds trained to drag down any intruder and fang-slay him.

There was a huge oaken door set flush with the cobblestones of the street. Niall studied it for a moment, hitched at his sword-belt, then walked toward it. With the pommel of a dagger, he rapped on the plankings.

After a time the door swung open and two men with naked swords in their hands stood scowling at him. "What want you at the walls of Maylok, stranger?" asked the larger man.

"Money to put in my pouch." Niall grinned and rattled the little leather sack so they could hear his few coins clinking. "I'm told the wizard pays well." His eyes ran over their fleshy bodies. "Men say also that those who work for Maylok eat only thort steaks and pasties, and drink wine instead of water."

"Maylok has enough servants."

"None like me."

The man went to close the door but Niall put out his brawny arm and held the door open, using his eyes on the neat grass and carefully tended bushes that formed these outer gardens. He noted that the men grew angry, but he paid no heed to that, for he was noting the thickness of the walls and surmising that there would be rooms between outer and inner walls.

The other man came to add his muscles to the first, but Niall was a strong man whose full strength had never yet been tested, and he held that door open against both of them.

"Well, if he won't, he won't," he muttered, and released the door.

It banged shut and Niall grinned. He had seen enough. When darkness was upon Angalore he would return. Somehow, he would find a way inside that palace.

He walked around the walls and noted that a big tree grew outside a portion of those parapets. A nimble man could climb that tree, move out along a thick branch. It would be a good jump from the branch to reach the wall, but he could do it.

Whistling, he moved off toward the river gate and through it to the quays where a dozen ships were loading or unloading cargoes. He watched them, savoring the hot sunlight on his back, and fell into converse with two seamen munching on some fruit.

"Your crew works hard," he commented.

"This is Angalore. The sooner out of it, the better."

Niall pondered that. He asked slyly, "Is it because of Maylok?"

"Aye. The mage is like a spider in its web, peering out and taking that which he covets, be it gold or silver or a man and a maid. Right now he may be listening to us."

"I tried to gain employment from him."

"Count yourself lucky you didn't. He'd offer you up as a sacrifice to his demon-gods, in time."

"I think I'll sail with you, then. I'm for Urgrik to the north."

"We lift anchor tomorrow, a little past dawn. Ask for the Hyssop, bound for the cold countries. We make a stop at Urgrik."

Niall ate at a seaside tavern, using his ears to feed on words as he did his mouth to savor the kama-fish flavored with leeks and spices. He heard one man tell how he had seen a pretty girl being pushed into the wall-door of Maylok's palace just before down, a girl in ragged leather tunic and with black hair almost to her haunches. Six men had hold of her, were forcing her along.

"She's dead by now," someone muttered.

14

"Too bad. She was a pretty thing."

Niall did not betray himself by the slightest quiver of flesh, but fury was alive inside him. He had liked Lylthia. By the War-god! She had been a fool, but his flesh had lusted after her. If she'd been sensible and spent the night in his arms, she'd be alive, now. Aye, and happy!

It might be too late to save Lylthia, but maybe he could find a way to avenge her.

He sat on a piling and watched the sun sink, telling himself that he was as much of a fool as Lylthia herself. Old Thallia had warned him that demons would carry him off in Angalore. If he were sensible, he'd walk over to the Hyssop right now and get himself a good sleep in a hammock below-decks, and forget Lylthia.

Still, no one had ever praised his brains.

When the quays were in total darkness outside the faint starlight, Niall began his walk. He was in no hurry, indeed, he was rather reluctant to clamber onto that wall. He could think of better ways to die than to be captured by demons. Still! A man had to do what he felt was right.

The tree was big, but his muscles carried him up the thick bole and in between the heavy branches as though he were a monkey out of the jungles of Poranga. He ran out on the branch he had selected earlier in the day and paused.

The gardens were dark, the wall was empty. Lights were on in the palace, he could see flickering candles and torches through open windows, and once he thought to hear a scream of agony, dulled by distance and the palace walls. He trotted forward, swaying as the branch moved, and leaped.

For an instant he was in the air, then he was dropping down onto the parapet, clinging to its rough stone with both hands and swinging himself onto the wall-walk where he crouched, peering about and listening.

There was no one in sight, neither guards nor watchdogs, that he could discover. It might be a trap, but he had fought his way out of traps before. And if by any chance Lylthia were still alive, then he would bring her out of this pile of stones and carry her with him to

Urgrik. His hand loosed Blood-drinker in its scabbard, made certain that his Orravian dagger was ready to his grip, and then slid forward between the merlon-shadows.

No sentinel walked these walls, as far as he could tell. Now why was that? Did some awesome fiend patrol these pathways after dark, lurking to attack and perhaps devour — or carry off — some luckless trespasser? It might be Maylok's whim to use demons as his watchdogs. His hand tightened on the dagger-hilt as he moved.

At length he came to a doorway set into a tiny shed built against an inner wall. His hand opened that door, he stepped into Stygian darkness and down a flight of worn stone steps. His war-boots made no sound, nor was there any clank of sword-chain or link-mail, yet the hairs at the base of his neck bristled.

It was too easy!

There should have been an alarm, an attack, before this. The wizard was no simpleton, he must have known that the tales of his ill-gotten treasures would tempt thieves and foot-pads They would be protected, by what grim guardian he had no way of knowing.

Men and hounds he did not fear. His steel could handle those. It was the thought of demons which bothered him. Sooner or later he would meet some snuffling cacodemon in this blackness and be forced to fight for his life.

Yet he strode on, down the ancient steps and along a narrow corridor which must run beneath the gardens. From far away he could hear the dripping of water and nearer at hand the click of rats' nails along a stonework floor. Rats? Or — devil imps?

He lifted out Blood-drinker and moved with the blade always before him, as a blind man uses a wooden stick. He saw nothing, the ebon gloom was everywhere, pressing in upon him. And yet — as he turned a corner of the passageway, he beheld a redness up ahead.

It was only a wink of light, shifting, quivering. It seemed like a tiny corner of the Eleven Hells of Emelkartha broken free of the barriers that kept them from this world. Yet it served as a beacon to draw his footsteps forward.

He came into a low-ceilinged chamber, the walls of which were purplish in the radiance of flickering torch-flames set into that stone. A carved and ruined altar stood upon a dais reached by stonework steps, and on the flat surface of that shrine to devilry lay a naked woman.

Niall took a step forward, and another. He growled low in his throat. That lifeless body at which he stared belonged to—

Lylthia!

Chapter Three

Dead she lay, unmoving, with one arm flung limply over the edge of the altar, her eyes wide and staring upward at the low dome above that was marked with strange and alien signs and sigils. Her black hair was dark and wet, her skin the pallid hue of death itself. No! Even more! Her smooth skin was so white it almost hurt the eyes, as though every last drop of blood had been sucked from her flesh.

Niall glared about him, sword up and ready to thrust, to slay as Lylthia had been slain. Yet there was no foe, no enemy to cleave. It was quiet as a tomb, this charnel room, with only his own breathing to break the stillness.

His eyes went over that face, lovely even now in death. Her lips had lost their redness, her cheeks their tinting. But the traces of beauty lingered, and something inside the Sell-sword sorrowed to its sight. They had reaved her tattered leather tunic from her, her body was nude. As she had come into the world so she had gone from it.

"He'll pay," Niall whispered. "Somehow, I'll find a way to make him pay."

He touched her hand, squeezing the cold flesh just once, then moved on, past the altar to an iron-bound door that opened beyond it into another corridor. This passageway was lighted by torches at distant intervals, and as his eyes raked it, he saw that it was empty — or was it?

For as he walked he seemed almost to see a blackness in the darker shadows, a blackness that flitted ahead of him, that ran and curved and leaped, seemed almost to — beckon. Niall growled in his throat. He did not like such shadows, that went before him so enticingly.

He followed that shadow, dogged its fluttering steps, for the urge to slay Maylok was strong within him. He must pay the warlock with the same fate he had given little Lylthia. Nothing less would satisfy the barbaric urge to slay that rode him with his every heartbeat.

When he came to a curving stone staircase, he paused, but it seemed that the shadow was still before him, lifting an arm as if to urge him onward. With a grunt, the Sell-sword raced up those steps, his blade ready for instant use—

—and burst into a vast chamber.

He slid to a stop at sight of the lighted bowls about the room, at sight of the pentagram glistening red in blood, within which stood a tall man cowled in purple robe on which were stitched in golden threads the secret symbols of the demon worlds. Rigid stood the necromancer, his face pale and almost skull-like under the cowl that covered his head, a grim smile upon his thin, cruel mouth.

"Welcome, Niall of the Far Travelings. I have waited for you, even since you came through the land gate, two days hence."

"You slew Lylthia. For that you die."

Maylok chuckled. "Do I, Far-traveler? Behold!"

From beyond the blazing bowls men came rushing, big men in chain-mail and with swords and axes, maces and war-hammers in their hands. They rushed at Niall, and their weapons gleamed redly in the bowl-lights. Niall snarled and went to meet them.

This was why he had been born, to fight, to slay, to wield a sword as though it were a scythe of Death itself. Maybe he was allied to Death, for Death rode where Blood-drinker cut and slashed. With a roar, he fended off a blade and hewed his steel through a neck.

He was in the midst of his attackers, then, whirling, darting, dodging a blow from mace or ax, freeing Blood-drinker to this feast of flesh which had been provided for it. He did not fight as an ordinary man fights, with care and caution, as ready to ward off a blow as he might be to strike one.

Nay! When Niall fought, he sought only to kill. His eyes saw an opening, his arm controlled the sweep of his sword, and when that blade fell, it was already lifting to strike again.

Pantherish were his leaps, lion-like his bellowed challenges. Men fell away before the onslaught of his steel, men died where they faced him or backed away. Yet always the swords and maces hammered at him, though more often than not he avoided their blows.

From his eye-corners, he saw Maylok moving restlessly about the pentagram, crying out encouragement to his guards. Yet there was a palsied fear upon the wizard; never had he seen a man battle as Niall fought now, with a reckless disregard for his own safety, concerned only with slaying all those he could reach with that long blade.

More men rushed from behind the lighted bowls, they hemmed Niall in, they offered their flesh to his blade in order to bring him down. The flat of an ax took him across the side of his head, a mace thumped his sword-arm, numbing it.

When he had no more room to swing Blood-drinker, he -dropped it and clawed out his Onavian dagger and buried it in chest and throat and belly. His other hand he used to sink iron-strong fingers deep into throat-flesh and choke out life from the man he held.

Even his massive muscles tired, after more than three hours of such battling. There were dead men on the floor, and pools of their blood on which his war-boots slipped. Once more a mace thumped his arm, again the flat of a blade landed on his skull. He went to a knee, half-conscious, but still he fought. Not until hands caught his arms and held them and someone swung a war-hammer did he go down.

Half-dazed he lay there, held by bleeding, desperate men who panted and sobbed in their tiredness, seeing Maylok as through a rheumy veil approach, to stand above him.

"No man has ever fought like you, Far-traveler," whispered the exultant wizard. "Your blood shall be a strong elixir in my vials and alembics. Take him below to the dungeons and chain him there against my need."

They dragged and half-carried the still-struggling Niall out of the spell-chamber, down the worn steps and into the deep pits below the palace, where the stink of rotting flesh warred with the moans of men and women imprisoned here, kept for the torment and the blood-letting.

To huge chains inset in the stone walls they fastened Niall, his arms apart, so that they seemed almost to be torn from their sockets. He could stand only with difficulty, for those links suspended even his giant frame a little. And then they mocked him.

"The wizard will make you pay for what you've done," one said with a grin, blood running down his gashed face.

"He'll keep you alive a long time, torturing you from day to day, to test your ability to suffer."

"I've known him to cook a man alive, over two weeks, burning a little of him at a time."

"Another man he flayed over the period of a full month, to pay him for a slight."

They hit him with their fists and kicked him with their boots, but he stood stoically, with his eyes wide and glaring. One man carried his dagger and Blood-drinker in his hands, and these he thrust into his scabbards with a mocking laugh.

"I'll leave them here with you, but where you can't reach them. So near and yet out of reach. It may add to your torment, having them so close yet unable to use them."

They went away after a time and left him in the blackness where only a distant torch shed any light. His head drooped, he was feeling the cuts and slashes now, the batterings he had taken from mace and war-hammer. Pain was an agony along his flesh and veins, and a raging thirst dried his throat and tongue.

He tugged at the chains, but they were tight-set in stone, and massive. His arms were stretched to their fullest length so he could exert little or no strength. His legs were tired of standing, yet he could not sleep for the manacles about his thick wrists dug their steel into his flesh when he would have relaxed. He stared into the darkness and muttered curses beneath his breath.

He sought to doze but the rats came, gray monsters that stood on their hind legs and sought to bite his knees and thighs, bared above his war-boots These he kicked away, killing some by the force of those kicks, but they remained away for only a short time, being driven by starvation. He heard men scream, and women too, from somewhere off in these pits, and he knew that Maylok was supervising their torture.

His time for that would come, he supposed, and made a wry face. He did not mind a clean death, but torture was repugnant to him. Fury at the wizard burned inside him, and his body shook in his rage so that the chains rattled.

Something touched him, soft as thistledown, so that it seemed not so much a touching as a faint caress. And his tiredness welled up in him so that he hung in his chains and slept. No rats came now to nibble at him, he heard not the screams of dying men and women. Deep were his slumbers, and dreamless.

When he woke, he was refreshed. His wrists hurt him where the manacles had held his sagging body, but there was a renewed vitality in his great muscles and he stood defiantly, as though daring his captors to approach. He had no knowledge of the time, but that distant torch still glowed, though only fitfully, enabling him to see a little better around him.

Once more that thistledown softness touched him and now he glanced sideways, and his flesh crawled for a moment. The shadow was with him!

It was little more than a deeper darkness against the blackness of the dungeon, but he could make it out. Was this some fiend sent by Maylok to bring him some undreamed-of torment? But no. Or if it was, it did nothing but stare at him.

Niall stared back and now — but faintly — he could make out greenish eyes in that umbrageous shape. He shook himself, the chains rattled.

"What are you?" he rasped. "What?"

The shadow did not speak, but stretched out a slim arm at the end of which was a shadow-hand. And at the tips of slim fingers, greenish balls of fire began to glow.

His torture would begin now, the Far-traveler knew. Curse Maylok by all the eleven hells for —

The green balls touched a manacle, not his flesh.

And where the manacle had been was only — rusted powder. That powder fell away, the chain dropped and his mightily thewed left arm was free. Again those green balls moved, to touch the other manacle and Niall stepped away from the stone wall.

"My thanks," he growled. "Whoever you are."

The shadow danced before him as if to lead him away from the dungeon wall. Niall put hands to his sword-hilt and his dagger, lifting them half out of their scabbards, and then he went after that flitting shape.

It ran before him, dancing almost in its eagerness, luring him as once before it had beckoned him on. But there was a difference in the shadow-being now; it did not slink but cavorted, spiraled and swayed — more gracefully than any dancing girl he had ever seen. It reminded him almost of that dream he had had, in which Lylthia had danced for him.

The shadow moved and where it went, Niall followed. To a small chamber it led him, and touched the iron bars and locks of its vast oak door with the green balls at the tips of its fingers. Niall put a hand to those plankings and pushed the door inward.

Chests lay piled one atop the other here, with small coffers and caskets above and beside them. The shadow gestured and the Sell-sword lifted the cover of one and then another.

He saw diamonds piled high in one, emeralds in another, golden coins in yet a third. Again the shadow-being waved a hand and Niall filled his money pouch with jewels and golden coins until it overflowed. There were treasures here gathered during Maylok's lifetime and the lifetimes of his father and grandfather, who had been famous sorcerers in their own right. He would have liked to take it all, but knew it was beyond his power to carry.

At the far door, the shadow waited, and finally Niall went with it, running after it as it picked up speed. Through winding passageways and up dusty stairways long forgotten did the shadow-being take him, until they came at last to a walled-up doorway.

With the green balls, the shadow touched those stones and the stones melted to run in molten slag down onto the floor. Beyond the opening thus made was a dark drapery. This, Niall pushed aside.

He stood on the rim of the necromantic chamber where Maylok could be seen through the smoke of the flaming bowls, head flung back and arms raised high, as he chanted in some Forgotten, phylogenetic tongue. He was not aware that Niall was in his necromantic chamber, he was engrossed in his incantation. The shadow danced forward, pointing to Maylok and gesturing the Sell-sword forward.

Niall went at the run, yanking out the Orravian dagger. He would not bother to use his blade on the wizard, deeming him not worth the trouble of lifting Blood-drinker. As he ran, the shadow went with him and now he felt again that thistledown softness of its touch, where it clasped his wrist.

Maylok whipped around, startled by the faint sound of war-boots on stone. His eyes opened wide, his lips parted to scream.

Then Niall was over the blood-wet pentagram and raising his dagger for the death stroke. But the shadow was ahead of him, reaching out with its dainty hands for Maylok and the wizard screamed indeed when he saw that graceful blackness reaching out to gather him into its embrace.

Niall could not move. He paused in mid-stroke, not wanting to harm the shadow — not even knowing if he could — but seeing that shadow now as that of a pretty girl.

"Lylthia," he whispered.

"Not Lylthia, no. But once I was — yes," hissed a voice. Laughter rang out, cruel and mirthless.

The palace swirled about Niall as he swayed drunkenly inside that pentagram, feeling feeling the floor shift under his war-boots, knowing a dizziness induced not by blow of weapon but by some demoniac spell. Faster the palace moved, faster, faster. He could not stand, but reeled and would have fallen but for the cool hand that caught and held him.

He stood in redness.

Beneath him the floor was of scarlet stone, faintly hot. Around him rose gargantuan walls of a brilliant carmine streaked with slashes of deepest ebony, on which were hung strange tapestries and golden vessels. Massive columns of black and vermilion rose upward toward a distant roof half-hidden by redly glowing mists.

A thin high squealing caught his ears. Maylok was groveling on the warm stone floor, beating at it with his fists and scratching with his nails. His purple cloak and cowl were already smoking, his body writhed as though he were in torment.

"Save me, Far-traveler," he mewled. "Save me and my treasure is yours. All the jewels, all the gold that my forefathers and I have gathered together, shall all be yours. And I — Maylok the Mighty, the wisest wizard in the world, shall be your slave!"

Niall growled, "I ought to kill you, you foul slug."

"Yes!" Maylok screamed, struggling upward to his knees and presenting his scrawny throat. "Slay me! Slay me and take my treasures. Only do me this favor, Niall of the Mighty Arms — kill me, kill me!"

Soft laughter floated through the vast room. It mocked and taunted and when it touched the necromancer he grovelled on the floor.

"Great Emelkartha — spare me," he bleated.

"Too late for mercy, Maylok. Nah, nah. You pay the price."

And Maylok screamed.

In the midst of that screaming, a woman came forward, clad in diaphanous robes of crimson streaked with jet through which Niall could see the flesh tints of her body. Long black hair floated down about her shoulders and her green eyes blazed with fury. On her full mouth was a cold, cruel smile.

"Lylthia," he whispered.

The green eyes slid sideways from the cringing necromancer to touch the Sell-sword, and it seemed to him they softened. "Not Lylthia, no. Not any more. Know me, barbarian, for Emelkartha herself."

Niall said boldly, "Too bad. I think I could have loved Lylthia."

Her mouth lost its cruelty, grew softly amorous. "The woman part of me knows that, Niall of the Far Travelings, and — thanks you.

"At first I was angry with you for saving me from Maylok's men. I wanted to be taken by them, to be drained of blood, so that I could become — a shadow being. Yet you did me a favor and for that I am not ungrateful.

"You could pass the pentagram. Not even I could do that, not as Lylthia nor as her shadow. Yet by touching you, your strength drew me along — to catch Maylok in my arms and bring him here to my eleven hells, as men name this domain over which I rule."

She was silent and Niall scanned her features, finding them more beautiful than ever, with broad brow and tip-tilted nose and those full lips exerting a sensuous appeal that shook him to his marrow. He licked his lips. Old Thallia had been right. A demon-woman had carried him off the world and into her abode. He wondered if he would ever return.

The green eyes glanced at him slyly.

"Well, Niall? Would you stay with me and be my lover?"

He found himself nodding, and she smiled but shook her head. "Nah, nah, you may not — though a part of me would like to keep you here. This place is not made for — human flesh. It cannot endure the heat and mephitic vapors for very long — without pain."

Maylok screeched and banged his head against the hot floor.

Emelkartha whispered and now eerie shapes to which Niall could not put a name ran from the walls to lay tentacles upon Maylok and lift him to his feet. He was sweating, gasping for breath, trembling as with the ague.

"You made a mock of me, magician," whispered Emelkartha, and how her voice burned the eardrums with its rage. "For that you shall suffer. As you have made your fellow-man suffer, so now shall you, from the first to the last of my eleven hells. You shall be tortured to death, yet shall be reborn after each death so that you may suffer even worse torments. Eleven times shall you die, eleven times shall you be

25

reborn, to begin anew — until the end of Time itself!"

Maylok screamed and screamed. His body contorted and twisted, but he was helpless in those rubbery tentacles that held him. In this manner he was dragged across that hot stone floor toward a distant doorway through which Niall could glimpse blazing fires and up-reaching flames.

They drew the wizard through the doorway.

For an instant he seemed to come to a dead stop, with his sandals digging in at the stone floor. Peal after peal of agonized fear burst from his throat when he saw what lay before him. Then he was gone and steam rose up to blot out the sight of what was being done to him.

The demon-woman looked at Niall inquiringly. "You do not approve," she whispered. "Yet Maylok has sinned against the demon world for too long a time, holding us in thrall. Soon — he would have been too strong for me to act against him, for he intended summoning up mega-demons known to me who would have prevented my disposing of him. His incantations are incomplete, and so my world — and yours — is safe from him, forever."

He nodded, he knew what wickednesses Maylok had done, of girls ravished and tormented, of brave men broken and tortured into mindless hulks, of treasures taken from rightful owners. Maylok deserved these eleven hells.

There was nothing he, Niall, could do about it, anyhow.

His eyes ran over her body, so much revealed in the black and scarlet transparencies she wore. He sighed, and with that sigh, the woman-demon floated closer, tilting up her head and lifting her bare arms.

Niall caught her in his embrace, held her a moment, and kissed her. He would never forget that kiss. It burned deep into him, seemed to lift him out of his flesh into another state of being where pleasure was almost unendurable. His arms held this lissome woman to him, and something inside him told him that no mortal woman could ever afterward affect him as did this one whom he had known as Lylthia.

"For now — farewell," her voice whispered...

She was gone and he stood alone inside the pentagram in the palace of the doomed wizard. A cold wind was blowing through the building, that chilled and refreshed him. He shook himself, touching his sword-hilt for reassurance that he still lived, that he was back in his own world.

His heart still thudded with the excitement of that last embrace. Whatever else she was, Emelkartha was a woman, her mouth had whispered to him of indescribable delights in that kiss. He shook his head, telling himself that he had gained a rich treasure in the gold and diamonds in his money pouch, but had lost something worth much more.

"Lylthia," he whispered as he walked through the forsaken halls of the ancient palace. "Lylthia..."

Would Emelkartha ever appear to him again — in human form? As — Lylthia? She had the power, certainly, being a woman-demon. But would she? He did not know, all he could do was hope.

He walked out into the gathering dawn and made his way to the wall-gate, unmolested. It was as if, with the wizard's death, his servants had all fled away. Or — been destroyed.

A river breeze had sprung up. He moved along the street toward the Hyssop, which would carry him to Urgrik. Yet there was a sadness in him, despite the wealth in his pouch.

"Lylthia," he whispered once again.

But the sea-wind caught the name and carried it away.

BEYOND THE WIZARD FOG

Chapter One

The ship lay becalmed on the great river. Its sails were motionless, limp and heavy. Men sat on the oar benches, the oar-handles gripped in massive fists, waiting for the clang of the overseer's hammer. Silence lay upon the Hyssop, as men turned their heads toward the great white fog that waited for them, spreading across the wide reaches of the waterway and up onto the land itself.

Niall of the Far Travels was uneasy. That uneasiness was a coldness down his spine, a restlessness in his every nerve. He stood leaning against the starboard railing, eyes seeking to pierce that shrouded whiteness which crept slowly but inexorably across the water and its shorelines.

They were three days out of Angalore, almost halfway to the great city of Urgrik, where he was to take service with Lurlyr Manakor who ruled those lands under his eagle banner. There should be no danger along the river Thalamar, ships plied its waters every day. There had been no word of trouble. Not so much as a rumor.

Yet danger lay ahead. A barbarian sell-sword out of Norumbria to the far north, almost an animal in his instincts, Niall scented that danger. He did not know what that trouble might be, yet it waited there for the ship and for all the men on it.

A shadow touched the railing. Edron Hobbort, who was captain of the Hyssop, stood scowling at his side. "I don't like this. It smacks of magic."

Niall shrugged. "Magic? Aye, it could be. Or warm clouds touching the land. I've seen fogs like that, here and there across the world where I've wandered."

The captain eyed him respectfully. He had heard tales of this Niall of the Far Travelings in the alehouses back at Angalore, from men who had seen him in the palaces of the Kings of the South, or riding with the dreaded Swordsmen of Chandion, or even — so one old man had whispered — consorting with the demon-priests of Farfanoll at the

Unmentionable Oasis which bestraddled the scarlet sands of the Inner Desert.

He seemed young for someone to have done all that, Edron Hobbort told himself. Yet there was a shadow in those gray eyes, a sensitivity on his sun-bronzed face, that told the captain this youth had been many places in his short lifetime, and had done many things.

He asked now, "What would you advise, Niall?"

"Turn back. I smell wizardry."

Edron Hobbort scoffed. "There's been no wizardry along this river for a thousand years. Except for Maylok, back there in Angalore and — you disposed of him."

"There is magic here. I can almost smell it."

"Come you to my cabin. I have charts of this river and its surrounding lands. Old charts and new charts. You can see for yourself."

They made their way to the cabin and after Edron Hobbort had lighted an oil lamp and unrolled parchment scrolls, they bent above these scrolls and eyed them carefully. One after the other Niall discarded, until only one was left. This last one was very ancient, cracked and marred by Time, and it crackled as he unrolled it.

"There," Niall said, jabbing his finger. "Those ruins..."

"...are only ruins," scoffed the captain.

"Na, na. They're more than a pile of rocks. There's evil there, Edron Hobbort. Ancient evil."

"Now, how can you know that?"

Niall straightened slowly. He tried to think, yet could not. Almost dazedly, he passed a hand across his broad brow. "I — cannot say. And yet — I know. It's as if — something whispered into my mind. But it told me of an evil that has come recently to life, back across eons of Time — and made its home close by this river."

Edron Hobbort snorted. "Nonsense. That ruin has been uninhabited since Porthia Malvia was queen in Angalore, and that's about ten centuries ago. We'll go on. If the sails won't work, the oars will."

He stalked from the cabin and Niall could hear him bellowing to the oarsmen, to the overseer, who began the beat with two bronze

29

hammers in his hands that he banged upon the drum before him. Instantly the oars dipped, bit into the water, and Niall could feel the forward surge of the ship beneath his war-boots

He still leaned upon the table, his palms on that old parchment map. Yet, uneasiness was strong inside him, as though — as though some inner voice were warning him of danger. He shook himself, angrily. Was he turning into an old woman, to dread whatever lay ahead of him? Na, na! He was a warrior, a sell-sword. Had he not faced awesome dangers in the past? Was he to be fearful of a fog now?

Almost unconsciously he rolled up that parchment map and thrust it into its niche. Then he moved forward into thick grayness, saw that grayness creep across the deck to hide the rowers on their benches, the piled crates of goods being shipped northward from the lands of Korybia and Strumathis, the overseer, as he banged away on the timing drum. Even Edron Hobbort vanished.

And then those mists touched Niall.

He felt them sting his flesh, exposed where his mail hauberk and fur kaunake did not cover him. It stung his legs, naked above his fur-trimmed war-boots. He opened his lips to bellow his anger, for it seemed almost as if a thousand tiny teeth were biting at his skin.

The little bitings ceased.

Those gray clouds still surged about him, buffeting his flesh, blinding him, seeking to crawl down inside his throat — or so it seemed — yet there was a calmness in him, an acceptance of that fog as if it were known and recognized from long ago. From — another time.

"Sisstorississ' work!"

Now where had that thought come from? Had he, in his far travels, come upon that name? He did not think so. He moved forward, to stand beside Edron Hobbort

The captain stood there, with legs apart, staring straight ahead. He did not turn when Niall touched his arm; he did not move. Niall drew back the hand that had nudged at the captain. His flesh had been cold. Cold! Now he peered more closely at his face and saw that his skin was white as the snows that cover the tip of the tallest mountain peaks in Norumbria in the dead of winter.

30

Niall put up his hand, passed it across those staring eyes. Edron Hobbort did not blink, did not turn aside his eyes. "Wizardry," whispered the Northumbrian as he made his way down the coursier which ran between the banks of oarsmen.

Every oarsman was white as falling snow, as blind.

He made his way to the fore-deck and stood there with the wind blowing in his face, swirling the fog about him. It seemed that he could hear tiny voices in that fog, voices that cried out against him. Underfoot, he felt the forward surge of the Hyssop.

No wind bellied out the sail, no oar moved. Yet the ship moved on slowly, through those river-waters. Niall felt an iciness creep up his spine. He put his hand on Blood-drinker, his sword, and brought it out of the scabbard. He waited then, as the Hyssop moved slowly forward.

In time he saw gray stones, where a wharf had been, long ago. Here the mists were less, they did not shield what lay ahead as they had done. It was as though puffs of wind came up suddenly to disperse them. Or — as though someone had whispered a command!

When the ship bumped against the wharf-stones, Niall heard movement behind him. Skin crawling, he watched the oarsmen rise up from their benches, turn and begin to walk. He drew back, staring at those blank faces and empty eyes. He watched them leave the ship and walk onto the wharf and then along a broken causeway upward onto a hill.

When Edron Hobbort came toward him, Niall fell into step beside him. He sheathed his sword, he walked as the others walked, as though asleep or under a necromantic spell. Yet his eyes went this way and that, and he searched the fog for some foe that might attack.

Ahead of him he saw the stark lines of an old tower, the crumbling ruins of buildings that were a part of that tower. They stood stark and empty beneath the gray sky; there was a menace about them that made his flesh creep.

They came at last to what had been a courtyard in days long since forgotten, and there the men stood unmoving, as though awaiting a command. Niall did not stand with them, but where he saw the outlines of a door set between stone uprights, he moved toward it.

Beyond the doorway, there was no fog, only the empty desolation of the past. Niall walked swiftly, eagerly, and in time he came to a flight of stone steps leading downward. He took those steps, moving as warily as a wild beast.

From far ahead, he heard a cry.

It was a wail of utter terror, of hopelessness.

Niall ran. He fled down the steps and along a subterranean passageway, past many doors, until he saw pale light ahead of him. And now he could hear, mixed in with those wails, a harsh scrape of something on stone, and a fearful hissing.

He came to an opening, he stood before a vast chamber with a great opening in the floor, rimmed with stone. Hung in that opening was a girl, caught by chains dependent from the ceiling. Her long black hair fell toward the opening, she writhed and twisted in the manacles that held her by wrists and ankles.

Those chains were lowering her slowly into that pit.

Niall ran forward crying out. The girl heard him, turned her head, stared with disbelief at his mail-shirted body, at his long yellow hair, at the anger on his face.

When he came to the rim of that pit, he stared downward and cried out in horror. A mighty snake was coiled in the depths of that opening, its fanged head rising upward, jaws gaping. Niall could see a forked tongue, glittering white fangs, multi-faceted eyes.

"By Emelkartha herself!" he rasped.

"You can't save me," the girl wept, still struggling. "Nothing can!"

Niall felt his muscles tense. He crouched on the rim of that pit and his eyes went upward to the chains, saw them lowering the girl slowly. Slowly! It was as if whatever evil brain had put her there wanted that girl to know the agonies of approaching death long before death touched her.

Niall leaped outward, over the pit.

The huge snake hissed in fury, fangs glittering to catch him when he fell. His hands caught those chains, they slipped, and then they clung.

The snake lifted upward.

Only for a moment did Niall rest motionless, clinging to those chains. Then he was swinging them, pulling with his arms, pushing with his feet. Back and forth he swung them, toward one edge of the pit and then the other. He could hear the links rasping to that strain, he heard the pit-demon hiss in outraged fury.

The girl hung motionless in her manacles, staring upward at him.

Like a pendulum, Niall swung those chains. They were dropping him more swiftly now, soon that gigantic serpent would be able to reach the girl with its fangs. Whatever he was going to do — he must do soon!

He heard a link scrape on the stone rim. One more swing! His muscles bulged in arms and legs and back as he put all his weight, all his strength, into his swinging.

Then he leaped. With one hand he held the chains even as he swung outward toward the pit's rim. His war-boots landed, scraped. He fell full length. But his hand still held a link, and the girl fell beside him onto the cold stones.

She sobbed, she wept with relief.

But they were not yet done with danger. Upward over the pit's rim came the fanged wedge that was the serpent's head. Niall cursed and yanked his steel free of its scabbard. With Blood-drinker naked in his hand he leaped to the edge of the pit, swung the sword.

Steel grated on a serpent's tooth, snapped it. Instantly, even as the head was drawing back, Niall curved the aim of his blade, cut upward under the jaw of the massive snake. Through bone and sinew and flesh went the edge of his blade.

The reptile hissed. That hiss was a susurration of rage and fury, of pain and agony. It reverberated from wall to wall, from the bottom of the pit upward.

Forward lunged that bleeding head. Outward swept the forked tongue. The fangs glinted cruelly in the faint light of the chamber. Niall could see the brownish scales, which seemed like armor plate, tinted greenish, here and there, as that flat head darted toward him.

Niall swung Blood-drinker, drove it in an arc of bluish light straight for that head. Deep into the skull went the blade, the shock of the blow ran up Niall's powerfully muscled arm into his shoulder.

The giant reptile hissed out its pain and anguish, its fury.

Bracing his thickly thewed legs, Niall tore the steel from its living bed. Yet in that moment he felt hate surge up about him, almost like a scarlet mantle: not his own hate, but that of another. It was a human hate, mingled with fear, and it shook him for a moment as he yanked free his steel and watched the skull-smitten reptile draw back, sink downward.

He whirled, sword in hand—

—yet there was no one there, only the girl who crouched naked on the stones of the flooring, half hiding her face behind a veil of fallen hair. His eyes went from her to the chamber in which he stood panting, blood and ichor dripping wetly from his sword-blade to the pavement.

"The wizard," he muttered. "Who is the wizard behind all this?"

The head of the girl jerked up so that he could see her eyes through the spill of black hair, vivid and fearful, tinted a pale yellow.

"Ulkarion," she whispered, and with her whisper a chill came into the air.

"Is that his name? The name of the warlock who inhabits this ancient pile of stone?"

He knelt beside her, lifting out his dagger and using it to pick the locks that held the manacles to her slender wrists. She shuddered away from him but he smiled at her.

"Na, na. There's no reason to fear me, I'm just a traveler on my way to Urgrik. Something bemused my fellow travelers and—"

"But not you?" she asked wonderingly.

Niall frowned. "No, and that's a strange thing. They all became like the living-dead, but whatever it was did that to them didn't affect me at all."

As the last manacle fell from her ankle, the woman rose up, proudly naked in the dim light, and raising her hands, parted her hair so that she could see him the more clearly. For his part, Niall did his own staring. She was beautiful, her black hair was almost like a robe that hid a part of her nakedness from his eyes, and her yellow eyes softened as they regarded him. Slowly she shook her head.

"We can never escape Ulkarion, you know," she said softly. "He is a very potent wizard, he has searched for many years for this place." Her hand rose, indicated the vast stones of the walls, the viper pit, the dark

34

entrances that lead into this vast room.

Niall rose to stand beside her. "What can you know of this mage?"

She shrugged. "Ulkarion needs sacrifices for Sisstorississ, the snake-like god who dwells in labyrinthine hells far out in space. Long ago, Sisstorississ was worshiped here in Kor Magnon." She caught the bewilderment in his eyes and smiled faintly.

"Kor Magnon is the name of this place where we stand. Long and long ago, it was the lair of a race of serpent-men who were worshipers of Sisstorississ. They stole human sacrifices to offer the snake-god, until the peoples of this region rose up and attacked it.

"Kor Magnon fell, everyone in it was put to death. From that day on, it has lain empty, abandoned, until all record of its location was forgotten. Yet Ulkarion searched for it, hampered only by the efforts of another wizard named Iphygia. Eventually, he defeated Iphygia and came here to worship Sisstorississ, so that the snake-god would make him powerful and almighty."

The girl shrugged. "I was to have been the first sacrifice to Sisstorississ — until you came along. I — am grateful."

Niall eyed her cautiously. "You know a lot about this magician."

"I was hand-maiden to Iphygia. When he destroyed Iphygia, he captured me, Kathyla. I was to have been his first sacrifice to the snake-god."

The Far Traveler grinned. "Looks to me as if he needs a new god. That one who came for you is dead. I clove in his brain."

The girl shrugged. "That was only the manifestation of Sisstorississ. Sisstorississ himself is — beyond death. Nothing can kill him."

"Then we'd better get out of here."

"It's no use. There is no escape."

Niall shrugged. "Stay here if you want, then. I'm leaving."

Chapter Two

He moved toward one of the exits, black and yawning in the stone. Behind him the girl stirred, called, "Not that way, Traveler! That door

35

leads to certain death. There is a trap door somewhere ahead of that walkway. If you put foot on it, the stone slab would turn and drop you into everlasting fire, into the very bowels of the planet."

Niall turned; asked, "Then where?"

She ran ahead on bare feet toward a different adit. "Our only hope is by this way. It may take us to safety."

He moved toward her, his eyes running up and down her bared legs, her hips, the tilted breasts half-hidden by her long black hair. "You seem to know a lot about this place."

"My mistress — Iphygia — did her own research. She also wanted to find Kor Magnon and set herself up as priestess to Isstorississ. She failed. Yet I have talked with her about Kor Magnon and I know it almost as well as does Ulkarion."

"Lead on, then."

He followed her swaying haunches across the tiles and into a narrow tunnel-way Darkness closed in around them, for it was black as deepest space where they walked, and Niall could not even see the girl ahead of him, nor could he hear the footfalls of her feet. Yet his animal senses knew she walked ahead of him, proudly yet warily, and once he felt the brush of her hand, though only faintly, against his arm.

"Beware here, Traveler. There are hidden traps in all these corridors."

He strode more warily, and after a time the walkway rose upward at an angle, before it turned suddenly and he could see the girl now, and also a round room with two doors at its far side.

She started forward and as she did, out of both of those entrances came a dozen liches — dead men clad in scraps of burial garments, wielding in their skeletoned hands rusted weapons that had been buried with them long ago — and as they caught sight of Niall and Kathyla, weird ululations broke from their skeletal throats.

The girl shrank back even as Niall leaped forward. Blood-drinker in a hand — not one of these mummified liches had blood, but that made no difference — he ran to meet them. They moved slowly, as though not yet aroused from the sleep of death, as though they still dreamed in the sepulchers in which they had been entombed.

Niall swung his sword, he ravened in among them with his steel always moving, slashing, darting. He was like an enraged panther in the fury of his fighting. Skulls rolled, clicking on the tiles, bony arms dropped where they were severed. In moments, those skeletal figures flopped and rolled across the floor, dismembered but still under the spell of some awful wizardry.

The Far Traveler paused, glancing about him. With his war-booted foot he kicked away a skull that sought to bite him, then tramped hard on a bony hand that still held a sword.

"Come along. There must be a way out of this hellhole, away from magicks such as this."

The girl shook her head, smiling faintly. "There is no escape from Kor Magnon. Nor," she added darkly, "from Ulkarion, either."

"If he's flesh and blood, he can die."

Her slanted yellow eyes slid sideways at him, mockery in their depths. "Do you think you can defeat Ulkarion, barbarian?"

He shook his bloody sword at her. "If he's human, he can die. If there's a way, I'll find it."

She whispered, "Perhaps you can, at that." Her hand lifted, she beckoned to him. "This way, now. If I remember the old scrolls, there should be safety down this passageway."

They stepped over the still flopping forms of the liches and moved into a narrow tunnel which led upward. Niall still held Blood-drinker in a fist; at any moment he expected attack. He had no way of knowing how Ulkarion could trace their movements in these subterranean tunnels, but apparently he could. The attack of the liches seemed proof enough of that.

Upward they walked, with the girl leading the way. Once she paused, her hand held high. They listened, but even though they heard only the silence of these long-unused corridors, Niall tightened the grip of his hand on his sword-hilt.

He had no knowledge of how long he had been without sleep, but even his gigantic muscles were showing the effect of his constant walking, fighting. His eyes slid sideways at the girl. She had stumbled once or twice lately, he saw lines of tiredness on her face.

"We need sleep," he muttered.

Her eyes were fearful as they turned toward him. "To sleep in

37

Ulkarion's lair is to die."

"And if we don't sleep, we die from exhaustion."

She paused, thinking, "There is a place — mayhap. It is not far from here, off one of these corridors. There we may sleep a while, reasonably safe."

Now Kathyla ran ahead, her black hair flying, and Niall trotted to keep up with her. Along two ramps they went, and then they came to a room off a short corridor, a room hung with arrases and drapes, quiet as a tomb, and almost as dark. Only a tiny candle which Kathyla found and lighted, enabled them to see.

The girl said, "You may sleep here, Niall. Without fear."

She settled herself in a corner of the room and closed her eyes. Niall watched her a moment, shrugged, and lay down himself. In moments, he was asleep.

Later, Niall was to recall that he dreamed of Emelkartha the Evil, that demon-goddess whom he had known as Lylthia in Angalore, and whom he had followed into the halls of her Eleven Hells. She came to him in his dream, as lovely as he had remembered her, and she put her hands upon his closed eyes as downward she bent, to kiss him with her blood-red mouth, soft and fragrant. Niall stirred under that kiss, he strove to put his arms about her nakedness, to hold her to him.

He struggled, but he could not move.

Emelkartha ran her hand down his side, to where he kept the jewels she had given him when, as a shadow, she had freed him from the manacles with which Maylok's warriors had fastened him, and later brought him into a strongroom and told him to take what jewels and gold he would. Niall protested, mumbling. Did Emelkartha want those gifts back?

The demon-woman laughed, and her merriment rang in his ears as his eyes snapped open.

Kathyla was crouched beside him, trying to open that pouch at his belt in which he carried those jewels. His hand stabbed downward, caught her wrist.

"What's this?" he mumbled. "Robbery?"

She tried to free herself, but he was too strong. Kathyla stared at him with her yellow eyes, and for an instant — before her eyelids fell to cover those lemony eyes — Niall would have sworn he saw anger and stark fear in them. She tried to draw away from him, but his hand was like an iron band, holding her.

"Na, na, girl. Would you steal from me and run away?"

She shook her head, but her eyes still widened in that fright which seemed to grip her. "There is something about you — something I can sense — that terrified me."

He laughed. "And do you think to discover the secret in my pouch?"

Niall put his hand into that leather pouch and lifted out a handful of the gems he had taken from Maylok's strong-room. He held them on his palm so that the candlelight glittered on them.

To his amazement, Kathyla shrank back, averting her face.

"What's this? Do you fear a few jewels?"

"Put them — away. I have seen — enough!"

Niall did as she bid, but his eyes rested on her averted face. He was curious. There was nothing so terrifying about a few rubies, diamonds and emeralds. What was there about them that so frightened the girl?

He rose to his feet, shook himself. "I know not how long we've slept, but it's time to go. I have a hunger in me to see blue sky and green grass. I've been in these pits long enough."

Kathyla rose also, but she hung back, away from him.

"Come along, if you don't want to spend the rest of your life within these walls."

He walked with swinging stride, his hand ever near his sword-hilt, his eyes searching the dark passages down which he strode. Behind him, Kathyla came at the trot, and he could hear her rather harsh breathing. What was it about him that so frightened the girl? Niall thought about other girls he had known in his travels, and could think of none that shrank away from him.

When they came to a branching corridor that led upward, Niall waited until the girl came up beside him. "This place is a labyrinth of walkways," he grumbled. "I've been going upward, but I can see no way of escape."

"We are near the subterranean dungeons of that building which served as Kor Magnon's temple to Sisstorississ. Here were the victims fed to the snake-god, here the people of Kor Magnon worshiped that evil being."

Niall nodded, putting a hand on her wrist, gripping it. "Good. Once inside that temple, we'll find a way out of it."

She shrank back, using her weight to hamper him. "It is the temple of the snake-god. There, Ulkarion will seek to rouse him from his far-off worlds, to bring him here to — destroy us!"

Niall scowled. He did not like this talk of demon-gods and warlocks. He was a warrior, a sell-sword, more used to fighting other men than battling with demons and their hell-inspired desires. Yet he understood that by going into that temple to Sisstorississ, they would be risking a confrontation with the serpent-demon. His broad shoulders shrugged.

He could not stay in these pits forever. Besides, he was growing hungry.

"Do what you like, girl. But I'm for the sunlight and some fresh air."

He moved upward along the ramp and into a cellar where dampness and mildew glittered on every stone of the walls. It seemed that he could hear a thick chanting, which rose and fell in mesmeric harmony, though faint and very far, far away. Those rhythms seemed to seep inside his flesh.

Kathyla was there beside him, whimpering.

"Ulkarion is worshiping! He calls on Sisstorississ to rise upward from the lands where he dwells, to come here and greet his worshipers!"

"Now how can you know that?"

"I have studied the ancient scrolls, the forgotten writings of the ancients. As handmaiden to Iphygia, that is."

"Perhaps now, while Ulkarion is busy, we can get away."

"There is no escape," Kathyla moaned, but she ran beside him on bare feet, sobbing softly to herself.

They turned a corner, they ran up worn steps hollowed out by the feet of long-dead men and women, they slid against walls wet with dew, they came at last to an archway. They peered in at a great altar of blue stone set beneath what seemed to be a round opening in the wall behind it. The wizard Ulkarion, in flowing robes of black and silver, stood with upraised arms before that black opening, chanting those words which had been old when the world was young.

Niall ran, with the girl beside him.

No one paid them any heed. The people who stood chanting in the great temple, Niall was with sickening revulsion, were as dead as the liches he had cut apart with Blood-drinker. They stood in their serements, the flesh shredding from their bones, eyeless sockets dark in the candles' light, and the sound of their singing was as the wind whistling past a forest of gravestones.

But with that eerie chanting—

—there was another sound!

Very faint it was, as if it were coming from the depths of ancient earth itself. It moaned, it wept, it cried out with soft whispers that promised unknown delights and pleasures. Yet beneath that cacophony of sound there was laughter! As a man might laugh as he crushed an insect, as a monster might laugh as it prepared some fiendish torture for a helpless woman, so was that laughter.

Niall slid his sword out, yet there were drops of perspiration on his forehead. Whatever made those sounds — was coming closer! Closer!

Beside him, Kathyla moaned.

It came to Niall that the chanting in the temple had stopped, by now. He heard a whisper of sound and turned. The dead were also turning away from the altar, toward him and the girl. Their eye-sockets were empty, but it seemed they watched them.

Beyond them was Ulkarion, on the dais before the altar.

He was smiling cruelly and his arms were making strange gestures.

"Fools," he shouted. "Fools! None can escape the vengeance of Sisstorississ! Behold — your doom!"

Chapter Three

Niall whirled, sword up. He could see nothing as yet, nothing but the entry way of the temple, dark and ominous. Yet always the sound of those invisible voices — and that eerie laughter — grew louder, louder, until it drowned out every other sound.

And then he saw them.

They were gray in color, and they rotated swiftly, like tops with which some demoniac child might play. They were twice as tall as a man and there were so many they hid everything that was behind them. They came on slowly, twirling faster and faster, and here and there in all that grayness, it seemed that Niall could see glittering red eyes. Eyes that taunted, eyes that gloated!

Kathyla moaned.

"These are the demon-things that serve Sisstorississ! Spawned in the depths of some unknown hell, the serpent-god sets them free to do his will! We are lost, Niall — lost!"

"Not yet," he growled, and lifted Blood-drinker.

He hurled himself at those eerie servitors. His bluish blade circled, swung. Through those gray bodies went his steel, and it seemed to him that where his steel touched them — green flames danced!

Something screamed. It was not a human voice, whatever made that sound. It seemed to come from far away, yet it pierced his ears, it reached deep into the soul of him, it fingered his nerve-ends. There was no pain, only an — awareness. Yet even as Niall swung his blade, he felt a numbness come upon his arms, his legs. He fought that numbness as he fought those twirling graynesses.

On the high altar, Ulkarion still chanted.

High and shrill were his chantings, filled with fright and worry. Never yet had Ulkarion summoned up the demon-god Sisstorississ, he knew only from his readings of ancient scrolls what Sisstorississ might do. He had no control over that awesome demon, he stood in no pentagram, he knew no words with which to control that which he had summoned up.

Yet as he watched, he grew more hopeful. For Niall was weakening. Aye! His sword-stroke were not as crisp, as sure. And where he faltered, those twirling imps surged in upon him, at times almost

42

hiding him from Ulkarion's straining eyes.

Niall raged. Were these things men, they would have fallen away before the sweep of his sword. Yet though some were damaged — he could see them lying on the flaggings — there were so many others they were all about him, touching him, weakening him, drawing his vital life force from his body.

He tottered, nearly falling, and he heard Kathyla scream in fright. He fought to put his back against a wall and used his blade to destroy those gray wraiths that swirled around him. But he could not keep on fighting. The mere touch of that grayness sapped his strength, weakened his muscles.

It grew harder to use his sword-arm, more and more of the twirling things darted in under his blade, touched him to weaken him still further. And now he heard the faint whisper of burial garments as the dead of Kor Magnon moved toward him, their bony hands outstretched.

Out of the corners of his eyes, Niall saw those dead things put their skeletal fingers on Kathyla. She screamed and fought them, but she did little more than tear a burial garment or shred a bit of rotting flesh from bone. They overcame her, lifted her into the air and held her there with skeletal fingers as the others came on toward Niall himself.

The Far Traveler rasped a curse as he sought to spring from the wall at his back and reach the girl. But the whirling gray imps had expected this, they swarmed upon him and where they touched he felt the sting of their grayness, weakened under it. Even as he weakened, the dead stretched out their arms and put their bony hands upon him.

He was lifted upward, still fighting. But now he fought as a babe might fight, weakly and without purpose. His right hand still clasped his sword but Blood-drinker was like a weight attached to his arm. He could not use it, it just hung there.

Like that, he and Kathyla were carried toward the blue stone altar.

The skeletal hands put them down, to stand before Ulkarion. The mage was rigid with triumph, it glittered from his eyes, it could be seen in the width of his smile.

"You die this day, both of you! You are my first gifts to mighty Sisstorississ! The woman for her beauty and her wisdom, the man for his strength and the might of his sword-arm!"

His black eyes studied Niall where he stood, upheld in his weakness by those many bony hands. Faint was Niall, and only dimly aware of what went on about him. Wizardry had sapped his muscles, turned them into water. He knew this, knew also there was no sense in fighting against it. If he was doomed, then he would meet death as bravely as he had in the past.

To one side of him, Kathyla was whimpering. She shuddered from moment to moment and on her forehead were beads of sweat that testified to her terror. Yet she was still beautiful, still lovely, with that black hair and those burning eyes, and her body — where the candle-flames' light touched it — shone as enticing as ever.

Ulkarion stepped aside, gesturing.

Golden chains lay on the tiled floor, fastened to plates of gold screwed into rock. There were many such chains, but two in particular were foremost among the others, and it was toward these that the skeletal figures pushed them.

One by one, golden manacles were lifted, clamped to their wrists.

They stood chained, after a time, and were aware that Ulkarion walked around them, nodding his head and smiling.

"The victory is mine," he said softly to the woman. "It is to my call that Sisstorississ shall come, and not to yours. You have had a few hours more of freedom, but that does not matter. The demon-god will come for you soon. You he will take first, and then this barbarian swordsman who has made himself your champion."

The black eyes slid sideways, touched Niall, and in them was a faint shadow.

"As for you, sword-man, I do not know how you escaped the fog. No living thing is safe from it. Unless one receives aid from the gods." His lips quirked into a mocking smile.

"Did you, swordsman? Have you invoked the protection of a god? But that I cannot believe! Who are you to have caught the fancy of some demoniac being? Pah! The mere thought is ridiculous."

His gaze went to the length of Blood-drinker.

"A good weapon, that. I shall make it mine — after Sisstorississ has come for you. The demon-god has no need of swords."

Niall eyed him coldly. Were he free, were his weakness gone from

44

him, were those golden chains that bound him fallen from his wrists — ahh, then he would leap with his hands outstretched and his fingers would fasten in Ulkarion's throat and the world would be without one more wizard. Something of this Ulkarion saw in his eyes, for he drew back suddenly, and his face was pale.

"Enough," he rasped. "It is time for the Summoning."

He turned, his black and silver cloak swinging wide. Upward went his arms, in invocation. His voice swelled, rose upwards, reverberated from wall to wall. As magicians had stood since the birth of Time, so stood Ulkarion and intoned his words and phrases, that formula which would unlock the barriers of space.

Niall listened, his body sick, his mind numbed.

Soon now, he supposed, Sisstorississ would come from the void where he dwelt, through the unimaginable abysses of deep space, to make his way to this adit which had been created by those who served him so many millennia ago. No man knew how old was this temple, this stronghold above the river Thalamar. Even the myths that surrounded it were old. Old!

And yet—

He felt it first in his muscles. They seemed to gather strength, they seemed to swell, to harden, to band outward as they had always done. No longer was that weakness so rampant in him. His mind cleared, too, free at last of that paralyzing pall which held him in its grip.

The powerful fingers of his big right hand worked on his sword-hilt

Not yet, Niall. Oh, not yet, my warrior!

Shock held him frozen. That voice! Yet it had not been a voice, not as a human would understand a voice. It had spoken in his mind. But — with the sweet tones of Lylthia, whom he had met in Angalore! Lylthia — who was merely the human manifestation of Emelkartha the Evil!

Soft laughter filled his ears.

You remember, do you? Know then, that neither have I forgotten!

Niall stood bemused, only half believing what was happening. It was not like him to hear voices where there was no body to make them. Yet he knew that Emelkartha was close beside him. Emelkartha, who men named The Evil One, yet whose beauty was like a flame

45

inside Niall of the Far Travels. It was she who had carried him to the threshold of her Eleven Hells, then sent him back to Angalore. It was she who had taken him in her arms, there in her Eleven Hells and kissed him as no woman had ever kissed him.

Aye, she had put her mark upon him!

He waited, every muscle tensing, and listened with half his mind to the somber chanting with which Ulkarion sought to summon Sisstorississ. The rest of his attention was concentrated on Emelkartha.

Why was she concerned with Kor Magnon? Or was she concerned only with her own safety? Could he care what happened here? Did the fact that Sisstorississ was emerging from his own dwelling space into the boundaries of Earth worry her?

"Why?" he whispered.

Inside him an anger was growing, very faint and small. It was as if some strange fury — a godlike rage — was deep in his innermost parts. He shook to hat fury, quivering like a hound at the end of a leash. His right hand clutched Blood-drinker.

Not yet, my love. There is a time to wait.

His muscles eased, yet he was ready.

Ulkarion had finished his chantings. He stood with upraised arms, his black and silver cloak hanging motionless from his shoulders. A silence grew upon that vast chamber where he stood, as though all creation held its breath.

Faintly and from far away, there came the sound of something slithering against the stone walls. The hackles on the back of Niall's thickly thewed neck stood up. A faint reek of slime and corruption came to his nostrils and he tensed, there in his golden chains, waiting.

Ulkarion took a step backward. A shiver seemed to run through his body, so that his black and silver cloak rippled.

Beside Niall, Kathyla sobbed, eyes wide and staring.

Only that sound broke the funereal silence, as vast coils rasped and churned against cold stone. The coming of the snake-god grew louder with each moment, and now Niall could hear a distant hissing, rightful and unnerving.

Sisstorississ comes! Be ready, Niall of the Far Travels!

What could he do, linked as he was to these golden chains and manacles that held him prisoner to the floor? He shook those chains so that they rattled, and fought as if to tear them from the tiles to which they were riveted. Yet inside him that anger swelled upward, almost as if it were something alien, something foreign to his nature.

Closer that rasping came. Closer!

Now in the deeps of that black hole above the altar, Niall could see — a something. Red eyes, glittering with hate, with fury, glowed in that ebon darkness. Nearer they came, until now he could make out that herpetologic head covered with scales, win horns rising upward from the brow, the flickering tongue twice the size of a tall man.

That head filled the hole, slid through it.

Kathyla screamed, a throbbing ululation of utter terror. Even Ulkarion fell back a few paces, awed by the sight of that which he had summoned up. And Niall felt the fury rise up inside his flesh, until it seemed to choke him.

All eyes were on that awful head.

Only Niall noticed that a strangely greenish mist was rising up about him. It seemed to come from inside his body, stretching outward. Like a verdant smoke it rose about his chest — moved outward.

This is my power, Niall! Be not alarmed!

With awed eyes he watched that green fog slide about him, and where it touched the manacles on his wrists, it ate the gold. That gold it turned to powder, so that the powder fell away from him and his arm was free. In seconds, the other manacle was gone, as well.

Niall rose to his full height, shook himself.

Now, Niall! Strike for Emelkartha!

He leaped forward like an arrow released from the bowstring. One big hand hit Ulkarion, knocked him to one side. Onto that black altar he leaped, his sword held high, and like that arrow, he launched himself at Sisstorississ.

As he swung his blade, he saw that the green glow covered the blade. It touched the snake-head even as his steel clove through the scales on that head, drove deep into the brain-pan.

Sisstorississ wailed. In that wail was an agony beyond words, and a paroxysmic rage that seemed almost to shake the very altar on which Niall had planted his war-boots That vast mouth gaped wide, the red eyes flared hatred at the man who muscles bulged as he sought to tear his blade from that skull into which he had driven it.

The sword came free, glittering greenly.

Again Niall struck, and again.

Blood and a colorless ichor spewed forth, like a fountain shedding its waters. Where that blood and ichor touched, steam rose upward and a faint hissing. Drops fell on Niall, but he did not feel them for that verdant tint covered his entire body.

Twice more he struck before that titanic head was withdrawn, back inside the hole and out of sight. For an instant, Niall heard the scrape of scales against distant stone, and then there was only silence.

Sisstorississ has fled! The victory is yours, Niall!

He turned, his sword-blade dripping blood and ichor onto the top of the altar. He stared at Ulkarion who glared back at him disbelievingly. The arch-mage was shivering, but with fear or with anger, Niall did not know. Nor did he care.

He came down off the altar and moved toward the magician.

Ulkarion lifted his hands, began to make archaic symbols in the air. Niall felt a coldness touch him, but even as it did, he leaped, swinging Blood-drinker in a wide arc.

Ulkarion sought to turn, to flee.

Yet even as he did, the length of Blood-drinker swept at him, its steel edge honed to razor sharpness. Through meat and gristle, blood and bone, that edge drove — and Ulkarion's head leaped from his shoulders and went flying through the air.

The body remained on its two feet for an instant, then collapsed.

As the body fell, so also did the dead bones and serments of the dead whom Ulkarion had raised from the grave to be his worshipers. There was a vast sigh throughout that chamber, and then a whisper of sound, a click or two as grave vestments and dried bones collapsed.

Niall found himself staring at a chamber empty of life, save for himself and Kathyla. The dead lay in heaps upon the tiles, and

Ulkarion's body rested lifeless at his feet. The girl was staring at him with wide eyes in which fright lurked with awe.

"You — drove Sisstorississ away," she whispered.

"Not I. I had help from Emelkartha."

"The Evil One? The Mother of All Wickedness?"

Niall grinned. "She's not so evil. I have the notion that she fights for that which she considers to belong to her. Or maybe it's her pride. What difference does it make? She helped us, and I honor her for it."

He moved toward her, reached for his dagger. He began to work the steel point against the golden rivets that held the manacles to Kathyla's wrists. In time he loosed one, and then the other.

"We can go now. There's nothing to keep us here."

Kathyla glanced down at the dead body of Ulkarion. "He would have slain me," she breathed. Her eyes lifted, touched Niall.

"Go you, Far Traveler. I will stay here in these ruins for a while."

Niall eyed her wonderingly. "Now why should you stay here, Kathyla? The world's out there, waiting for you, and this is a dead place, filled only with the dead."

She shook her head. "Trust me, Niall."

He shrugged and turned away. He walked toward the far end of the chamber, but it seemed that as he walked his body grew more tired, so that occasionally he stumbled. Once he paused to lean against a pillar, letting his head hang. His eyelids were so heavy! His brain so bemused! It was almost as if there were some sort of spell on him.

Now — he heard singing.

It was a chanting such as Ulkarion had made, and as he heard it, his very bones seemed to turn to water. His hand clung to the pillar against which he leaned, and his legs trembled. He could not move. He tried, but his muscles refused to listen to his mind.

Bare feet came running.

Kathyla stood before him, eyes glowing. "Fool," she whispered. "Did you not suspect — when Ulkarion sought so hard to kill me?"

He eyed her dully. His brain was numb, but he remembered the manner in which this girl had shrunk away from him, the first time he had seen her, still in those chains. She had never touched him, or very lightly, nor had she permitted him to touch her. It was a puzzle, one he could not solve.

"I am not Kathyla, but — Iphygia! Aye, Iphygia the enchantress, the witch-woman, mortal foe of Ulkarion. He and I sought to come here to these old ruins, to what had been Kor Magnon. Ulkarion knew! And so he tried to slay me, to offer me up as sacrifice."

Her lips smiled, but it was a cold and deadly smile.

"Ulkarion trapped me with his wizardry, would have given me to Sisstorississ, but for you. I owe you a favor for having saved me, for having rid me of Ulkarion.

"And yet — were I to favor you, I think you would find a way to slay me. And this must not be. For now Sisstorississ will serve — me! I will give you to him, to do with what he pleases. It will not be a nice death, Niall. The snake-god will be very angry with you."

Her laughter rang out, mocking.

Deep inside himself, Niall felt again that hatred. He knew now it was not he who hated, but Emelkartha herself, whose demoniac powers were represented by that green cloud which had come from him. She waited now, deep inside some corner of his being, and he sensed that she was smiling even more cruelly than Iphygia.

He shook his head. "Do you think Emelkartha will let you kill me — when she stopped Ulkarion and drove Sisstorississ back into his far abodes?"

Iphygia stared at him. "What are you talking about."

"Didn't you see that green cloud that ate my manacles?"

She touched tongue-tip to lips. "I saw no cloud. I — didn't see how you got free." She shook herself. "Why bother talking to you? Turn around. I'll put you back inside those chains and then summon up Sisstorississ once again."

Emelkartha was stirring. Slowly she was expanding inside him, as once before she had lifted out of him and along his arms to shed his golden bonds and coat the blade of Blood-drinker. He could sense the hate, the fury in her. As she hated Sisstorississ and Ulkarion, now she hated Iphygia.

He could do nothing. He understood that, dimly. He was only a focal point for her power. As that verdant power grew within him, he lost his bemusement, his lassitude. He saw that green fire flow out of him, along his arms, covering his chest, his legs. And as it expanded, it drove out the magical spell under which Iphygia had placed him.

She did not see the verdant flame. Her expression was merely puzzled, for Niall was straightening, rising away from that pillar, and he was smiling down at her.

He raised his right arm. He held no weapon in his hand, but he could see that his arm was green, that it glowed. Iphygia stared at that arm, at the fingers of his extended hand.

From the tips of his fingers, tiny green balls fled outward. They touched Iphygia, ran over her like a malachite slime. And now Iphygia threw back her head and screamed. Agony was in that scream, and a deadly fear.

"No! Niall — save me!"

He cannot. You have offended me, Iphygia, you and Ulkarion! You would have brought back into being That-Which-Was-Conquered! For that, you must die!

Niall watched, unable to move, as that green tint ate at Iphygia. In moments it consumed her, as it had consumed the golden manacles. A bit of dust drifted to the floor, where she had been.

Go on, Niall of the Far Travels! My work here is done.

He stood alone in the ancient temple. A cool wind came off the river and moved through the halls, the vast chamber. Niall shook himself, touched the hilt of his sword, and walked past that which had been Iphygia.

In the outer courtyard, Edron Hobbort was stirring, as though rousing from a deep sleep. All about him his men were staring, looking this way and that. As Edron Hobbort caught sight of Niall, he came forward.

"What is this place? How came we here?" he asked.

"Wizardry. I'll tell you of it, on the way to Urgrik."

Yet as he followed Edron Hobbort and his men along the old

causeway to their ship, he turned and stared back at those crumbling ruins. He thought of Emelkartha and her powers, and he told himself that he would sacrifice a fowl to her, once he came to Urgrik.

He owed her more than that, but what sort of gift could a mere man give — a goddess?

THE STOLEN SACRIFICE

Chapter One

The man moved silently through the shadows, keeping always to the darkest places. He moved as an animal might, his body poised for instant action, a big hand on the hilt of the long-sword by his side. His eyes darted from a doorway to the far corner, where the wind blew a length of scarlet silk hanging from the wall. Caution was in his great body, for he knew that should he be seen this night, death would be his reward.

Niall of the Far Travels was not afraid, though he knew that he would be killed, and in no pleasant way, should anyone discover him, or guess where he went — and why.

For fair Amyrilla of the golden hair had been condemned to die by order of Thyra, queen in Urgrik where Lurlyr Manakor was king. Amyrilla was the favorite concubine of Lurlyr Manakor, and Thyra was jealous of her barbaric beauty. And so Thyra had prevailed upon Lurlyr Manakor to offer her up to the grim god Korvassor in his splendid temple in Urgrik.

Amyrilla was not yet dead. Her death would come in hours, when the priests of Korvassor gathered in the temple to summon up their god. There would be no eyes to see that death, other than those of the priests of Korvassor. Amyrilla would be dragged screaming into the maw of the grim god, to be devoured, and only Lurlyr Manakor would grieve for her.

Well, that was not quite true. Niall would grieve as well, for in the weeks that he had been here in Urgrik, serving under Lurlyr Manakor, Niall had come to know pretty Amyrilla, and had loved her for her gentle ways. Yet now she was to die, abandoned by all save Niall himself.

His huge hand tightened on his sword-hilt Ahead of him, he could see the temple. Its tall towers rose upward almost to the low-hanging clouds, and where the moon shone with silver. The great oaken doors of the temple were locked and bolted; it would be no easy task to win through those doors, to release Amyrilla from the golden clasps that held her and then take her out of the temple, and even out of Urgrik.

Sweat touched the brow of the giant youth. It was not a warm night, the breezes sweeping the streets carried in their touch the hint of coming winter. Yet the sweat stood out on his forehead, for he knew the price he must pay were he to be discovered.

His fur-edged war-boots made no sound as he ran from one dark shadow to the next, nor did the chains that held his scabbard jingle. Nearer he came to the temple, ever nearer, and from time to time he paused to stand motionless listening.

No man save himself walked these deserted streets, due to the edict which Lurlyr Manakor had issued. This night of sacrifice must be a silent one. All Urgrik must weep as Lurlyr Manakor wept for the loss of Amyrilla. No man must venture forth upon the streets; only the guards which patrolled them, to make sure the edict was obeyed.

So far, Niall had seen no sign of the guards.

Yet they were here — somewhere.

He paused now at the wall which ran around the vast temple. One leap at that wall and he would be over it, into the temple grounds themselves. From the ground to the temple would be a quick run. Ah, but could he escape discovery in that brief time? Did eyes watch the temple grounds for any rescue attempt?

He did not know. He cared only because he must avoid discovery.

Niall drew breath. It was now or not at all. He must make the attempt, he must rush that wall and go over it, and if he were seen, why then — he would have to fight. And a fight meant he would never rescue that girl with the long golden hair.

He ran. His hands went up to the coping of the wall and next moment he was outlined against the sky. Then he was over and dropping down into a bed of gorgeous pimalotus blooms. He dropped to his knees and waited, heart hammering.

These was no outcry, no rush of soldiers, of guards. He heard no weapons drawn. Slowly he rose and moved forward, and now he went with more confidence, to the nearest temple doorway. His hand touched the great iron handle, and he turned it. The door swung outward and he slipped inside.

There was ebon darkness in here. Only up there by the altar was there any light. Pallid candle-flames glowed there, surrounding an almost naked girl who hung in golden chains between two ivory posts. Long yellow hair covered her features, for her head hung low, as though she slept.

This was Amyrilla.

Niall sighed. Then he moved forward, his war-boots making no sound on the paving-stones. As he walked through the darkness, his hand fumbled in the leather pouch at his side, in which he had put the pick-lock that he had made earlier this day against the moment of need.

In the last bit of darkness he paused, studying the temple. It was not yet time for the priests to come with their prayers and exhortations to Korvassor, to entice him out of the worlds wherein he dwelt, but that time was soon. He would have to act swiftly, without thought to consequences.

Niall sprang forward. In a bound he was before the girl, was fumbling with the golden manacles about her wrists. His touch roused her, she lifted her head and stared at him through the golden strands of her long hair. Her blue eyes were wide with terror. Yet that terror faded at sight of him.

"Niall," she breathed.

"Be quiet, girl," he growled.

He worked swiftly, thrusting in his pick-lock, turning it until he heard the metallic click that told him the manacle was opening. With his left hand around Amyrilla, he held her even as he probed at the other manacle with his right hand.

In moments, she was free.

Yet as she slumped against him, to be lifted against his chest, he heard the faint chanting of the priests. They were coming now, with their incense burners and their acolytes, to summon up Korvassor.

Niall muttered under his breath as he lifted the girl and tossed her over a shoulder. His eyes went to left and right of the great altar where stood the gigantic statue of dread Korvassor. For an instant, he seemed as though turned to stone.

I cannot carry her out the way I came! We would be seen, and herself recaptured when the guards came to slay me. His thoughts ran in a circle, like mice chasing their tails.

Behind the altar, Niall! And — quickly!

The voice sprang to life inside his head, but — he knew that voice. It was the sweet tones of, Lylthia, that girl he had met in Angalore! But Lylthia was not human. No! She was the flesh and blood manifestation of Emelkartha the Evil. Emelkartha, who had taken a fancy to the big barbarian who had aided him in the ruins that had been Kor Magnon, months before!

He leaped. Like a wild animal he leaped, and he ran as runs the wild tiger, gracefully and with easy strength. Straight for the altar he went and then he dodged around behind it.

Amyrilla groaned. Niall grinned, for he knew what a jouncing she was taking, perched on his shoulder like a sack of meal. Well, he couldn't help that. She had to ride where she was, if they were to get out of this alive.

Yet when they were in the darkness behind the high, altar, almost under the splayed feet of the statue of Korvassor, he let her slide down his body so that she stood before him.

"If you want to live, girl, you'll be silent."

He felt her nod, even as she shuddered.

The floor, my love. The floor!

He dropped and felt the paving-stones with gentle fingers. Ah, here. His fingertips went over the faint crack, then searched about until he discovered the sunken handle. He plucked at it, felt it rise up. Gripping the handle, he yanked upward and a section of the floor rose.

Niall reached downward, felt a step. Then he caught at Amyrilla, shoved her into that dark opening. Sobbing to herself, she went down the stairs. Instantly, Niall was after her, turning to bring the trapdoor down behind him so that it fitted level to the temple floor.

As he did, he heard a faint shuffling, far below.

Chapter Two

Amyrilla shrank back against him, whimpering.

56

Niall growled low in his throat as he pushed past her, lifting his blade from its scabbard. Whatever was down here in these underground lairs was something not quite human. Oh, he had heard tales while he drank with the other guards in the city taverns; there had been whispers of the strange beasts which the priests of Korvassor kept, to be fed with sacrifices, with slaves who had displeased them in some way.

He had no idea what these beasts might be like. He chuckled, thinking that it might be best if Amyrilla could not see them. If they were as hideous as was rumored, she might well scream and so alert the priests as to their whereabouts.

He went down stone steps, half dragging the girl behind him. Always, his sword was out in front, ready to be used against whatever might hurl itself against them. Now that there was an enemy to face, Niall was calm, ready.

He heard nails scrape stone and then something flung itself at him. He could not see it, but neither could it see him. If it had been kept in this darkness for very long, its eyes might be weak. Ah, but its hearing would be fantastic.

Something struck the wall a foot away from him. Niall was aware of an awful stench, and then he was thrusting with his steel. Straight forward he ran his blade, felt it drive into flesh.

Something spurted out and splashed up on him.

He drew back his blade, slashed with it, felt its keen edge going into meat. He had no idea of what this beast was shaped like, yet it lived, it breathed. And it could die.

Twice more he drove in with his sword, and each time he struck home. Now he heard a faint dragging sound, a hushed and labored breathing, and then the sound as of a body falling. Niall reached behind j him, caught at the soft hand that lay against his shoulder, and moved down the stairs.

They came to the bottom of the stairs and moved along a stone floor in that utter darkness. To a far wall they went, and grouping along it, Niall discovered a closed door. Fumbling, he found the latch and lifted it.

Brightness came in at them, from wall torches hung here and there along a corridor. Niall urged the girl through the door and closed it behind him.

"Now where?" she whispered. "Where can we go where there is any safety for such as us?"

"Na, na. Don't despair. We'll find a way."

Her eyes were big in her pale face. "How? The queen hates me. She wants me dead. Do you know what they will do to you for trying to rescue me?'

He grinned, showing his white teeth. "We aren't dead yet, girl. I just wish I knew a way out of these catacombs."

Then he shrugged. "We might as well go this way as any." His hand indicated a stretch of lighted corridor before him. "Come along, now."

They went swiftly, with Amyrilla half running to stay even with him. Along one walkway and then another they went until even Niall, with his barbaric sense of direction, confessed himself lost. He had not the slightest idea of where they were, except only that they must be somewhere within the temple grounds.

Yet something told him that they had come too far for that. Surely, they must have passed from under the garden walls that surrounded the temple. And if they had done that, if they could discover an exit, they might find themselves in the city itself.

In time, they came to a tiny staircase that led upwards. Niall mounted it with Amyrilla at his heels. To a door they came, and here Niall paused, debating within himself whether to open it.

What lay beyond this oaken barrier? More danger? Would there be an attack from the city guards? Or would the priests themselves be waiting for them?

Shrugging, Niall caught the handle, moved it. He stepped out into the night air. High above, the broken remnants of what had once been a moon shone down, the clouds since fled westward. The wind was cool on their faces, with a faint remnant of salt in it.

The river lay not far away, then. And on that river would be boats.

Niall paused to scratch his head. His eyes slid sideways at the girl. He had come far these past few months; from distant Styrethia to Angalore, and then on to Urgrik by way of the river Thalamar. Now he could scarcely stay in Urgrik any longer, certainly not with Amyrilla.

Therefore, he would risk the river.

"Stay close beside me," he muttered. "It's death for anyone to be caught out of doors this night."

She nodded understandingly and half-ran beside him as he angled his long stride toward the riverfront. The smell of salt grew stronger the closer they came to the docks, and now they began to hear the gurgle of waves against the pilings.

At his side, Amyrilla turned to stare back the way they had come. And she gasped, her fingers tightening on Niall's arm. A whimper grew in her throat.

"What's amiss?" he asked, swinging about.

Two red eyes gleamed in the night sky, above the temple to Korvassor. Unblinkingly they stared, and it seemed to Niall that they looked right down inside him, those eyes, studying this man who had dared to snatch away the sacrifice that belonged to the god of Urgrik.

There was no body to those red eyes, just the eyes themselves, and bile rose up in Niall at the sight. The priests did not know where their sacrifice had gone, and so they had enlisted the aid of their god. To good effect, too. Those red eyes had seen him, had glimpsed the girl also. Soon now, the priests would learn where they went.

Niall wasted no time on curses. Their only hope now was the river and a fast boat to sail on it. He swung Amyrilla up in a brawny arm and began to run. He went swiftly, as though he might outrun the stare of those unblinking eyes.

As he ran, his eyes slid across the boats anchored in the river, observing their shape, the set of their masts. He wanted a small ship, a fast one, and he found it with his stare, after a time. He angled his run toward an old pier, half rotted, and carried the girl with him out onto those boards.

An instant he paused, to ask, "Can you swim?"

"Like a darson," she panted. "But it's no use! We—"

He left the pier, plunging downward into the water. As he did, he released Amyrilla. They went deep, and when they came to the surface, they struck out toward the little ship Niall had marked for their own. Behind them, the city was silent. Too silent, Niall found himself thinking. Surely, the priests knew where they were, now.

Korvassor would have told them.

Why then, was there no pursuit? No alarm?

He clambered up onto the ship, reached downward to help the girl, dragging her up onto the deck. For an instant they stood together, dripping water on the deck-planks, staring at those red eyes that watched them.

Niall ran for the sail, curled about the spar. He shook it free of its ropes, then caught at the ropes to raise it. A wind sprang up behind them, filling out the sail.

'The anchor," he growled, and the girl ran forward to catch hold of the chain and lift it upward.

The boat began to move, slowly at first, then more rapidly as the sail filled out and her keel slid through the water. With a hand on the tiller, Niall stared off toward the temple.

The red eyes stared, unblinking.

The priests would be moving now. They would come for their prey. There would be no escaping them.

Chapter Three

The wind blew even more strongly, and now the little craft skimmed across the water, heading northward. Niall stood by the steering-post, his back buffeted by that wind which was intensifying almost to the proportions of a gale. On the deck at his feet, Amyrilla crouched, quivering and moaning. Above and before them, the sail was being strained almost to the ripping point by that monstrous gust, while beneath them the ship fled like a terrified thing.

They headed into darkness, where even the keen eyes of Niall of the Far Travels were almost blind, for without the pale light of the ring of matter that once had been a moon, high above his world, the night was an ebon blackness all about them. Yet the ship sailed on, rushing through the water, as though demon-borne.

Yonder, Niall! There where the light gleams soft and pale!

Aye, that was Emelkartha again, whispering in his mind. He stared through the darkness and saw at last a tiny flicker of light, high up on what seemed to be cliffs. For all his far travels, Niall had never been in this corner of his world before, he knew nothing of its shape. Yet those were cliffs, he felt certain, and he swung the rudder-pole.

Now that wind abated, grew to a mere breeze, and within seconds his keel was grating on tiny stones. Above him and at a distance, he saw that pale fight beckoning. His hand went downward, caught hold of the girl, raised her to her feet.

"Up there," he growled. "There we can find safety."

Her head swung about so she could see where he was looking, and the breath caught in her throat. She shrank away from him, lips quivering.

"Not there — no!" she whispered.

Her fear made him glance down at her. "And why not, girl?"

"There are ruins there — old, old ruins. Men tell tales of those ruins, and always they speak in whispers."

"Tales to frighten little children. I tell you, we're safe enough. It comes to me that our only means of escape from Korvassor is to go there, to hide."

She fought him, trying to escape the hand that held her wrist. Fright looked out at him from her eyes, a deadly terror that made him pause even as he tugged her toward the gunwale. Her face was contorted, her lips drawn back, her nostrils flaring outward.

"They say — they say that Death waits for anyone who enters that temple. Hideous death!"

Niall shrugged and nodded back the way they had come. "Look behind you, Amyrilla. Look!"

She turned her head, saw the distant red eyes hanging above the temple. Far away they were, yet they watched. The girl shuddered. And now she could hear sounds behind her, the rasp and grate of oars in their locks, the swish and swirl of water rushing past the prows of ships.

"Men come for us," growled Niall. "Would you be taken back to Korvassor, to be — eaten — by him?"

She whimpered, but she no longer fought the tug of his hand. She ran beside him to the gunwale, was lifted and tossed over-side onto the pebbled beach. In a moment Niall was beside her, catching her hand and leading her across the beach and toward the cliff.

He could make out a vague path carved out of the rock itself, leading upward to the top of the cliff. He went up it slowly, his sword Blood-drinker in his hand, and with a prayer to Emelkartha on his lips. Behind him, Amyrilla came, reaching out to touch him with soft fingertips, to make certain that she did not lose him.

Now as they went higher and yet higher, he could feel a difference in the air about him. It was colder, and seemed filled with tiny motes of fight, like fireflies almost, that seemed to whisper about them as they climbed. The girl began to whimper aloud now, and came even closer to his big body.

'The realm of the evil spirits that dwell in the ruined temple," she breathed.

Niall scowled. He could not contradict her, for all he knew, she might be right. Yet Emelkartha had bid him come here, and to that place where the pale fight glowed he was going. It seemed to him that he was moving more swiftly, now that he was in among the tiny lights. They flared and surged, they seemed to — beckon — to urge him on in the very faintest of whispers.

He could not understand those whispers, yet he sensed their friendliness. Once he looked back toward the river, and saw three warships filled with soldiers, moving toward his beached vessel. Three warships! Whoever captained them was complimenting his fighting abilities. Not even with his sword Blood-drinker could he hope to withstand so many warriors.

But perhaps he would not have to fight them. It might be that in that ruin up above, he could successfully hide from them. What was it Amyrilla had said? That Death waited for anyone who went into what was left of the temple up there? Well, death waited for them below, too. They couldn't escape it, apparently. Still, Emelkartha had brought them here, and he trusted that goddess.

They came to the top of the cliff, and in the darkness which was lighted by the tiny little glowings, he made out a stretch of crumbled rock, of tiny stones. A dead place, surely! Yet ahead were white columns and broken bits of wall which once had been — long ages ago! — the fane of some god.

He walked toward it, sword out and the girl half-running beside him. Behind him, the warriors of Lurlyr Manakor and his queen were coming ashore, their weapons out to capture them. And always the tiny, elfin voices of those faint fights urged him onward, bidding him hurry, hurry!

Then he was at the rim of what had been a temple, long ago.

The brightness he had seen from the river shone eerily, here. Wisps and bits of those tiny fights in the air outside seemed almost to have coalesced inside the temple, forming a brilliant nimbus of cold fight. It hung a few feet above the tessellated floor, shimmering, incandescent, and it appeared to whisper as the tiny fights had whispered.

"What is this place?" Amyrilla whispered.

"I thought you knew," he growled.

"I know only what the rumors say. That ages ago it was a temple to some god or goddess, that it had been abandoned. Yet — yet here Death waits for any who enter, who dare to — profane it."

"And that fight?"

The girl shook her head. "I never heard of that."

Niall stared more closely at that strange, glowing globe. There seemed to be a fife to it — inside it — as sentient as he himself. He grew aware of a vast intelligence, it appeared almost to whisper out at him, urging, commanding. There was an imperiousness to it that reached outward toward him.

It wanted him to do something.

Yes, he knew that, suddenly. But — what?

He heard faery laughter.

Foolish one. Do you think he can understand you, after so many eons in which you have lain sleeping? Na, na, Devolian!

There was an utter silence. Yet outside that silence there was — danger! Something in Niall stirred to it, and a corner of his mind whispered to him that while he stood here before this eerie fight, armed men were climbing cliffs for him.

Unless Emelkartha aided him, he was doomed. Alone, he would never be able to drive away those warriors who were even now coming for him and Amyrilla.

"What?" he growled. "Gods! What do you want me to do?"

Reach inside the light, Niall! Reach and — grasp!

Niall was dubious. The light surged and waxed even blighter. It was not hot, but it was cold, numbing. He could feel that cold, it made him shiver.

But if Emelkartha wanted it—

He shifted his sword to his left hand and reached out into that brilliance with his right. He touched nothing, he felt only a paralyzing coldness, an arctic chill that ran up his arm and into his very heart. He swayed, eyes half closed, knowing that in a moment, he was going to collapse. No human flesh was ever meant to stand such cold.

And then—

His fingers tightened on something hard.

Draw it forth, Niall of the Far Travels. Draw it forth!

He yanked his arm free of that brightness. Clutched in his big hand was a piece of what seemed to be crystal. It was shapeless, and yet—

Niall scowled. There was shape to this thing. Inside himself, he knew it. Yet it had been fashioned in a world which was not of his. As his fingers went over it, as his eyes studied it, and he found himself remembering that in his early youth, just when he had taken up his profession of sell-sword, he had seen something akin to this thing that he held in his fingers.

It had been in Styria, when he had ridden with the Red Guards of Falfarran. They had made a long ride across a corner of the Lomarrian Desert, which was reputed to be what was left of a fertile land that had existed a hundred thousand years before. There had been a ruined temple in that desert, a thing of broken columns and shattered walls.

In a part of that ruined fane, he had come upon a shattered statue. Now if that statue had been whole and unbroken, it might look like this crystal thing. Very much like it.

"Devolian," he whispered.

And in answer, or so it seemed, that crystal thing grew warmer and comforting. It grew brighter, radiant, and from within it, he heard the faint music of a million bells thinly chiming...

"Niall!"

He dragged his eyes from the crystal statue to stare at Amyrilla. She was looking behind him, at the cliffs edge, and there was utter terror in her blue eyes.

Niall swung about.

Moving toward him were several lines of swordsmen, their blades naked in their hands, their faces dimly seen beneath their helmets. On their armor he could make out the basilisk insignia of the kingdom of Urgrik. They came slowly but steadily, for their prey was here in the temple of the forgotten god, Devolian. There was nowhere for them to run, no place to hide. All that was needed to do now was attack and subdue them.

Niall grinned. Cold was his grin, and unpleasant. A few of the men in that front line who saw his grimace, shuddered and knew fear in their hearts. Aye! They knew the way of Niall of the Far Travels with his sword Blood-drinker. And they were not eager to be the first ones to test his sword-arm

Yet they came on, urged by their officers and by the weight of the men who came behind them. Sweaty hands worked on sword-hilts, getting a firmer grip. Soon enough they would stand before Niall and that sword of his. Soon enough.

Niall awaited their coming, his own sword ready. Slightly behind him was the girl. She was breathing harshly, yet she was no longer whimpering.

Niall chuckled. "A cleaner death, girl, than being taken by Korvassor. A couple of slices from those blades, and we'll stand together before Father Thimugor, waiting for his judgment on our lives."

"They won't kill us," she whispered. "They want us — alive!"

He thrust the crystal into his belt-pouch, closed the hasp. Then he moved forward to the edge of the broken pavement, sword in his hand. Behind him came Amyrilla.

They came then, in a coordinated rush, pale light glimmering on their sword-blades These were veterans of the wars of Lurlyr Manakor, who had fought the savages of the eastern frontiers, who had battled against the troops of Queen Thalmyra, who had stood off the hordes of Omar Khan.

Niall went to meet them, sword swinging. Two men went down before that first sweep of the blade, then another, and now he stood surrounded, the ringing clash of steel on steel drowning out the gasps of and curses of the fighting men. Niall was everywhere, leaping, dodging, ducking a blow and thrusting.

He fought carefully, without seeming plan. Yet always he maneuvered his path toward a great pillar, crumbling away under the weight of the eons, until at last he put his spine to it so that no man could come at him from behind, and now he fought as does the wounded bear, snarling beneath his breath and thinking only of killing as many of his adversaries as was possible.

His great, rolling muscles shifted under his tanned hide as he moved his sword one way and then another, catching a man rushing in boldly or driving out to draw blood from another as that man was seeking to outflank him. He felt a tug at his belt and knew that Amyrilla was lifting out his dagger, using it to stab those who came within reach of that sharp Orravian steel.

The battle was hopeless, of course. Yet perhaps because of its very hopelessness, Niall fought as he may never have fought before. No beginner, he, to the clang and clash of weapons. All his life he had fought, it was a way of life for him. He took rash chances, sometimes leaping from the broken pillar to transfix two men before any could guess his intent, then leaping back to rest his giant frame against the crumbled rock obelisk.

Yet he did not die. Swords cut into his flesh, but these were minor wounds. Blood ran down his shoulder and sides, and his legs bled too, where sharp steel had sliced him. Yet he stood tall and firm, and his sword-arm seemed untiring. But there was a growing weariness inside him, in his blood, in his muscles. Not much longer could he stand here against a small army.

There were no arrows shot at him, no spears appeared, they wanted him alive, to offer him up to Korvassor. He and the girl, these were to be the sacrifices.

Dawn was in the air, a brightness to the east, when they rushed him. Half a dozen lines of rested veterans came forward at the run, shields up. The men he had been fighting drew back to give them room. Niall saw them coming, saw the tilted shields locked together. There would be no escape.

He smiled bitterly. "It ends, Emelkartha," he whispered.

His sword came up and he struck with it, but he hit only those shields, knowing as he did so that these veterans were using not swords but ropes against him — nets that would cling to him, that would hamper his sword-arm He felt their touch, he tried to evade them, but could not.

They fell about him, faster and faster, as those veterans flung them. Entangled in those strands, his sword-arm useless, nevertheless he battled on as best he could until the haft of a dagger struck him between the eyes.

Niall dropped and lay motionless...

He opened his eyes to the movement of a boat through water. Amyrilla knelt beside him, his head on her thigh, her head bent and her tears dropping slowly on his face. There were many men around them, armed men. When they saw his eyes staring up at them, they grinned and moved closer.

"Man, you're a fool," one said.

"To risk your life for a dancing girl!"

"But — gods! How you can fight!"

There was no enmity in them, only a mild envy. And a grim sympathy. They knew how he would die, chained to those ivory posts, when Korvassor came to claim him. It would not be a nice death, absorbed into the god-being.

"More than a score of men dead, two score with wounds," one man was muttering, shaking his head. "I thought no one man could ever cause such havoc against such fighters as we have in the Borstyrian Guard."

"It's a waste of a good man," another murmured.

"You've angered Lurlyr Manakor," a captain nodded. "Bad enough to offend the queen, which you did when you stole the girl. But the king — ah, that was a true mistake."

Niall growled, "What difference does it make? I'll die. A man can die only once."

"But you won't die. That is, not actually die. Whoever is absorbed

67

into Korvassor becomes a part of him and — lives on."

Niall shuddered.

Chapter Four

He hung from golden chains between two ivory posts. Beside him, so that he could see her by turning his head, he could make out the naked body of Amyrilla, slumped down so that she would have fallen but for the manacles clasped to her wrists.

From the girl, his eyes went around the temple. It was dark here, except for the few tapers that were lighted here and there on the altar. They were the only ones in the temple. They were the sacrifices, those who were to be offered up to Korvassor.

Soon now would come the priests. And after them, Lurlyr Manakor and his queen, Thyra of the Midnight Hair. The king and queen would come here to see them taken by the god-being. They would want to know that their vengeance was complete.

Niall rattled the golden chains that held him prisoner. The sound of their clashings was loud in the stillness of the temple. Sweat came out on his forehead but it was not the sweat of fear but rather that of fierce fury. He had never been so helpless. Never!

For a moment he thought of biting his wrists, of letting his blood run out of his body, so as to kill himself and cheat Lurlyr Manakor of his vengeance and Korvassor of his flesh. Yet the will to live pounded strongly within Niall of the Far Travels, he was not a man to yield himself so shamelessly.

But he did not want to die!

Nor shall you, Niall. Not with myself beside you.

The words were in his mind even as he saw a faint shimmering, as though faery lights were gathering before him. And then, shrined in that pale brilliance, he saw — Emelkartha No, not Emelkartha but — Lylthia!

Aye! The goddess stood before him in her human guise, as once she had appeared in Angalore to the south, clad only in that bit of rag she had worn there, when he had rescued her and then, slept as she fled

68

away to die — apparently — on the death-stone of the wicked mage, Maylok

She stepped toward him, smiling. Her arms came up to go about his neck and her red lips were pressed against his own. For an instant, he knew utter bliss. His senses leaped and quivered to the delight of her caress.

And then, smiling up at him teasingly, she stepped back, lifting a hand and shaking a finger at him in mock anger.

Do you think I would let Korvassor take you? Do you, Niall? Na, na. Emelkartha is no wanton, to toss her lover to the gods. There is a plan, Niall. And you must play a part in it."

"What part?"

"Nay, now. This I cannot tell — lest you betray to Korvassor what I have in mind. Just be easy. Act as though you knew me not. Is this agreed between us?"

Niall scowled. "Agreed," he muttered.

The ways of a goddess were strange to mortal men. He wondered what was in her mind. Yet he did not wonder long, for she came forward, pressing herself against him and kissing him again, and once more Niall knew that strange ecstasy which only Lylthia — or — Emelkartha — could bring to him.

He heard a distant sound.

At once, Lylthia drew away, laughed softly, and began to fade. But just before she disappeared, she raised pink fingers to her mouth and blew him a kiss.

The sound grew louder and now Niall knew it for the strum of sistrums, the tinkle of bells, the musical clangor of cymbals. Voices too, he heard, raised in song.

That chant grew louder and now he could make out, at the far end of the temple, the procession of priests who came toward them, served by acolytes. Candles swayed, lighting their way. Their chant grew more solemn, raised in worship of the god.

Niall stood firmly on his war-booted feet. He would meet these priests as he met warriors: head up, with no fear in his heart. His eyes slid sideways, toward Amyrilla. The girl was conscious now, rising to her full height. Yet her lips quivered, and he saw tears gathering in her eyes.

"I'll save you," he muttered. "So stop worrying."

She gasped, turning to eye him in stunned amazement. "Save me? But how? You're chained just as I am."

He could not tell her of Lylthia, nor of her promise. And so he muttered, 'There will be a way. Just trust me."

Amyrilla sighed, but the color came back into her cheeks, and she stood more bravely than before. Indeed, as Niall thought, they both seemed far more defiant than the occasion warranted. The priests of Korvassor sensed this defiance, and on their pale faces smiles sprang into being. Only the high priest, an old man with long white hair and a beard, gazed at them dubiously, as though he sensed that their defiance was based on something other than mere human courage.

The priests took up their places before the altar. In low voices they chanted on, but still they waited. Now the great doors at the far end of the temple opened, and down the broad aisle came armed men, fanning out as they approached the altar. Behind them, in gilded palanquins, came King Lurlyr Manakor and his queen, Thyra the Dark one. They were here to witness the fit punishment of those who had transgressed against them.

Lurlyr Manakor stepped from his palanquin when it came to a halt, and walked forward toward the altar. He was a big man lately run to fat, but the huge body and the iron will, which had made him a conqueror of nations, could still awe the onlookers.

Toward Niall he walked, though his eyes swung sideways toward the naked body of Amyrilla. In happier days, she had been his favorite. But since he had wedded Thyra of the Midnight Hair, he had been forced to put Amyrilla aside. Even to offer her up to Korvassor as a sacrifice.

The king sighed once, then twice, and then he looked at Niall. There was no hate in his eyes, only pity. In a low voice so that neither the priests nor the acolytes might hear him, he spoke to the Sell-sword

"I am sorry you failed. If it were up to me, neither of you would die. I would, set you free and pay you good gold to see you on your way." He shook his head. "But I no longer reign in Urgrik. The priests of Korvassor rule this city."

Niall said nothing, yet felt pity for this man in his heart. He was a conqueror, a fighting man, yet in his crown city, he was subject to the priests and to his wife, the Queen Thyra. Lurlyr Manakor eyed him a moment, then turned away.

Now the curtains of the second palanquin moved, fluttering. And out stepped Thyra, clad all in ebon robes, with her long black hair bound with diamonds and pearls. She was a beautiful woman, everyone acknowledged that — yet Niall thought to read cruelty in her hard eyes, in her pale face. She stood a moment as slave-girls lifted off the jet robe in which she was swathed. Now she was revealed in a thin garment of purest black silk in which threads of gold were cunningly woven. Golden sandals were on her small feet.

Thyra moved across the flaggings, smiling almost to herself. Toward Amyrilla she walked, and at her every step her cruelty became more manifest. Her lips were drawn back, her eyes became slitted.

She came to a halt. Her hand darted out, clapping hard against the face of the girl in the golden manacles. Loud and sharp were the sounds of those slaps, and Amyrilla's head was knocked sideways by their force.

Then Thyra turned toward Niall and now he could see the hard eyes, the distorted lips. She came toward him, and for a moment their eyes locked. Hers were haughty, proud, and still cruel.

"You dared?" she breathed. "You dared to try and rescue her for whom I had decreed death. Well, you shall pay the penalty along with her. Remember Thyra wherever it is that Korvassor takes you."

She turned and moved away, and now the sistrums and the flutes began to wail again, very softly. In was an eerie tune they played on their instruments, and a cold chill went down Niall's spine.

They were summoning Korvassor. He had learned enough about Urgrik and its ways since he had arrived here to take service with Lurlyr Manakor to know that much. In hushed whispers over goblets filled with Kallarian wine, men had spoken of the temple and that which came into it when the music played and the priests chanted.

Now the priests were chanting in some long-forgotten language. The sound of those words made Niall even colder. What they did here was obscene, frightful. They were summoning up dread Korvassor, were offering to him the bodies of a man and a woman.

Niall rattled his chains as he stretched his big body. Fury grew inside him, a raw heat that seemed almost to lift him upward. It was not a human anger, but rather a rage that seeped into him from outside.

"I defy Korvassor!" he bellowed. "Let him come. I shall destroy this god you worship."

There was a silence after his outburst. Even the sistrums and the flutes had stilled. The priests looked at one another, then at the high priest who stood motionless, eyes hollowed in his head. Those eyes burned at Niall, filled with fury and with — what? Foreknowledge of some awesome doom? Fear?

Queen Thyra moved from where she had stationed herself beside Lurlyr Manakor. Her right hand came up, imperiously. "The man is half-dead with fright. Why do you hesitate? Continue the ritual."

The sistrums woke to life, and with them the cymbals. Loudly they sounded, as though they might drown out the words of this giant who hung in the golden manacles. Niall moved his eyes from the musicians to the priests, to that high priest who regarded him so dubiously.

There was doubt in his eyes, and worry.

Lurlyr Manakor too, looked uncomfortable. Yet his queen stood regally proud, her head held high, her eyes burning with the hate she had for Amyrilla and this barbarian who hung in the golden chains.

Heat gathered on the altar. Niall felt it as he might a hot fog, creeping over the tiles, seeping upward about his legs and hips. To one side, Amyrilla moaned, as she too felt that awful heat. Soon now, Korvassor would emerge from whatever worlds he inhabited and — take them.

Words whispered in his mind, and in answer to them, Niall stiffened his body, stood upright and shook the golden chains that held him.

"I defy Korvassor," he bellowed. "I defy the wicked one — in the name of Devolian himself!"

The high priest gasped.

And the heat fled back, away from Niall. It retreated, almost as though fearful of him. The sistrums strummed and the cymbals clanged, even louder. The priests chanted with harsh voices.

Slowly the hot mists crept back. Slowly, slowly. They surged about his feet, ran up his legs to his hips and higher. It grew hard to breathe, for those mists were strangling him, almost suffocating him. Niall shook himself, rattling the chains.

Now he saw that those before him — the musicians, the acolytes, the priests themselves — were drawing backward, away from the high altar. There was fear in their, eyes as they stared at something behind Niall. Fear and awe and something of — horror. Only the high priest stood firm.

Niall swung about, stared.

Something was forming behind the altar, in the curved niche that reared high above the statue of Korvassor. Shapeless and formless it was, black and evil. Menacing! In the middle of that amorphous bulk, two red eyes shone forth, unblinkingly.

A coldness settled in Niall.

This was Korvassor, summoned from his hells, eager to devour that which was being offered to him. This was the wicked god of Urgrik, he who came from beyond Time and Space. He-who-devours.

Fear not, Niall! I am with you!

Ah, that was Emelkartha, whispering again in his mind. Ha! Easy for her to say, not to be afraid. But by all the Gods! This thing was something out of nightmare, something which should never have been born.

What defense could anyone have against it?

The hot mists were all over him now, stifling him. Yet it seemed to Niall that those mists did not sting him as fiercely as they had done. It was almost as though he had become immune to them, or that he was — protected.

Korvassor bulked huge now, filling the space behind the altar. He was beginning to flow forward, emerging onto the altar tiles themselves. Shapeless he was, and of no certain outlines, yet the menace that emanated from that gross bulk was as palpable as the flagstones on which Niall stood.

Ah, now Korvassor was completely out of that far-distant world he inhabited. His bulk was moving, sliding — oozing — across the tiles, straight for his victims. The red eyes studied them hungrily. Almost, the hulk seemed to drool.

Faster it flowed. Faster!

A tentacle touched Niall, paralyzing him. Agony stabbed inward from his skin, around which that black tentacle was clasped. Yet Niall did not cry out. Rather, he stood firm, almost defying this god-being who had come for him.

Korvassor felt that defiance and was puzzled.

The red eyes grew angry.

More and more of that black bulk flowed forward. It hovered high above Niall, and paused, waiting. In another moment, it would dart downward to surround him, absorb him.

Something stirred, close to Niall. Stirred and — waited.

Korvassor swooped downward. His tentacles fashioned arms that stretched out to gather him in. Swiftly he moved, blotting out all sight from the waiting Sell-sword Then those dark arms closed on him.

Niall felt the pain, the agony. He opened his mouth to scream. No mere man could endure such pain! His heart pounded, the sweat ran out of his pores. And yet — and yet — he still stood. And now — that agony was receding.

Something was flowing out of Niall, something that ran with the swiftness of water rippling over brook-stones It went to meet Korvassor, went eagerly, almost singing as it flowed. Niall shuddered, knowing suddenly that this was Devolian — Devolian, whom he had brought here from that abandoned temple, in that crystal shape.

I am here, black one! You of the red eyes, I am come at last!

Korvassor screamed.

There was agony in that scream, and despair. Niall felt those emotions as a distant part of himself, and he knew that just as Korvassor was experiencing them, so he was himself, since he was a part of that god-being.

Then, abruptly, Korvassor spewed him forth.

Niall crumpled on the tiles, staring. No longer were the golden manacles on his wrists, they lay beside him on the floor.

High above, the blackness which was Korvassor wrestled with the thing that was Devolian. Fiercely they fought. Fiercely! Korvassor sought to retire into that curving space out of which he had come, yet always Devolian was there before him, to prevent it. And now, slowly,

Korvassor was weakening. Less furious were the rushes he made, not so brilliant were his red eyes. And always, that which was Devolian closed in about him, surrounding him.

Niall glanced back at the priests.

They stood as though under a spell, only their eyes being alive. The high priest was very pale, very frightened. The fear in him was like a living thing. And to one side, Amyrilla lay unconscious in her golden manacles.

Now Korvassor merely writhed in the watery tentacles that gripped him, squeezing him. The red eyes were dimmed, almost to extinction. In another moment, they would disappear.

And then — suddenly — only Devolian stood upon the tiles.

Transparent he was, a shimmering curtain of brilliant lights. Niall heard those lights whispering joyously, radiant with delight, with power. Forward moved that curtain, quivering, sentient! It poised a moment above Niall, almost as though contemplating him.

Downward stretched an arm of those lights, touched him.

My thanks, man of this world. But for you, I should never have been able to trap Korvassor, to destroy him!

Niall had never felt so energetic. The power of Devolian swam through his flesh, his veins. He straightened, all the agony and its memory gone from him. He put a hand on his sword half-lifted it from the scabbard.

"I have enemies too, Devolian. Let me—"

Nay, now. These are my enemies as well.

Forward swept that living curtain, toward the priests and the acolytes of Korvassor, and when it touched them, they became shimmering motes of brightness that faded into nothingness. The high priest screamed and whirled to flee but Devolian swept forward, rushed over him — and the high priest no longer existed.

The curtain poised, moved forward.

Thyra the Dark screamed once, a high shrilling that reverberated from wall to wall of the temple. She turned as had the high priest, but the curtain of lights surged forward, touched and enveloped her.

Niall heard a faint, distant keening. Then — silence.

Slowly now, the curtain faded, and where it had stood was emptiness.

Niall growled and moved toward Amyrilla. But he was too slow. Lurlyr Manakor raced forward, his hand getting a key out of his pouch. It was his hand that inserted the key, his arms that caught the girl as she stirred and looked up at him.

"Can you forgive me? It was not I but Thyra and the high priest who condemned you. They worshiped Korvassor, it was they who insisted on restoring the old worship, the giving of sacrifices."

Amyrilla smiled faintly. "There is nothing to forgive, Lurlyr. Yet there is thanks to be said — to Niall."

Lurlyr Manakor flushed and glanced sideways. "There is that, of course. And you know how deeply I am indebted to you, Niall. Ask what you will of me. Except Amyrilla. Her I mean to marry, to make my queen."

Niall shrugged, remembering that he had acted because of Emelkartha "No thanks are needed. I did what — I had to."

"You shall be given half my kingdom."

Niall only shook his head. "I'm no ruler. I'm only a warrior."

"Then you shall be made general of my armies. I shall build you a fine castle, I shall fill your chests with gold and jewels. Come now, walk with us out of this temple which is no longer a temple. Come, Niall."

"In a moment."

He watched them move down the aisle, arm in arm. Aye, they were going to be married, to rule together in Urgrik. But he? He who had helped bring this all about? What was there for him that he wanted?

It was a whisper in the air, no more. Yet every part of his body quivered to the sound of that voice. "Where are you?" he asked hoarsely.

"Soon I shall come to you, Niall. Soon, now. Be patient."

She came out of the shadows, almost naked, still wearing those bits of rag which she had worn in An-galore. She was smiling, she was holding out her arms. And Niall stepped into them.

He held her for a long time, kissing her. Oh, he knew she would never stay here with him in this world where he lived. But to have her like this, sweet and warm and scented, her soft mouth under his, was reward enough for him who was a sell-sword

Even when she went away from him, blowing him those kisses, he did not despair. Some day she would come to him again. For that he lived, for that he would wait in patience.

THE THING FROM THE TOMB

Chapter One

Niall of the Far Travels reined in his big gray stallion, lifting his right hand to halt the long column of riders who followed him across this comer of the Baklakanian Desert. In front of him, and far away, he could make out a dark blotch on the golden sands toward which he was moving.

The blotch did not move.

Yet it had moved, for a brief second, just then. Niall, who had been watching it as soon as he had caught sight of it, was certain of that. His hand went to his side, loosed his sword Blood-drinker in its scabbard.

Niall was commander of the armies of King Lurlyr Manakor of Urgrik. His robe was of saffron silk and it blew in the lazy winds that swept across these stretches of bleak and empty sand. His mail was silvered and bore the basilisk insignia of Urgrik. He was riding to make an inspection of the desert forts which served his king, to replace the troops stationed there with the men who rode behind him.

But now—

Caution w;as alive in him. Again and again he scanned these sands, seeking some explanation for that dark blotch. The hairs on the back of his neck stood up, and he sensed, with an animal awareness, that there was danger here. Or — had been.

To the lieutenant who rode at his right elbow he said, "Keep the men here."

He toed the stallion and rode forward, and as he went, he drew his blade. Niall did not know what that dark blotch might be, but he would be ready for trouble.

He rode slowly, the hooves of his mount kicking up little puffs of sand. As he came closer to the blotch, it resolved itself into the shape of a man, a man w;ho had been cruelly attacked, wrenched about and torn as if by gigantic bands. Sympathy touched Niall, made him snarl under his breath and urge the big gray horse faster.

He swung down from the saddle to kneel above the dying man and turn him over onto his back. The man w~as a grizzled veteran of Urgrik. His face was scarred with old wounds, and his body was clotted with blood from more recent ones.

The man opened his eyes.

"Death," he whispered. "Death came in the night and—" He choked and his eyes closed. Niall leaned closer, his arm about the man, half lifting him as if to ease him of his pain.

The soldier smiled, nodded. His eyes opened once again. "Beware the fort. They're all dead, inside it. Only I got away. Crawled. Crawled until I — could crawl no more."

His hand closed on Niall's wrist. "Beware the tiling in the fort. It cannot — be killed..."

The man shuddered and writhed as pain ate inside him. He gasped at the hot desert an and stared upward into the face of the man who bent above him.

"It began when they were di-digging ... digging to find more water. They — uncovered an old-tomb. And then..."

The man shuddered once more, violently, and then Ins body sagged. Niall looked down at him with pity in his eyes. Pity and — admiration. If this man had not struggled and fought to crawl out this far away from the frontier fort, he and his men would have ridden into untold danger.

He straightened and let the man down gently on the hot sand. He stood up and waved Ins column forward.

When the lieutenant stood before him, Niall said, "This one came from the fort. Apparently he is the only one left alive. His comrades dug for water and seemingly uncovered a tomb — or so he says. Death came out of that tomb and killed the entire company, excepting only him."

Niall scowled. His eyes ran along the column, studying the faces of these men he led. He could not take them into the fort, not without discovering what danger lay before them.

"Go back to Urgrik," Niall said slowly. "Tell Lurlyr Manakor that I have gone on alone to discover what this danger is. If I don't return," here he shrugged, "then I would advise that he consult magicians to try and learn what it is that has come up from the ground to slay his warriors."

The lieutenant would have protested, he would have urged that the entire column go on with their commander, but Niall would have none of it.

"I am one man. I may discover what the thing is that has killed. One man may hide where many cannot. Besides, now that I command the armies of the king, mine is the duty to protect them."

He would hear no argument. He waited until the dead man was wrapped in a blanket and slung across one of the pack mules. He stood and watched the column as it swung about and headed back toward Urgrik.

Only then did he mount up and urge the gray stallion onward. As he rode, his eyes were forever busy, staring out across the sands toward the low line of mountains in the distance, toward which he went.

What was this danger that could wipe out an entire detachment of hard-bitten soldiers? Each man of them was used to weapons, used to fighting the hill tribes, accustomed to swift forays or long battles. Yet something had destroyed them.

Unease lay along his muscles. Niall had met many foes, he had always defeated them, whether they were of the robber kingdoms that lay along the shores of the Aztallic Sea or the trained legions that swore allegiance to the Great Kham. He knew of nothing that could destroy an entire garrison and leave wounds on its victims such as those he had seen on the man who had crawled across the desert.

"By Emelkartha's pretty toes," he muttered. "I may be riding to my death."

Well, he had known that when he had sent back his troops. There was no need for more than one man to die, if die he must. No sense in condemning an entire troop to that method of dying.

He growled low in his throat and rode on.

In time he came to where he could sit his saddle and stare at the high walls of the frontier fort. Nothing stirred there except for the flags that bore the basilisk standards of Urgrik, limp in the still air. No man walked the walls. The big wooden gates were wide open, affording him a partial view of the parade grounds, but these were empty.

Sighing, Niall rode on.

He came up to those open gates and moved between them. In utter silence, he swung down from the saddle and moved here and there, studying the ground. Then he walked into the barracks.

There were bodies here, torn and mutilated as the dead man on the sands had been. Niall let his eyes run over them, trying to imagine what demoniac power could have done this to living men, to men accustomed to fighting. A cold chill ran down his spine.

He heard a whisper in the air and his head snapped up even as he drew his blade. Something was here in the fort. Something deadly, something hateful.

Niall was about to take a step forward, to go in search of whatever it was that quested through the halls and barracks of this frontier fort. Something touched his wrist and held it.

Do not go, Niall: It waits for you!

Ah! That was Emelkartha the Evil, goddess of the eleven hells. Niall grinned and felt himself relax. It has been some time since he had faced death on the high altar in the temple to Korvassor, with pretty Amyrilla beside him.

Now Amyrilla was queen in Urgrik, being wedded to Lurlyr Manakor. And he himself was commander of the king's armies.

"Well? What am I to do?" he asked softly. "Wait here for that thing to come and kill me?"

Anger was in the voice that whispered in his mind.

Do you think I would let you be killed? I felt your trouble and I came as swiftly as I could, to help you. I do not know what it is you are to face and so I must be — careful.

"I'd like it better if you became Lylthia, if I could see you," he growled.

You would only want to kiss me.

"What's wrong with that? I love you."

The anger was gone from that inner voice, it held only tenderness

81

now. Perhaps. In a little while. After I learn what it is that quests for you.

The whispering in the barracks grew louder. Niall swung about, almost forgetting Lylthia. The danger that had killed an entire garrison was after him, now. Would he be wrenched about and twisted, cut up as those others had been? Would even Emelkartha herself be able to save him?   It came slowly, whispering more loudly. Through the passages of the barracks and the fort it made its way, hunting him. Niall's band was fastened tightly to his sword-blade, but of what use was a sword against something like this? Those dead soldiers had had swords and had undoubtedly used them.

Niall gasped.

A ball of blue fire hung above the floor, motionless. It had moved out of the hallway and into this larger room, and now that it sighted its prey, it paused, seemingly to gloat over him.

Even Emelkartha was silent, as though stunned by what she was seeing through his eyes. Then he heard her whisper very faint.

It cannot be! I dream! This thing was destroyed five thousand centuries ago!

The bluish ball moved forward, whispering more shrilly, as though already it were tasting the blood of this man who stood before it.

Niall! Let me!

He felt something run along his veins, felt it slip out of his hand. Instantly the steel blade of Blood-drinker blazed with crimson light. It was as though a million tiny fires blazed within its hardness.

Fight now, Niall! Fight and — destroy this thing!

He hurled himself forward, and harsh laughter-eager laughter — rose up from the blue ball to gloat at him. The blueness rushed, even as Niall swung his sword.

Into that blue ball he drove his crimson steel, felt it bite. He wrenched it out and drove in forward again, barely aware that the blueness was screaming as though in mortal anguish.

Into the ball he stabbed his blade and heard again that keening cry of wild despair. Before his eyes it seemed to shrink, sought to turn and flee.

Do not let it go, Niall! After it!

He ran as swiftly as any Thort deer and as he ran he swung Blood-drinker again. Through the blue ball he drove his crimson steel, again and yet again.

The blue ball wailed. No longer did it whisper so hungrily, for now it was shrinking, as though it were losing shape. Its roundness disappeared, jagged edges came into view. Niall stabbed again.

Suddenly the blue ball was gone.

From somewhere far away, something screamed.

Chapter Two

The crimson faded from his blade as Niall lowered his sword and stared around him dazedly. Where was the thing? Had he really destroyed it? He grew aware that sweat ran down his back.

He heard a patter of feet and swung about.

Emelkartha ran toward him, wearing those same ragged garments she had worn in Angalore. Into his arms she threw herself, to be clasped and kissed more hungrily than Niall had ever before kissed a woman.

For a long time he held her, caressing her, whispering words of love into her ears, half hidden by her long black hair, as dark as Corassian ebony. Then her bands were on his muscular shoulders, pushing him back and away.

Green eyes gazed up at him fondly.

"So. You have not forgotten Lylthia?"

"How could I forget you? Don't you know I dream of you, night after night?'

"You are a very foolish man, you know," she chided him. "You rush into dangers the way a bull rushes at a red flag."

He grinned down at her. "I always have you to protect me."

"That is only because I like you very much. But you must not expect me to be around you all the time."

"Only when there is nobody to see you. Like now."

"And because you are in trouble." She pouted. "Much trouble, if I am not mistaken." Her eyes went up to stare into his. "Do you know where you are, right now?'

"Of course. In a frontier fort that belongs to the kingdom of Urgrik."

She nodded. "Yes, of course. But it is something more. I did not realize it myself until just a little while ago. You are standing where once bloomed the ancient land of Pthest."

Niall turned the word over in his mind. "Never heard of it."

"You would not. It has long since been forgotten by mankind. But five thousand centuries ago, it was famous all across the world. Sosaria Thota lived here, where it was a garden world."

"Oh? And who was Sosaria Thota?"

"A most famous witch. Some said she was the daughter of a demon, She ruled this part of the world with cruel fingers. Kings and emperors paid her fortunes to have her cast spells for them."

"Well, she's dead now."

"Is she, Niall? I begin to think she still lives — or hopes to."

He stared down at her. It was on the tip of his tongue to tell her that this was nonsense, but he was remembering other times when he had encountered magic and the effects of magic. But why would this Sosaria Thota come alive again? How could she?

It was as if Lylthia read his mind when she murmured, "Because she has made a bargain with the wicked ones who dwell in mega-space, who wait outside the world you know, seeking a way to enter it."

Niall shrugged his brawny shoulders. He did not care overmuch for demons, he had a wholesome regard for them and their powers and if it were up to him alone, he would avoid them. As commander of the armies of Lurlyr Manakor, it was his duty to put this frontier fort into operation, however. He could not do that if this demoniac witch were to send her powers outward to destroy the men who inhabited it.

His eyes touched Lylthia. She was staring at the door through which the glowing blue ball had come. Was she expecting another manifestation of the powers of this Sosaria Thota?

"Well?' he asked softly. "What now?'

She turned her head and smiled at him, yet deep within her green eyes there was worry. "By rights, I ought to go back to my eleven hells. But I dare not leave you unguarded." She sighed, "You are a worry to me sometimes, Niall."

He gave a bull bellow of laughter and dragged her in against him, almost smothering her in his embrace. Lylthia tinkled laughter, but there was an undertone of concern in her throat

"You must not take things so lightly, Niall," she scolded. "No matter if I am here to guard you. There are those in the mega-worlds with powers as great — if not greater — than my own."

"The thing to do then is find out how strong this witch-woman is. We'll go exploring."

His hand caught hers and like that, with Lylthia tripping lightly along beside him, he moved from the big barracks room out into the corridor and walked past the doors of other rooms, rooms in which weapons and other gear were stored.

Silence lay like a pall on this fort which usually resounded to the curses or laughter of the men who were stationed here. It seemed to lap about them, surrounding them with menace. Niall grumbled and shifted his shoulders restlessly, and his hand was never far from his sword-hilt

They came out upon a wall-walk and stood with the hot wind off the desert brushing them. To the south lay the vast expanse of the Baklakanian Desert, and beyond that the cultivated lands of Urgrik. Westward were the vast steppes between Urgrik and the lands of Noradden. Niall had never been to Noradden, but he had heard tales of its bazaars and the ships that fled across the waters of the Pulthanian Sea. He turned and stared eastward, and could make out, dimly enough, the Mountains of the Sun, that marked the boundary of Urgrik.

Lylthia touched him with a shoulder, and he put an arm about her. The winds were cool up here, and he felt her shiver.

He swung about and looked northward toward the high hills. Whatever evil had come upon this fortress had come from those hills, where the men of this fort had been digging for water.

"I have to go there," he muttered.

85

Lylthia stirred. "No. It is certain death. I know that much, Niall."

"It is my duty."

She drew back and stared up at him. "You men, with your ideals of duty and what you must do!" She sighed and laughed. "Perhaps that is why I like you so much, though. But you shall not go alone, my love. I will walk with you."

"First we will eat and sleep."

They turned — and suddenly froze.

In the long shadows of this late afternoon, they heard a strange and eerie keening. It was like the wail of a lost soul, rising and falling. The sound came from the north, in among those hills.

Niall swore and half drew Blood-drinker. Lylthia listened, eyes wide and head up, as though something in that sound touched a chord of memory deep inside her. After a moment, she shuddered.

"She has strange powers, that one," she whispered. "Ancient powers, long forgotten by this world." Her lovely face twisted in a grimace. "Indeed, I myself had forgotten all about them — until now."

Niall glanced down into her face. "Are you telling me that you're afraid?"

Her green eyes glowed. "You would be well advised to know fear. Such a woman as Sosaria Thota has never been known since she died."

With a hand at his fingers, she drew him down off the wall-walk They found a commissary room equipped with freezer units and with stoves. In moments, Niall had two big steaks roasting over the flames while he poured red Kallarian wine into two big goblets.

They ate without a thought for anything but the food. When they were done and sipping at the wine, Niall grinned. Lylthia eyed him suspiciously.

"Last time I took you to bed with me —in Angalore, you'll recall — you mesmerized me."

Laughter twinkled in Lylthia's eyes. "I did not know you so well, back in those days. To me, you were only someone who was interfering with my vengeance on Maylok the magician."

"And now?'

The girl shrugged. "We'll see," she muttered, and laughed. "I have a fancy to know something of this emotion you humans call love. It might not be amiss..."

Niall lifted to his feet, reached for his wine-cup and drained it. Then he reached out for Lylthia. He put an arm about her slender waist and hugged her to him. Like that, they walked out of the commissary room and up a short flight of stairs to the bedrooms of the post officers.

The room was dark, but Niall found tapers of yellow wax and lighted them. In their light, he saw a big, wide bed, together with a bureau and a desk and chair Lylthia was staring around her with wide eyes, almost as though she had never before seen a bedroom.

"Now you shall dance for me, as once you danced in a dream," he said softly.

She shook her head. "I do not feel like dancing, Niall. There is danger here — great danger. I can feel it, inside me."

"What sort of danger?'

"I know not. But it is here. Somewhere. Just — waiting."

She turned and walked toward an open window, without glass, with only a leather curtain on a rod drawn back, freeing that opening to the winds. It was a still night, no breeze stirred, and there was a heaviness in the air.

Niall stared at this woman he loved. It was not like Lylthia to be given to worry. If she were concerned, there was reason for him to be, too.

He moved toward her, stood beside her looking out into the night. High above, the ring of shattered matter that encircled their world reflected back the brilliance of the sunlight that touched its edges.

It was a beautiful sight, and on more than one occasion Niall had looked up at it, wondering what it was, where it had come from.

"If you—"

"Wait!"

There was urgency in her, and he could feel the tenseness of her body where he touched it. Her eyes were wide, her arms were by her side, yet rigid. It was as if she searched with senses unknown to him somewhere out there in the night.

And then —

A beam of light shot skyward. It was pure white, almost blinding in its brilliance. For a moment it paused, as though seeking, and then it flashed downward, straight at them.

Lylthia gave a little cry.

She whirled and thrust at him with both arms, driving him backward and into the darkest shadows. Then the pale light was all about her, enveloping her.

Niall shouted, with agony in his soul.

The blazing whiteness was all around Lylthia, eating at her, dissolving her. From where he stood as though paralyzed, Niall could see her shimmer, glow with unearthly brilliance, then fade out.

Only the whiteness was left.

That whiteness sang joyously. It whispered and laughed, or so it seemed to Niall, and then —slowly, slowly — it withdrew, back into the night from which it had come.

Lylthia was gone.

Eaten.

Niall lifted his head and bellowed out his grief, his rage.

Chapter Three

Dawn found the Far-traveler moving upward along the slopes of the hills that lay north of the fort. He felt frozen inside him, dead. Lylthia was gone. So too, was her other self, Emelkartha of the Eleven Hells.

He would never see her again, never know her laughter nor the touch of her body. A rage burned inside him, cold and deadly. As he walked, his big hand fondled the hilt of his sword.

He would find this witch-woman, this Sosaria Thota, and he would run cold steel into her flesh. Lylthia would be avenged! He cared nothing for what might happen to him, nor did he pause to reckon at any odds.

He was a barbarian sell-sword All his life had been given to using a sword in battle. He was walking toward his last battle, now. If he could avenge Lylthia, if he could kill this witch-woman, he would be satisfied. Even if he himself found death.

Life meant nothing to him any longer. Not without Lylthia. Or Emelkartha He loved that woman who was also a goddess in her demoniac worlds. He would revenge her death. Then he would die, himself.

He plodded on and upward, his great muscles rolling under his sun-bronzed hide. He felt no tiredness, no weariness, though he had been walking since early dawn. Up there in the hills, the men of the frontier fort had been digging for water, to make a stone pipe which would bring water into the fort.

And they had unearthed — Sosaria Thota.

He would search and find that tomb where she had been buried. He would run his steel into her body and destroy her. Nothing else mattered.

Sometime after high noon, he rested on a flat rock and ate the food and drank the wine he had brought with him. His eyes searched the tree-covered heights toward which he climbed as he ate, striving to discover where it was the men had been digging.

He sighed and rose and began walking again.

Toward evening, he sighted an open gap in the ground where it had been dug up, and several tools lying there, neglected. Niall moved forward.

He came to the opening, and stared down into it.

He saw rock-work and bricks, part of a subterranean chamber. Yet much dirt and rocks lay there, hiding any way in or out of it. The first thing he must do was to dig out that rubble, find a way into that structure.

But not now, not tonight. Tonight he must eat and sleep, to be ready for the morrow.

He stood before that opening, grieving. Never to see Lylthia again! Never to hear her soft laughter or be aware of the brightness of her green eyes, staring up into his with so much love! It was not a burden he could carry for the rest of his life.

No! As soon as he had killed the witch-woman he would leave this place and walk westward. He would walk until he dropped of exhaustion, and there he would die. Niall of the Far Travels no longer wanted to live.

He sat down and ate the remainder of the food he had carried with him, and finished the wine in the skin. He lay down and drew his cloak more tightly about him. In a moment, he was asleep.

When he woke in the early morning, it was to a brilliant sun that covered him with warmth. Niall lifted off his mail shirt, his other garments, until he stood almost naked, with just a bit of cloth about his loins. Then he reached for a shovel.

He began to dig.

Apparently there had been a landslide here, for the dirt was loose. Shovelful 1 after shovelful 1 rose upward, and as he worked, Niall saw that he was uncovering the door of the tomb.

It was a bronze door, covered over with strange signs and sigils. Niall stared at it a moment, scowling. There was an aura of evil about that door that was almost tangible. He scowled blackly, shrugged and put out a hand to it.

The door opened slowly, its hinges creaking. He had to apply all his strength to opening that door, for it had been closed for uncounted centuries.

When it was open, he waited for air to go into that dark chamber which lay beyond it. As he stood there, he bent to lift up his sword and draw it from the scabbard.

Then Niall stepped into the tomb.

His attention was caught by what seemed to be a glass case, under which lay a body. The case was on a table of ebony with carven legs, about which were entwined the bodies of demons. Niall stared at it a moment, before turning to look around him.

His eyes wandered here and there, seeing strange and unusual objects of metal, objects the purpose of which he could not understand. There was something that resembled a great glass globe mounted on golden balls, and to one side of it there was another object which consisted of slender rods and golden stars. Not far away was a great metal square with antennae rising upward from its top.

Niall turned back to the glass case.

He moved forward and caught his breath. He stared downward at the body of a woman with long golden hair, a woman so beautiful that something inside him choked up at the sight of her. Her eyelids were blued, yet were closed, and her golden lashes lay like tiny fans against her cheek.

She wore a single garment, something of diaphanous silk through which he could see the gleam of pale flesh. Her breasts pushed upward into this cloth, and for a moment, Niall thought to see those breasts move.

But no, that was merely an illusion.

This girl — or woman — was dead. There was no doubt of that. But — could this be the Sosaria Thota whom Lylthia had mentioned? How long ago was it she said the witch-woman had lived? Five thousand centuries?

Ha! If that were so, then this could not be she. This woman looked as though she had just fallen asleep.

He put a hand on the case. It felt warm, and seemed almost to quiver under his touch. Niall drew back, scowling.

There was wizardry here. He could almost smell it.

Niall waited. He could not believe that a woman as lovely as this could be as dangerous as Lylthia had suggested. Yet if she were Sosaria Thota, she had killed the woman he loved. With some sort of magic in this tomb.

He eyed those strange objects warily.

Maybe he ought to lift out Blood-drinker and use the flat of his blade to smash those queerly glittering things. There was evil in them, and a strange power which he could sense.

His hand lifted out the blade and he took a step forward.

"No!"

The word exploded inside him. There was strength in that word, spoken by a tremendously powerful will, Niall whirled around.

The woman lay as she always had, motionless. The chamber was quiet, with his breathing making the only sound. The hair rose up on the nape of his neck. More sorcery!

Niall growled low in his throat, swung back toward the strange objects. His huge hand tightened on his sword. By Emelkartha of the Eleven Hells! He was going to smash those things, destroy them forever.

He took another step, and froze.

Behind him he heard a whisper of sound. He did not know what that sound might be. he had never heard it before. With it came a sharp scent to his nostrils.

Niall wanted to swing around, to look behind him at that ancient catafalque, but he could not move a muscle. Yet his every sense strained to hear, to listen to those sounds which were like nothing else he had ever heard. And with the sounds, came that sharp acrid smell.

"You fool!"

The words were sharp, bitter. They had been spoken by a woman. Niall gave a rumbling growl. Was that corpse behind him — alive? Was that woman he had seen breathing? Could she have spoken to him?

Slowly, slowly, the rigidity went out of his muscles. Now he could move, and he swung about, staring.

The transparent covering was gone. Melted away? Evaporated into nothingness? The woman was sitting up and looking at him with calm gray eyes, very wise eyes and very old, or so he thought. She was beautiful. More beautiful than any woman Niall had ever seen.

Those gray eyes went over him from his worn war-boots to his kilt and fur kaunake that covered his mail beneath the saffron silk cloak, upward to his face. The gray eyes widened at sight of his rugged good looks, his mop of thick yellow hair.

"Who are you, who come blundering in to disturb my sleep? From whence do you come?"

"I am the commander of the armies of Lurlyr Manakor, king of Urgrik," he growled. Then he asked, with a snarl in his voice, "Are you the one who killed Lylthia?"

Mocking laughter rose upward into the air as the woman on the spotted furs of the catafalque threw back her head. Amusement was written plainly enough on her face. "And if I were? What is that to you, man? Do you not know who I am?"

She paused and stared at him. In a softer voice she went on, "No, perhaps you don't. Something tells me I have been asleep for a long time. A long, long time. Even your speech is different from the way people talked when I lived before. What is the year?"

"The fifth year of the Bear in the Cycle of the Twelve sigils"

"All of which means absolutely nothing to me."

Niall remembered what Lylthia had whispered in his mind.

"You have been dead for five thousand centuries. If you're who I think you are."

The woman gasped and sat up straighter. "You lie! So much time could not have elapsed."

"What would I gain by lying?"

She considered him, her head tilted sideways. Those eyes seemed almost to weigh him, to look deep inside him. They made Niall uncomfortable. He still held his sword in his big right hand, and he told himself that if he could get close enough to this woman, he would bury its steel in her throat.

"Do you know who I am?" she asked softly.

"Sosaria Thota."

Alarm and amazement came into her features. She swung her legs forward off the catafalque and stood upon the stone floor. Her breasts rose and fell as though to deep emotion.

"How could you know my name?" she whispered. "If what you tell me is true — that five hundred thousand years have passed since I was last here — no man could possibly have remembered me."

Niall shrugged. He was not about to admit that it had been Lylthia who had whispered that information into his mind.

She moved forward, as graceful as the hunting leopard, and — or so Niall thought — as deadly. She was beautiful as Lylthia, but there was something about this woman that chilled Niall, deep inside him.

He stood waiting, his hand still holding his sword. As though she sensed his thought, Sosaria Thota laughed softly.

"Would you kill me, man?" she asked.

"Aye. I would."

She laughed gleefully and clapped her pink palms together in an almost childish glee. She was close now, and despite the hate he felt for her, he was aware of her as a desirable woman. The garment she wore was revealing, being woven of some silken strands that seemed almost transparent.

"You are an honest man. Good! I like that. And you are a brave one. I like that, too. It will make your subjection that much sweeter."

She paused, the green eyes laughing up at him.

"Do you think you can buy your sword in my flesh, man? Do you? Try it"

He could not look away from those eyes which seemed to hold him in thrall. His knees grew weak, suddenly, and he groaned, unable to move his sword-arm She was a witch-woman, all right, this Sosaria Thota. In her hands he was like a helpless babe.

"There now," she smiled, speaking in a soft voice. "You appeal to me, whoever you are. I need a companion, a living companion. I have been too long — asleep."

She sighed. "I would look upon the world again, see it as it was, so long ago. Come you with me, man."

Sosaria Thota turned and without looking back at him, made her way out of the tomb, climbing over the loose rubble and the rocks, the wind blowing her drapery about her flesh so that at times it seemed she was almost naked.

Niall went after her, sheathing his sword. No sense in carrying Blood-drinker in his hand, if he could not use it. And he knew he could not, against this woman.

They came out upon the lip of the diggings, and the woman stood as if frozen, staring out across the desert sands. Her eyes went this way and that, as though seeking something that had been here, and was here no more.

Niall stood beside her, so close that her bare arm touched his. From her flesh rose up a sweet, stirring fragrance.

"Gone. All gone," she whispered. "No longer is there a land of Thilmagia. Instead — only dead sand."

She whirled and stared up at him with those disturbing gray eyes. "Is it like this all over the world?"

"Of course not," he growled. "This is the desert. Out yonder," and here he flung up a hand, "are the wild hordes of Pugarsk. To keep them at a distance, Urgrik has built these forts."

He turned and now his arm swept northward, toward Urgrik. "There are cities that way, and to the east and the west. There live men and women. No one but soldiers stay in such places as this."

His mention of soldiers made him think of the men this woman had killed with her devilish lights. She must have caught the anger in his throat, for she smiled faintly and nodded.

"Yes, I slew all life around me, once I was—disturbed. I lay asleep and dreaming for many centuries, it seems. Yet when men came and began to dig, I became aware of it, and sent out my messenger to kill them."

"As your messenger was slain."

Her hand stabbed out and caught his arm, her long red fingernails biting into his flesh. "Aye! Something destroyed Messarib. Was it you? No, no. You have not the power. Then —who was it?"

Niall shrugged. He was not about to tell this woman anything, though it could make little difference, since Lylthia was dead. At that thought, a fierce anger began to burn inside him, until it became a rage that made him tremble.

Her eyes were wise, they saw the fury in him, and she laughed softly. "I sent the vilaspa light to search the barracks when Messarib was destroyed. That light touched a living person — ate him. Who was that person, Niall?"

He shook his head, knowing that those eyes were on him as though they might read his mind. Let her look, let her try to discover what he knew. He would not tell.

Sosaria Thota sighed and turned away, her stare going over the desert lands once again. She stood as though she did not feel the desert winds that touched her lone garment and blew it about her. Niall wondered what she might be thinking.

At last she said, "These lands where men do live in these days — be they far?"

"A few marches away."

"Then lead me there, man."

"Not I, lady."

She turned and looked at him, haughtily. Her lips opened as if she would speak, but then they only curved at their corners into a grim smile.

"Go and fetch horses, then. One for you, one for me, and two more to carry those things I shall need. Go now."

Niall turned and walked toward the fort. In the stables there would be horses. Yet he told himself he would not take the witch-woman into Urgrik City. He would lead her out upon the desert, but in a direction away from the populated places.

There in that desert, without water, she would surely die. Of course, he would die with her, but what was his death compared to the lives of the people he would save? Sosaria Thota would kill and slay all who stood in her way. She would not rest content until it was she and not Lurlyr Manakor who ruled in Urgrik.

Aye, and in other cities as well, until with her wizardous arts she controlled all men and their lives. His big hand clenched into a fist. He would not permit it. In some way, he would find a way to kill her.

He saddled two horses, one of them the big gray stallion he had ridden here. He also selected two pack animals. He fed them and the other horses which would be left behind, and made certain they had plenty of water.

Then he brought the mounts toward where Sosaria Thota waited. He might not be able to draw and use steel against her, but she would not suspect that the desert sands might kill her.

It was his only chance.

Chapter Four

They began their march at a walk, with Niall out in front on his gray horse. He set the pace, it was an easy walk, for he was in no hurry. Apparently Sosaria Thota was content with that, for she made no comment.

All day they moved across the hot sands, until the sun sank in the west and a breeze sprang up. Only then did Niall turn and glance back at the witch-woman who sat her saddle with the ease of olden days.

Her eyes were very bright as they studied him.

"Always you move westward, man," she said softly, and her eyes were narrow and angry. "I ask myself if you are trying to trick me."

Niall shrugged his broad shoulders. "Now why should I do that?"

"Because you are loyal to this king you serve, because you don't want to lead me into this city of Urgrik." Her lips curved into a cruel smile. "I will play your little game with you, for a time."

She leaned forward in the saddle, her hands clutching its pommel, and her eyes blazed at him. "Think not to fool me, man. I am Sosaria Thota!" She moved back then, and let her laughter ripple on the air. "You take me westward, and I want to go north. Am I such a fool that I cannot see the sun?"

Niall swung down from the kak. "We'll make camp here."

The woman stared around her, brows wrinkling. "One spot is as good as another, I suppose. One can eat and sleep here."

She came onto the sands and walked back and forth, kicking little sand-puffs at every stride. From time to time she threw back her head and stared upward at the darkening sky. Then, as though making up her mind about something, she moved toward one of the pack horses and began to fumble with the straps.

Her hands lifted down an apparatus consisting of many slender rods, each of which was surmounted by a golden star. This she set down very carefully on the sand and stood a moment, brooding at it.

She turned and stared at Niall.

"I have had men flayed alive for lying to me, man. Others I have had my torturers spend a week over, making certain that the manner of their dying was extremely slow and painful." She sighed. "I should not care to order you to die in any such manner."

"In those days, you had many servants. Today you have only me."

She laughed at him. "Fool! Do you think I cannot summon up help? I can call on the denizens of the outer darknesses, which are all familiar to me, who obey my slightest whims."

Niall shrugged and turned back to the little fire he had made and over which he was cooking meat he had brought from the fort. Inside him was a coldness that seemed to stretch inward to his very bones. How did a mere man deal with such a witch? From what Lylthia had hinted, this beautiful woman who stared at him so coldly had strange and mighty powers.

Her hands did something to the rods and stars, and instantly Niall saw a dark cloud spring up about them. It was dark at first, as black as the fabled pits of Aberon, yet slowly that ebon tint faded, was streaked with brilliant scarlet — then faded.

Now he stared at a dead world. Dark were the cinders on which he crouched, lifeless and sere, while above him was a sky shot with crimson fires. It seemed that he heard a whisper, very faint, yet one which grew louder she listened.

It was the beat of wings.

The thing came on widespread wings, fluttering a moment, before it settled down near Sosaria Thota. Its three eyes were brilliant with evil, and Niall shuddered when he saw that this demoniac being eyed him hungrily.

"Can it be Sosdria Thota?" the thing croaked.

"None other, Alphanor. I am awake again, you see. I have slept a long time. Now I appeal to you for help."

"Leave the man-thing for me, and I shall be at your service."

"Na, na, Alphanor. This one I need — for a time, at least. Yet you shall be paid. This I vow."

The bird-being took its beady eyes from Niall to glance at the witch-woman For a moment it seemed to hesitate, then its armored head nodded.

"What is it you seek?"

"Long ago — in my other lifetime — the gods of the outer darknesses promised me their aid. Yet at that time they were unable to help me — and so I waited. Now my time of waiting is at an end."

She stood proudly before that black bird-beast, her head flung back, and Niall had to admire her at that moment. She was a human being, or had been, and she trafficked with demons in their own lands. Great must be her powers, great her courage.

Alphanor hesitated. "There are other powers," he grumbled. "They too, are powerful, mayhap even more powerful than we dark beings. Over the years when you have been sleeping, those others have extended their abilities."

"Are you saying you cannot help me? Or will not?"

"It is not easy. If those other powers were to guess—"

It seemed to Niall that the bird-thing shivered.

"Enough," Sosaria Thota snapped. "If you fear to aid me, there are others upon whom I can call."

The bird-god shook himself. "Look around you," he croaked. "Once this land was fair, with trees and grass and animals abounding, all over it. That was before you called on me and I — aided you.

"Those others came then and destroyed my world, even as they forced you into an eons-long sleep. Do you care to risk their wrath a second time, Sosaria Thota?"

"I do. I shall"

Her hand touched the rods and stars and instantly the dark, dead world was gone and there was a moment when Niall swayed while all about him madness cracked and thundered. Then the ground under his feet settled, and he saw that he stood in a massive hall, so large it seemed to stretch away almost to infinity.

There were tiles underfoot, and a warmth everywhere. Niall swung about, stared at a great throne upon which — something — stirred and seemed to rise upward from slumber. He could not make out its form, there was something alien and non-human about it.

"Who comes?" a voice whispered. "Who dares disturb the dreams of Xinthius?"

"I dare, great one. Long ages ago, I worshiped thee in the lands I ruled. I am Sosaria Thota!"

There was silence, then something rustled like dry leather. "I remember you. Aye. But that was long, long ago."

"And now? Are your powers so faded you cannot aid me again?'

"What is it you wish of me?"

"Help me attain to my old powers! Help me rule the world of my birth as once I ruled it?"

"Na, now. Things have changed while you slept, girl. We dark worlders are not so powerful as once we were. There are those who would contain us."

Sosaria Thota sneered. "And you fear them?"

"I do, and rightly so. I am content here in my halls, where my word is supreme. Here I sit and dream, and I enjoy my life. If I were to aid you in your plans, all this might be taken from me."

"Must I seek out Abaddon himself?"

"Go seek him, woman. I will not help. I am content with my dreamings."

Angrily, Sosaria Thota stabbed out a hand, touched the rods and stars. They glittered and gleamed and gave off a faint music. Niall swayed to the dizziness that touched him, and then he stood on rocky ground riven by great fissures. Upward from those fissures came white steam.

Yet in the near distance, Niall could make out grassy slopes and trees heavy-hung with fruit. His head turned as he stared about him. This land was like a paradise. The air was sweet, it was filled with bird-songs

"Carry that," snapped Sosaria Thota, gesturing at the rods and stars.

She turned and walked away from the rocky ground, moving steadily toward the nearest grass. Niall bent and lifted the rods and stars and carried it easily in his muscular arms. Only when Sosaria Thota halted did he set it down.

"Who intrudes on Abaddon in his domains?"

It was a whisper from the very air. There was no shape around, nothing which could have spoken. Yet the words rang in his ears, and he knew that the witch-woman heard them too, for she stiffened and glanced around her.

Was it his imagination, or did her beautiful face mirror an inner fear? No matter. She flung back her head and cried, "I come for help, Abaddon. I am Sosaria Thota, who worshiped you long and long ago as the father of all demons!"

"I remember."

"Then aid me now, great one! Restore to me those lands which once

100

I ruled."

There was laughter all about him, Niall realized, as though the very air itself were amused. Slowly that mirth died away and there was a silence.

Then: "If I do this which you ask, what is to be my reward?"

"Anything you ask."

"Then this is my demand: that all men shall adore me, on your world. There is to be no temple to any other god or goddess. I alone — Abaddon! — am to be sole god."

"It shall be done."

Niall stirred restlessly. Was this to be the end of his world as he knew it? He had heard of the powers of Abaddon, they were whispered of by priests and initiates of other gods and goddesses. He was The Black One, the Dark Destroyer. All power was his, he was supreme among the evil ones.

His hand touched the hilt of his Orravian dagger and he half drew it. Yet he knew that he could never use steel against Sosaria Thota. It was an order that was impressed upon his very brain by her wizardous arts.

Around Sosaria Thota the air seemed to glow, to brighten intensely. Swiftly that brightness shrank until it encompassed her body and then seemed to merge with it. She turned her head and stared at him, and now it seemed to Niall that another was inside that body, looking out at him.

"Come, man," said the witch-woman, and gestured at the rods and stars.

Obediently, Niall lifted the contraption. There was an instant of intense cold and darkness, and then they were standing again on the vast stretch of sand that formed the Baklakanian Desert.

Sosaria Thota was looking around her, as though considering. Niall watched her closely, then reached for his dagger. Could he throw it at her? An old warrior with whom he had served in the forces of Sensenall to the south, had taught him the way of it. Still, he was long out of practice.

He hefted the dagger in his big hand. Should he risk it?

Na, na, Niall. That is not the way.

Niall of the Far Travels froze. His heart leaped and thudded inside his great chest. Was that Lylthia? Or — to give her her true name — Emelkartha of the Eleven Hells? But — Lylthia was dead!

Sosaria Thota turned and stared at him and at his dagger. Her lips curved into a grim smile. "Are you thinking of using that against me, man? You cannot, remember. I have forbidden it."

Niall said, "Our meal is done. I was about to slice off steaks.

He knelt about the flames and lifted off the piece of meat he had brought from the fort. He sliced off pieces and handed one to the witch-woman She accepted it, her gray eyes grave on his face, as though she weighed whether or not to let him live.

You shall live, Niall. Neither Sosaria Thota nor Abaddon himself know this world. It has been eons since they were here. You do know it. You are invaluable to them.

Niall hunkered down, chewing his steak. He was at peace, within himself. Now that Emelkartha was back with him, nothing else mattered.

When he was done eating, he wandered away from the little camp to attend to the horses. He fed them, he gave them to drink from the water-skins he had brought from the fort. Then he turned and looked back at his campfire, where the witch-woman sat before it. staring into its flames.

"What shall I do?" he whispered.

Nothing. Only — wait.

Niall came back to the fire, stretched himself out and wrapped his cloak about him. Sosaria Thota glanced at him, but her eyes were lidded so that he could not see their great depths.

Niall slept.

He woke in the early dawn, when the sun was tinting the desert sands a reddish hue. Sosaria Thota was standing beside the dead embers of the fire, her body rigid, arms by her side, her head flung back. Beside her was the machine with the tall, thin rods.

Her hand touched it.

All about them there was a shifting of light, of vision. No longer was there any sand but instead green grass grew, and at some distance,

Niall could see a great white wall and behind it the tops of buildings.

Yet this vision lasted only a few moments. It shifted then and faded away, and only the desert remained. Sosaria Thota sobbed.

"What is it? What's wrong?" she wailed.

"I do not understand. Always the amanathor has performed as you requested. It has great powers, has the rod-thing." That had been the voice of Abaddon.

"I saw my little city, I did. And the lands that were wont to surround it when I lived — before."

"Yet now they will not stay. Some other power is making them disappear, setting at naught the power of the amanathor."

Anger touched the witch-woman, distorted her features. "You are the father of evil, the grandfather of all devils! Help me!"

"I — cannot. There is great power here allied against us. I am seeking for it, but it is hidden."

Soft laughter rippled through Niall's mind.

They search for me, yet they do not suspect you hold me within you, as Sosaria Thota holds Abaddon. Nor shall they.

Sosaria Thota began to pace up and down, kicking sand with her feet at every stride. Confusion and fear touched her face. She halted at last and stared down at Niall where he sat on the sand.

"What power rules this desert, man? Answer me!"

"'No power I know of. It is only a desert."

The witch-woman shock her head. "No. There is something here. Some great and tremendous strength, against which I am helpless."

Her hands clenched into fists. Her green eyes blazed. "It shall not defeat me. Nothing shall do that. I will not permit it."

She turned and walked away, toward the pack horses and their burdens which Niall had put upon the ground last night She walked up to the metallic thing that held the huge glass globe mounted on golden balls. Her hand touched it, set the balls in motion.

Faster those golden balls rotated. Faster, until they seemed almost to disappear. And as they whirled, the interior of the glass globe darkened, then brightened. Tiny lightnings shot outward from it.

Break it, Niall!

Sosaria Thota stood with her back to him. Niall lifted out his Orravian dagger, balanced it a moment, then hurled it with all his strength. Straight for that glass globe hurtled the steel blade.

Claaanngg!

The sound of breaking glass was loud in the desert stillness. Niall saw pieces of that globe fly to and fro through the air. Sosaria Thota whirled and screamed.

Raw was her fury, black her rage. Her arm lifted and she leveled her fingers at him. From the tips of those fingers flaring blue light sped at him.

Sped at him and—

Parted as that light was about to touch him! On either side of him it went, and faded out.

The witch-woman stared, mouth open and eyes wide.

"Who are you?" she whispered. "What are you? No human could so turn my power."

Niall found himself saying —knowing that Emelkartha was making his lips and tongue fashion those words, "It is useless, Sosaria Thota. Even your evil gods cannot help you. Can you, Abaddon?"

Her last three words were bugled, ringing clearly and loudly. Sosaria Thota shrank back as if hit, and fear lay written on her beautiful features, distorted now by terror.

"You are a demon, a god," she breathed.

Niall said, this time in his own voice, "I am only what you have named me. A man."

She shook her head so that her long golden hair flew about her head. "No! You are more than that. You have driven Abaddon from me. He has fled away, back into his own lands. He has left me to face you alone."

In a broken voice she asked, "What seek you of me?"

"Your death, Sosaria Thota."

She leaped at him, fingers curled to claw at him. With one sweep of his arm, he hit her, drove her reeling backward until she fell and lay upon the sands.

"You struck me," she breathed. "You lifted your arm and struck me. You could not. I had forbidden it."

Niall lifted out his sword. Her eyes went to it, to his face. There was insane terror in her eyes now.

The witch-woman whimpered, "No. You cannot. Look at me, man!"

Look you, Niall, as she commands.

Those gray eyes fastened on his, as though they would devour him. Had not Emelkartha been inside him, he would have done what those eyes were bidding him to do: lift out his sword, put its point to his chest, and fall on it.

Yet he did nothing more than stand there, staring back at her, his sword in his right hand.

And then Sosaria Thota whimpered. Her eyes grew bigger, as though something within his own eyes were speaking to her. Slowly she rose upward, to stand before him.

As she did, Niall lifted his sword and pointed it at her, as an inner voice commanded. His blade began to glow whitely, so brilliantly that its glare blinded him.

That brightness gathered in the steel, focused at its point, became a ball if incandescent luminescence. Sosaria Thota shrieked, the agony of death alive in her throat.

From his sword that blazing radiance leaped forward, straight at the witch-woman It hit her, seemed to burst so that it enveloped Sosaria Thota. For an instant, her body was outlined within that shimmering refulgence.

A voice inside that brightness wailed.

Then the whiteness was gone, and the witch-woman with it.

Niall stood alone upon the sands, with only the horses to keep him company. He lowered the sword, and was aware that there was wetness on his forehead. He shook himself, like a great bear newly wakened from his winter sleep. Then he sheathed Blood-drinker and looked around him.

Emelkartha was gone from inside him—

Yet even as he turned, he saw Lylthia standing a dozen feet away, laughing softly.

"I thought you — dead," he whispered.

"And so did Sosaria Thota. I wanted her to think that, Niall, for she had sent one of her messengers to slay someone whom she suspected of being in the fort."

She strode toward him and he opened his arms and caught her to him, kissing her soft red lips hungrily.

When she could, she said, "We shall spend a few days together in the fort, Niall. Before you return to Lurlyr Manakor and tell him that the danger here is done with. Eh? Would you like that?"

Niall gave a great roar of laughter, lifted her high on his chest and began to kiss her even more hungrily.

THE EYES OF MAVIS DEVAL

Chapter One

It was her eyes flat drew his stare as he sat astride the high-peak saddle of his stallion, there on the edge of the huge slave market. They were a brilliant green, those eyes, and it seemed to Niall of the Far Trawls as he looked, that there was a tiny flame glowing in each pupil.

Niall stood in the stirrups, lifting his giant body upright. Clad in the silver chain-mail of his rank as High Commander of the armies of Urgrik. with the scarlet cloak hanging from his wide shoulders, he was ignorant of the men and women who turned to regard him.

All he was aware of was the girl.

She stood on the slaw-seller's dais, all but naked with a bit of torn sackcloth hiding her flesh. Her head was up-tilted there was a faint smile on her full red mouth when she saw how she interested him, and her breasts rose proudly as if to tempt him.

The flames were gone from her eyes, now. Her long black hair hung down her back, almost to her buttocks. There was a wild, untamed look about her. and a pride which seemed to reach out and caress him

Niall urged his stallion forward. The people gathered there made room for him; they all knew him and how he was much honored by Lurlyr Manakor. their king. He paced the stallion to the very edge of the dais, and his upheld hand summoned the slave-seller forward.

"The girl off there to one side, where she stands alone." Niall rasped. "How much is she?"

Kavith Monalong was torn with greed. His black eyes slid toward the slave girl, then turned back to the High Commander. Never before had he known Niall to be interested in a slaw. The thought touched his mind that he could make a very great profit here, but the cold stare of the High Commander turned his insides to water.

"Ten durakins. highness. Or say — eight."

Niall fumbled at a bag at his belt, loosing it and tossing it to the slaw master. He did not watch as Kavith Monalong fumbled with the coins he poured into his palm, selecting several, and when the pouch was handed back to him he did not look at it but only tied its drawstrings to his belt.

"Come, girl." he called, waving an arm.

The girl ran to him with light steps, a happy smile on her mouth. She came to his stirrup and stared up at him with those bright green eyes mat seemed to look deep inside him

Niall put a hand to her, lifting her easily upward behind him onto his stallion's croup. Then he turned and nudged the horse with a toe. walking it away from the crowd. After a moment he felt two soft arms close about his middle.

"How are you named, girl?" he asked.

"I am Mavis Deval, highness."

He waited, but she gave no more information. Then he said. "You come from the South-lands, I would guess. From Cassamunda. Torel Cabbera. or perhaps even from Sensanall."

"You are very wise. I was born in Carthia. which is not far from Sensanall. I was working on a farm when raiders came and captured me. But I escaped from them, fleeing away in the night, and wandered about until I came on a slow caravan." I felt her shrug. "I was too exhausted to run any more. They fed me, chained me, and brought me here."

Niall paced the black stallion slowly over the cobblestones of the city, wondering at the eldritch impulse that had made him buy tins girl. He owned no slaves, he did not believe in slavery, though it was practiced everywhere in his world. Well, that was easy enough to handle. He would free the girl give her some gold, and send her on her way.

And yet—

There was something about her that appealed to him. He had never paid much attention to women, except for a tavern girl now and then, to assuage the hungers of his flesh. Perhaps it had been the sort of life he had, wandering here and there across his world, mat had made him lead this almost monastic life.

He shrugged. He had enough to keep him busy, as High Commander of the armies of Urgrik, without bothering his head about some wench.

Of course. Urgrick was at peace, there were no wars to draw his attention, and sometimes a man found Time lying heavy on his hands.

But, no. He would feed the girl, put some decent clothes on her, and then send her packing. His shoulders straightened; his mind was made up.

Yet he was very aware of those arms about him, and from time to time he felt the weight of her head where she laid it against his back, almost caressingly. It was too bad he could not look into her eyes. They had fascinated him, from that very first moment when he had thought to see glowing flames inside them.

He toed the stallion to a canter.

When he was within the walls of his citadel, he caught her and lowered her gently to the cobbles. She stood there looking up at him, and her eyes and her lips smiled at him. Almost lovingly. It was as if she considered him to be her very own.

Niall swung down and guided Mavis Deval toward a huge oaken door. It creaked slightly as his hand moved it inward. The girl slipped ahead of him and walked with a lissome sway to her hips that caught his eye.

They went up a flight of stairs and into a chamber hung with thick drapes. Flames burned from a log in a huge fireplace. There was heavy furniture here, of rich mahogany: big chairs thick with pillows, a long table piled high with manuscripts, a vast oaken highboy that took up much of one wall.

Mavis Deval paused to look around her. "You must be a rich man, to own such a home."

Niall grinned. "Rich? Not I. All this belongs to the king. I just live here."

He was about to drop his cloak when the girl ran forward to take it from him, to fold it neatly and carry it to the highboy. As she walked, she looked back at him over a shoulder.

"Would you like to be rich?" she asked softly.

Niall barked laughter. "What man would not?"

She put his cloak inside the highboy and straightened, to regard him soberly. "I know where there is a treasure. A very big treasure. You can have it, if you want."

He grinned hugely. The idea of a slave girl telling him how to become wealthy amused him. "Now how would you know of such a thing?"

She looked sullen. "I have ears. I heard men speaking on the caravan that brought me here."

Something stirred deep within Niall of the Far Travels.

Beware, Niall my love! Beware this—woman!

Sheer surprise held Niall motionless. Aye! That was Emelkartha the Evil, the strange goddess of the eleven hells who had taken a fancy to him long ago, and who now loved him as devotedly as might any earthly woman.

But what would cause Emelkartha to be with him right now?

Mavis Deval walked toward him. She had a pulse-stirring walk, one that made him realize suddenly that she was a very beautiful woman. Something about her green eyes held him.

She put her hands palm down against his mailed chest She was very near; he could smell the perfumes of her flesh, the scents seemingly woven into the texture of her thick black hair. He had been a long time without a woman, and this slave girl was very close, and seemed almost eager for his embrace.

Emelkartha stirred jealously within him.

Beware, Niall—you foolish one!

"You could have all that gold," Mavis Deval whispered. "There is so much of it! And —-jewels, as well."

Almost bemused, he asked, "Why should you offer so much riches to me?"

"You bought me. You are a good man. You will make a good master."

He shook his head. "I'm setting you free. I'll feed you and put some decent clothes on your back, and give you many golden ruplets. You will be able to go where you want, do whatever it is that pleases you."

She inched nearer, so that he could feel her body against his own, and she shook her head, sighing. There was no doubt about it. This girl had an animal appeal to which his own body responded.

"I do not want to leave you, Niall." How was it that she knew his name? Kavith Monalong had not spoken it, nor had he. "You bought me. I belong to you."

"There is no room in my life for a girl."

Her smile was subtle. "There might be — if I make myself very pleasing to you."

Somehow his arms had gone around her body, holding her close. In something like surprise, he did not hear Emelkartha whispering angrily to him. Emelkartha was a very jealous goddess. She did not like Niall to hold or caress any other female but herself.

He was gazing down into her eyes when once again he saw those tiny flames deep within them. Just for an instant, a mere wink of time. Those flames seem to leap upward, as though in joy.

Niall drew back. He could not help himself, he was so surprised. Then—the flames were gone, and it was only Mavis Deval smiling alluringly up at him.

"This treasure," he made himself say, "Where is it?"

The girl laughed softly. "I shall take you there, master. Oh, so gladly! Then you shall be rich, you shall be able to have whatever it is you most want."

"But where can it be found?"

"In the mountains of Kareen, that lie a long distance away. We shall need horses and much food, but the trip will be well worthwhile. And you must bring extra horses, to carry all the gold and jewels."

To Niall, it seemed much too easy. He had not become High Commander of the armies of Urgrik by being a simpleton. There was someone he must see, and soon, about this.

"Go, girl. Upstairs you will find a bath. Cleanse yourself, and by that time, I'll have something better for you to wear than that bit of sackcloth."

She thrust herself against him, but he pushed her away gently. He needed time to think, and he could not do that with Mavis Deval so close.

The girl laughed up at him softly, as though she felt he was afraid of her beauty. She turned and moved away, haunches swinging

111

invitingly. Niall watched her go, and there was a thin film of sweat on his forehead.

When she had gone, Niall moved to a small table set against the wall, on which stood a massive oak chest. He lifted the lid and reached in for some of the golden coins that lay there. He filled his leather pouch, drew a deep breath, and closed the chest

This night, he must see Danko Penavar, the wizard.

Chapter Two

The moon was high and silver, far above the city rooftops, as Niall of the Far Travels walked the cobbled streets of Urgrik. Emotions warred within him. He told himself that he was a fool, there was no treasure in the mountains of Kareen, that lay so far away.

And yet—why should Mavis Deval speak of it, if it did not exist? Ha! He had offered her freedom. Why had she not accepted that freedom, and gone herself for all this gold? It was a puzzle he could not solve.

Yet if there were such a treasure, he wanted to own it. All his life, he had been a carefree sell-sword, laboring where his talents at fighting and at swordplay put coins in his moneybag. It was time now for him to think of himself, of his future.

He came at last to a doorway hidden in thick black shadows. He raised the knocker there, carved in the face of a demon, and banged it

A soft wind that held a chill in it swept up the narrow lane. It made him shiver, so that he drew his cloak more closely about his big, thickly muscled body. His hand touched the hilt of his sword, Blood-drinker. Its firmness seemed to reassure him.

The door creaked open. He stared into a vast room, a room filled with golden censers and thuribles burning incense, with athanors cold now and empty of coals, with vials and cruets and flagons containing strange and mysterious elixirs. There a fire glowing in the hearthstones, and by the red glare of the flames, Niall made out an old man, gigantic of build, who sprawled in a huge oaken chair.

The old man chuckled. "Enter, Niall. I have been expecting you."

112

"Have you, now?"

Niall entered the room, closing the door. He wondered how it had opened; the old man could not have done it, he was too far away, and there was no sign of any servants. Well, he ought to have expected nothing else from Danko Penavar.

The old man chuckled. "I have my ways of learning what goes on in the city around me. And elsewhere too, I might add. Little escapes my notice. Sit yourself, my general."

His hand indicated a footstool, off to one side. Niall nodded, lowered himself onto it. His hand lifted his moneybag and put it between his war-booted feet.

"There is much gold there," he said slowly. "The gold is yours. Just answer me a few questions."

Danko Penavar smiled at him. "You bought yourself a girl today, general. You want to know who she is, where she comes from, eh?"

"Can you tell me?"

"Oh, yes. But why do you want to know? Isn't she attractive enough? If I were your age, I would be in bed with her, not talking to an old man who has more years to his life than you can imagine."

"She has mentioned a treasure in the Kareen mountains—"

Danko Penavar started upright, so swiftly that he started Niall, who had not thought him capable of such movement. His eyes stared hard at Niall, and a little breeze seemed to ruffle the hairs on his head, and those of his long beard.

"Kareen," he whispered, "Kareen!"

His big, thickly veined hand came up to stroke at his beard, and then he shook his head. "It has been long, long since I have thought of Kareen. So! There is a treasure there, is there?"

He was silent, his thoughts turned inward, as though he were tracing out the long years of his life and what he had learned in all that time. He shifted slowly and lay back against the cushions, shaking his head.

"It is not good, that treasure, Niall. Be advised. Forget about it." Niall grinned. "But there is a treasure?"

"Oh, yes. But it is cursed. Sisstorississ himself lays claim to it, and Sisstorississ is a jealous god."

113

Niall nodded gloomily, remembering. He himself had fought Sisstorississ, back there in the ruins of the Kor Magnon, on his way to Urgrik. How long ago had it been? Ten months? A year? Yes, all of that. There had been the girl Kathyla, who was also Iphygia the enchantress, whom he had rescued from the reptile in the pit, and who had later turned on him—after he had fought Sisstorississ himself—and tried to deliver him up to the snake-god.

Emelkartha had helped to rescue him, since she hated Iphygia.

He spoke of Sisstorississ and of Iphygia, but not of Emelkartha The old magician listened, chin on hands, eyes half-closed. When Niall was done, Danko Penavar nodded.

"Yes. It makes a good tale, one to stir the blood. But you made a terrible enemy, Niall. Sisstorississ is not a demon-god whom it is safe to defeat. Hate will live in his soul—if he has one—and that hate will stir within him an appetite for vengeance. Be warned. Stay far away from the mountains of Kareen. Far away."

Niall of the Far Travels was not a man to turn his back on danger, especially when there might be a profit to be made. Often enough he had fought for nothing more than an ideal or a whim. He moved his shoulders, and his left hand went to the hilt of his great sword.

"If there is gold there, and jewels..."

Danko Penavar shook his head. "There is also that which is worse than death! If Sisstorississ should discover that you are after his treasure, he will move all the Hells there are to come at you!"

Niall moved his foot, toeing the heavy purse forward across the floor. "Read the future for me, mage. Tell me what waits for me in the Kareen mountains."

The old man shifted his weight, as though uncomfortable. His veined hands toyed with his robe, rearranging it over his knees. Twice he opened his mouth to speak, but closed his lips. Wearily, he shook his head.

"I shall read the future for you if you ask, Niall. But —I want no gold for it. This is not a task I relish. There is doubt in me, and worry..."

Softly, Niall asked, "Is it then so dangerous?"

"To you—yes. Perhaps to me as well." Danko Penavar sighed and

114

lurched to his feet. "However, I admit to a curiosity in me. I will summon up some imps and have speech with them. Come you with me."

Niall walked slightly behind the old man as he moved toward the rear of the big room, where there was now only darkness and a hint of golden objects off which candlelight and fire-flames reflected. He stood and watched as Danko Penavar went toward a prie-dieu and opened a massive volume, thickly bound in leather.

"Come you and stand beside me, Niall, safely within the pentagram."

As he stepped forward, Niall could make out the markings of a pentagram, inlaid in ivory in an ebony floor. He watched as the mage extended his finger and candles overhead burst into flame. He had not seen those candles in their holders hanging by a chain from the ceiling. He wondered at the powers of this man who could cause fire by the mere act of stretching out a finger.

"Be quiet now. Do nothing more than breathe, and if you value the life you have, stir not a muscle. Stay always within the pentagram."

Niall waited, breathing softly. He saw the magician bend above the tome he had opened, watched as he scrutinized the words limned there in human blood. Slowly, Danko Penavar began to read, sonorously and with music in his voice.

The air around them grew warm, then hot. Overhead, the candles seemed almost to bend as though weary of their own weight. Here and there tiny flames sprang up in the outer darkness. Those flames grew and spread. The heat became almost intolerable. Sweat ran down Niall's cheeks.

Slowly... slowly... something began to take shape.

It was the figure of a demon. He could not see it all, not yet, but he could guess at its contours and he felt like retching. The flames blazed higher, the figure grew even clearer.

There were fangs jutting from the great, misshapen mouth. Thick skin hung in ugly folds over vast muscles. The thing was bald, its head was grotesque, and its three hands played nervously, as though the thing wanted to reach out and rend them both.

"I come, sorcerer, to your call," the being croaked thickly, as though its lips and tongue could scarcely mold themselves to fashion human speech. "What is your wish?"

"It has been long since I summoned you, Vokkoth. Not for many years. I seek to know about the mountains of Kareen, and what awaits a man named Niall."

The demon lurched forward a shuffling step, but drew back when its toe—or what served it for toes—came close to the edges of the pentagram. Hell-fires blazed in its eyes.

"Niall! Ha! I have heard of him, even in the Hells where I dwell. Sisstorississ seeks for him, everywhere. He asks for help. Imagine! The great Sisstorississ has even asked me to lend my powers to his quest."

"And what is that quest?"

"He would do anything to get this Niall in his power. Anything! Already he has hunted in the many Hells there are for some hint, some way of drawing Niall to him, that he may get control over his body."

The misshapen head shook so much that the loosely fleshed jowls swung ponderously. "Be warned, Danko Penavar. Have nothing more to do with this man."

The old magician sighed. "Tell me, Vokkoth, out of old friendship. What waits for Niall in the Kareen hills?"

"No one knows. No one can know. It is hidden. Hidden so deeply that I fear Sisstorississ has flung a veil across that portion of the future."

Niall sighed. If things were as dangerous as that, if Sisstorississ were waiting for him to get control of him, he would forget about all the gold and jewels that were reputedly hidden in those mountains.

"I've heard enough," he told the mage.

Danko Penavar nodded his white head. "Indeed, I think you have," he murmured in a soft voice. More loudly, he called to the demon swaying before him, "Go now, Vokkoth, back into your worlds. I shall trouble you no more."

In an instant, the heat was gone, the demon with it. Overhead, the candles blazed more brightly, though their shapes were oddly distorted. The magician heaved a deep sigh, put a hand to the tome and closed it.

116

"It is done. Now you know," he said heavily.

Niall chuckled. "I know, old man. And you have all my thanks. I am glad I came to speak with you this night."

"I'm not so sure I am," the magician mumbled, leading the way toward his vast chair. He sank down into it, regarded the man standing before him. "Forget the gold, Niall. Nothing is worth risking the vengeance Sisstorississ has in mind for you."

"I agree with you. I'll tell the girl I've made up my mind. I stay in Urgrik, where—hopefully—Sisstorississ cannot touch me."

Danko Penavar smiled. "It would be best."

It was colder, once Niall stepped outside the great doorway which closed by itself behind him. For a moment he stood sniffing the salt and wind blowing off the river, carrying with it the iciness of the high peaks of the Kalbarthian mountain range to the east. Then he drew his cloak more tightly about him and began to walk.

He was grateful that he had come this night to the old mage, and glad that he had left his money pouch on the floor, so that Danko Penavar should find it and have the spending of the gold coins in it. The old man had done him a great favor.

He walked more briskly. It was quiet in these late hours. There were no walkers abroad, nothing seemed to stir within the city. Here and there in a house window, candles burned, but for the most part, the moon above gave the only illumination to these streets.

Niall came into the citadel and made his way up a wide staircase to the upper floors. He turned into his bedchamber and halted.

The girl lay sleeping on his bed, the fur coverings half off her body. She was beautiful as she lay there, the moonlight making her ebony hair even darker and silvering her soft skin. She seemed more innocent, too; there was none of the wantonness in her now that her earlier actions with him had hinted.

Niall took a few steps forward, bending to lift the fur cover and draw it more fully over her. As he did so, she stirred and turned on her back.

Her eyes were closed, yet Niall would have sworn that those eyelids were transparent. Almost he could see her green eyes—and in them the lambent flames that he had noticed earlier. The flames blazed upward, filling those eyes until they were a mass of flames.

And the flames began to whisper to him....

Chapter Three

Niall woke to the warmth of the body snuggled so closely against his own. His arm was about her, her own arm was thrown over his chest. He smelled the perfume of her hair, knew the softness of her flesh.

There was something he sought to remember—and could not. There was danger; some remote corner of his mind whispered this to him, but it fled away as the girl stirred and, lifting her head, looked down at him.

"We ride today, Niall of the Far Travels," she murmured. "To the hills of Kareen," he nodded.

What was it, hidden deep within him? A warning of deadly danger, a hint of abominations to come? Niall tried to run down that furtive memory, but could not. He sighed and his arm tightened about Mavis Deval, holding her close.

She bent and kissed him, and her mouth was as soft as warm, moist velvet. It stirred fires in his big body, that kiss, making him realize that he was going on a long journey with this witch-woman, that he would have her with him under the stars at night, beside glowing fires, and riding beside him day after day.

His big hand clapped her on the rump as he laughed. "Better stir ourselves, then. There will be matters to attend to, food to be put into bags, horses to be made ready."

She laughed and ran from the bed to don the garments he had provided for her. Niall watched her, wondering at himself. He ought to be more eager for this holiday, be anxious to get out on the road with the wind whispering past him, his eyes on the girl, and golden coins waiting for him to discover them.

Yet there was almost a reluctance in him. It was as if he had been warned about going to the Kareen hills, told that there was only deadly peril awaiting him.

Bah! He was a fighting man. He did not fear danger.

He clad himself in his fur kaunake and mail shirt, girded on his great sword. He had fought across his world, he had faced the Swordsmen of Chandion and battled the Dark Guards of Korapolis. No need to fear anything in the hills of Kareen!

They left Urgrik a little before high noon, mounted on two big stallions, and a third behind them carrying such goods as they might need. Mavis Deval was filled with excitement and laughter. She shifted in her saddle to stare back at the towers and rooftops of the city, then faced forward to run her eyes over the low-lying hills in the distance, and the great grasslands that spread out on all sides.

They rode for hours in the hot sunlight, pausing only at a stream of cold water where they got down and lay on their bellies to drink beside the horses. They chatted as they lay on their backs, staring up at the sky, relieved to be out of the saddle for a time.

"What will you do with your share of the treasure, always providing we find it?" Niall asked.

"The gold is yours, all yours. I shall stay with you, and help you spend it."

Niall thought about that for a time. It might be fun, having this girl with him. And yet—

Emelkartha was a jealous goddess. It was Emelkartha, in her earthly guise of Lylthia, whom he loved. Uneasiness ate in his middle. Emelkartha was nobody to fool around with. She had awesome powers, and she regarded Niall of the Far Travels as her property, as her earthly lover.

She had been strangely silent. Usually when he found a pretty girl, Emelkartha was there inside him, scolding him. When she felt that he had been tempted enough, she would appear to him as Lylthia, and they would make love for weeks at a time, before she had to go back to the Eleven Hells she ruled.

It was not like the goddess to let him run off this way with a pretty woman. Niall felt very uneasy about the whole thing. Still, there was that treasure to be found. If it were anything like what he suspected, and he could lay hands on it, he would be one of the richest men in all Urgrik.

It was a nice thought.

They rode on, day after day, deeper into the grasslands until the low-lying hills were before them, and then at their backs. They came now, into wilder country, where tumbled rocks lifted upward and deep chasms made furrows in the earth.

At long last, they could make out the hills of Kareen, far away in the blue distance. They were old, those hills, and rounded with age, and their slopes bore sparse vegetation. Somewhere in among them was the golden hoard.

Now Niall began questioning Mavis Deval more closely. "Are you sure you can find where it is hidden? If all you heard were a few words spoken by travelers...."

She turned her eyes upon him, laughing softly. "Do you think I would have brought you so far if I could not?"

Niall grunted. He could discover no other reason, search his mind as he would, why the girl would want to take such a long trip with him unless she knew—by what manner he knew not—just where the treasure was to be found.

"The hills of Kareen are long and wide," he muttered. "They are very ancient. There are tales that there was a kingdom there, long ago, and a band of men who hunted down other men, and women, to make them slaves. It was very long ago, I realize, but—"

"The city was called Granolure," the girl murmured, staring straight ahead. "It was one of the richest cities of the world, in its time. The people who lived there were robber barons, preying on the surrounding territories. Until a coalition of neighboring cities was formed and sent a vast army against it, it thrived. The people there worshiped a god—"

She broke off suddenly, starting as though she had said too much. Mavis Deval turned her head and looked at him, but Niall rode with his gaze on the rocky terrain before them.

She smiled with a subtle curving of her lips.

Niall stood upward in the stirrups. He had paid little or no attention to the girl's last few words; he was certain he had seen movement off there to the west, along the edge of the Kareen hills. Movement meant people—or wild animals. From what he had seen, there was more than one—thing—out there.

"Saw you anything just then?" he asked.

She stared at him in surprise. "Something living, you mean? But there is no life in those hills. They are dead, forgotten alike by animals and mankind."

"I saw something. I was not mistaken."

It was the girl's turn to stand in the stirrups and to put her gaze out there where the hills seemed purple, where sunlight glinted on barren rocks and loose shale. Mavis Deval shook her head until her thick black hair swirled.

"There is nothing. All you saw was a shadow." She added musingly, "There can be no life in those hills. All is dead there, and long since forgotten."

Niall shrugged. He knew what he had seen, and he loosed his blade in its scabbard. Just as well to be prepared. Others might have heard of the treasure and come looking for it.

As they moved onward, he used his eyes. From hilltop to hilltop and in between, in the low valleys, he ran his gaze. There was no more movement, none at all. Still! It paid a man always to be on his guard.

It was sunset when they came to the foothills, and stood a moment to blow their horses. It was cool here, and the night would be cold.

"We'll make camp," Niall said.

"We could go on. It isn't far now." Niall shrugged. "There's no hurry."

Mavis Deval would have protested, but his face was grimly set, so she shrugged and stepped down from the saddle. It had become her task to prepare their food every morning and evening, and she set about it with practiced dexterity.

Out of the corners of her eyes, she watched Niall. He was restless, moving back and forth, scanning the hillsides, the empty land around them. It was as if he feared that men would rise upward from the very ground and rush to attack them.

She saw him sniff the air, and called, "Now what will you be smelling?"

"Human sweat," he growled. "Men have been here, men who have gone long without bathing." When she scoffed at him, he swung about to look at her. "Girl, I know of what I speak. I've fought too much not to know that stink when it comes to me."

She got to her feet in excitement. "But it cannot be! No one ever comes here!"

"How would you be knowing that? Or did those men you overheard at the caravan also tell you that?"

She shook her head and knelt again to lift the steaming meat from the fire-flames On a board she placed it and began slicing it into thick slabs. She gestured at it, looking at Niall.

"Come eat. There is hot bread, too, almost finished baking."

Niall found that there was an avid hunger in him. His strong teeth tore and chewed at the charred meat, and it seemed that he had never enjoyed anything as tasty. There was red wine from Calmanar in the skins, and of this he drank deeply.

When he was done eating, he looked away from the fire into the darkness. There was something—alive—out there, and something— evil. He had no way of knowing what it was, but he had fought too often not to be able to sense foemen, even in the dark.

"Go to sleep," he told the girl. "I'm restless, I want to walk a little."

She shrugged and lay down close to the flames, drawing a cloak about her. Her eyes rested on Niall's brawny figure as he loomed huge beside the fire. He was a handsome man, she thought as her eyelids closed for sleep. It was too bad, in a way, that he was doomed ....

Niall strode away from the girl, walking easily in his furred war-boots. He did not look at the fire any more; instead, his eyes were directed outward toward the hills. There was a moon, and by its light he could see a good distance.

He would sit there, with his back against a rock, and stare out into that moon-swept land. If anything moved, he would see it in time to defend himself and the girl. His sword lay across his thighs, its blade naked, his hand wrapped about its pommel.

You do well to be on guard, Niall!

The Wanderer started. Had that been Emelkartha, speaking inside him as she was wont to do? He had dozed a little, sitting here—it had been a long, hard ride all that day—but he felt certain that he had not dreamed those words.

Na, na. You did not dream.

"Where have you been?" he whispered, almost to himself. "You warned me about the girl and then you stayed away."

I have been searching, witless one. Searching in the demon worlds for word of — Sisstorississ

Niall growled low in his throat.

So you remember Sisstorississ, do you? And how you drove him back to where he belongs, that time in Kor Magnon?

"I remember."

Do you imagine that evil one has forgotten you? Ah, no. He hates you with a fury that will not be satisfied by your death. No, no!

Emelkartha went on whispering inside him, telling him of the raw fury that consumed Sisstorississ when he thought of Niall of the Far Travels. She spoke of his vengeance, long plotted and now about to come to pass.

He shuddered, listening to what the evil one planned to do to him— for all eternity. The sweat came out on his skin and a tremor ran through his huge body. It was always bad to offend the gods, and most especially one like Sisstorississ.

However, there is hope. You may die before Sisstorississ gets his claws in you, unless you use your eyes!

Something in that voice brought Niall to sharp wakefulness. His hand tightened on Blood-drinker. He stared out into the darkness and it seemed that he could make out shapes that ran, hunched over, and the glint of moonlight on drawn weapons.

Niall grinned. "My thanks, goddess," he whispered.

Men with weapons he could understand. He had faced up to swords since he was big enough to lift and swing one, it seemed. Back there in Norumbria, where he had been born, men lived and died by the sword. He had been one who had lived, who had waxed stronger and greater every day, until his skill with a blade was almost proverbial.

He lay down and crawled on his belly over the ground. Those men were close now, very close. In another few moments, they would be at the fire, and at Mavis Deval. Niall grinned and shifted his weight, drawing up a leg under him.

They loomed up, their weapons at the ready.

"Haaaaaah!"

The screech came upward out of Niall's guts. It was a blend of delight and fury, a warning and a paean of joy because he had an enemy to face. He erupted from the ground and came at them like a maddened beast.

Blood-drinker caught the reflection of the fire on its blade an instant before the steel was buried in human flesh. It came out, dripping blood, and swung again at a second man.

A head rolled past the fire, as that which had been a man collapsed to one side.

Niall, stood with widespread legs, his blade humming as he swung it, and a tiny smile played about his lips.

"So then! You came to rob, did you? Well, I am here. Rob me—if you can!"

The remaining men flung themselves at him, but Niall had learned his trade of swordsman long ago, and had practiced it forever since. His muscles were as iron, tireless. He battered down the blades that faced him and drove his own steel in a web of death at the men before him.

One by one, he slew them.

The last man died with a scream gurgling in his throat, as Niall drove Blood-drinker through his belly. He fell and lay twitching, bloody hands clawing at his ripped entrails, body convulsing.

Niall stood over him, staring down.

Were these men only cut-purses, landless robbers who preyed on whatever moved this far away from any city? Or were they demons gathered by some evil god such as Sisstorississ to slay him?

No, no. What was it Emelkartha had said? Sisstorississ wanted an eternal vengeance on him. He would not, therefore, send mere men to kill him. No, he would have planned something else, some way of luring him into his clutches so that he could snatch him into the hells where he was the supreme ruler.

The sound of a sob swung him about to stare at Mavis Deval.

The girl was standing beside the fire, her robe having fallen from her. A hand was lifted to her mouth and her eyes were enormous with terror.

"Are you—all right?" she whispered.

Niall grinned. "It takes more than such as these to bring down Niall of the Far Travels. They were after our gold. And you too, I should guess. In this wilderness a man doesn't often see a woman, especially such a beautiful one as you."

Emelkartha stirred inside Niall. He could feel the heat of her anger, the coldness of her jealousy.

Mavis Deval nodded slowly. "Yes, you saved me. I am grateful. Those men are vermin. They would have..."

She shuddered and turned away, staring into the fire. It seemed as though she would speak again, but she did not, only lifting her eyes and looking at him, and for an instant, Niall thought to read pity in her stare.

Chapter Four

Next day they were into the hills, riding upward over rocky terrain, picking their way with the girl in the lead. Niall watched her as she rode unerringly—as though she had committed this trackless wilderness to memory—without glancing to left or right, but only moving straight ahead.

When they had come to a rock outcropping, she reined in and turned to him. Her arm lifted, finger pointing.

"Over yonder, where there is only scorched earth and tumbled rocks, is the entrance to what was once a great stronghold," she told him.

Niall could see nothing that suggested any entryway, and said so. Mavis Deval shook her head.

"There is nothing to see; the door that is there is blocked by stones. But it is there, believe me."

The Wanderer shrugged, toed his mount off to one side, to descend a slope which would bring him to the heaps of scattered rocks. When he came there, he swung down and, putting big fists on his hips, eyed the boulders.

"I'll need an army to move those things," he growled. The girl came up to him, touching his arm. "You can do it. Only try."

He laughed and moved forward, putting his big hands to a huge rock. It was impossible to move that boulder, his common sense told him, yet he felt it shift as he applied his strength, and then as he put his full weight behind it, the rock tumbled to one side.

To Niall, it smacked of magic.

Still, the biggest rock was out of the way, and the smaller ones ought to give way even more easily. He bent and pushed, and one by one, the stones slid where he shoved them.

He could see a massive door, of oak and iron bands, half hidden beneath a bit of stone that hung above it. There was a great lock, rusted now, that once would have defied any effort to open it.

Niall picked up a rock, lifted it high, and smashed it down against the lock. He heard metal snap and wood creak. He took a few steps forward, put his hands to the door and heaved. The oaken beams of the door protested with muffled crackings, but the door swung inward upon blackness.

The girl was at his side. "There! You see? It was not so hard, was it?"

"It was too easy," he growled.

Aye! Too easy. It seemed almost as though unearthly powers had been used to let him clear the way into this crypt. Well, this was what he had come for. There remained only to enter, to see what it was he had come so far to find.

He took a step forward, and then another. Sunlight shone into the crypt through the open doorway, and Niall could make out, as he stood on the threshold, that this was a vast room, seemingly filled with chests piled one upon another, with smaller caskets here and there. Where one such casket had fallen and opened, he could make out the gleam of fabulous jewels.

The air was stale in here, but if he waited, it would clear. Far in the background there was blackness, yet he thought he could see something like a walled-up archway, filled with bricks and cement. He would need a torch to examine it, and the contents of all those chests and coffers.

"Enter," said the girl at his elbow. "Go in and feast your eyes on all those riches which are now yours."

Niall struck sparks from flint and iron, lifted the end of a dried bit of wood that he found off to one side. With the torch in hand, he moved into the crypt. Mavis Deval came at his heels.

He moved toward a chest, threw back its lid and gasped. The thing was filled with golden bars, glittering in the torchlight. His eyes lifted to stare at the other chests. If all were like this one, he would be the richest man in all his world. The breath caught in his throat, and his heart began to hammer.

"Did I not speak the truth?" the girl whispered at his side. "All this gold, all the jewels in here are yours."

Niall shook his head. There was something wrong here. He did not know what it was, he could put no name to it, yet the tenseness inside him, the tautness of his nerves and the worry in his mind could not be disregarded.

"Why?" he asked softly. "Why have you given all this to me?"

He whirled and caught her by an arm, bringing her up closer to him. His blue eyes blazed down at her. "You could have claimed all this yourself! Yet you give it to me. Why?"

"You rescued me from slavery."

"Na, na. There is something else. But what?"

She rubbed her arm where he had clutched her, pouting a little. "How could I, a mere girl without money or anyone to befriend me, have come here? Those men last night would have raped me, probably killed me."

All she said made sense, but Niall was not so sure. There was something lurking behind her eyes, some secret which he could not fathom. Those eyes that stared up at him so worshipfully hid her thoughts. Ah! He recalled now how he had seen flames in those eyes, too.

She turned away and moved toward the oaken door, still rubbing her arm. When she came to the door where it hung on its bronze hinges, he caught hold of it and slammed it shut.

127

For an instant, the only light in the crypt was from the torch Niall held. And then—slowly—faint reddish light began to gleam everywhere inside the vault. Mavis Deval stood proudly, head high, her eyes glinting boldly, and the fire-flames were alive in them.

Niall swore, "By Emelkartha! There is something wrong about all this—"

He reeled. His head seemed to explode for an instant, then come back to normal. Dazed, he stared around him. He remembered, now: remembered his visit to old Danko Penavar, and his warning.

He laughed harshly. He had been mesmerized by those eyes, when he had returned from seeing the mage. Hypnotized, and made to come here—to fall into the clutches of Sisstorississ!

Niall tried to leap forward, to spring at the girl, but his muscles were locked tight. He could not stir so much as a finger. And the reddish light blazed more brightly, triumphantly.

Behind him he heard something surge against the bricks of the far wall. Those bricks fell and shattered and now he could feel heat on his back, fantastic heat that was unendurable.

"You belong to me, Niall of the Far Travels," came a booming voice. "Turn now, and see your master for all eternity!"

He swung about.

Sisstorississ was there, just as he had remembered him in the temple at Kor Magnon. There were the red eyes, glittering with hate and an all-consuming fury! There also was the herpetologic head, covered with scales, the twin horns rising upward from the brow and the flickering tongue that was twice the size of a man.

When he had beheld Sisstorississ that other time, Emelkartha had been inside him, to shield him with her powers. Ah, where was she now? Without her to aid him, he was doomed forever!

Those great jaws lunged forward, parting.

That huge red tongue wrapped itself about him, lifted him upward as those jaws closed about his body. Niall could not speak, nor cry out.

He was drawn swiftly toward the bricked-up doorway which now was gaping open. Downward he was drawn... ever downward... into a redness and a heat that was intolerable....

Chapter Five

He lay on a flat surface that was like the red-hot top of an iron stove. His first impulse was to leap up, crying out in agony, but the pain seemed to subside even as he felt it, and though the stink of his scorched flesh was still in his nostrils, he felt no other discomfort.

Niall opened his eyes. He lay on the steaming floor of a huge chamber walled with flames. Everywhere he stared, there were fires, leaping, dancing upward. Sweat rolled down off his flesh, but he found he could move, and so he stood, his right hand moving toward his sword and lifting it out of the scabbard.

He shook his head.

He was nowhere on earth. He was in a demoniac hell, a hell ruled by Sisstorississ. Niall groaned. Aye, he was in the clutches of that evil godling. He would be put to the torment, then rested, then tortured again, for as long as there was Time.

Strange. He felt no especial discomfort, though he knew that steam rose upward from the floor where he was standing. Now, how could that be?

His eyes lifted to the flames, and Niall started. Were his eyes playing tricks on him? For he could see, as though partially hidden by those flames, other eyes that stared down at him almost, it seemed, in sympathy.

Then—the eyes were gone.

He heard slithering across the tiles of the steaming floor, and whirled. Sisstorississ was there—gigantic, looming high above him, triumph shining in those red eyes. Suddenly, along with the triumph, there was—doubt. Even—worry.

The snake-god hissed, "You belong to me now, Niall! Mine you are, to torture and agonize for all Time."

Niall held his sword up. "Come then. Take me if you would torture me."

The scaled body writhed undulantly forward. "Take you? I have already done that. Yet you still defy me? Good. I like that. It will make your breaking that much more pleasant. Behold."

He was in a great cauldron of bubbling metal. The bubbles of iridescent bronze broke with a popping sound, steam rose upward all around him. By rights, he should be screaming in agony, writhing and twisting as that molten metal ate away his flesh and bones.

Yet he felt no pain. It was as if he were in thick, viscid water. He began to swim laboriously to the rim of the cauldron, then gripped its edge and hauled himself upward onto that rim.

Something protected him. Niall knew that much. No man— without the help of magical forces—could have lived through that bath of liquid-hot metal.

Ah! So you realize that, do you?

His relief was so great he almost fell back into the stuff that bubbled beneath him.

"Emelkartha! I thought you'd deserted me." Soft laughter was his answer.

You are my proof, beloved. The gods would not believe that Sisstorississ had disobeyed their injunction. I had to let the snake-god take you and bring you here for torment.

Niall growled in his throat. "Am I a plaything of the gods? It's a wonder I didn't die of shock when Sisstorississ caught hold of me and dragged me here."

I protected you from pain. My protection is still around you. The snake-god must be punished. We can only do that through you.

Niall shrugged. There was no point in arguing. Better to fall in with Emelkartha's plans. "What do you want me to do?"

Only be yourself.

The voice faded and he was left sitting alone on the cauldron's rim. How long he sat there he was never to know, but suddenly he was standing on the steaming metal floor of the chamber where he had been lying when he recovered consciousness.

He sat up to find Sisstorississ staring at him with his malignant red eyes. There was fear and rage in the snake-god's voice when he spoke.

"What's this? You are unharmed! How can that be?"

Niall sprang to his feet and rushed upon the demon-god, Blood-drinker held high to swing. He drove its edge at the head of Sisstorississ and saw the being dart backward, slithering along the hot, metallic floor.

There was panic in the crimson eyes of the demon-god, raw fear and awful horror in them. It was as if it saw its doom staring at it. "What gives you this power?" it hissed.

Again Niall slashed, driving it backward. He had no way of answering the demon. By rights, he should be dead by now, or reduced to a quivering mass of melted flesh and bones. Yet he had all his strength. Indeed, he felt invigorated, filled with muscular power.

He knew he had enjoyed the help of something beyond the human.

Ah! So you know that, do you?

Niall slid to a halt, grinning. "It was you, Emelkartha!" he said almost to himself.

Of course. You have served me well, Niall. But follow Sisstorississ, follow him no matter where he goes!

He leaped forward even as the demon-god slithered backward into a great opening in the flame-wall. As Sisstorississ went even further backward into that recess, Niall sprang. Deftly avoiding that snapping jaw, those rows of razor-sharp teeth, his hand caught a horn projecting from its scaly forehead and he swung himself up onto the thin, sinuous neck.

Instantly, Sisstorississ seemed to go into convulsions. It whipped its titanic body about, writhing its neck and flinging its great head back and forth, seeking to dislodge this human who clung so tenaciously to him.

When Niall clung to him, driving his sword's edge down upon its head, the demon-god retreated even further. Backward it slid, down a dizzying slope, and then plunged deep into a sea of molten metal.

Niall closed his eyes and drew a deep breath. Next moment he was beneath the surface of that molten metal sea, clinging to that horn, riding this nightmare moment with his legs locked about a scaled neck.

Where was Emelkartha? Why did she not help him?

I am here, Niall my darling—waiting!

131

If she didn't help him soon, he was going to topple off, be helpless in this thick quagmire of smoking, seething metal. He would be fair prey for those jaws, then!

Down went Sisstorississ, downward, ever downward. It was as though it sought to find the bottom of this sea, where it might find a purchase for its clawed legs. Ah, then it would turn and rend this mere human, this servitor of the gods who were aligned against mighty Sisstorississ!

Niall was blind and helpless. He dared not open his eyes, he was fearful lest the molten magma blind him. Yet he could breathe, his body did not feel the awesome heat of the molten metal. He still retained his strength.

"Emelkartha," he shrieked in his mind. "Aid me!"

Not yet, my dear one. Not yet—but soon.

Sisstorississ found the bottom. Its claws dug in, its neck whipped about. Despite the hold he had with his hand on that horn and his legs about the neck, Niall felt as though he were about to be flung off.

Aye! Flung off—then to be snapped at by those terrible jaws— swallowed alive! Could anything save him, then?

His legs loosed their hold, sliding. His hand was wrenched from that sharp horn. Beneath him, Sisstorississ was flinging itself about like a mad thing, emitting great bellows that sounded dulled and muted through the molten magma.

Now, you other gods! Strike—now!

The voice in his mind was like a clarion call—sharp, bugling— imperious and commanding.

Something bright and golden sped downward through the seething metal. It was joined by other golden lightnings—until they formed a shower of aureate energy striking at Sisstorississ, hitting it.

Niall could hear the violence of those blows thudding into the vast body to which he still managed to cling. Through his flesh he could feel the shuddering of the demon-god as those darts of yellow light struck against its scaled hide.

Sisstorississ bellowed in agony.

It forgot the man still hanging onto him. Upward it surged, seeking any avenue of escape it could find. And ever those golden lightnings played about its scaled body.

Those yellow forkings weakened it. Niall could feel some of the titanic strength of the body seep from it as he clung. From somewhere inside Sisstorississ there came a prolonged wail of despair, almost of resignation to what was about to happen to it.

To a rocky edge of this metal sea came the demon. It reached to that stone and clambered out upon it and lay there, its sides heaving. It did not seek any longer to dislodge Niall but crouched downward as though waiting for some final blow.

Now Niall could make out, high above and scattered about in this rocky cavern, tiny globes of white light that grew and grew until within them he could make out faces. They were cold and implacable, those faces—the faces of the gods, of the potent lords of the realms beyond the world Niall knew.

Awed, he stared upward at them, knowing a vast inferiority, a mighty humility. The eyes regarded Sisstorississ, and in their stare their was no pity.

You have sinned, demon. You have risen up against our will!

A soft voice that sounded feminine whispered, Now you must pay the price for your disobedience!

Niall saw the face of the womanly creature who had spoken. Her glowing purple eyes were turned away from Sisstorississ to look down at Niall.

So this is the human who has served us. He has done well. Emelkartha was right in her judgment of him. He must be rewarded.

And so he shall be, sister!

That was Emelkartha, laughing deep inside him.

The womanly being who stared down at him from so high above nodded slowly, a tiny smile playing at the comers of her mouth.

Good. I approve of it, Emelkartha See to it, please.

Niall slid down off the great bulk of Sisstorississ, at a whispered command from deep inside him. Still clinging to his sword he moved backward, backward, feeling the rough stone of this vast shelf under his war-boots

He went backward until he felt rock at his spine and there he crouched, scarcely breathing.

From the globes of light he could see arms projecting. There were many fingers on the hands at the ends of those arms, and each finger was rigid, pointing.

Now from those fingers spread something black and ominous, like tiny droplets of molten ebony. They grew as he watched, grew and grew until they seemed to fill the entire cavern. As one, the blackness hurtled at Sisstorississ.

The demon screamed, and then those black bolts were upon it, hammering it, pounding in upon it. The sound of their beatings filled the cavern with dreadful thumpings. The buffeting deafened Niall. but he could hear Sisstorississ screaming now in utter agony.

There was no escape. The demon could not move, as those blacknesses thundered down upon it. Under their onslaught, its very shape seemed to change, to flatten, to swell in bubblings, to be driven backward against the stone wall of the cavern It screamed, thickly at first and then more thinly, until its shriekings became only a thin wail lifting upward.

"Gods," breathed Niall.

Sisstorississ was being hammered into a pulp, out of which oozed a stinking greenish ichor. Hammers and sledges of that blackness drove upon it, pounding its flesh into the very rock on which it stood.

There was little left of Sisstorississ now, but even those scraps and shards of quivering flesh were being beaten into nothingness. Pound and pound and pound, until those poundings became a litany of destruction.

Niall rose from his crouch, aching in every muscle. It was done.

Nothing was left of Sisstorississ.

Now he heard vast creakings, saw the stone half-riven, even as the great walls of this cavern began to split.

Now, Niall—now!

Instantly he was whirled upward, as though caught by a gigantic whirlwind. He experienced a moment of abysmal nausea, he began to retch—

Then he stood in the cave with the chests and caskets still catching the gleams of die dying sunlight. Dazed, he drew a deep breath. Had it been a dream?

Laughter came from a comer of the crypt. Niall whirled, then grinned. Lylthia came toward him, clad in her short tunic, rent here and there to show the tints of her flesh. Never had she seemed so beautiful.

"Take what you will of the gold and jewels, Niall." she smiled. "You have earned your reward."

"Never mind the gold and jewels," he chuckled moving toward her. "Who can look at those when you are here?"

Lylthia laughed, her head thrown back. "I like that! You make a good lover."

He caught her. kissed her hungrily. After a time, she stirred in his embrace. "We have plenty of time for this, Niall. I shall ride back with you. all the way to Urgrik. And—we shall take our time."

A thought touched the barbarian, and he lifted his head to stare about the crypt. "Mavis Deval. Where is she?"

Lylthia "s fingernails dug into his arms. "What is she to you, that woman?"

He chuckled. "Nothing. But if she should try any of her tricks on me..."

The girl-goddess laughed and nestled against him. "She will not. When Sisstorississ was destroyed, so was she. You only have Lylthia now."

"I wish I did have you," he grumbled, then brightened. "But I suppose I should appreciate the moments when you come to me like this. And to show you how much I appreciate them—"

He caught her to him again, kissing her. And Lylthia, who was Emelkartha snuggled up against him, quite content to forget for a time that she was a goddess.

THE CUBE FROM BEYOND

Chapter One

Sword in hand, Niall of the Far Travels raced down the long palace corridor. All around him in this city of Bar Gomal, rising and falling in cadence, were the sounds of battle. As general of the armies of Lurlyr Manakor, lord king of Urgrik, he was leading his men against the stronghold of Thavas Tomer, magician-king of this strange land which threatened the safety of Urgrik itself.

For three weeks, his army had besieged the high walls of Bar Gomal. For three weeks Niall had hurled the might of his army against those walls. Only this morning, under shelter of a storm of war arrows, had he been able to mount to the top of a scaling ladder and lead his men to the ramparts.

Now Thavas Tomer was a doomed man. He had fled down the halls and corridors, seeking sanctuary—where no sanctuary was to be found. At his heels had come Niall, his great sword Blood-drinker in his hand, seeking to make an end to this magician-king who had slain and raped and robbed all those against whom he had sent his mercenaries.

Now the end was close.

A flutter of a cape, a brief glimpse of a sandal, and Thavas Tomer was gone around a corner. Where was the man heading? To throw himself from the top of a tower? Now he was mounting a curling stairway toward the very topmost part of the palace.

Niall went after him, grinning wolfishly. Already the sounds of battle had died down. The mercenaries in Thavas Tomer's employ did not want to die for the man who had hired them. Seeing that the battle had turned against them, knowing that their commander had fled, they would be throwing down their arms.

Up the staircase Niall went, always upward.

He came at last into a small room, the windows of which looked out over the city and the plains stretching in all directions beyond it. Thavas Tomer was standing beside a large blue cube dotted with a myriad of bright little specks that looked like imprisoned stars.

The magician-king was tall, almost as tall as Niall. He was broad of shoulder and lean of waist; he looked more like a warrior than a magician. There was a cunning smile on this thin lips.

"No more, Niall," he rasped. "I flee no further."

"Then surrender."

Thavas Tomer laughed: harsh, mocking laughter it was, as he drew himself to his full height. "You can never make me surrender, general. Na, na. I have a way to get away from you, even here and now, with you so close."

His laughter rang out as Niall started forward. With the ease of a trained athlete, Thavas Tomer leaped upward to the top of that big cube — and began to sink into it.

Niall rasped a curse as he too leaped upward. His war-boots landed on top of the stone, and remained there. Surprised, Niall stared downward at the cube. It was hard, adamantine.

How in the name of Emelkartha of the Eleven Hells had the magician-king disappeared inside it? For he had gone into it, Niall had seen that much. With the sharp point of his steel sword, Niall jabbed at the stone. It resisted his every effort.

He sprang back onto the carpeted floor, paced around the queer cube, eyeing it suspiciously. He replaced the sword in his scabbard, put both big hands to its edge and tilted it. The cube was heavy, but it moved under the pressure of Niall's great muscles.

There was no trapdoor under it, just the thick rug.

Obviously, then, Thavas Tomer was inside the cube. Ah, but how could that be?

Magic, of course. There was no other answer.

A sound swung Niall around. Haifa dozen of his men were crowding into the room, weapons in their hands. Niall grinned at them wryly.

"He's inside that," he growled, gesturing at the cube, "by some trick of an evil god. Pick it up, carry it back down to the ground. I'll take it back to Urgrik with me. Thavas Tomer isn't going to escape from me that easily."

He watched as the burly man bent to their task. He walked with them, supervising their carrying of the cube. His eyes never left its blue surface, never turned away from the tiny white stars imprisoned inside it.

Out in the sunlight, he watched as other men came with hide wrappings and bound up the cube inside them. Ropes were knotted all about the hides, and then the whole thing was lifted onto a cart.

"We'll take it back to Urgrik with us," Niall growled. "I don't want it unguarded or unattended at any time. If Thavas Tomer comes up of it—by some devil's trick—run your spears into him."

He detailed men to watch the cube, standing about the wagon. No one was to be allowed near the cube, under pain of death for the men watching it. He had the king-mage in his grasp, and Niall was not about to let him go.

For a full week he remained in Bar Gomal, razing the city and scattering salt on the gardens which had furnished it with food. When he finally gave the signal to march back to Urgrik, Bar Gomal was only a memory.

Niall rode at the head of his troops, the captured mercenaries, the women and children. Everything worth taking that had been in Bar Gomal was being brought back with him. From time to time Niall stood in his stirrups and directed his gaze at the farm cart which held the strange cube. It was still wrapped as he had seen it wrapped. There had been no sign, no hint of Thavas Tomer.

They came into Urgrik to the singing of the crowds watching as he rode at the head of his armed columns. Music blared everywhere, mingled with the shouts of the populace. They screamed in delight as the captives swung past, at the sight of the vast treasures that had been in the city of Bar Gomal.

"Thavas Tomer," they screamed.

"Where is he?"

There was no reply to that, and Niall made none. Only to Lurlyr Manakor would he make answer, and he did not know whether or not he would be believed. In one way, his failure to bring the king-mage back in chains spoiled his sense of triumph.

Yet when he stood before the king and made his report, he knew

138

that he was being foolish. Lurlyr Manakor came down from the throne and put both hands on his shoulders, smiling at him.

"You have done what no other man could do, Niall. You have destroyed Thavas Tomer, you have made him flee into some magical place where—we hope—he shall remain forever."

Niall shook his head. "You are too kind, majesty. I fear such a man as Thavas Tomer. I doubt that he'll be content to stay lost inside that cube. I mean to find a way to bring him to justice."

Lurlyr Manakor shrugged. 'The cube is yours. Do with it as you like. But for now, forget everything but the victory celebration. There are many of my noblemen who wish to congratulate you."

Niall brought the cube to bis little palace and set it up in an otherwise empty upstairs chamber, cutting away the ropes that bound the hide to it. For hours he would stand and study that cube, and he noted that the tiny white dots moved, that they followed a set pattern, swinging through the blue spaces of the cube as do the stars on which he looked every night from a balcony of his palace.

There was no answer to his problem.

For a time he lost himself in the feasts and banquets which Lurlyr Manakor held to honor him. He listened as men made much of him, and he smiled as the lovely women of the court flattered and flirted with him. Always at the back of bis mind was the strange cube and the man it held in its grasp.

Then on a warm spring night, he had his servants carry the cube down to the courtyard and place it in a cart. He himself took the reins of the big draft horse and urged the horse and cart through the city streets until he came to a section of the city that was close to a hundred centuries old.

Here the houses leaned against one another, weak with age, and the windows were narrow and small. There were slops in the street here, and ordure, and Niall told himself that only for one reason would he come to these haunts.

He came down off the cart and knocked at a narrow doorway. When the door opened, he saw no one there, but in the flickering light of a fireplace, he saw a stout old man wrapped in richly ornamented robes, lying back in a vast chair.

The old man chuckled and waved a hand. "Enter, Niall of the Far Travels. What brings you to my humble abode?"

Niall moved into the vast room with his pantherish stride and came to a halt before Danko Penavar. He had no eyes for the golden censers and silver athanors, for the chests heaped high with strange and almost unobtainable magical condiments. All his attention was concentrated on the old man who sprawled in the big oaken chair.

Niall began to talk. He spoke of Thavas Tomer and of the manner of his escape. As he talked, he saw that old Danko Penavar seemed startled, then highly interested. The big old man actually rose up straighter in his chair that so much resembled a throne, and his eyes glistened.

Almost under his breath, the old man whispered, "I have heard of it. In very ancient tomes have I come upon faint hints of it, fearful references to that cube."

He shook his head until the white hairs of his head and beard swayed lazily. "Never did I think to lay eyes upon that thing. I believed it lost forever."

"Well, what is it?'

"It was created long and long ago by a great magician. It is a universe unto itself, that cube. It is protected by secret sigils and enchantments that have long since been forgotten."

"Not by Thavas Tomer, it seems."

The old man smiled wryly. "I wonder where he found it? Where he discovered the way in which to make it work for him?' "Can I go into it, as Thavas Tomer did?"

Danko Penavar scowled. "You would be advised not to. I know nothing of what might await you inside that thing-always assuming there is a way into it. For you, I mean. It would be best for you to forget the cube—and Thavas Tomer."

Niall scowled. He was not a man to relish defeat, nor to accept it lightly. And Thavas Tomer had defeated him. His gaze went around the room, studying the dusty old tomes that lay on the shelves, tomes that held the magic of uncounted centuries. It seemed strange to him that nowhere in all those old archives was a way to enable him to enter the cube after the king-magician.

"He could stay in there for a century, and then reappear. If he were not too old," Niall announced at last.

Danko Penavar nodded. "He could, yes. He would not age in there, I think. According to the old legends, anyhow."

The old man sighed. "When Tarj Needal invented that cube-or created it, rather—it was to act as an escape for him, in case he ever needed it to escape the vengeance of some king or emperor. Whether he used it or not, I have no way of knowing. No one does, except perhaps Thavas Tomer."

Niall stalked up and down the room. He was troubled. He knew the evil of the king-magician, knew that if he himself abandoned the quest for him, the man would escape, perhaps to return to this world when everyone now in it was in their graves.

If he did that, with his powers he might rule the world. Niall shuddered at that thought, for Thavas Tomer was a cruel, haughty man with no consideration for anything but his own desires.

There must be a way. There had to be!

He turned and moved toward the door which opened for him by itself. Framed in the doorway, he turned and regarded the old man.

"If ever I find a way into that cube, I shall go," he growled. "No man escapes me when I have marked him for death."

Danko Penavar said, "Be advised, Niall. I like you. I have always given you good advice. Leave the cube. Lock it up somewhere. Buy it in the sea or in the river. Forget it—and live. You are too young to die."

Niall grinned coldly. "We shall see," he muttered.

All the way back to his little palace he sat hunched forward on the cart seat, the reins all but forgotten in his hands. There had to be a way to go into that cube. There had to! If Thavas Tomer had done it, so could he.

Ah, but if old Danko Penavar, who knew the secrets of the ages and of all magic, could not tell him how to do it, who could? Niall sighed and shook his head.

When he was back in his palace courtyard, he called to his serving-men and with their help carried the cube up the stone steps and into a small room fitted out with thick rugs and a pair of comfortable chairs.

He dismissed the man, went around the cube, just touching it with his fingertips.

He would not be defeated. He would not let himself be beaten. "Emelkartha," he whispered.

She could help him, the goddess of the Eleven Hells. Always she had come to him in his world, to lend her aid. She would not refuse him now. Or—would she?

She was a wayward goddess, was Emelkartha Ever since that day when he had accosted her—in her human guise as the maiden Lylthia—she had come to him in his hours of need, to lend her assistance-aye, and her love.

Niall grinned at his memories. She was a jealous one, was Lylthia. She did not like him to pay attention to any woman other than herself. Ah, but she had kept him alive on a number of times, when he had been beset by demons as powerful as herself.

"Maybe I ought to summon a maidservant to me," he grinned. "That new girl from the farmland country, for instance. She's made eyes at me, she would come."

"There's no need for that," said a cold voice.

Niall swung around.

Lylthia was sitting in one of the chairs, arms wrapped about her knees, scowling at him. She wore a leather garment, much shredded and rent so that he could see her pale white skin through the tears. Her long black hair was piled on top of her head, with some of it hanging down past her cheeks.

"You're a fool," she snapped. "Forget Thavas Tomer. Enjoy life. Why must you always be poking your nose where it will only get you into trouble?"

Niall gave a great shout of delight. He leaped toward her, caught her bare arms and yanked her up against him. He kissed her hungrily even while she struggled—but not too hard—to evade him.

When he had kissed her until she clung to him, he said, "Help me, my darling. I want to go into that cube and fetch Thavas Tomer back to stand trial for his crimes."

Tears came into her eyes.

"I dare not," she whispered.

Chapter Two

Her palm stroked his cheek tenderly.

"You big foolish man! Why won't you be guided by me? I tell you no one—no one!—knows what is inside that cube."

"But you are a goddess! You know—"

"Yes, yes. I have great powers. But where that cube is concerned... sit down, Niall. I want to tell you about it."

He drew her with him, onto his lap with his arms locked about her as she nestled against him. He nuzzled her soft throat, kissing it, until she laughed and pushed him back.

"Behave yourself. This is important. Now listen!

"Long, long ago when Tarj Needal lived and was a mighty magician, he sought the help of the gods to make for him a world into which he might go from time to time when dangers threatened him here on this world.

"They worked together, did the evil gods, to make the cube. Into it they poured their powers, fashioning it of the stuff of the god-worlds where they lived. They snatched stars from other dimensions and embedded them within the cube.

"When they were done, they told Tarj Needal that they had made a masterpiece, incapable of destruction, incapable of being made again. There was only one cube like that. There would never be another."

Lylthia sighed and shook her head, cuddling closer to the man who held her. "They spoke the truth, did those evil gods. They had made a masterpiece. And they told Tarj Needal the one and only way of entering and leaving it."

"But Thavas Tomer entered it."

Lylthia sighed. "Then Tarj Needal must have left a record of it, and this magician you seek found out where he had hidden that record. Perhaps it was with the cube when he found that."

Niall growled, "I can't believe no one among the gods knows the

143

way to enter that thing."

Lylthia smiled sadly. "Oh, I know the way to enter it, all right—but I can't tell you how to get out of it."

"I could make Thavas Tomer tell me that."

"No! You must not risk it. It would be too dangerous."

Niall eyed the cube where it stood close to the flames of the fireplace. It seemed to mock and taunt him as those tiny stars slowly revolved and swung in their courses. Anger built in him. If Thavas Tomer could go into that thing, so could he. If Thavas Tomer knew of a way out, he would force him to tell it to him.

Ah, but he must not let Lylthia suspect what he meant to do.

He sighed, saying, "I guess you're right. I'll leave well enough alone. "

A soft hand caressed his cheek. "Now you're being sensible." Laughter made the corners of her mouth quiver. "As long as I'm here, I might as well stay the night. Take me to your bedroom, Niall."

When he woke in the morning, Lylthia was gone. Niall lay a moment, breathing in the fresh spring air, remembering the night and the goddess who had shared his bed. He grinned slowly. Well, Lylthia was gone, now.

And the cube waited for him, downstairs.

During the night, as they had talked, Lylthia had divulged the way to enter the cube. She had whispered the magical words almost under her breath, but Niall had heard and memorized them.

He rose and dressed himself in worn leather garments, over which he pulled a chain-mail shirt. His belt and the scabbard attached to it that held his sword he buckled about his lean middle.

Niall moved down the stone staircase, scowling blackly. He knew he was risking his life by trying to enter the cube. Emelkartha had warned him, as Lylthia. In the world within that cube, her great powers could not reach.

And yet—the idea of allowing Thavas Tomer to escape the consequences of his robberies, rapes and killings was too much to endure. He had to make his try. If he failed. . . .ah, but he would not think of failure.

144

He turned into the room that held the cube. It waited almost sullenly, its deep blues and the twinkling dots that seemed to be stars quiescent, almost inert. Niall approached it, and with a lithe bound, leaped up onto it. He drew a deep breath.

"Tamalka frathanis devor, hoppolis entrala porvor," he growled.

Almost instantly, the hard surface of the cube seemed to melt away under him. Suddenly he was sinking downward, slowly at first, and then more swiftly. His open eyes beheld a vast firmament of dark sky and brilliant stars through which he was being swept as by a godlike hand. He felt no cold, no warmth. In a way, it was almost as though he were dead.

Downward he was pulled, ever downward.

Faster those strange stars seemed to rotate in their courses, faster, faster, until a sort of dizziness overtook him. He closed his eyes, he gasped for breath.

Then—his feet were planted on a flat, white rock, and he opened his eyes, staring around him. He looked out upon a lush land covered with green grass that grew to the height of a tall man's knee. Here and there upon that sward were great trees, thickly boled and heavily leaved.

Niall blinked. It was a pleasant land over which a soft, sweet wind blew fitfully, carrying with it the scents of flowers and growing things. He drew a deep breath and stepped off the rock.

Gods! This was like the Nirvana of which the priests of Urgrik sometimes preached. He took a step, and then another, turning to scan the horizon. Far away there were mountains, dim with distance and faintly blue.

How could he find Thavas Tomer here? This world seemed to be as large as the one he had left The magician-king might be anywhere, half a continent or more away. Still! The man had come here through the cube as he, Niall, had done. The man had to walk as he himself was going to do. If he were here, he would find him.

Niall began to walk.

He walked for a long time, until the tireless muscles of his legs began to feel the strain. There was no night here, apparently. Everywhere the light—softly glowing—as all around him. There was no sun, none that he could discover, anyhow.

The trees under which he moved at times were huge, multi-branched, shedding their shadow over the ground beneath them. When he was tired, Niall lay down under one of those trees and fell asleep.

He woke to a faint sound moving across the grasslands. Sitting up, he listened, hearing the baying of wolves. Niall scowled. Could this be? Were there wolves in this paradise?

Rising, he loosed Blood-drinker in its scabbard. Just as well to be prepared. Standing beneath the tree, he let his eyes roam out across the grasses.

There was movement out there. Something or someone was running toward him. He could not make out what it was, it was so far away. He heard the wolf-cry louder now, savage and hungry, and he drew out his sword and held it in a big hand.

Now he could make out the shape of that which ran before the wolves. It was a woman. A girl, really. She seemed young, lithe, shapely. There was a mane of yellow hair on her head that ran out behind her in the swiftness of her running.

She came closer, closer. She had seen him, he knew, and she lifted an arm, waving it, as she turned and came toward him.

"Run," she called, "run! The wolves of Thavas Tomer are on the hunt. "

Niall grinned. He could fight wolves, and slay them. He stepped out from beneath the tree and waited as the girl stumbled now in her running, moving toward him. She was exhausted, he could see. Only the Gods knew how long she had been running like that, with the fear of death in her throat.

He moved toward her, caught her as she was about to fall. Her soft body lay pressed against him as she fought for breath.

"He wants—to kill me,"she gasped. "He came to the Citadel and now he—rules there."

"Thavas Tomer?"

Her eyes studied his face. They were purple, those eyes, and they were filled with fear and wonder. "Who—are you?" she whispered. "Are you a magician such as Thavas Tomer?"

"Na, na. I came here to kill him. The man's wicked."

She lifted a hand to brush away some of the tumbled hair from her face. That face was beautiful, Niall told himself. By the Gods, she was as lovely as Lylthia herself. But who was she?

When he questioned her, she shrugged. "What does it matter who I am? I am soon to die." Her hand waved back in the direction from which she had come. "The wolves are on my trail. They will be here soon, to kill us both."

He shook his sword. "We will take some killing. I am not afraid of wolves. "

Her eyes studied him more closely. "There are more than wolves that obey the lord of this world. Devils! Evil things that crawl and fly." She shuddered. "Nothing can defeat them."

Niall felt the despair in her. He shook her a little, trying to rouse up her courage. "I've fought wolves before—aye, and demons, too. I'm still alive. "

In the back of his mind was the realization that at many of those other times, especially when he had been dealing with demons, Emelkartha had been there to help him. She was not here now; she could not be, she had said.

No matter, He had depended on his wits and his skill with a sword before Emelkartha had come into his life. He lifted his head and stared out across the grasslands.

He could see them now, big wolves and well fed. They were strong and powerful, and their tongues lolled in their open mouths. Their fangs seemed huge.

They saw the man and the girl near the tree and now they howled no longer but ran with silence, even faster. They came swiftly, heads low, and a lust to kill shone in their greenish eyes.

Niall pushed the girl behind him and set himself with his sword up, to defend her and himself. There was a calmness about him now, as he was always calm before a fight. And there would be a fight He could count ten of the great beasts as they coursed the grass to come at him.

Foremost among the wolves was a great beast even larger than the others. It came swiftly, running low to the ground, and then it was gathering its muscles to make the leap that would carry Niall backward off his feet. When that happened, the rest of the pack would close in.

The wolf leaped. Niall swung his sword.

The sharp steel almost split the wolf in half. Its body fell and twitched convulsively on the ground. Then the others were upon him.

Niall fought as savagely as he had ever fought. His great steel blade swung in blazes of light, darkened as the steel went through a great, furry body. He shouted in the fury of his onslaught His arm was tireless as he drove the two edges of his blade back and forth, sometimes turning the point into the chest of a beast as it sprang for him.

Sharp fangs gashed his thighs, his calves. They seemed to be everywhere, those great beasts, and their fangs were sharp as knives.

One beast who sprang chest-high he caught with his left hand at its throat and that beast he choked to death, holding it out at arm's length, even as he plied his steel to kill the others which attacked him. When the wolf went limp, he dropped it.

As he fought, Niall backed up toward the big tree, crowding the girl behind him, growling orders at her between his teeth.

"To the tree, girl! Hurry, hurry! These aren't your ordinary wolves. They're demons of some sort. Back up, I say. And hurry if you want to stay alive!"

With the tree-bole to his spine, he did not have to worry about one of the animals getting behind him. He wished he had thought to bring his dagger. He could have given it to the girl, who might then have been able to help him.

Now he fought more carefully, thrusting savagely when a wolf leaped, slashing fiercely when two came at him at once. There were many dead wolves now; their bodies lay quivering here and there half-hidden by the tall grasses. Behind him he could hear the spasmodic breathing and the occasional frightened sobs of the girl.

Three wolves left, now! Niall grinned into their snarling faces as they paced back and forth before him, working themselves to a final attack. Niall rested his back against the tree-bole, gulped in air.

They came in a rush, all three at once, leaping high and low and in the middle. Niall cleaved downward with his blade, felt bone give and flesh split under its edge. One wolf he decapitated, another he cut

148

across its back so that it lay and flopped about, unable to rise. The third took his point in its chest and hung a moment, slavering, before it fell away.

Niall dropped Blood-drinker's point to the ground, dragging air into his lungs. By the Gods! This had been a fight! He was gashed and torn, but his wounds would heal. He was alive, at least.

He sank downward to sit at the base of the tree. The girl crouched near him, her purple eyes wide and wondering.

"You killed them all," she whispered. "I did not believe anyone could harm those wolves. Who are you?"

"Niall of the Far Travels," he muttered, and looked at her more closely. "And you?"

"My name is Parlata. I have lived here in Norlana for all my life."

His eyes scanned her face. "Your folks? Your father and mother?"

She shook her head. "I do not know what you mean. What is a father? A mother?"

He explained what he meant, but she only looked the more puzzled. "I have always been like this, for a long, long time. I was never a child. I can remember far back, to the days when Tarj Needal came here from time to time."

Niall blinked. "Tarj Needal! But he lived thousands of years ago."

Parlata shrugged. "I do not know about that. I have lived in this world all my life. Yet I know there is another world beyond this one, a world to which Tarj Needal went and from which Thavas Tomer came. And you also, I suppose."

So, then. She was a creation of magic. A plaything to amuse Tarj Needal who had made her. Niall wondered how she spent her days.

Parlata smiled. "I roam the grasslands. I lie down and sleep when and where I will. I tire of the palace."

"What do you eat?"

She shook her head. "I do not know what you mean. Eat? What is that?"

"You must have food."

She could not understand, no matter how Niall sought to explain it.

149

When she explained that there was no need to swallow anything, that the very light here gave her all the sustenance she needed, Niall began to realize that he himself had felt no hunger since entering the cube.

It was beyond him. But then, all magic was. And this cube and everything in it had been created by magic, the powerful magic of Tarj Needal. Somewhere in this land, Thavas Tomer was hidden. It was up to Niall to find him.

"It's time to go," he said slowly, rising to his feet.

Parlata stared up at him. "Go where?"

"To find Thavas Tomer. I have to kill him, or take him back with me to his own world."

The girl went white. "It is impossible! You don't know his powers." She stared around her as though half expecting demons to rise up from the very ground. "He has great powers. He can call on evil beings to aid him. Nothing can overcome him while he is here."

Niall grinned, extending a hand to her. "We'll see about that. His wolves didn't get us, did they?"

She let him pull her to her feet, but she was visibly shaking. "The wolves were only sent out after me," she told him. "He wanted this world all to himself. He said the sight of me offended him. He—he gave me a head start, and then he let the wolves loose."

Parlata shivered. "Who can guess what things he will send against us now?"

"Well, we can't just stay here forever. We can begin walking."

"Not that way,"she begged, pulling back. "That way leads to the palace, where Thavas Tomer is."

"It's the way I'm going," Niall told her and let go of her. If she did not want to accompany him, there was no way he was going to force her.

He strode off, moving with slow, deliberate steps. After a few moments, the girl called to him and ran to catch up. "I am afraid to be alone," she admitted.

For a long time they walked across the grasslands, until Niall saw how tired Parlata had become. She staggered as she walked, and there were strain lines on her face. It was then that he pulled her down onto the ground.

"Sleep now," he ordered.

There was little tiredness in him. He lay back on the grass, his hands beneath his head, and he stared up at the whitish sky that was flecked, here and there, with blue clouds. A strange world, this, stranger than any land he had ever been in. He thought of Emelkartha, and of how she had told him that she herself could not enter into this world.

Whatever magic had made the cube and this land inside it, it must be very powerful to be able to keep out Emelkartha of the Eleven Hells. Niall wondered if he himself would ever be able to get out of it.

As he thought, his eyelids grew heavy and he slept. It was a dreamless sleep, and refreshing. When he woke, all tiredness was gone from him. Parlata was sitting up, eyeing him from under knitted brows.

"We are both of us dead, you know," she said slowly. "It is just a matter of time until we actually die. Thavas Tomer will want us dead, and he will find a way to kill us."

"He hasn't yet," Niall grinned.

The girl sighed. "You are very stubborn. In the old days, that were so long ago I can scarcely recall them, Tarj Needal used to bring his enemies into this world. He would set them free to run, as Thavas Tomer did to me. Then he would send his—servants—to run them down and slay them. Sometimes he would have those servants capture them and bring them back to the palace for torture."

The girl shivered. "I did not like it, then. I could hear the screams. I was always ill after times like that I would run away and wander the grasslands for a long time, hopefully until Tarj Needal had gone back to his own world. "

"All that was a very long time ago."

"But I remember and—I am still afraid."

Niall stared at her, frowning. "Why did Tarj Needal create you? Why did he leave you here?"

She shrugged. "He told me once he liked company, even such company as mine. Oh, he would amuse himself with me. He told me once he made the most beautiful girl in any world because he liked to look on beauty."

151

"You're very beautiful."

Parlata smiled at him. "Am I? I have no way of knowing. I have never seen another woman."

Niall sighed. It must have been almost unendurably lonely for the girl, living alone in this world, all by herself for so many thousands of years. It was a wonder she had not gone mad. Perhaps when Tarj Needal had created her, he had made her in such a manner that she would never know loneliness.

They walked on, side by side, across the rolling grasslands. They came to some low mountains and moved over them, and then crossed over more grasslands. Niall marveled that Parlata could have run so far to escape the wolves.

"Oh, Thavas Tomer caused a spell that lifted me out of the palace and put me down somewhere on the grasses. He said it would give me more of what he termed a sporting chance."

She shuddered. 'Thavas Tomer is very cruel. Crueler even than was Tarj Needal. At least Tarj Needal liked me."

Parlata was close to tears. Niall felt tenderness well up inside him. He put an arm about her shoulders, drew her against him.

"I'll see you safely out of this. You won't have to worry about Thavas Tomer once I get my hands on him."

She gasped, lifting an arm and pointing. "You will never do anything to him. See there, low on the horizon. Thavas Tomer knows where we are. He has sent the coorjas to find and kill us!"

Niall stared where she pointed and knew a moment of awed wonder.

Chapter Three

Giant birds were flying low in the sky, barely slamming the tops of the grasses. They were quite the most gigantic birds Niall had ever seen. Indeed, they were as large as men, or perhaps even larger.

They came in a great cloud of swiftly moving brown wings. They skimmed the ground, and they headed straight for Niall and Parlata. Since there was no cover on these vast prairies, they must be quite plain to see, even from a distance.

Niall growled low in his throat and yanked out his sword. He was vastly outnumbered, there seemed no chance for him at all. Yet he was determined to sell his life dearly. If those bird-men managed to kill him, there wouldn't be many of them left.

As they swooped in closer, he saw that each bird-man carried a long, slender spear. They held those spears before them like a fence of steel points. They would spit him on those sharp barbs and he would wriggle out his life on them.

They darted in—

Niall fell flat, knocking Parlata down with him.

As he did so, he thrust upward with Blood-drinker, slashing savagely. The spear-points skimmed over them, but the sharp edge of his blade bit into flesh and blood. Three of the bird-men fell, either slashed or with their wings hacked off.

The wingless ones flopped helplessly. Niall ran to them and stabbed at them, dispatching them as the others wheeled in the sky and came at him again.

Niall ran, drawing them toward him and away from the girl. He had no experience in fighting such creatures, yet he knew they were not at home on the ground, only in the air. He dove under their spears, stabbing upward, catching one and then another.

Their cries of rage and pain were sharp and shrill, and they looped upward into the sky, to come at him again. Those he had slain lay on the ground near their fallen spears. Niall eyed those long, slender spears calculatingly.

He knew how to fight with spears. He ran to one, lifted it, hefting it. It was perfectly balanced. Niall smiled grimly. Now as the bird-men circled to dive at him again, Niall stood to meet them, half a dozen of their own spears in his hands.

He waited, seeing them come. Then he swung up a spear and hurled it. Straight it went, as might an arrow from the bow. It pierced one of the bird-men; Niall could hear his scream of agony as he plummeted groundward.

Again he hurled a spear, and again.

Each spear was perfectly balanced. Each spear flew as he wanted it, and where it went, a bird-man died.

Niall ran to where their bodies lay, snatched at the spears near them. He had destroyed half their number and those others who still lived had drawn off, flying about in the air, speaking to each other with weird and alien cries.

Parlata ran to Niall, eyes wide and worshipful. She wrapped her arms about him and pressed her body against his.

"No one has ever stopped the bird-men before," she babbled. "I did not think it could be done."

"We aren't out of it yet," he growled. 'There's more of them to slay. "

It seemed that the bird-men had had enough. They still circled in the sky, but they made no move to attack. It was almost as if they were waiting for something.

Niall picked up what spears he could, giving some to Parlata to carry. Then he gripped her wrist and began his walk.

"They won't attack for a time," he told her. "We'd best be moving onward to where I can find Thavas Tomer."

"It is not far now," Parlata murmured, but she shuddered as she spoke, and as she walked, she held back as if reluctant to accompany him.

"Now what ails you?" he demanded, turning to look down at her.

"Frightful things will happen to us if we go forward," she breathed. 'The magician has strange and awful powers in this world."

Even as she spoke, the ground began to ripple as though it were a rough and choppy sea. Niall went sprawling, with Parlata to one side of him. Up and down they heaved, with the ground bucking and falling beneath them. Sickness churned upward from their middles, and nausea ate inside them.

"By Emelkartha of the Eleven Hells," Niall rasped. "I can't take much more of this."

Parlata was being sick off to one side, and Niall felt like joining her, but he fought off the illness, clamping his teeth together, and he managed to bellow out his defiance. He rolled over and got to his feet, and his legs kept him upright. It was like standing on the deck of a ship during a terrible storm, he decided.

Gradually the shaking earth quieted under them. It seemed to Niall, as he bent to assist Parlata to her feet, that he could hear mocking laughter from a long way off.

With his arm about her middle, Parlata quieted her shakings. She lifted a hand and brushed back her tumbled hair.

"Thavas Tomer is amused," she whispered. "He but toys with us."

For the first time since he had entered the world of the cube, Niall began to have misgivings. What could he do against a man whom even the very ground obeyed? He wished that Emelkartha were with him. What was it she had said? Yes. She could not enter the cube, that the very enchantment which had brought it into being was strong enough to keep her out

His jaw firmed stubbornly. He was not yet beaten. Thavas Tomer would have to send something more dreadful than wolves and bird-men against him, if he wanted to defeat him.

He yanked Parlata forward. "Come on. Let him do his worst. We'll see what happens."

They moved now toward an up-jut of land, covered with grass and with here and there some underlying rock showing. That land rose upward into the air; it would make a good point from which to scan the surrounding countryside.

To the top they climbed, and when they stood on that great precipice, Niall made out in the near distance another height of land, even higher than this, and on its top there stood a castle. He knew, without being told, that this was where Thavas Tomer had taken up his residence.

He glanced down at Parlata, "Is it?" he asked. "Is that where the magician lives?"

She nodded dumbly, crowding closer to him.

"Even now he will be preparing some new danger for us. I can almost hear him laughing to himself as he does."

"If I can get inside that castle, he won't be able to create many more magic spells. My steel will remove his head from his body."

Parlata shook her head. "No. You will never be permitted to enter. Look! Even now Thavas Tomer is sending more of his creations to do battle."

Niall saw them coming from the castle, a long line of centaurs, with the bodies of men above the waist and the bodies of horses for the rest. Each centaur carried a net. They came at a gallop across the castle causeway and down onto the grasslands, and they rode straight for the height of land where Niall stood with Parlata.

"He intends to capture us and bring us into the castle," she whimpered.

"First they have to catch us."

Niall glanced around him. They stood on high rocks, here, and anyone who tried to get at them must move up the grassy slope which slid away into the vast grasslands over which they had come.

Oh, it would not be easy. He knew that. But he meant to fight as he had always fought, without thought for anything but the slaying of as many of his enemies as he could reach. He checked the number of spears they still had and rested them butt down in the ground for easy snatching.

He watched the centaurs galloping. They were big, bulky, and the thought came to him that they might be a little clumsy. His lips widened into a grim smile. Clumsy or not, there were a lot of them, and they would take a lot of killing.

Fortunately, those men-horses had to come up a rise to him, which would slow them. He bade Parlata sit down, to hide herself as best as she could behind some rocks.

"They will throw those nets at us," he explained. "Don't let yourself be caught in one."

There was no more time for talk. The centaurs were coming up the hill at them, their nets swinging overhead, ready to be hurled. But the men-horses were too close together, some of the nets tangled in others, and it was then, at that moment of disarray that Niall leaped forward.

Sword in hand, he ran down the slope and his blade winked in the pale light as he swung it. He thrust and cut, and every time he moved his blade, it was bloodied anew. Hands reached for him, the centaurs sought to loop their nets over him, but he was too quick, too spy.

He hacked and stabbed, he cut and slashed, and as the blood flew, he saw centaurs drop stricken in their death agonies. For long moments he leaped and darted, always slaying, and then he ran back up the slope and left behind him dying things that threshed out their life's blood on the grass.

Niall stood then, and waited, hearing the blood drip from his sword onto stone. More than half of them he had already dispatched, no more than a dozen yet remained.

"You are a great warrior," Parlata whispered from his feet, where she lay crouched between two big stones. "The greatest I have ever heard of."

"Let's hope Thavas Tomer realizes it and surrenders himself to me."

"He will never do that. He is too strong, too powerful. He has only been playing with us, so far. Soon now he will tire of it and then we shall die."

"You're a cheerful little thing," he grinned.

Aye, almost as cheerful as Lylthia, warning him of this cube-land. Where was she now, that woman who was also a goddess? Could she see him where he stood, surrounded by enemies, a bloodied sword in his hand, awaiting the next charge of those centaurs?

Now the men-horses began to move. One stood forth and then another, each one swinging his net They formed a line, one behind the other, and while Niall knew what they meant to do, mentally he congratulated them on their clear thinking.

The foremost came up the hill at a gallop, the net waving over his head. In a moment it would belly out and open as it flew toward him. He must act—and fast!

From the ground where he had planted them, butts down, Niall snatched up the nearest of the spears. He lifted it and hurled it, and saw it fly through the air almost as swift as any arrow.

The centaur tried to dodge it, but he was too slow. Full in the chest it took him and the keen point slid out the other side, an inch to one side of his backbone. He stumbled, his hooves slipped on the turf and he went sprawling. Dead before he hit the ground.

The next centaur in line came racing forward, his net swinging high above his head and opening. Again Niall reached for a spear and hurled it. The centaur went down, dying.

They came swiftly, until all the spears were gone.

Niall gave a great shout, yanked out Blood-drinker, and ran down the slope as fast as any deer. His sword made a great arc of light in his hand as he swung it.

Sight of him may have confused them, for instead of rushing forward to meet him, the centaurs drew back and tried to hurl their nets as one man. Those thrown nets met in the air, became entangled, and as they drooped, Niall ran under them, his blade already stabbing.

One centaur went down, and then another. The balance would have turned to flee, but Niall gave them no time. Upward onto the back of one he leaped and from that vantage point, cleaved a second's head from his neck and drove his blade full length into the chest of another.

Next moment the man-beast he straddled was staggering, Niall's sword between his shoulder blades. Niall leaped aside as the centaur fell.

He turned his eyes toward the citadel that he could see in me distance. No doubt Thavas Tomer stood at one of its windows, staring out at him as he himself was staring. Niall lifted Blood-drinker and shook it.

"I'm still alive, magician! Try and kill me—if you can!"

There was a silence over all this curious cube-world. Nothing moved, there was no sound. And then, as clear as a bugle call upon the still night wind, came a voice.

"I see you, Niall of the Far Travels. I hear your voice. Now—hear mine! I vow your death, general. You have invaded the sanctity of this world where I have come to live for a while.

"For that, you shall be stripped of life. Ah, but not easily, not lightly! The time for a swift death is over. I have but toyed with you, thinking to dispatch you—and that little witch with you!—so that I may be about my studies.

"Yes, yes, I have much to learn, much to decipher of the incredibly ancient scrolls and parchments which Tarj Needal kept here for his own study and amusement. There is so very much that is new to me.

"You have become an infringement on my study, Niall. You annoy me. And so, I must use my arts to bring you to your knees in abasement, to surrender your person to me so that I may torture it throughout all eternity."

Laughter rose up, harsh and hateful, and Niall felt his flesh crawl at the sound of it. There was madness in that laughter, and sharp triumph. It seemed to rise up out of the very air and beat against the eardrums.

"Watch now," bellowed that voice.

Slowly, almost imperceptibly, the air about them seemed to darken. Blacker it became, until one could see little more than a foot or two away. Now there were violently scarlet streaks of what seemed to be living fire in that air. Those red lightnings shot here and there, thin and vicious, and where they streaked, Niall could hear a sharp crackling.

The voice went on, "Dodge, if you want, but those fiery bolts of mine will seek you out, no matter where you try to hide!"

Then there was silence, except for the crackling of those blood-red lightning bolts. Parlata was screaming beside him, clinging to him, and even Niall felt the hairs on the back of his thick neck stand up.

What could he do against such magics?

If only Emelkartha were here, to offset them with spells of her own! But he was on his own, now, and so he caught the girl and dragged her down in among the rocks.

There was shelter here, of a sort. If the lightnings hit at them, they would strike the rocks first. Niall kept an arm about Parlata, and an eye on the black sky which rained down those fiery bolts.

He never knew how long that eerie bombardment went on, yet after a long time it slowed its anger, the air began to lighten once again, and gradually everything went back to normal. Niall sighed and lifted the girl, standing on top of the rocks.

"We live," he breathed.

"Of what use is living? Better to have let those bolts hit us and relieve us of this torture."

Grimly, Niall shook his head. He still held his sword, he had life in his body, and there was an enemy to catch.

"Come," he growled. "We go forward, up to that castle."

Parlata stared at him with huge eyes. "Are you mad? He will capture us, torture us—forever! There is no escape. None."

But he was moving forward, his hand holding hers, and she was dragged along at his side. Down they went off that pinnacle of rock where they stood, and began striding toward the distant lair where Thavas Tomer made his home.

They were halfway to the mountain on which the castle stood when Niall saw a black cloud forming above one of its spires. It swirled, that cloud, faster and faster, and then it darted forward, straight at them.

Parlata screamed. Niall lifted his blade and as that menacing cloud swept down and around him, he struck out at it. His blade went through the darkness, and now that cloud was all about them, lapping at their bodies, lifting them upward off their feet, swinging them around and around.

They went through the air, gripped by that black cloud, heels above their heads, parallel to the ground, rotated like spinning wheels. High into the upper air they were swept, faster and faster, until they were no more than leaves in a strong gale.

This is the end, Niall thought. There is no way I can fight anything like this! His doom was upon him. They would be hurled groundward, smashed against it, crippled and helpless. It was useless to fight any longer.

Yet even as he consigned himself to death, Niall felt the fury of the cloud lessening. No longer did it rotate so swiftly; its swirlings lessened, grew feebler. Yet still it sped on, always onward.

Now the cloud began to relax a little, come closer to the ground. Niall felt a foot touch the earth, then was swept upward again. When next he was driven groundward, he caught hold of Parlata, wrapping his arms about here, and hurled himself sideways.

They tumbled across the grass, and lay flat.

When Niall raised his head, the cloud was dissipating into thin wisps of blackish smoke. And mad laughter filled the air.

"You are back where you started from, Niall of the Far Travels. How did you like that way of traveling? You have it to do all over again. And next time, you shall face even worse dangers."

Mad laughter rang out. "Oh, I am enjoying this. I wait to dream up more dangers for you to overcome. So come at me, Niall. Come at me again and again until at last you crawl to me on your belly, begging my pity. Ha! Ha! Ha! Ha!..."

Niall shook himself, staring about him. Yes, Thavas Tomer was right. There was the rock on which he had stood when he had first come inside the cube. It loomed before him, flat of top and of a whiteness that almost hurt the eyes.

Parlata shook beside him, crawling closer so that his big body might shelter her own. He put his arms about her and held her, his eyes still fastened to that white rock.

"I have been thinking," he said slowly. "It is useless to try and fight Thavas Tomer any longer. He is too strong for us."

Eyes wide, she stared up at him. "But what can we do? No matter where we go, he will follow and torment us."

He dragged her to her feet, urged her along the grasses until they came to the white stone. Lifting her in his big hands, he put her on its flat top. Then he joined her.

"Tamalka frathanis devor, hoppolis entrala porvor," he breathed.

Then he was rising upward, seeming to expand....

Once again, he stood in his own palace, beside the strange blue cube with the stars. Beside him, shivering and staring around her, was Parlata. Her eyes were large and fearful as she swung them toward him.

"Where are we?" she whimpered.

"In my palace. Now, now, there's no need to fear. You're safe enough here. Thavas Tomer is inside that thing, along with the world from which we've come."

She stared at the cube, brows wrinkled. Niall pushed her gently into a chair and began to explain all that had happened ever since he had attacked Thavas Tomer in his stronghold.

"But—but—what am I to do in this world? I know nothing about it—or even where it is! What does it hold for me?"

"I'd like to know the answer to that, myself," said a cold voice.

Niall swung around. Lylthia was sitting in a chair to one side, her arms wrapped around her knees. Her eyes were angry, her cheeks flushed.

He threw up his arms. "What could I do with her? Leave her to be tortured to death by Thavas Tomer? I brought her with me, as I'd have done with anyone that demon planned to kill!"

His eyes locked with those of the woman he loved. Lylthia sighed softly, then turned her eyes toward the shrinking Parlata.

"Well, perhaps you did the right thing. I say perhaps, mind. I don't like the idea of your keeping her under the same roof with you. She's too pretty."

"What is this 'pretty'?" asked Parlata, leaning forward.

Niall growled, "Quiet, both of you. I have more important things on my mind, right now. Mainly, what am I going to do about Thavas Tomer?"

Lylthia smiled wryly. "There is that problem, isn't there?"

Niall went on scowling at her. Even as he did, his scowl began to relax and his lips curved into a big grin. Lylthia straightened up, frowning.

"What's so funny?" she snapped.

"I just thought of the perfect way to dispose of him. Now, now. I'm not going to tell you yet. We have something else to discuss, you and I."

"Oh? And what's that?"

"What do we do with the girl? We can't leave her to starve to death. You don't want me to take care of her. So what do we do?"

"Turn her loose. Let her wander our world."

"Penniless? Oh, come now, Lylthia."

The goddess glared at him. "Well? What would you suggest?"

"Let's make her a rich woman. You have hoards of gold and jewels in those eleven hells of yours. Be free with them. Give her some gold, some jewels. Let her buy a house here in Urgrik—or even better—let her go roaming this world and learning all about it as a rich traveler."

Lylthia turned her green eyes upon Parlata. She studied her beauty in the torn garments that did little to conceal her body. Slowly, she nodded.

"Yes. I think that might be best. What do you say, girl? Would you like to be rich, to wander as you will wherever your fancy might want to take you in this world that is so new to you?"

Parlata stared back at the goddess. Their eyes met and their minds seemed almost to speak, one to another. Then Parlata smiled and nodded.

"Yes. I do not love this big man who came so suddenly into my life, though I do admit my gratitude to him for having saved that life for me. I find there is a curiosity in me to learn more about this world into which he brought me. I should like to wander over it, to see it, to learn all I may about it."

"Good, then that's settled. I'll see that you have enough gold and jewels to last you a lifetime. Oh, by the way. You will age in this land. It isn't magical, as the cube-world is. You will grow old. You will die, some day. "

Parlata shrugged. "I would have died in the cube, if Niall hadn't saved me."

Lylthia turned her stare at Niall. "And now that's settled, what do we do about Thavas Tomer?"

"I give him to you, my darling. He's all yours." The goddess blinked. "All mine?'

"Of course. Take the cube into one of your eleven hells. You are immortal. It doesn't matter when Thavas Tomer emerges from his cube. You will be there to greet him and let him have the taste of every one of the hells you rule."

Lylthia burst into laughter and clapped her hands. "I shall love it! Oh, what a solution to our problem. You know, Niall—sometimes you prove yourself smarter than I think you."

She ran to him, hurled herself into his arms and was soundly kissed. They forgot about Parlata, they enjoyed the pleasure of the moment.

Only when she coughed a little, to remind them of her presence, did they break apart and look at her.

"What is that which you two do?' she asked. "I find myself oddly affected by it."

Lylthia tinkled laughter. "It's love, girl. Go find yourself a man and let him teach you what I mean." She pushed away from Niall and turned toward the cube. "I'd better be about my business. The sooner I take the cube away with me and return with some gold and jewels, the sooner you can leave and I can have Niall all to , myself."

Niall grinned, calling, "Hurry back."

Lylthia nodded soberly. "Oh, I shall-believe me."

Then she was gone, and the cube with her.

THE CUP OF GOLDEN DEATH

Chapter One

His fingertips brushed gently at die earth surrounding the curving edge of something that glittered with golden fire under the rays of the hot Lurydian sun. His heart thudded wildly under his mail shirt and leather jacket For a moment Niall of the Far Travels drew back away from what he had found and stared about him.

Everywhere his eyes went, he saw the flat moors, a wild desolation of empty land where once had stood part of the kingdoms of the Five Gods. Nearby were the tumbled stones of a citadel, long ago abandoned by whoever had inhabited it. Gone were the men and women of that kingdom; only remained now the fables and the legends.

Niall was hunting for one of those legends.

His huge hand went out to the sand, brushed more avidly at it. The tiny grains flew away, disclosing a rounded bit of metal. The breath came short and fast now to his lungs; excitement was awash inside him.

"Maralia!" he bellowed.

A girl came running across the flat moorland, her red hair glinting in the sunlight. She wore a thin, short skirt and a vest, and little more. The vest was held together by silver chains, and it was decorated with silver thread that bespoke her rank as high priestess of the god-being, Humalorr.

She fell to her knees beside him, her eyes hungry at the sight of that which he had partially uncovered. Her tongue came out to moisten her ripe, red lips.

"Have you found it? Is it the—cup of the god?"

Niall grunted. "Who knows? I'd stake my life on the feet that it's a ceremonial cup of some kind, but whether it belongs to your god or not, you yourself have to decide."

Maralia slid her eyes sideways at this big blond youth who was the warlord of Urgrik and a great favorite of its king, Lurlyr Manakor. He was also held in high regard by Queen Amyrilla, for was it not Niall of the Far Travels who had saved Amyrilla from the death promised her by Thyra, who had been queen before her? It was also whispered that Niall of the Might)' Arms was oddly favored by the demon-queen Emelkartha of the Eleven Hells.

Maralia was afraid of Niall.

Yet she was sworn to do what had been whispered into her ears by the high priest short days ago, when they had been last in Urgrik. Niall was to go with her to the moors of Lurydia. There they were to find the ancient cup which once had been used by the wizard Yellixin, in the ancient days when there had been a citadel standing where they now knelt.

After that—

Maralia swallowed. She was to kill Niall and bring the cup back to the high priest, to Aldan Hurazin himself. And Aldon Hurazin would hide the cup so that it might not be used to save the life of Lurlyr Manakor.

She whispered, "I can't tell. It's half hidden by the dirt. Remove it, Niall."

He put out his big hands, dug his massive fingers into the ground, tightened them about the cup. As he did so, his flesh tingled, and something in his brain whispered to him that this cup was evil. Evil!

Niall shook himself. No need now to won)' about any evil. He and the girl were all alone, far out here on the moors. There were no enemies about Even if there were, Niall did not fear them. Not if they were human enemies, anyhow.

The cup came upward out of the ground and the sun blazed down on it making it shimmer, making it seem to draw brightness from the sunlight, so that it shone as if with inner fire.

Maralia stared, whimpering.

Oh, she had heard tales of this cup! She knew how it was used by Yellixin long, long ago, of how it helped him perform some of the mightiest magic that had ever been worked by man. Now she was to take the cup, bring it to Aldon Hurazin.

Yet first, she must kill Niall.

He would never let her take the thing to the high priest. Pundor Event, who was the king's physician, was awaiting the cup, hoping to use it and its magic power to cure Lurlyr Manakor of the illness which was slowly sapping his strength, slowly killing him.

Pundor Everit had tried everything else, to no avail. The king still lay in a deathlike trance. If something drastic were not done, he would die. And so, by order of Queen Amyrilla, Niall and she had set out far the moorlands of Lurydia

Let it go, Niall! Now! At once!

His big hands opened and the cup fell to the ground.

Ha! That had been the voice of Emelkartha speaking to him, the goddess of the Eleven Hells, who had first come to him in human shape as Lylthia. Since then, the goddess had been protector and lover to him, and looked with jealous eyes on any who sought to take Niall for her own.

He waited, but the voice spoke to him no more.

Maralia cried out and reached for the cup, catching it in her hands almost crooningly. She bent over it and stared down into its bowl, as though she sought to read the future in it. Niall eyed her wonderingly. Why should she be able to hold this thing and he not?

He sighed. It was a question to which he really wanted no answer. Sufficient for him was the fact that Emelkartha thought it dangerous to him.

Maralia lifted her eyes to stare at Niall. They were black, those eyes, and it seemed to Niall as he met them that they were merciless. But that was silly. What could a girl like Maralia do to him? True, she could slide a dagger between his ribs while he was asleep, but he did not believe her capable of that. No, he was being overly imaginative.

He rose from his knees, brushing the moor dirt from them. "We have the cup. Time now to be returning. The king is dying; we must hurry."

Maralia still knelt there, clutching the cup to her bosom. She seemed so little, so helpless, there on the ground. She was a pretty thing, too. Her body was well-rounded and her legs were very shapely. The vest was partly open, to show a swell of breast.

Niall! She is dangerous!

167

He had to grin. Trust Emelkartha to keep an eye on him when he went traveling across half a world with only a pretty female beside him. He wondered if she had been watching ever sine they left Urgrik.

Indeed I have. For your own protection.

He could almost hear her sniff.

"You going to kneel there all day?" he asked.

Maralia shook her head so that her black hair swirled about her shoulders. "No. No, of course not."

She got to her feet and walked ahead of him toward their little encampment. His eyes dwelt on her swaying hips, her curving legs. His eyes left her almost reluctantly, but he knew better than to make Emelkartha angry at him. Something inside him made him vaguely aware that he would need that goddess very desperately before he got back to Urgrik.

As he came up to the small fire he had built to cook their evening meal, he said, "Well sleep the night here, then make an early start."

She did not hear him. She was seated on a stool before her tent, bent over the cup, staring down at it with wide eyes, as though the golden bowl were communing to her. Niall watched her a moment, then shrugged.

He busied himself with thort steaks, with a wine-sack They had plenty of food, enough wine. He had expected to be here far longer. It had been sheer luck that had made him see the rim of the cup where it projected above the moorland, its gold caught by the rays of the sun.

Or—had it been luck?

Were there forces here at work that he did not understand? Was some god anxious to cure Lurlyr Manakor? Could that be why he had found the cup so easily? Niall felt uneasy. He did not like gods and goddesses —— excepting always Emelkartha, of course! They were too selfish, too unconcerned with the well-being of humans.

He cooked the steaks, giving them all his attention. There was a hunger in him for meat, for wine. It may have been because he had not eaten since dawn, and it was almost sunset now. He turned the steak over and watched as the flames seared it.

He glanced over at Maralia.

She was not there. The stool stood empty.

He rose to his feet and turned.

The girl stood within three paces of his back, and there was a long dagger in her hand. In her other hand she held the cup.

Their eyes locked, and Niall told himself that Maralia looked murderous, almost as if she had been going to plunge that long Orravian dagger into him. But that was nonsense.

He grinned at her. "You going to cut me—or that steak I'm cooking for your meal?"

She seemed to emerge from a daze. "What? Oh. The steak, of course. What else?"

Her feet carried her past him to the fire. She bent down to slice a portion of a steak. Niall eyed her curving rump. He ought to slap that pretty rump of hers, bring her back to the world around them. She seemed almost to be sleepwalking.

He watched her move toward her stool and seat herself, clutching the steak with both hands and biting into its succulent meat with strong teeth. The cup was between her feet. Well, let her guard the cup, then. He didn't want anything to do with it, except to get it back to Urgrik in time to save Lurlyr Manakor's life.

They ate silently, Niall relishing the thort steak and the swallows of wine he took right from the sack itself. The girl ate nothing beyond that first piece she had sliced off. Well, that was all right with him. He could eat it all.

The stars were out now, and as he eyed them, he felt tiredness creep into his muscles. They had come fast and far from Urgrik, they were mounted on the best horses the palace could supply, and they had made good time. But now his big body was tired.

He rose to his feet, stretching.

Maralia was still crouched on her stool before her tent, clasping the cup and staring down at it. Niall said, "I'm going to sleep."

She paid him no attention. It was as if she did not hear him, that her thoughts were far away. Niall studied her a moment, then shrugged. Let the girl dream. She could sleep in the saddle tomorrow.

He lay down on the blanket that was both mattress and pillow for him, and his eyes closed. In moments, he was asleep...

Niall—wake!

His eyes snapped open. Maralia was crouching by him and that long Orravian dagger was uplifted, about to plunge into his throat.

Niall was like a wild animal in his movements. All his life he had fought, had been faced with danger. Now he reacted like a panther. His left arm lifted, hit the hand that held that dagger, drove it sideways. At the same time his right hand came up and clouted the girl on the side of her head.

He knocked her across the tent where she fell in a limp huddle. Niall had risen to his knees. His hand reached for the dagger that he had driven from her hand and tucked it into his belt. Then he rose to his feet and crossed to where she lay.

She was breathing; he hadn't killed her with that blow. But her cheek would show the mark of his hitting for a few days.

Niall caught up some rope and tied her hands behind her back, then hobbled her ankles. Let her sleep, he told himself. In the morning he would tie her on her horse and, like that, take her back to Urgrik.

He walked out into the night and scowled down at the fire. Why had the girl tried to kill him? Had this been the second time she had attempted to do so? She had been right behind him with that dagger before they had eaten. Of course, she had said she was merely going to cut the steak. But that might have been an excuse thought up on the spur of the moment.

But—why? Why should she want to kill him?

"You're a big innocent fool, that's one reason," said a voice off to one side.

Niall whirled, his hand going to the hilt of his great sword Blood-drinker. A woman stood in the shadows, barely revealed by the fire-flames. She wore a torn garment that clung to her body here and there, and exposed more of it than it hid. Long hair, as black as Corassian ebony, hung to her shoulders.

"Lylthia!" he bellowed, and ran toward her.

Laughing, she sought to dodge him, but his arms were too quick. He caught her soft body up against his own and covered her mouth with kisses. She clung to him with her arms, urging her body into his, but after a moment she tried to push away, banging on his broad shoulders with both fists.

"Let me go, silly! You're worse than a Porangan bear! You'll snap my ribs."

His arms eased their hold on her a little, but she snuggled up against him, her head resting on his chest. "Have you missed me?"

"As I've missed your kisses, your caresses."

"Ha! You've been eyeing that wench you have with you often enough."

He grinned. "She tried to knife me, the little tart. I think she's gone mad."

"No, no. She was ordered to kill you, just as soon as you found the cup."

"But why?'

"Because Aldon Hurazin wants the cup. He saw his chance when your king fell ill. He talked the physician into agreeing to send you and the high priestess for the cup."

Lylthia sighed. "The girl was to kill you and bring the high priest the cup. And so I warned you, woke you from sleep to make you save your life."

She leaned against him and shook her head. "We have a pretty tangle here, my love. Aldon Hurazin wants the cup—and so does the god he worships, Humalorr."

Niall scowled. "Maybe my wits have abandoned me, but if the god wants it, why doesn't he ask his high priest to get it for him?"

"Because if Aldon Hurazin gets his hands on that chalice, it will give him great power over his god. Humalorr will have to grant him all his wishes."

Niall sat down on a stool and drew Lylthia down beside him. His arms were about her, holding her to him, even as he asked, "So what do we do?"

"First of all, I have to keep you alive. I haven't decided about the cup. I may give it to Humalorr as a favor, or I might keep it in one of my eleven hells—just to make certain that Humalorr doesn't try to blame you for what may happen."

Niall ran his hand up and down her smooth thigh. Lylthia whispered, "You are very foolish. You should be worrying about what may happen."

His grin was infectious. "I'd rather think about you. It's been a long time since you came to me."

She sighed and kissed his lips. "Later, my big barbarian. When all this trouble has been removed." She scowled at him. 'You worry me, you know. You don't take danger seriously. And there is danger. Much danger."

"But not now," he said softly, his hand caressing her back.

Lylthia sat up straighter, pulling away from him. "The cup. Where is it?"

"Somewhere about. Maralia never lets it get far away from her,"

"Go look for it, Niall. But on your life, don't touch it."

He sighed as she rose from his lap and then got to his feet. "It ought to be somewhere around. You wait here."

She did not stay where he had told her, but walked with him as he padded about the camp. The cup was nowhere to be seen. Niall stared at his tent, where he had left the girl. Could she have brought the cup into his tent while on her mission of death?

Niall walked forward, vaguely aware that Lylthia walked in his footsteps. He strode to his tent, drew back the flap. Instantly his eyes went to the figure of the tied-up Maralia.

"By the Eleven Hells!" he rasped.

The girl at his side whispered fiercely, "The cup, Niall! Throw a blanket over it—or the girl will die!"

The cup was gleaming with brilliant golden fire that reached out in all directions. But mainly it seemed to be stretching out aureate tendrils toward the unconscious girl. And where those tendrils touched her—

Her skin was tinted golden!

Chapter Two

Niall moved like a striking panther. His hand shot out, caught up a blanket, tossed it over the cup. Instantly the tent was dark, with only the faint red flames of the fire outside it touching its interior with reddish light.

The gold that had touched the girl was still upon her. Niall crouched, moving forward, hand out. His fingers went to her arm, which shone like the arm of a golden statue in the fire-flames. He touched what seemed to be cold metal.

Yet, even as he touched, warmth came to his fingers and he saw that the golden pallor of her skin was fading.

Above him, Lylthia whispered, "There was not enough time for the cup to do its task."

Her words made Niall shudder and he turned to stare up into her eyes. "Are you telling me that—"

"Yes, yes! Of course I am! Do you think me so weak as to be frightened of any normal thing? I tell you that cup is evil. Evil! Just as evil as Yellixin the wizard was evil.

"A thousand centuries ago, Yellixin dwelt here on this moor, in a castle the ruins of which have sunk into the soft ground over all the years. Yellixin, who searched the stars and the gulfs of space about them for gods to serve him.

"He found Humalorr and learned how to take control of him through a cup made of this special gold, gold he found in a big lump in a cavern deep in the Kalbarthian Mountains. He hammered out that gold himself after melting it down with special incantations. Melted it down and shaped it, always whispering spells, as though to seal each magical word into the very shape and metal of the cup."

Lylthia clutched his hard shoulder. "There is a tale told of how a man who worshiped Humalorr came to Yellixin and stole the cup. It was after the cup was stolen that Humalorr destroyed the castle Yellixin had built and all within it, and took the magician off into the worlds of Humalorr to torture him for all eternity."

Before them, Maralia stirred and murmured in broken words, and her face was a mask of awful fright. Her lids went up, her black eyes stared at Niall.

"You live," she whispered. "Oh, thank all the gods! I—I tried to kill you because Aldon Hurazin wanted you dead. I was to bring the cup to him and—the cup! Where is it?"

"Hidden under that rug. Rest easy, now. You're safe enough."

His hand touched the thick red hair of the high priestess, and as he caressed that hair and the eyes of the girl gleamed up at him, Niall felt Lylthia's nails bite into his arm.

Suddenly Maralia noticed Lylthia. Her eyes focused on her, and it seemed to Niall that they were terrified eyes. "Who is—she?' Maralia whispered.

"A wanderer on the moor," said Lylthia slowly. "I was ill and half out of my mind when I saw your fire and came toward it."

Maralia glanced at Niall. "I am afraid," she whispered. "Afraid of the cup—yet just as afraid of Aldon Hurazin and what he will do to me when I come back to him without it. He will kill me slowly by tortures."

She shuddered. Lylthia slipped past Niall and knelt, her hand to the girl's forehead. "Sleep now. No harm will come to you."

Maralia closed her eyes. In moments, she was asleep. Over her reclining figure, Niall stared at Lylthia.

"What now?" he whispered hoarsely. "Now that we have the cup, what are we going to do with it?"

"Carry it with us, until 1 can make up my mind what ought to be done with it."

Lylthia moved away from the sleeping Maralia, bent to wrap the cup more securely in the blanket. She carried it out to the fire and put it down. She stood then, staring down at it, frowning thoughtfully. Niall came up to her, put his arm about her shoulders and brooded with her at the cup....

Morning dawned across the Lurydian moorlands in a blaze of crimson sunlight. It tinted the few rocks a dull scarlet, and the edges of the thick heather a leaden bronze. Soon now those colors would change as the sun turned golden, but for now there was a dreaminess, an unreality, across the land.

Niall woke Maralia, told her to go eat while he folded their tents and made packs for their horses. It took him only a little while, then he went to squat down beside Lylthia and reach for some of the meat she had been roasting.

"We will travel fast," he told them, noting that Maralia edged closer to him. "There are roving bands of outlaws here and there on the edges of the moors. They live here because it is a lonely, abandoned countryside, yet it is close enough to the caravan routes to make it profitable for them."

"Suppose we meet these bandits?" Maralia whispered, eyes wide.

"Then well have to run—or fight." Niall shrugged. "We have fast horses. We may be able to outdistance any pursuit. But we must remain together."

He helped Lylthia up into the saddle, then did the same for Maralia. A moment he paused, looking up at the high priestess.

"I'll tie the blanket that holds the cup to my saddle," he told her. "Don't try to touch it again. If you do, it means your death."

She looked down at him, her eyes hooded. Niall could not read those eyes, but he told himself if she were fool enough to try and hold that cup again, she deserved the fate that would overtake her. That cup was devil-spawned. It was accursed, filled with all the magics with which Yellixin could imbue it.

His great shoulders shrugged. He had warned her; he could do no more. His head lifted and he stared north and eastward in the direction of Urgrik. They had a long road yet to travel.

He swung into the saddle and with Lylthia riding easily beside him, he headed away from the ancient ruins of the City of the Five Gods. They rode at a swift canter, then at a gallop. From time to time, Niall slowed the horses to a walk, to conserve their energies. If they were to meet danger, he did not want to be astride a tired horse.

All that day they rode, until the moorlands changed slowly into great, rolling plains where the grass was high and swayed easily to the wind which swept across them. They did not stop for a noontime meal; Niall was in too much of a hurry for that. These grasslands were the home of the bandits who preyed on the caravans following the roadway between Urgrik and distant Noradden on the shore of the Pulthanian Sea.

As he rode, Niall scanned the prairies, alert for the slightest hint of movement. As yet he had seen nothing and no one, but he was too much the realist to believe that he might go a second time unseen through these lands.

When he had crossed them on his way to the City of the Five Gods—or what was left of it—he and the high priestess had traveled at night. He might have waited until the stars were out to come this way a second time, but there was an impatience in him to be rid of the cup.

Niall did not like gods or magic. He was a man and he would have preferred to fight a dozen men than have anything to do with necromancy. Still, he lived in a world where magic was almost away of life, and so he had always to be on his guard.

As the sun set and long shadows began to creep over the prairie, his left arm lifted to signal a halt to his companions. Maralia drooped in the saddle, and even Lylthia showed some of the strain of the long ride in her lovely face.

"We camp here," he told them. "It's as good a place as any." His arm moved to call their attention to a stand of great rocks, off to one side, where a few trees grew. "That's likely to be an oasis of sorts, with water. Well stop there."

They walked their horses closer to the rocks. Niall swung from the saddle with a warning to the women to stay where they were. He drew Blood-drinker and advanced cautiously, bent over a little, his eyes scanning those tumbled rocks and the somewhat stunted trees. He leaped onto the rocks, moved from one to another with great bounds.

Then he was on the lip of a flat stone, staring downward at a tiny pool of water surrounded by grass. It was a beautiful place, unsuspected by chance passersby, a haven for the weary, a tiny fragment out of Paradise. Exultation swelled in Niall's chest. Here they would spend the night. Here they would rest for the rest of their journey back to Urgrik.

He did not notice the tiny mist that swirled lightly above the pool waters.

He went down the rocks and to the women.

"Come. We sleep here the night. There is water to drink and grass for the horses. We can build a cooking fire that will not be noticed because of the rocks around."

They led the horses up the lowest of the rocks. The animals had to scramble, but Niall was always there to lend a hand or a push at a mount's hindquarters. Within moments, they were inside the rock-bowl and standing on the grass.

They drank the pool water, then led their horses to it. Niall built a fire and Lylthia brought the thort steaks to the flames. Maralia went off by herself to a rock at the edge of the pool and sat with her bare feet dabbling in the water.

The stars came out clear and bright overhead, and there was a cool breeze whispering about them. Maralia yawned and sought her blanket. Lylthia leaned against Niall and let him caress her.

The mists upon the water thickened slightly and stirred, moving this way and that. From where they sat, staring into the fire-flames, Niall and Lylthia did not notice.

Finally the girl yawned. "I'm sleepy," she admitted. "It was a long ride and I'm not used to such things."

Niall nodded. "I can sleep myself. But let's lie here, close beside each other."

They stretched out beside the fire. Their eyes closed. They slept.

Slowly now the mists gathered, oozed slowly outward from the water, onto the land and toward the three sleeping humans, almost as if in curiosity. They touched Maralia, slipped from her feet upward onto her thighs and rounded hips, her breasts. The high priestess stirred, moaning faintly.

Her eyes opened, dreamily. She felt very relaxed, so much so that she did not want to move. And yet something in the back of her mind nagged at her. What was it that was so important? She stirred restlessly.

The mists went also to Niall, enveloping his giant frame. And since his arms were about Lylthia, holding her to him, they touched her as well.

For long moments the mists dwelt upon these invaders of their poolside. They swirled and danced, they crept into all the pores of these human bodies, and as they did, they sang softly, almost silently....

Maralia rose and stood wide-eyed, dreaming.

177

Niall moved his hands upon the body of Lylthia, and the girl sighed faintly, moving her body closer to that of the man she loved. Niall caught her up, drew her closer, and his lips descended on her mouth. Lylthia arched her back and murmured deep in her throat.

There was silence everywhere about the little oasis, except for the soft cries of Lylthia and the deep rumblings of the big barbarian, Maralia made no sound as she moved across the grasses to where a blanket was twisted and folded about the golden cup.

Maralia squatted down, her hands going to the blanket, lifting it away from the chalice. Now the cup was free, seeming to gather brightness from the very darkness about it.

The chalice gleamed as if with inner fires. Ever more golden it became, until it glittered so brightly it might have blinded the eyes.

Yet it did not blind the high priestess who knelt before it, hands outstretched, She gloried in that golden effulgence, gathered it to her as she might a perfume with which to salve her flesh.

The golden brightness sang to her, causing her to forget everything about herself: her name, her rank among the priestesses of the god Humalorr, her very self. Kneeling there, her arms outstretched, she became aware of nothing but that golden light....

Morning came slowly to the man and woman still stirring together lazily upon the grass. They had been and still were asleep, but this was a deeper sleep than any either had enjoyed. It was a sleep not only of the senses but a sleep as well of the spirit.

Niall opened his eyes. He held the sweat-drenched body of Lylthia tightly to his own. Their limbs were intermingled, they lay as lovers upon the grass. Waking so, ordinarily he would have been delighted, but there was a vague memory within him, a recollection of something which had taken possession of him so recently.

Lylthia opened her own eyes, staring into his own, He saw a sick awareness in those gray eyes that looked up at him. She groaned.

"We have been slaves to the evil gods this night!" she whispered.

Niall nodded: "I think so myself. But how did it happen? Why?"

Lylthia pushed away from him, rose to her feet. Her eyes went to the pool waters, to the rocks about it, and her palms clapped together angrily.

"Fool that I am," she breathed, "I should have known this place! It is haunted by the spirits of the dead godlings who have been cast out of their heavenly homes. They live here, weakened and almost helpless, but there is given to them at times the power to enter into people to grant humans what they most desire...."

Niall grinned. "Well, I can believe that, I want you most of all, and last night I—"

"Niall! Look!"

Her outstretched finger brought his eyes across the remains of the little fire. Niall stared.

Where Maralia had been crouching before the golden cup, there was now a golden statue. It was Maralia, but a Maralia turned from flesh and blood into solid gold!

Niall rasped a curse. Were his eyes deceiving him? But no. Maralia—or what had been Maralia—was solid gold. His hand touched her, felt the metallic hardness of what had been her flesh. Even her garments had been altered, were now also gold.

He snarled, reached for the fallen blanket, tossed it about the cup. Niall drew a deep breath, staring at what was no a statue. No longer the breathing, living Maralia, but a dead thing, an inanimate object. His eyes lifted to Lylthia.

"Can we—restore her to life?" he asked.

She shook her head. "No. What the cup touches—it takes. She is dead now, her flesh and bones changed miraculously."

Niall shook himself. "Let's get out of here while we can."

Lylthia gestured at the statue. "And that?"

He shrugged. "We leave it here. We can't carry it."

He moved towards the horses, It was at that moment that his eyes caught movement off to one side, toward the rim of the little oasis, Niall straightened, his hand going to his sword-hilt

Men were moving along the rim of the oasis, men on horses, hard-faced men in ragged clothing some in mail shirts, all of them heavily armed, He glanced here and there and as he looked, more and more of these ragged desert riders came into view, until they surrounded the oasis.

They sat in their saddles, staring down at him. Lylthia stood frozen, eyeing them, turning her eyes to Niall and then up at the rim, where those horsemen stood like a wall.

Niall's sword came out into the morning sunlight, even as Lylthia sighed. She shook her head at him, saying, "It's no use. You can't defeat them all."

One man among all those at the rim moved. He was an older man, with streaks of gray in his hair and beard. He was a handsome man, broad of shoulder and tall, and the hands that held the reins of his horse were sun-bronzed and powerful.

His eyes flitted from Lylthia to Niall, and then they settled on the golden statue. They widened, and he leaned forward in the saddle the better to scan that aureate figure. The breath seemed to hiss in his throat when he straightened up.

"Where did you get it?" he asked.

Niall grinned. "We brought it with us."

The older man let his eyes study the three horses. "It would be a tremendous burden for one mount," he said softly. "Unless one of you walked, and the statue was carried between two horses. I am afraid I do not believe you."

The barbarian shrugged. He was content to talk with this man, even as his brain tried to resolve the question of how they might win free of his little army. Niall was realist enough to know that on this desert where the bandits ruled supreme, there were few travelers who met them who ever returned to tell of it.

Baradon smiled grimly. He was the captain of this outlaw band—the most powerful of the thieves who dwell upon this desert world—and he ruled them with a hard hand. In the tent-city which was his home, he had gathered the fruits of many years of raiding upon the caravans. Yet nowhere in his several tents was there anything as valuable as this golden statue.

"You brought it to me, and for that I am grateful," the bandit chief said slowly. "You also brought that one." His hand gestured at Lylthia. "For that, I am grateful, too."

Baradon chuckled. "I shall take the statue and the woman and your horses in exchange for your life. You are free to go."

Niall grinned. On foot on these sands, a man would not last long. A man would die under the heat of the sun and with only the water he might carry. If Baradon permitted him water, that is.

His sword flashed out.

"I have a better idea," Niall called. "Send your dogs to kill me, or come yourself, I refuse your offer."

Baradon whirled his horse and lifted his arm. At that signal a dozen riders came charging down the slopes, swords swinging in the sunlight.

Lylthia cried out, but already Niall was moving, circling about, making the riders rein in to follow his movements. As they did so, Niall leaped for the nearest rider. His great sword whirled, came down to split a man's skull. Instantly, Niall was in the saddle, driving the horse against the mount of his closest antagonist.

The blade sheared an arm; then Niall was in among the others, driving Blood-drinker this way and that, cutting into faces, lopping heads from necks, driving forward into chests. He fought like a man maddened by drugs, and the heavy sword seemed like a feather in his huge hand.

Men died, toppling from their saddles, and ever Niall evaded the cuts and thrusts they aimed at him. Laughter burst from his lips, together with taunting words.

"Is this the best you can do? Do you call this fighting? Fools! Every one of you are dead men! Dead men sitting their saddles, waiting for the moment my steel takes you."

The men fought him as best they could, but Niall was no common man. Born in the far north-land, in Cumberia, trained to the sword since earliest childhood, he was at once master of it and proof against it. His reactions were akin to those of the wild animals of his world. He was lightning in a human body.

As the last man fell before his steel, he drove his horse straight for Baradon. The outlaw king rasped an oath and whirled to flee. He was too slow.

The flat of Niall's blade took him across the back of his head. Baradon pitched from the saddle to lie flat on the ground. Even as he fell, Niall was dropping from the saddle to land beside him.

The point of his sword touched Baradon's throat.

"Back!" bellowed Niall. "Go back or your leader dies!"

The bandits who had come charging down the hill reined in now, sitting and glaring at this madman who could fight like the fiends of Farfanoll Their faces were grim, their eyes hard.

Let Niall kill Baradon, those grim eyes said silently, and he would die. Powerful hands gripped the hilts of their swords, but they did not use them.

Baradon stirred. Slowly he moved, his eyes opening. Over him crouched Niall, a grim smile on his mouth. "Do you want to live, Baradon? Or shall I kill you here and now?"

"If I die—you die, barbarian!"

"I die anyhow, according to your word."

Baradon chuckled. "It seems like stalemate, then."

The sharp tip of Blood-drinker touched Baradon's throat, drawing blood. Niall growled. "I am not a patient man. Die if you want. It matters not to me."

Baradon had dealt in his life with many men. He had come to know them, to understand their individual weaknesses. But in this huge barbarian crouched above him, he saw no weakness. The man spoke truth. He would as soon plunge his blade into his neck and take his chances with his men as not.

"Wait," the outlaw gasped.

The sword tip moved away, but only slightly.

Baradon growled, "I agree. My life for yours."

"And for the girl's. And for horses to carry us away out of this forsaken desert."

"Agreed."

Niall smiled grimly. "The statue I give to you. It shall be the price of my life." He paused. "There is another gift I give you, Baradon. A golden cup."

"What cup?"

Niall rose from his crouch, moved across the grass to where he had thrown the blanket about the chalice. His hand raised the blanket so that Baradon might catch a glimpse of the golden bowl.

"This thing. You can have it, if you want it."

Baradon rose to his feet, suspicious. "Now why should you give me that? You could have snatched up the blanket that wrapped it and gone away. I am always suspicious when men give me gifts I do not ask for."

"Then I'll keep the cup."

Baradon laughed. "No, no. You made an offer. I accept it. The statue and the cup for your life—and that of the girl."

His hand waved and his men put away their swords in their scabbards, turned their horses and rode to the top of the oasis rim. Baradon himself walked toward his horse, mounted it. He sat and watched as Niall went to Lylthia, clasping her arm and leading her toward her mount, assisted her to rise up into the saddle.

Niall did not trust Baradon, yet the outlaw chief made no motion to his men, but sat and watched as Lylthia and the barbarian urged their horses up the grassy slope of the oasis and out upon the desert sands. They rode swiftly, with Niall glancing back over his shoulder every now and so often.

The barbarian grunted. "I cannot believe we are alive," he growled. "I mistrust Baradon. He will come after us, I am sure."

Lylthia shook her head. "It may be that he is satisfied with the statue of Maralia and the cup."

Niall grinned coldly. "Let's hope he unveils the cup and takes a good long look at it. If he does, his followers will have another statue to make them rich."

The sun rose higher in the molten sky, beating down at them with sullen heat. They had a long ride before them, Niall knew, before they reached the forests of Malagon. Even there, they would not be completely safe.

Lylthia said suddenly, "What will happen to you when you do not bring back the cup? Pundor Everit, the king's physician, has said the cup was needed to cure Lurlyr Manakor."

"Then Pundor Everit is either a fool—to believe what Aldon

Hurazin has told him of the cup's curative powers—or a villain who works hand in glove with the high priest to encompass the king's death. I wish I knew which it was."

They rode on through the long day.

Chapter Three

Niall slept well that night, when they had made camp and eaten. He dreamed as he slept, and in that dream he walked along a road that twisted through the mountains and led toward a great black castle high atop a massive rock.

He was being drawn forward in his dream, drawn by a power against which he could not fight. Useless to him was his great sword, though it rested in its sheath. His great muscles tried to fight the forward tug which was drawing him, but they were as if turned to mush.

Step by step he advanced. Now the great rock was before him, steps carved into it. He mounted those steps, came at last to a mighty doorway. The huge door slowly opened, silently, and Niall saw a long entry hall before him, and at its far end a sullen, reddish glow.

Toward the glow he walked.

Then he stood in an archway of a great chamber. The floor of the chamber was of polished black tile. The walls were hung with thick scarlet draperies on which were worked, in black-gold stitchings, strange signs and sigils, the sight of which made Niall's flesh crawl, and caused the hairs on the back of his neck to rise straight out.

There was a vast throne at the far end of the room, and on the throne sat—

Niall was not sure what it was he looked at. It seemed to be an enormous blob of blackness shining brightly from the reflection of the dark candles lighted here and there about the throne. There was no shape to that mass, yet Niall sensed the extraordinary intelligence which dwelt inside it.

"Welcome, Niall of the Far Travels. Long have I admired your daring, your warlike skills. Now I have summoned you to me, to command you to my use."

The voice was booming; it echoed from the four walls of the great chamber. Niall had the vague feeling that if the black blob had wanted to, it could have blasted him just by the sound of its inhuman voice.

"How may I serve you?" Niall asked slowly.

A chuckle was his answer. "You know me not. Yet you are willing, perhaps, to be my servant. I like that in you, Niall. It shows you are a clever man.

"This then, is what I want. You found the cup Yellixin fashioned. You gave it to the bandit Baradon. I want it. Find it, take it to my palace in Urgrik, and hold it there for me. Give it not to Aldon Hurazin, on your life!"

Niall growled, "And how am I to take it from Baradon? He is an outlaw chief with masterless men about him who obey only his voice."

"I shall be with you, I promise. Go, now. Go!"

Niall woke to the first faint rays of a cold dawn. He lay in his blankets, shivering a little, not from the cold but from the memory of his dream. It had been so real! To one side of him lay Lylthia, eyes open and staring at him.

"You dreamed of Humalorr, my love."

Niall ran thick fingers through his mane of hair. "Was that who it was? A blob of darkness on a throne in a great, dark hall?"

"Aye. that would be Humalorr. He sent for your soul last night, and brought it to his stronghold. He wants the cup, doesn't he?"

"He does. He says I am to get it for him."

Lylthia nodded. "Then let's be on our way."

Niall stared at her as she sprang to her feet. 'You would go get the cup and give it to Humalorr?" he asked in astonishment.

Her mouth smiled slyly. "I would get the cup. As for giving it to Humalorr, I'm not so sure. But come. Mount up and ride."

"After I eat."

She stamped her foot. "Ride now. You can eat later. This I promise you."

Niall shrugged. He was used to obeying this god-woman whom he loved. He rose to his feet and moved toward the horses to saddle them. Lylthia walked beside him, head down, frowning in thought.

All that day they rode, back to the oasis. As the setting sun threw long shadows, they drew rein before the oasis, sitting their tired horses and staring down at the pool of water—and at what they could see grouped together to one side.

Where there had been one golden statue, now there were almost thirty. Baradon was there, turned to gold, with every one of his bandit riders. They crouched or stood, their eyes riveted to what lay in the ground before Baradon.

Niall sighed. "The fools."

"They did not have me to warn them, Niall."

"No, I grant you that. But now I have to go down there and get that accursed thing."

Lylthia slid from her saddle. "You wait here. I shall fetch the cup." Her lips quirked into a wry smile. "Its magic will have no effect on me."

He growled low in his throat, but one glance at those golden statues changed his mind. Lylthia was a goddess. If anyone could safely fetch the cup, she could. He dismounted and waited at the top of the ridge as she went down the slope and walked toward those aureate statues which had once been men.

He watched as she moved between those golden figures, lifting the rug and tossing it over the cup. She caught it up in her hands and brought it back up the slope, walking slowly, thoughtfully. Niall wondered at her thoughts.

They rode off then, side by side, and now Lylthia rode with her head bent as if communing within herself with whatever spirits the gods and goddesses spoke with, from time to time. Niall eyed her carefully, knowing that at such times he must not interrupt her train of thought.

At last she raised her head and smiled.

"Tonight we will camp and try to raise Humalorr," she announced.

186

"Are you giving him the cup?"

"Not yet. Not just—yet."

When the campfire was blazing, after they had eaten, Niall sat off to one side and watched as Lylthia knelt down and drew strange sigils in the earth. As she did, the air about them grew frigid, so that hoarfrost seemed to hang in space.

Niall shifted uneasily and drew his fur cloak closer about his shoulders, wondering how Lylthia could stand that eerie coldness, clad as she was in that patchwork ragged garment she was wearing.

He was about to call out to her when a deeper darkness began to gather on the other side of the little fire. An ebony blackness grew in size, shapeless yet with a strange malignancy about it.

"I have come, Emelkartha What is it you want?"

Niall felt the hairs rise up on the back of his neck. For the life of him, he could not move a muscle. This was Humalorr, drawn from the hells he inhabited to this remote area, speaking in his booming voice.

Lylthia who was also Emelkartha began to speak, yet for the life of him, Niall could not understand what it was she was saying. He could see them both, and knew vaguely that Humalorr was responding to whatever it was she was saying to him. Maybe the gods spoke in a different tongue than the people of his world, but whatever speech it was, Niall could not follow it.

They spoke long, Humalorr objecting at first, then grudgingly agreeing to whatever it was Lylthia was suggesting. In time, the dark god began to chuckle and then roared with strange, obscene laughter.

Niall was relieved to hear him laugh. He had not thought him capable of it....

Then Lylthia was shaking his shoulder, waking him from sleep, and smiling down at him gently. "Everything is arranged, Niall. I have convinced Humalorr that the plan I have in mind is a good one."

"What plan is that?"

"It will be revealed to you in time. Now move over, I have a need in me to sleep close beside you this night, to be held in your arms and loved."

Niall grinned. His sleepiness fled away as his arms went about the soft body of this woman-goddess he loved. To Acheron's dread pit with the cup! This night he meant to forget all about it.

In the morning when he questioned her, Lylthia put him off with a hug and a kiss. "Forget what you saw and heard last night, Niall. It was talk between the gods, and not right for a man to understand."

Niall shrugged. That was fine with him, but he did need to know what plan they were to follow. "Am I to give the cup to the king's physician? Will it cure Lurlyr Manakor?"

"No to both questions. Just ride. Let Fate decide what has to be done."

He chuckled. He was hungry after what happened last night between Lylthia and himself. He lifted out what was left of the thort steaks and began to cook them over the fire. With Lylthia beside him, he told himself, he really didn't have to worry about a thing.

All day they rode and all the following day, and now they came within sight of the outlying hamlets and towns of the great kingdom which Lurlyr Manakor rules. No one paid them the slightest attention, they seemed to be just two wanderers lazily making their way along the dusty roads.

It was not until they were riding into Urgrik, with the darkness of night wrapped about them and only the reflected light off the shattered rings that encircled the planet to give a ghostly light, that the attack came.

Men rose up out of the shadows, swords and axes in their hands, and came at them. Niall cursed; his hand swept to his sword-hilt and drew Blood-drinker out into the night air. His knees urged his horse forward to shield Lylthia, and then he swung his blade.

He was not facing war-hardened warriors, he saw that at a glance. These were ruffians hastily gathered from the alehouses, cut-purses and thieves. But their very numbers—there must have been twenty of them, at least—gave them courage.

He bellowed and swung his long sword, and he lopped off a hand, then cut into a neck before he thrust the sword-point into an open mouth. His horse joined in the battle, as it had been trained to do: Its hooves lashed out, it bit into a soft neck, it trumpeted its battle-rage.

Niall's blade was everywhere, like a web of steel about him. He had no need to worry about Lylthia: no man could touch the goddess unless she so willed it. Besides, he gave them, no time to think of anything but fending off Blood-drinker:

He slashed and cut, and from time to time he bellowed in his battle-fury. These ruffians had never seen Niall of the Mighty Arms in battle; they had no way of knowing that against such enemies as they, he could have slain twice their number. Half their number were groveling in the dirt of the street, wounded or dying. The others were too concerned with tying to save their lives to worry overmuch about slaying this man, who fought like a demon out of Hell.

They broke and ran, tossing aside their weapons.

Niall watched them go, grinning. He had enjoyed this fight; it had torn the cobwebs of tiredness from him, it had made him glad to be alive. He turned and looked at Lylthia. She sat watching him with a faint smile on her mouth.

"You were born to fight," she said softly. "You revel in it."

His great shoulders shrugged. "When I'm attacked, I do. I have the thought that the high priest sent these tavern dregs to attack us and wrest the cup from me."

She nodded slowly. "Yes. I agree with you. Now we shall go on to the temple, to his house, and deliver over the cup to him."

Niall scowled blackly. "Give the cup to Aldon Hurazin? After all the trouble I've had getting it—and keeping it?"

"Humalorr and I are agreed. It is what must be done."

"I thought Humalorr was afraid of his getting the cup."

"He was. He is afraid no longer."

Niall sighed and shook his head. It was hard to follow the reasoning of the gods. Sometimes they made no sense at all. His eyes slid sideways at Lylthia. She was a goddess, too. In human form right now, but always a goddess. He supposed she knew what she was doing.

He hoped so, anyhow.

Chapter Four

It was close to the Hour of the Basilisk when Niall and Lylthia drew rein before the house of the high priest which was set close by the huge Temple of Humalorr. Niall came down out of the saddle and with the pommel of his sword beat upon the thick oaken door. Echoes sounded, yet they had to wait a little time before the door creaked open.

A lesser priest stared out at Niall, eyes wide. "'Wha—what is it? What do you wa—want?"

"I am Niall, general of the armies of the king. I have with me a cup, which is a present to the high priest."

He put his hand on the door and pushed it open. The priest might have pushed back, but Niall's great size convinced him that he would have little chance of keeping him out. Besides, there was a woman just behind the general whose eyes looked deep into the eyes of the priest caused him to know a great fear.

The priest scurried ahead of them, down a corridor and up a marble stairway. He began to run after a time, but when he slowed at the doorway of a room in which many candles blazed, Niall and the woman were right behind him.

Niall pushed the priest aside and strode into the room.

Aldon Hurazin had been studying the stars, etched out on sheets of vellum. At the interruption, the sheets fell from his hands and he started to his feet. His face was white, his eyes bulged.

"Niall," he breathed.

The barbarian grinned. "I've already met your welcoming committee," he said slowly. "They were a trifle impolite and I had to chastise them."

Aldon Hurazin swallowed hard. His eyes went to the hilt of the sword this big man carried at his side. If Niall knew that he had sent those assassins to slay him and steal the cup, why didn't he drag out that sword and cut him down?

"What do you want?" Aldon Hurazin whispered.

Niall felt the goddess enter into him, controlling his voice. "Why, to give you what you sent me for. Unfortunately, your high priestess—died—along the way. But she told me that you wanted the cup and so I brought it to you."

He lifted the rug that held the cup and placed it on the desk beside the tumbled parchments. The lamplight caught the cup and made it gleam. Aldon Hurazin stared down at it, eyes wide, his throat dry.

This golden bowl would give him everything he wanted! Power unbelievable, power to rule Urgrik no matter who sat the throne. All he had to do was give his orders, and the god Humalorr would be forced to obey him!

"Yes," the high priest whispered. "Yes. You have done well, Niall. I am a grateful man. I shall reward you for this, beyond your wildest dreams."

Niall said, "I seek no reward. It is enough for me to have served you."

The high priest shot him a glance. Had he misjudged this huge barbarian? Was Niall ready to give allegiance to him, instead of to the king?

Aldon Hurazin shook his head. "You are too modest. Yet I like that in a man who serves me. You shall have much gold, whatever women you may desire. But go now. Leave me with the cup."

His eyes ate at that golden chalice, as though they might absorb it His hands quivered with the desire to lift and fondle it.

Niall turned and with Lylthia beside him, moved out into the hall, where the priest was waiting, still shaking. It was Lylthia who touched the priest, whispering, "Go now to your bed, and sleep, Sleep well and deeply."

The priest turned and walked away. Lylthia swung about and looked at Niall. Her hands came up and made strange patterns in the air, and where they moved, something bright and shimmery came into being.

A veil hung from her fingers, gossamer-thin but oddly bright, as though glistening stars were embroidered into its material. She lifted her hands and tossed the veil into the air, where it hung across the doorway.

"Watch now," she said softly, "but move not if you value life."

Niall stared into the chamber, seeing the priest bending above the cup and staring down at it, a malicious smile on his lips.

Aldon Hurazin was muttering an incantation under his breath. "Come to me, God of the Lesser Hells, Humalorr the Mighty, the

Cruel, the Evil! Come to my abode to serve me as once you served the great Yellixin."

There was silence in the chamber then, except for the harsh breathing of the priest. Niall knew a sudden fear, not for himself, but for Aldon Hurazin. The fool! If he stared so on the golden bowl, the same fate would overtake him as overtook the high priestess and the bandits.

He would have said something of this to Lylthia, but her hand on his arm, suddenly squeezing, cut off all speech.

A blackness was gathering in the chamber where Aldon Hurazin stood. In his dream, Niall had beheld a blackness such as that, formless and shapeless, and knew it for Humalorr. As he stared, that darkness grew—and grew.

"Who calls Humalorr from his Lesser Hells?"

"I do! I, Aldon Hurazin, your high priest! Long have I worshiped you, great Humalorr. But now it is time for you to serve me, as once you served Yellixin, long ago. Aye, it is I you shall serve and obey!"

The blackness oozed forward, slowly but relentlessly.

"Say you so? And what is your command, Aldon Hurazin?"

The high priest looked vaguely startled, Niall thought. There was mockery in the tones of the black god, mockery and—jubilation. It was as though he toyed with the man who stood behind his desk and gave him orders.

"I seek wealth. Wealth and power. No longer shall Lurlyr Manakor rule in Urgrik. I shall rule. Aye, in Urgrik and in Angalore, in far-off Cassamunda and in the countries bordering the Aztallic Sea."

The black blob was closer now, much closer. It oozed along, and where it went, it seemed almost to absorb all light.

"Is that all? Yellixin wanted the entire world. He almost got it. But Yellixin was a clever man. He studied the ancient runes, the all-but-forgotten tomes. Have you done that, Aldon Hurazin?"

The high priest straightened. For the first time, there was a touch of fright on his face. "I have studied—yes. But what has that to do with you and me? I have the cup. You must obey him who owns it."

"You forget, priest. Or perhaps you never knew. There are words to

192

be spoken with the cup. Words that bind me to serve him who speaks them. What are those words, Aldon Hurazin?"

The face of the high priest was a mask of utter terror, now. He caught the power in the words that had been addressed to him, the malevolence and the derision. His eyes went this way and that about the room.

"You must obey..." he whispered.

A chuckle broke from the god who was now so close to the high priest. "Nay, now. If you know not the words—as your high priestess did not—then neither the cup nor I must obey.

"Fool!"

The god's words thundered out in the otherwise silent room.

The high priest screamed and turned to flee. But two great blobs leaped from that which was the god; leaped outward and closed about Aldon Hurazin.

At the touch of the darkness, the high priest screamed shrilly in utter agony. His body bucked and twisted as though red-hot pincers were being applied to his flesh. Again and again he screamed, trying to fend off that which was slowly but surely enveloping him.

"Come you with me, Aldon Hurazin. Come you with me down into my many Hells, each of which you shall experience again and again until time has no meaning for you beyond a pain that is everlasting.

"In those Hells I rule, your scream shall be forever. Pain such as you have never experienced shall be yours, as now it is Yellixin's. Forever, Aldon Hurazin. For all eternity...."

The high priest was gone, hidden within the dark god. Now Humalorr reached out for the golden bowl, and Niall saw it melt into aureate droplets and become absorbed within the god.

Then the chamber into which they stared was empty.

The shimmering veil disappeared.

Niall swore softly. His face was wet with sweat, and only now that Humalorr was gone could he breathe properly. Lylthia turned and smiled up at him.

"I made a bargain with Humalorr, Niall. I would give him the cup and Aldon Hurazin—in exchange for his future protection over you."

"Over me?" Niall was surprised, very much so. "You protect me. Isn't that enough?"

Lylthia snuggled up to him, and his arms went around her, "It never hurts to have another god watching over you. Besides, when you make love to me, I am very vulnerable. It's always best to be on the safe side."

Niall growled, "Well, I've done a lot, everything but what I was sent to do. I don't have the cup and the king is still sick, if he isn't dead by now."

The goddess smiled. "Oh, your king is all better. That was part of my deal with Humalorr. We cured him, he and I. Now you don't have anything to keep you busy."

Niall grinned. It was something of a wicked grin, Lylthia thought as she regarded it. "Nobody knows we came back to Urgrik. Why don't we just ride out for a week or two, just the two of us? Ill make up a story about the cup and how I had to make a deal with a god about curing him before I'd give the cup to the god,"

Lylthia laughed. "Why not, indeed?"

He put his arm about her waist, and like that they walked from the house of the high priest out into the cool night where their horses waited. By dawn they could be far away, close to the empty lands where they would camp and make love endlessly.

They mounted up and rode out of Urgrik.

OUT OF THE EONS

Chapter One

For long ages, the green light had burned within the narrow confines of four brick walls. It burned slowly, steadily, despite the fact that there was no air within the tiny space which contained it. It was waiting... waiting during the long years, the seemingly endless eons... waiting—for freedom.

Niall drove the sharp edge of his pick into the ancient yellow bricks of the sub-cellar wall. His muscles bunched and writhed as he worked, a tiny film of sweat grew on his forehead. Occasionally he paused, to study what he had already done—broken through his cellar wall only to disclose another wail behind it.

"By Emelkartha of the Eleven Hells," he grumbled. "I didn't know it was going to be all this trouble just to enlarge my wine cellar."

Still...

The mystery of that second wall intrigued him. He knew every chamber of this great house in Urgrik—-where he was Commander General of the armies of Lurlyr Manakor, king of Urgrik—and he knew there should be no second wall behind the one he had broken through.

There should be a large chamber behind it, yes. But not another wall. He grumbled under his breath as he stepped forward to attack that second barrier.

"What madman built it?" he asked the air about him. "What need was there for such a thing?"

No matter. The wall was here, and it had to come down if he were to have the added room he needed to house his wine bottles. The edge of his pick struck into those ancient bricks. Struck—and struck again.

That which was the green light blazed upward at the sound of those

195

blows. It quested here and there, scarcely daring to believe....

The pick arced again and again. The eon-old bricks seemed to fly apart under those furious blows. Chips flew through the air, together with yellow dust. Niall worked fiercely, savagely, almost as though something beyond himself willed it.

The pick made a hole in the barrier and Niall was aware of a faint green light glowing beyond this second wall. He stared, hunching his muscular shoulders. A light inside this sub-cellar? It made no sense, no sense at all.

He lifted the pick, drove its point again into the bricks. The yellow blocks seemed to explode as they shattered, raining brick and dust about him.

There was a larger opening now, one large enough for him to step through. Yet he did not move, instead standing transfixed as he beheld what seemed to be a large, green flame, burning steadily.

"By the eleven Hells," he growled.

The flame grew even as he stared, rising upward, broadening, waxing larger. It appeared to take shape before him, gathering together here and there, widening elsewhere, until it was shaped much like a man, with broad, fiery shoulders and a torso which tapered to sinewy-looking leg-shapes.

"My thanks," the thing whispered. "At long last—I am free! To dwell again among men, to have them bow down and worship me. Ahh, it has been long—long!—since the race of men knelt to Adonair!"

It rushed out, and instinctively Niall of the Far Travels drove his pick at it. The pick touched it—and disappeared!

Then the being was upon Niall, but touched him only with what appeared to be the ends of its fingers.

The Far Traveler went backward off his feet. He rammed hard into a far wall, crumpled up and slid to the floor. As he lay unconscious, the green thing raced past him, glowing more brightly, like a lost piece of some queer green star....

Niall shook himself. Like an animal he crouched in the semi-darkness, which was lit only by the glowing end of a taper thrust into the wall. His wits were addled. Something monstrous had taken place. He could not remember... ah!

Slowly he rose to his feet, stared into the opening he had made. There had been something green and glowing behind that second wall which he had opened. It had come out and—

"Emelkartha," Niall growled, and reached toward his hip, where his sword was usually hung. He carried no sword, he was within his own home. Here in Urgrik, there was no need for a sword within his walls. Or—was there?

He went into the cavity he had made, the second chamber which had held the green thing. His skin crawled. A dizziness came upon him, so intense that he reeled. There was evil here—or, at least, there had been. An evil so gross, so malicious, that human senses could scarcely perceive its magnitude.

Hastily he stepped back into the first chamber.

What had become of that which had rushed from here? Where was it now? What was it doing?

The sound of a footstep on the narrow, wooden stair behind him swung him around. He crouched in the reddish glow of the torch, waiting.

"I did not believe," a voice whispered. "I had to come and see for myself."

Niall saw white legs, naked up to the hem of a ragged bit of skirt. He saw graceful hips sway, saw an incredibly beautiful face—

"Lylthia!" he bellowed.

She shook her head, her long, black hair swaying gently. Her green eyes were worried behind their long lashes. "What have you done, Niall?" she whispered. "Have you broken through the ancient barriers we set about Adonair? Have you loosed him after so many eons?"

Niall could not move as she stepped past him, walked to the opening he had made and peered into it. Her eyes drank in the empty space behind the second wall. It seemed to the man who watched that her shoulders slumped in something akin to despair.

He moved toward her.

"What is it? What have I done? All I wanted was more room for my wine bottles. I broke down this first wall and saw another."

Lylthia looked at him. There was understanding and pity in her eyes. Her hands went to him, caught his hands. She shook her head slowly.

"You could not know. No man alive today could know—it was so long ago. So long, so long..." Her head drooped, and Niall almost felt the worry and the tension in her flesh.

Niall said slowly, "You spoke the word Adonair. What is he? Who is he?"

"A god-being from far away—so far that even we gods and goddesses have only heard faint whispers of his birthing place. He came here eons ago, liked what he saw about him and made this world his own."

She shuddered. "But he was evil. Evil! He made men his slaves, his—playthings. Against him the people cried out. We heard their calls, their prayers, in those other—spaces—where we dwell. We heard, we came. We fought Adonair and reduced him to a green flame, but we could not kill him. And so, as a green flame he has dwelt here for uncounted centuries."

Her black eyes looked up at Niall, troubled, worried. Slowly Lylthia crept closer, so that he might put his arms about tier. Some of the tension seemed to flow out of her upon contact with his great body.

"I had forgotten," she whispered, "that the city of Urgrik was built over the ancient ruins that were the dwelling place of Adonair. It has been so long. So many eons have passed since Adonair troubled this world. So many!" She pushed herself away, still clinging to his thickly thewed arms with her hands, and smiled tremulously.

"What are we going to do about him?" he asked.

Her shoulders rose in a shrug. "I do not know."

A terrible coldness rose inside Niall. If Emelkartha herself did not know, what hope did mere human beings have? His hand moved again to the hip where his sword was normally found. Sometimes he thought better with Blood-drinker in his fist.

"I must leave," she whispered. "I must consult the other gods, those who helped put Adonair within the brick cubicle. Perhaps one of them

198

will know what we must do to stop him."

His hands tightened around her shoulders. "No. Stay! With you beside me, there may be a way—"

Lylthia shook her head almost sadly. "I dare not. No one knows what evils Adonair may have dreamed of while he was imprisoned. Davolian, Humalorr, Kanadol, Thallatta—all the gods and goddesses—must be warned. I cannot delay."

A wistfulness filled her black eyes. Niall tried to hold her, to draw her in against him and kiss her. But even as his muscles tensed, he felt his arms move through nothing but air.

Lylthia was gone.

An anger grew in Niall. His gaze lifted toward the wooden staircase up which Adonair had raced, and down which Lylthia had come. His sword and his Orravian dagger lay up those stairs, in his small, private armory. He would belt his blades about him and seek out Adonair. He would do what he knew best: He would fight.

In the armory, he donned his mail shirt, then his sword and dagger. He did not expect any of this to help him survive—Adonair was too powerful for that, if Lylthia were to be believed—but if he could at least weaken the evil being, perhaps the gods could again subdue—or perhaps kill!—Adonair.

Niall walked from his house into a city of bedlam.

Everywhere men and women were gathered in tiny groups, white-faced and wide-eyed, staring about them. Upon sight of Niall, some ran to him, addressing him with terrified voices.

"Saw you that thing, General?"

"What was it?"

"It rushed down the street and when it touched someone, that person died."

Niall strode along Adonair's trail of death. "I saw it," he said. "I will find it."

He walked along the cobbled street, aware the clusters of people were breaking up and survivors were fleeing into their homes. Word of the monstrous being he had unleashed would be all over the city soon—even to the isolated palace where Lurlyr Manakor and his queen, Amyrilla, lived. He would go to the palace, then.

Niall walked deserted streets. A miasma of terror lay over the city. No one ventured forth. Even the shops were abandoned. As he went, his hand was on the hilt of his great sword. Die he might, if he were to meet that green being—but he would fight.

Knots of guards stood nervously as Niall came into the palace. At sight of him, they saluted, but their faces were pale, their eyes terror-filled.

"It killed those of us who sought to stop it!"

"With a touch of its hands—our comrades perished!"

Niall nodded grimly. "Where is it now?"

A warrior gestured. "In the throne room... with the king himself."

Niall strode forward. The throne room doors were closed, but they opened at a thrust of his huge hand. He stood a moment in the opening, staring.

Adonair occupied the golden throne of Lurlyr Manakor. The king stood before him, arms spread, his back to Niall. The silence in the vast chamber was broken by Niall's voice.

"Adonair, I have come to challenge you," he said harshly, and moved forward.

The green being lifted what was its head. Niall felt the impact of burning eyes. "So, then. You have followed me. That is good," it bellowed.

Niall felt those eyes move all over his great body, as though approvingly. The being moved upon the throne, seemed to stiffen and stare even harder at him. Niall felt forces gathering to oppose him, and he drew Blood-drinker.

Lurlyr Manakor scarcely breathed. Then he said, and his voice croaked, "He—he claims to have ruled our world long and long ago, Niall. Now he has returned to claim it once again."

"Only if he kills me."

Sword in hand, he stepped closer to the throne, until he stood side by side with Lurlyr Manakor. He raised his sword. As he did so, Adonair chuckled.

"A man with spirit. A man gifted with a great, strong body. I like that in you, man. I need a body. I shall take yours."

The green thing which was Adonair rose from the throne and stepped toward Niall. Down the three steps of the throne dais he came, and as he did, Niall raised his sword.

Onward came Adonair and now Niall moved. Swift was he as any wild animal. His blade slashed the air, touched Adonair, went right through its body.

Its head thrown back, the green being laughed. The laughter boomed loud in the throne room, echoing back from the arras-hung walls.

Even as that laughter rose up, Niall dropped his sword. His arm was as if turned to ice, so cold he could no longer hold Blood-drinker. The steel blade clattered on the floor.

Adonair studied him, its head held at a slant. He murmured, "You are brave, man-thing. You do not scream and run away from me. Good! I want that in someone who is to be my—shelter."

The greenness moved toward Niall then, as if to embrace him, its arms spread wide. Niall could not move. He could not fight.

At the first touch of the green thing, Niall thought he would die. Every muscle in his body seemed to wither. He could scarcely stand. There was a dizziness in his head, so that the room appeared to swirl about him, faster and faster. He was about to collapse.

No, Niall. No!

He knew the voice which whispered in his mind. It was Emelkartha Ah, she had not deserted him. Niall slowly straightened, knowing that he did not do it of his own will but that he drew strength and power from the goddess who was now within him.

Adonair drew back, a very little. He seemed to be studying Niall more closely. "What is this? Can one of your race fight me—and win? It cannot be!"

Almost angrily, he moved again to gather Niall within his embrace. But just as his arms were about to tighten, they were repulsed. Yet Niall stood with arms at his side, unmoving.

Niall felt the spirit of Emelkartha inside him. He knew she gave him a vast strength which he felt had never been fully tapped. He knew, too, that Adonair was mightily puzzled. An air of bafflement exuded from Adonair.

"So. Some power aids you," it whispered. "But—what power? It has been so long, I seem to have lost some of my own strength." His voice swelled powerfully. "Yet I will win. Whoever helps this man—understand that!

"I will win. Nothing can stop me. Nothing!"

Chapter Two

Niall slept in a chamber next to the sleeping chamber of the king. His great body tossed in its slumber, moving restless, as though it was aware that it should be somewhere else. Yet he dreamed on....

...and in his dream he stood in a vast chamber, a chamber so huge that he could see neither walls nor ceiling. In the tiles of the dark blue floor, tiny stars twinkled. It was as if he stood on the nighttime sky itself.

All around him were the gods.

He saw Emelkartha on an ivory throne with Davolian to one side of her, resting uneasily on a ruby chair. Humalorr was there, and Kanadol as well, while close beside Emelkartha was a woman with flowing red hair and a body seemingly carved from ivory. Lovely she was, as lovely as Emelkartha herself. This, he knew, was Thallatta.

It was Thallatta who spoke. "I see a man-being here, Emelkartha He is a big man, well endowed with muscles." Her voice grew soft. "Almost I envy you your lover."

"He is my lover, Thallatta. Mine alone. I summoned him here so that he might listen to our deliberations." Emelkartha turned toward a shadowy figure which rested on a magnificent throne comprised of diamonds and emeralds, rubies and sapphires, and of other stones of which Niall knew not.

"Great Father God, you who rule over us all—know that I have summoned this council because Adonair is free again. You do remember Adonair? It was long ago, yes—so long ago that no trace of him remains but in the minds of you gods and goddesses who fought

202

him—and won."

Thallatta smiled upon Niall and he felt his blood stir. In her musical voice, she said, "I remember, Emelkartha If the Father so wishes, I shall recall to his mind the—"

"The Father needs no help," a deep voice boomed. "I know all that transpires and—forget nothing." In a musing tone, the deep voice went on. "So. Adonair is freed at last. We have it to do all over again. I hope we may win as once we won, in those times past. Adonair is strong. Strong! He is of a different universe, a universe into which we have never probed."

"Probe now, All-Father," urged Emelkartha, clenching her fists. "Adonair wants the body of the man who stands before you. Once, I stopped him. Whether I can stop him again—I know not."

"Let me try next," smiled Thallatta, eyeing Niall. "I would like to enter into the body of this youth."

To Niall's surprise, Emelkartha did not respond as angrily as she had a moment before. Instead, she regarded Thallatta almost pleasantly, nodding her head. "If the All-Father agrees, why not?"

Emelkartha seemed to be almost gleeful, Niall thought. Thallatta herself saw this and seemed momentarily suspicious.

In his booming voice, the All-Father murmured, "Why not?

Let Thallatta try her strengths against Adonair. It cannot harm. Meanwhile, we shall take counsel among ourselves."

Thallatta rose from her seat, gathering about her ivory body the nearly transparent robes she wore. Her long, red hair trailed after her as she stepped toward Niall, hand outstretched. Behind her, Emelkartha watched, eyes narrowed.

Her hand touched his, held it. Niall felt his body seem to gather strength from that touch, which was almost a caress. He straightened, frowning slightly, looking at Emelkartha

Niall tried to focus his attention on what the gods and goddesses were saying, one to another, but he could hardly think, not with Thallatta beside him, touching him with hand and hip. He caught an attractive fragrance rising from her flesh, her garment

"I shall protect you, Niall of the Far Travels," she crooned. Was that laughter in her voice? "Aye, I shall be with you now, for a little while.

Or perhaps even longer."

Her hand ran up and down his arm. These goddesses! Did all of them consider a man a mere plaything? Not Emelkartha, of course; it was she whom he loved, but this Thallatta... he glanced down at her, saw her slanting eyes laughing up at him.

"Shall we go?" she breathed.

"I ought to stay and learn what it is the gods want of me," he muttered.

"Hah! I shall know—and tell you. Come, Niall."

He swirled backward down the slopes of dreamland....

And awoke.

He lay on the cot that had been given to him by Lurlyr Manakor. He was wide awake, though it was still dark about him.

Niall turned. A woman with ivory skin and long red hair lay beside him, one arm about him. There was laughter on the smiling red lips which were inches from his own. The blankets which covered him also covered her.

He could feel the warmth of her flesh against his own. Niall told himself that he belonged to Emelkartha—or to Lylthia, which was her human self—but the nearness and the beauty of Thallatta was disturbing.

"We ought not."

Soft laughter was her reply as she strained closer. "Why not? Emelkartha loaned you to me, did she not?"

"Adonair may—"

Her mouth stilled the words on his lips. Niall could not help himself. His arms gathered her in against him and he kissed her hungrily. He knew she was surprised; he felt her murmur something against his teeth. Then she was holding him, caressing him with her body....

Niall lost all track of time. He was whirled up into utter ecstasy, was shaken by that ecstasy so much that he felt lost from all contact with the world about him. Pleasure, so intense that it made him weak, traveled through every part of his mind and body.

Then—

A whisper grew upon the stillness.

"Come to me, man. Come!"

Ah! That had not been the voice of Thallatta. Instead—it was a summons from Adonair! Niall drew a deep breath, and suddenly Thallatta was gone.

Not gone, Niall! Waiting.

He rose to his feet. He walked from the chamber out into the hall and down the great staircase. The palace was empty of life, it seemed, except for himself.

He moved from the stairs to the hall floor and along it until he stood once again in the open doorway of the palace throne room. Adonair was still astride the great throne of Urgrik. A green arm lifted, beckoned. Niall strode forward.

"You have no weapon now, man-thing. And that which was in you is not, any longer. Come to me. Yield to me your body that I may have life as you have life."

Mocking laughter rose from the throat of the thing on the throne. It lured Niall, seemed to whisper to him to advance, to yield himself to that which would conquer him. And yet—that laughter appeared almost to plead with him.

Niall came to the first of the three throne steps. And there he halted. The green thing on the throne straightened, and anger blended with the curiosity with which it studied him.

"Advance to me. Come!"

Niall shook his head, not certain whether he was doing it of his own volition or whether something else was making him. Where was Thallatta? If she was going to help him, ought she not to be here with him?

"No," said Niall. "I do not obey you, Adonair."

The green creature was very still. For a long moment it stared down at the Far-Traveler. In a soft voice it whispered, "Now, how can you know my name? Certainly there is no mention of me in any human records. Men would never remember me after all this time. How can you know my name?"

It gathered itself, rushed upon him. Arms outstretched, it hurtled toward him. And—halted.

Adonair drew back. "Yes, you are protected again. I can sense it. But why should anyone protect you? You are only a man. A sell-sword. A mercenary, even if you are a general of the armies of the king." In a lowered voice, Adonair asked, "What else are you, man?"

A voice—Niall did not recognize it, though it came from his very throat—said harshly, "I am your doom, Adonair of another universe. In me you may read—your fate."

Adonair snarled. His arm lifted. From the tips of his fingers came flames of white fire, white fire that ran around Niall's naked body, that ate at it—or tried to. For long moments Niall stood frozen within those pallid fires.

The fires died down, faded out.

Adonair was standing now, staring at Niall with utter disbelief in his wide, red eyes. "Nothing can survive the flames of Xilth! Nothing—mortal! Who are you?"

"Men call me Niall of the Far Travels."

Adonair gestured. "Yes, yes. So men call you. But who are you?"

The Far-Traveler shrugged. He had grown more confident now. If Thallatta were within his body—as he had no doubt she was—then she was just as protective of him as was Emelkartha For that, he was profoundly grateful.

Do you think I would permit Adonair to hurt you?

There was tenderness in that voice which whispered silently to him. And even something more than tenderness. Guiltily, he thought of Emelkartha

"Answer me!" rasped Adonair furiously.

"I am only a man," Niall growled. "I have fought all over this world in which I live. What else is there to tell you?"

"Who aids you? What god?"

Speak no names to him, on your life, Niall!

Niall grinned. "What have such as I to do with gods? I am only Niall, a man."

206

The green being hesitated, then waved an arm. "Oh, begone! Back to your slumbers. I shall call you again in the morning."

Niall turned and walked away, vaguely aware that Thallatta was grinning delightedly inside him.

Now we have the rest of the night to be together, my darling.

He merely grunted. Something told him he was going to need all his strength when morning came.

As he came into his little bedchamber, movement on his rumpled bed caught his eye. Thallatta lay there, only partially covered by the blankets, her red hair spread across a pillow, an ivory leg bared to the hip, her arms and upper shoulders naked in the torchlight. There was a lazy smile on her full, red mouth.

Niall halted, staring at her. Inside him there was an eagerness to know again the delights she had brought him during the night. Yet he was fearful of how Emelkartha might regard this toying with her fellow goddess. He scowled blackly.

"Welcome back, Niall my love," she whispered.

"A few moments ago, you were inside me, protecting me from Adonair," he growled. "For that I am grateful, but—"

Thallatta waved a hand. "Yes, I know. You love Emelkartha" She stretched like a lazy kitten, laughing softly as much of the blanket fell away from her. "But Emelkartha is not here—and I am."

Her brown eyes glowed up at him. A slender hand lifted a corner of the blankets. "Come and rest, Niall of the Far Travels. There is much to be done before we can be safe from Adonair—if we can. But you must slumber now, restore strength to your body."

To resist her was asking too much of human flesh. He advanced to the bed, sank upon it. Thallatta reached up her arms to him, gathered in his body, brought it down beside her.

Niall sighed and surrendered....

When he woke, he possessed a vitality that surprised him. To be so alive, to feel so powerful, so strong—after such a night!—was incredible. Yet he had never felt so well. A little suspiciously, he raised his head from the pillow and looked around him. Thallatta was no longer in the bed.

Instead, she sat in a chair, her lovely legs crossed, smiling gently at him. She wore a skimpy garment of leather that displayed her body to perfection. Niall blinked.

"I let you sleep, to rest. We are going on afar journey" she said. "There is something the gods need before they can act against Adonair. And we must hurry."

Niall leaped from the bed, began to clothe himself in his garments, slipping on his mail shirt, then his broad leather belt that held his sword and dagger. He was ill at ease, regarding Thallatta. Was she going with him on this journey?

"Of course I am," she chided gently, rising to her feet and stretching. Niall blinked, wishing that leather garment were larger. It was entirely too revealing. She giggled, seeing where he looked.

"Come along," she smiled. "There is no time to waste."

In the light of early dawn they crept from the house into the stable. Niall saddled two horses, aided Thallatta up on one. Then he swung up to his stallion and let the woman-goddess lead the way out onto the cobbled street. He followed where she rode, making sure that his weapons were loose in their scabbards.

All day long they rode, until the sky darkened and the ring of matter that circled their planet where once a moon had been began to glow. Then Thallatta stood in the stirrups and pointed.

"Over there," she said. "We shall dine and rest."

He swung his stallion about and cantered with her toward a little hollow. When he came to its rim he stared down to where small, horned men and women labored over a glowing fire.

"My servitors," Thallatta explained. "They prepare our meal." Her brown eyes regarded him. "You must be hungry."

Niall did not remember the last time he had eaten. Eagerly he rode down the slope, dismounted, and would have unsaddled his horse to rub him down except that those horned servants of the woman-goddess shouldered him aside and took over his chores.

A soft hand caught his. "Come and eat, Niall."

Cushions had been thrown on the ground. As soon as Niall sat down on them, Thallatta was close beside him, her bare shoulder leaning against him.

The horned men and women came to serve them, and Niall told himself as he ate that he had never tasted food so succulent, so enjoyable. His eyes watched the horned people, saw how efficiently they went about their tasks. Who had summoned them? From whence had they come? Where would they go, once he and the woman with him rode on?

Ah, well. It made no difference. When one was merely the servant of the gods, one accepted everything that happened without question. Uneasiness was still in his mind, however. Did Emelkartha see him? Could she know what he was doing, and what he had done with Thallatta in that bed of his? He flushed faintly.

"We ride south of the Lurydian Moors tomorrow," the woman was saying. "There is a very old ruin there, forgotten by mankind, almost forgotten by the gods themselves. It is a long ride. You need your rest."

She leaned against him, kissing him, pressing him down into the cushions. Her fingers touched his face, his eyelids, closing them. Almost in that same moment, he was asleep.

Niall woke to the smell of cooking food. Again that same energy flowed through his veins, his limbs. As he sat up, the woman-goddess came striding toward him.

A troubled frown wrinkled her forehead.

"We must not delay," she told him. "Adonair knows you have left the city, though he does not know where you went. And he is raging. He has gathered the people of Urgrik to watch their king and queen die. Meanwhile—he feasts."

Niall shuddered. There was something about the way she had spoken that sent a cold, dread chill through his body. "I'm ready," he growled.

"We shall eat and ride. Eat well, for we shall not stop until we are past the moors."

Niall was not used to feasting on the war trail—and this was a war trail, if ever there was one—but he ate the meats and breads placed before him with a hunger that drew an approving nod from Thallatta.

Their horses were already saddled. They swung up into their saddles and began to trot. All day they rode, into lands where Niall had never been, following a narrow pathway through the Lurydian swamps. These were strange and deadly lands, Thallatta informed him. One misstep and man or beast would sink forever in these watery lands, drawn downward by a terrible, irresistible suction. No man knew the path through these lands, no one but a god or goddess. The swamps bordered the moor, placed there by the gods uncounted eons ago.

All this Thallatta told him as they rode single file along a very narrow stretch of solid ground. Niall realized that alone, neither he nor any other human could have penetrated as far as they were now. Death would have claimed them a dozen times over. Yet with the woman-goddess in the lead, they went smoothly, easily.

Then they were on the moor, cantering toward a little hillock in the distance. It was here Thallatta drew rein and pointed.

"Uncover what lies hidden there," she ordered.

Niall swung down, drew his sword. He worked swiftly, loosening the dirt, then scooping it up in his cupped hands, tossing it aside. Slowly he exposed old stones, linked together in a subtle manner. From time to time he glanced up at Thallatta, who stood still watching him. It seemed that she listened to other voices while standing there.

"Expose the top stone," she said at last.

When he had done so, she stepped forward—

As she did, a darkness gathered. It was utter blackness, a blackness so intense Niall lost all sight of her. Indeed, he could see nothing at all. It was as if he had been struck blind.

From the darkness, lightnings flashed.

Those lightnings struck Niall, toppling him forward. He lay as still as a dead man.

Chapter Three

Niall stirred, moaning. He ached in every fiber of his body. As he lay there, he vaguely recalled that Thallatta had screamed at sight of that darkness, calling upon the All-Father. What had happened after that, he did not know.

Slowly, life flowed back into his flesh. He rose to hands and knees, shaking his head. The blackness was gone; he could see again. Niall stood up.

Thallatta lay crumpled on the ground, her body across the stones he had uncovered. He bent over and gently lifted her in his arms. She seemed dead, but as he studied, her, her shoulders lifted and fell, and her eyes opened.

"Thanks to the All-Father," she breathed. "We still live! But haste, Niall. There is no time to spare. Loosen the top stone—quickly!"

He set her down, put his hands to the top stone, turned it as she bade him. The stone came loose; he lifted it and set it aside. The hole it left led down into a narrow opening. And in that opening stood a silver cup, filled with a glowing white liquid.

"Lift it, let me see it," whispered the woman-goddess.

Niall held it up to her. She inspected it, raised the lid. Her eyes narrowed as she regarded it, and then her head tilted to one side, as though she listened to voices from far away. Niall saw her hands tighten on the silver cup. Thallatta sighed.

"Take out your sword, earth-man," she whispered.

Niall drew Blood-drinker, held it out as Thallatta indicated. For a moment she paused, frowning, then dipped the tip of a slender finger into the glowing whiteness. Her fingertip came out, touched the blade of his sword.

Instantly that strange, white liquid spread across the surface of the steel blade. Like water it ran, yet it did not drop from the steel. Instead it seemed to cling to it, to move across its surface everywhere. For a moment that whiteness glowed brightly, then slowly faded away, as though the steel itself had absorbed it.

Thallatta sighed, then raised the cup to him.

"Drink," she breathed. "Drink it all."

Niall scowled. "What is it?"

Tenderness shone in Thallatta's brown eyes. "Do not fear, Niall. Long, long ago, the gods concocted this liquid. The All-Father, Emelkartha and the others." She sighed. "Even I helped to make it. It will not hurt you."

The Far Traveler shrugged. Why refuse? Deep inside him, he knew

211

he was merely the servitor of the gods. If they bade him drink, he would do so. He took the cup from Thallatta and raised it to his lips.

He swallowed. There was a faintly tart taste to the white liquid, but it seemed pleasant enough. He drank all that was in the cup and stood a moment, frowning. Something was happening inside him.

He could feel a new strength gathering within him. It was as though he were being reborn, revitalized. His muscles seemed to swell even more. And in his mind, there was a strange peace. He looked down at the goddess.

"What now?"

She smiled up at him. "We shall go to meet Adonair, you and I. You shall challenge him to battle."

His nerves crawled. Challenge Adonair? Did this woman-goddess think him mad? What could he do against such a being? Yet even as he felt a faint touch of terror, the liquid that was inside him warmed him, appeared almost to comfort him.

Niall shrugged and grinned. With an arm he hooked the waist of the goddess, drew her toward him so that he could feel the softness of her flesh. "We go, but not yet. Before I meet that demon, I want to savor more of the sweets which you can bring me."

Thallatta laughed up at him. "There is no time, Niall. Remember! Adonair sacrifices the king and queen of Urgrik. You would not have them die while you pleasured yourself?"

His arm dropped. "Of course not," he grumbled.

He walked toward the horses, expecting Thallatta to follow him. When she did not, he turned; he saw her kneeling, lifting the silver cup toward the sky.

"All-Father, take back that which you yourself have fashioned," the goddess-woman was saying. "I deliver it into your hands."

For an instant, a terrible quiet fell upon the land. Then from the sky flared a single bolt of lightning. It touched the cup—and where the cup had been was nothingness.

Thallatta sighed, rose to her feet and came toward him. There was a happiness upon her face which seemed almost to transfigure her. She came up to Niall, pressed herself against him.

"The All-Father approves. It is time now to go."

They mounted their horses and began to canter.

Though they went at a slow pace, it seemed to Niall that the land rushed past them. No horse could run that fast, yet once when he stood in the saddle, the hillock and the moor itself were no longer to be seen. Even as he stared, the land around him was altering, rushing past them.

It came to Niall that the gods were all about him, hurrying him along. The little hollow where he had eaten and slept was beside him. Then—it was gone.

The walls of Urgrik rose up before them and still they continued their unearthly fast pace. They moved through the great gateway and along the street. People were about them but none appeared to see them.

The palace gates were there, and suddenly Thallatta reined in. "We go on foot, now," she directed.

Niall grinned at her. There was a wild recklessness in him, fueled by that white liquid and the strangeness of that ride, and some inner voice told him that he had become—godlike. Not so much a human being was he now, but a god in truth.

He swung about and stared at the palace. No guards stood on duty. It seemed deserted. Yet from somewhere in that vast building came faint wails of utter terror. His hand moved toward his sword hilt.

Thallatta touched his wrist. "Go now—and hurry!"

He raced into the building, bounding down the long hall, seeing the big doors of the audience room flung open wide. To those doors and between them he ran, and as he ran his hand gripped the hilt of Blood-drinker, drew it forth.

It gleamed white as new-fallen snow, that blade. It glistened, glinted so brightly Niall could not bear to look at it as he raced into the audience room.

He slid to a halt, dumbfounded.

Lurlyr Manakor hung naked on a cross. Across from him, separated by a dozen feet, hung his lovely queen, Amyrilla. And all about them licked something which looked like greenish fire.

Adonair sat upon the throne, smiling at his enjoyment of their agonies.

For they were in agony, both of them. Amyrilla was screaming shrilly now as the flames ate at her pale legs. And Lurlyr Manakor bellowed as other flames licked across his hips. Over those terrible cries rang out the laughter of Adonair.

"Terrible are my flames," he shouted, "that eat and eat——yet do not devour. For long years you two shall hang there, suffering agonies the like of which no man and no woman has ever suffered. You cannot die and so end them. Ah, no.

"Each moment will be a century. A minute will be an eon. And those flames can never die—unless I will it!"

Niall moved forward. A hate such as he had never known was within him, a rage so vast it nearly blinded him.

"Adonair!" he bellowed.

The being on the throne stiffened, lifted its eyes from the helpless woman and man to stare down the length of the long hall down which Niall came walking, sword in hand. Slowly, Adonair rose to face him.

"Beware, you whom men name Niall," came the rumbling voice of the green being.

The Far-Traveler did not answer. Inside himself, he felt an alien power glowing, promising him strength. He turned aside, drew his dagger, cut Amyrilla from the cross that held her. Then he turned to Lurlyr Manakor.

His dagger slashed once. Twice And the king collapsed in his arms. Very gently, Niall placed him on the floor, then turned toward the throne.

Adonair stood erect. What passed for his face was contorted, grotesque with the fury that blazed in him. For a moment he studied Niall, then smiled faintly.

"Fool of a human! I can sense there is no one inside you now. You are rash, mortal, to dare Adonair! But I like that in you."

As though gathering itself together, the green being towered above the throne. Then, like a thunderbolt, it hurled itself at Niall.

Swiftly it came, but swift too was Niall. He raised Blood-drinker and swung it. In an arc of white steel that blade curved—and since Adonair was almost upon him, that blade bit deep.

Deep it went into the green being. Deep! Deep!

And Adonair screamed!

Rigid was its body as it felt that blade slide through it. Rigid! Motionless! From its open mouth came an unearthly cry, part wail, part bellow of agony.

Niall raised Blood-drinker to slash again.

But Adonair was a dozen paces away, fleeing. Fast it went, hurling itself along so swiftly that it seemed only a green blur. And then, with one last great cry, it was gone.

Niall lowered his sword. All his vitality seemed sapped. For a moment, he could not move. Then he sheathed his great sword and moved toward the king of Urgrik.

Lurlyr motioned him away. "See to Amyrilla," he said.

Niall bent, raised the unconscious queen in his arms, carried her from the throne room up the side staircase to her own chambers.

Niall put her down on her bed, raised his head and shouted.

Women came running, faces white with fear. In dread they stared at Niall, then at Amyrilla. Yet they crept forward toward the bed.

"Attend to her," Niall growled. "Make her as comfortable as you can."

He went down to the throne room, where Lurlyr Manakor was lying, breathing fitfully. The king opened his eyes, stared up at Niall.

"What you did I shall never forget, Niall."

Niall grinned. That was a good sign. He lifted a golden wine flask and carried it to the king, who grasped it and put it to his mouth. Long he drank, until he lowered the flask and stared at Niall.

"It will be back," he whispered hoarsely. "It told me enough about itself so that I know—it can never be killed!"

Tears glistened in the king's eyes.

Chapter Four

The palace was quiet. Niall sat alone at the royal table, dishes about him piled high with roasted meats, with delicacies. A serving maid stood at his elbow, in her hands a flask filled with wine.

As he ate, the girl watched him, awe and admiration in her eyes. She trembled from moment to moment, until Niall noticed it and, beckoning her, brought her trembling to his side. She stared at him with eyes that were so big he thought for a moment they might fall out upon her cheeks.

"What is it, Palora?" he asked. "Why do you stare at me so?"

"Lord, you drove away—that thing. Men say nothing on earth can stand against you and that sword of yours. They say also that if you desired it, you could rule the world."

Niall grinned. "Now, that's something for which I have no desire. I'm content to be the general of the king's armies." He thought a moment and chuckled. "It seems to be quite an interesting occupation."

Palora shivered. Her eyes roamed the big, empty dining hall. "Will it return, lord? That—thing?"

Niall shrugged. "Who knows? If it does, I'll have to fight it again. Now—fill up my beaker and go get some rest."

He sat with his wine for a long time, pondering. Adonair would return, yet the gods had not spoken to him since he had met it with his sword and driven it away.

Niall scowled. It was unlike Emelkartha to leave him so in the dark. She ought to have appeared to him, counseled him, advised him. Yet ever since he had fought Adonair, even Thallatta had not appeared.

He drained the goblet, put it down. He rose from his chair—and froze motionless. Fire-red eyes stared at him from the darkness beyond the candle flames.

Niall reached for his sword.

"Nay, now," said a voice. "No need to yank out that blade of yours. I am here merely to study you—and wonder." There was a faint sigh, and then the voice of Adonair whispered again.

"Man or god? Which are you? From whence have you come? These

216

are questions I must have answered before I can attack you again. That sword of yours bit deep. Ahh—but how?

"I am not of your world. Nothing of your world can truly harm me. There is some reason why—you can. I must learn that reason before we meet again."

The red eyes were gone. Niall found himself half standing, sword partly drawn from its scabbard. With an oath, he banged it back, then reached out a hand for the goblet.

It was empty.

Niall threw the cup, moved along the table. There was a flask at the far end which he carried from the dining hall. Lurlyr Manakor had insisted he stay in the palace from now on. It would allow the king to sleep easier. And the queen as well.

Niall grinned, wondering if Adonair could read his thoughts. But no. Adonair could not do that. Otherwise he might have learned of that strange white liquid in that cup.

Hmm. What was that white stuff? A brew made by the gods, of course. He knew that much. But how had they made it—and of what? Certainly it was no poison. Anything but! As soon as he had downed it, he had felt almost superhuman. And he still felt that way.

He wished Emelkartha would appear to him this night. As Lylthia, of course. There was so much he wanted to talk to her about. Uneasiness touched him. Maybe Emelkartha was angry at him for having made love to Thallatta. But he could not help himself; he was only a human. Thallatta was a goddess.

Tiredness was rising in him as he made his way to the room set aside for him. One glance at the huge bed made him realize just how deeply he could sleep. Clad as he was, with his sword and dagger close beside him—in case Adonair should make an attempt at him again—he lay down and was almost instantly asleep....

Or—was he asleep?

He stood again in that gathering of gods and goddesses, in that vast chamber where Emelkartha sat on an ivory throne and Thallatta close beside her. Once more the dark blue floor, through which stars appeared to shine, was under his war-boots.

"—and there is always a risk," the All-Father was saying in his deep voice. "Yet I feel inside me that it is the sensible thing to do." The shadowy figure on his jeweled throne sat up straighten "Providing, of course, that the human will agree to what we ask."

All the time the All-Father had been speaking, Niall had been watching Emelkartha She had not looked directly at him, but one or twice Niall thought he saw her glancing at him from the corners of her eyes. Almost angrily.

Niall felt ill at ease. He had no excuses to offer for what he and Thallatta had done. The goddess with the red hair seemed to lounge in her throne, one leg crossed casually over another, a smile on her full mouth.

The All-Father looked at Niall, and now he could feel all their eyes, staring at him questioningly.

The All-Father addressed him. "Do you agree to face Adonair for us—without sword, or dagger, or any weapon whatsoever?'

A coldness ran through the Far-Traveler. Face that demon without a weapon? It was not to be thought of! And yet—did he dare refuse?

His eyes were on Emelkartha Slowly she lifted her head, looked at him. She was angry, yes; but he sensed that she would also forgive him for what he had done with Thallatta.

He asked, "What does Emelkartha bid me do? I will abide by her decision."

The gods and goddesses looked from him to Emelkartha An angry frown touched Thallatta's face, which Emelkartha saw.

Emelkartha said sweetly, "Always I have done that which the All-Father counseled. I shall continue to do so." She rose from her ivory throne and walked toward Niall, her hips swaying.

Her hands she lifted and put on his shoulders. From this close, he could see very plainly the anger in her eyes.

"Do as the All-Father asks, Niall," she smiled.

It was not a nice smile, Niall thought, as he nodded dumbly....

Niall woke to daylight coming through a window of his room. Lazily he stretched, remembering his dream. Ah, but he felt certain it

218

had not been a dream. The memory of what had happened was too vivid, too real.

"So!" a voice hissed at him. "So that she-demon tired you out! It was as I thought."

He turned around, saw Lylthia standing by a window, scowling at him blackly. Her fists were on her hips; she looked like a woman insulted, deeply wronged.

Niall licked his dry lips. "You gave me permission—"

"Permission? Hah!"

It was his turn to scowl. Slowly he slid from the bed, moved toward her. She watched him come closer, glowering at her. Only when he was within a foot of her did she move, lifting her arm, striking out at his face.

Niall moved as swiftly, caught her wrist and bent it back even as his arm went around her. He dragged her up against him and kissed her, long and hungrily. Lylthia fought him savagely, but his strength was too great for Emelkartha in her mortal form.

In time, she lay against him, letting him kiss her, even kissing him in turn. But when he released his hold, she drew back and frowned.

"You made love to Thallatta," she accused.

"As you expected me to do," he grinned.

She looked away, shrugging. "If you had been true to me—"

"Thallatta would have deserted me, and Adonair would have taken over my body. Wouldn't he?"

Lylthia pouted. "You could have repulsed her."

"And angered her."

A smile touched the corners of her mouth. "It is true that I dared not face Adonair again. Someone else had to be inside your body. He— weakened me too much." Her shoulders lifted, fell. "I suppose Thallatta was as good as anyone else. She succeeded."

"Good. Now you shall stay with me."

"No. I cannot. I must leave you soon, as the All-Father wishes." Something akin to despair touched her face. "Even he is not certain that our plan will work."

This time it was Lylthia who stepped closer, putting her arms around him, hiding her face against his chest. In a muffled voice she whispered, "Adonair may kill you, Niall. And—we may not be able to prevent it."

Surprise held Niall rigid. "Not prevent it? But you are all gods and goddesses! Your power is—"

"—helpless against such as Adonair! He is from another universe. Only one thing may overcome him." She shuddered. "You must go to him, offer him your body! Go without weapons, naked. Let him enter you!"

Their eyes met; both were filled with despair. Numbly, Niall said, "Give myself to him. Let him take control of me. That's what you mean, isn't it?"

"It's our only hope."

"I—cannot."

He shuddered. Offer himself to that thing? Give his mightily muscled body to that demon? Anything else but that! "It is the only way."

He pushed her from him, walked up and down the chamber. Permit Adonair to enter into him? To rule over this world, make it and the men and women in it his slaves? Niall shuddered.

A gentle hand caught his arm, another touched his face caressingly. "It is the only way, Niall," Lylthia whispered.

"But—what will happen?"

Lylthia sighed. "We do not know. We can only hope. But this we do know: Unless you do as we bid, Adonair will certainly take over your world, make it and the people in it his own. Can you dare everything to try and stop him?"

He could not think with her body pressed so temptingly against his own. It was as if she were reminding him of all the pleasures that body had given him—and would bring him in the future—if he lived.

His heavy shoulders shrugged. "Always I have done what you asked. I suppose I will now." He grimaced. "You know what you're asking of me, don't you?"

"More than you do."

The room was silent. Niall stared out the window at the rooftops of the city. To give up his life! Never to see Urgrik again as he saw it now! No more to lead his warriors into battle! Lylthia would be lost to him forever.

Instead, to dwell in a form of living death, with Adonair within him. No longer to be in control of his body, his voice. No more to swing a sword or smell the cool air as it swept across the river Thalamar.

His hands lifted to his sword-belt Slowly he undid the buckle, let his weapons clatter to the floor.

Tears were running down Lylthia's cheeks. In a broken voice she whispered, "I did not think I would ever counsel you to do what you are about to do. I shall come with you, of course."

She put her hand in his, held it.

Lylthia tugged at his hand, drew him with her out of the bedchamber and down the hall to the great stairway. They went down the staircase step by step, slowly. Niall did not think. What use was thinking? He was giving himself up as a sacrifice.

He scowled. How the gods expected him to defeat Adonair by doing this was beyond him. The gods must try to help him in some manner. If they did not, he was doomed.

Now the open doors of the great audience hall were before him. Lylthia sighed at his side, and her hand that held his tightened.

To the doorway they moved and stood there, side by side. They saw the green thing which was Adonair again upon the throne. It sat, unmoving, as they advanced into the chamber. Yet Niall felt menace pulsing from it. Its anger throbbed outward at him.

"Have you come to mock me?" Adonair asked.

Niall strode forward, Lylthia at his side. "I have come to surrender," he called. "I ask only that you spare the woman I love from whatever it is you intend doing with the rest of the people of this city."

"Surrender?"

The word hung in the air between them as Adonair stirred, rising to what served it as feet. His red eyes glared at Niall, examining him.

"You bear no sword. What have you done with it?"

"Left it behind in my sleeping chamber. I come unarmed, to prove my good faith. My body in exchange for the safety of the woman I love."

"She shall be safe."

Was there mockery in the voice which answered him? Niall did not know, but he knew well enough that once Adonair was in command, Lylthia would die—assuming Adonair could catch her.

Yet Niall revealed nothing of what he thought.

He spread his arms. "Come take me, master."

Adonair towered over the throne. It seemed as if he gathered all his strength, all his power. Then he moved slowly toward Niall, appearing to float through the air.

Sweat stood out on the Far-Traveler's face. What was he doing, standing here without Blood-drinker in his fist? Weaponless! Helpless!

Adonair swooped.

His arms opened and caught Niall up within them. They held him motionless, unmoving. Then Adonair entered into him.

At that entry, Niall felt an awful fear. Every bit of his being rebelled against what was happening. He felt the awful alienness of Adonair, sensed something of its powerful mind. His muscles seemed to swell with agonizing pain and he opened his mouth to bellow out his agony.

Mine! You are mine now, man!

Triumph was in that voice, shouting inside his brain. Niall could feel the—thing—which was inside him as it expanded outward, seemed to fill every blood vessel, every muscle, every last inch of body flesh.

Laughter rang from Niall's throat. Maniacal laughter, which was filled with victory.

In a tiny corner of his mind, Niall asked: Where are the gods? What sort of help have they given me? Have they offered me up as a sacrifice without even putting up a fight?

Amusement was in the voice that answered him.

What kind of fight can even your gods make against such as Adonair? I am all-powerful!

And then—

Something that had been hidden began to gather within Niall. He could sense it, sense also the touch of doubt that was striking Adonair.

What is it? What is this thing I feel?

Not Niall but Adonair thought this, yet Niall felt the thought. Something swirled upward within his body, moving outward into all the places that Adonair had filled—and Adonair was helpless against it.

Niall screamed.

But it was not Niall's voice that uttered that frightful cry—it was Adonair's! Inside Niall, the will being twisted and turned, seeking escape.

It is here, hidden. It—waited—for me!

Niall was vaguely aware that Lylthia was watching, crouched down and staring, her hands clenched into fists, her eyes wide. Those eyes studied Niall, saw what was happening to him. They softened with tenderness, with pity.

"Soon now, Niall," she whispered.

The battle raged within him, though he stood absolutely still. That which was in him—whatever it was—was slowly eating at Adonair, slowly devouring him. And the evil being could do absolutely nothing against it.

Too firmly was he mired in flesh and bone! Too caught up in Niall's physical presence! Trapped!

Adonair screamed. Screamed again. And yet again.

Slowly the green being was dissolving, being eaten alive by whatever it was that was in Niall.

"The white liquid," Lylthia whispered. "The liquid that was in the cup you and Thallatta found. The same liquid in which you coated your sword!"

"The gods made it, long and long ago," Lylthia whispered. "They never used it; they first overcame Adonair another way. For eons upon eons it has rested in that silver cup, waiting. Now—it has been used!"

Niall stirred. He flexed an arm, a leg. He moved the fingers of his hand. Then he shook himself as might a giant bear upon rising from a long sleep. He stared down at Lylthia.

"Gone," he breathed. "It's gone."

"Thanks to the All-Father."

Almost instantly, Niall sensed the presence of the gods and goddesses. They were here, all about him, pressing close. Faintly, very faintly, he could hear their words, their laughter.

"We have won!"

"Adonair is no more."

"Gone—forever!"

Niall held Lylthia by a wrist, drawing her to him, sliding an arm about her body. He knew the All-Father was there—somewhere — looking down at him benevolently.

"My thanks," Niall growled. "My thanks to you all. And now—a boon."

The eyes of the gods and goddesses regarded him.

"What boon seek you, Niall?" one of them asked.

"Let Emelkartha—as Lylthia—stay with me for a time."

Lylthia chuckled. "Silly! I intended to do that anyhow. Ask for something else."

Niall shook his head. "I want nothing else."

The anger that had been in Lylthia faded away. She pressed against Niall, kissed him. "For that, I forgive you everything. But come, let us go. Adonair is gone; nothing more detains us."

She led the way toward the huge doorway. Over her shoulder she said, "We go to your house, not to that room in the palace where Thallatta slept."

Niall grinned.

When they reached the street, they began to run.

THE LURE OF THE GOLDEN GODLING

Chapter One

Niall came striding through the dark night, his head down and his great chest bowed slightly before the viciously biting wind that came sweeping in off the river and roaming the almost deserted streets of Urgrik. Ahead of him, half hidden in the black shadows, he saw what he assumed to be the shape of a man, lying motionless on the street cobbles.

A late drinker, one who had imbibed too much of the strong Kallarian wine? Or a man who carried gold in his pouch and had let it be seen by street robbers? No matter. He, Niall, would lend the man a helping hand, get him under a roof and into a room where he would be safe.

And yet—

As he neared the bundled body, it seemed to Niall that whoever lay there must be thin to the point of emaciation. For his garments flapped wildly in the breezes, and it seemed to the Far-Traveler that little swirls of dust rose with each blast of wind and were blown away. Intrigued, he quickened his pace, his hand going instinctively to the hilt of his long Orravian dagger.

Then he was staring down at what lay at his booted feet, seeing richly embroidered garments and a cloak in which golden threads were thickly interwoven to form strange signs and sigils. What he had supposed to be a body was no more than clumps of those garments.

Yet a living man had worn these clothes—and recently.

With a foot he dislodged a part of the cloak and found himself staring at a bearded face, a face that was open-eyed and open-mouthed, as though death had come in such a manner as to surprise this man, whoever he might have been. As he watched, the wind toyed with that face—and blew it away as though it had been fashioned out of dust itself.

"Gods," Niall whispered, awed.

He went down on a knee and put out a hand, as if by that action he might prevent the gusts from disturbing any more of this thing that had been human. As he did so, his fingers touched something hard and unyielding beneath the cloak.

Niall drew back his hand. Scowling, muttering a prayer to Emelkartha who was his goddess and his love, he flung back a part of the flapping cloak to disclose what he had touched.

His eyes saw a golden statue.

It was no more than a foot high, and had obviously been carved by a master craftsman. It showed something amorphous, almost shapeless, yet possessed of some strange, other-worldly power. Its rounded eyes seemed to peer upwards at Niall, as though promising him untold wealth and power even as a tiny voice whispered soothingly inside his brain.

Niall growled under his breath. He did not like these mysterious manifestations of the many gods that infested his world.

"Emelkartha—aid me!" he whispered.

Almost instantly he heard faery laughter from somewhere deep within him.

La, Niall! What is it now that so disturbs—

That voice broke off. Niall shivered as he sensed the attention of the goddess whom he loved and who loved him.

Korython! Oh, gods of outer space!

There was a strange silence. Niall shook himself and rose to his feet, still clutching the golden statue. One quick glance he gave it, then he thrust it deep into the leather pouch that hung at his sword-belt

He moved away from the bundle of clothes, shaking his huge shoulders as though to free himself from an intolerable weight. He cast a last glance back at the cloak and garments that lay shrunken now, stirring this way and that in the wind.

Niall breathed deeply of the cool, clear air off Thalamar River. Some of the wine he had imbibed at the palace with Lurlyr Manakor, who was king in Urgrik, and with his queen, Amyrilla, faded from his veins. He walked more soberly, more quickly, and there was a distinct uneasiness within him.

Once he opened the pouch as though to reach into it and bring out the golden godling, but his fingers fell away, then tightened the pouch's drawstrings savagely. He wanted nothing to do with gods and goddesses—always expecting Emelkartha, of course—for he had learned that to traffic with the gods was to traffic in misery for himself.

And yet—he did not want to throw away that statue. It was of solid gold, he was positive, and extremely valuable. It belonged to someone, and Niall meant to find out to whom it belonged.

He was nearing his palace when he heard the sound of running feet behind him. Niall grinned, and his huge hand fell to his long Orravian dagger. Foot-pads in the early hours of the morning? Ah, this he understood and was ready to meet.

He waited, waited....

When those footsteps sounded from right behind him, he whirled, his steel lifting from the scabbard. A woman was before him, sliding to a halt, her eyes wide and her mouth open in sudden fright. His dagger point was just touching her belly.

"Lord," she cried. "Stab me not!"

She was beautiful, Niall saw. Dark with the loveliness of the daughters of the southern deserts, with long, black hair flowing in the wind, with large black eyes and with a mouth the color of a scarlet flower, she poised there before him, palms stretched up and outward as though to fend him off.

"What seek you?" he growled.

"The statue, lord. The golden god."

Niall grinned. That statue in his pouch was worth a fortune. It was of solid gold, and it was of such a shape as Niall had never seen before. What was it that Emelkartha had called it? Korython Yes, that had been it.

Niall shook his head so that his golden hair swung. "Na, na. It was I who found it. I keep it."

The woman softened, moved a step closer. She was beautiful; there was a passion in her eyes and face that was reflected in the curves of her body where her clothing was pressed against it by the breeze.

"To you it means nothing, lord." Her eyes widened. "Seek you money for it? Then come. Come with me and you shall be rewarded."

There was a deviltry in Niall at the moment. Go with her? Why not? His life had been rather stale of late, with little for him to do as High Commander of the armies of Urgrik, with peace everywhere on the borders.

He slid his dagger back into its sheath, hooked an arm about the slender waist of this woman, drew her in against him. She was soft and warm, curving against him.

"Lead on, little one. Who am I to resist an appeal such as yours?"

She smiled up at him temptingly, her hand lifting to caress his face. "Come, lord. Be Thayya's companion for the evening."

Her soft hand caught his, drew him with her at a trot. They moved down the deserted avenues, past shuttered houses and locked doors, their footfalls sounding softly in the night. Once when Niall would have halted to question her, she pressed her body to his, putting her arms about him and lifting her mouth for his kiss.

Niall kissed her. He would not have been a man if he had refused that caress. But inside him something stirred with suspicion. What was so valuable about the golden god to cause this woman to offer him great wealth in exchange for it? Of course, she might be leading him into a trap. He half suspected this to be the case.

Yet there was a recklessness in Niall this night. He almost hoped that there would be a trap. His muscles needed exercise, and even the merest promise of a battle was all he wanted.

"We waste time," she murmured against his lips. "There is gold waiting. Much gold. All yours, lord—in exchange for the statue."

He turned her, hugging her softness to him as he did so, and half-carried her as they ran along the avenue. They came at last to an oaken door barred with iron, into the lock of which Thayya slid a key.

The door opened inward, into a large room lighted with a few fitfully burning candles. There was a big table there, on which rested velvet bags bulging with their contents. Thayya slipped away from Niall and moved toward the table to undo the drawstrings of one of those bags.

As Niall watched, she tilted the bag, and golden ruplets and durakins fell out on the tabletop. Astonishment held the Far-Traveler motionless. There was a fortune in that velvet sack. If the others held the same amount of golden coins, he was staring at a vast fortune.

"All yours, " smiled the woman. "In exchange for the golden statue."

Niall grinned. Nothing was worth all that gold. Nothing!

Be not tempted, Niall! On your life!

Ha! That would be Emelkartha again, warning him as she had warned him so often in the past. Himself, he cared nothing for all that gold. He had more than enough riches. Yet the woman seemed so anxious, so eager....

Slowly, he shook his head. "I think not. I have—taken a fancy to the little godling. I mean to keep it."

Fury blazed in the black eyes of the woman. Then that fury faded before her will. She came closer to Niall, again pressed her softness against him.

"All that gold—and me," she breathed.

The goddess stirred angrily within Niall. Emelkartha was a jealous woman, goddess though she might be. Slowly, the High Commander shook his head.

"I'll keep the statue," he growled.

Thayya stepped back, her mouth opening. She screamed, and as she did, a door opened off to one side. Men with swords and daggers in their hands came pouring into the room. Thayya stepped to one side to give them room, pointing at Niall.

"Slay him!" she ordered.

Niall bellowed with delight. His great sword came up into his hand and he swung it like a scythe. A head toppled from a neck, and then Blood-drinker was burying its keen blade into a shoulder, half severing it.

The Far-Traveler moved like a cat. He was half across the room even as he was freeing his blade from bleeding flesh, lifting it to swing again, and then again. At each stroke of that shining steel, blood spurted. Heads were cloven, arms were sheared. Only now and again did he use his blade as a shield to deflect the blows that were aimed at him.

Niall was in his glory, with the ring of steel in his ears and the sight of armed men coming at him. For this he had been born, to fight— and to fight even harder against such odds.

He heard Thayya urging on the men amid whispered prayers to whatever gods she worshiped She was backing slowly toward the door, eyes big with terror, as she saw how Niall fought.

Niall wanted to reach her, to take her with him to answer questions. But the mercenaries who fought him seemed to detect what it was he wanted. They flung themselves before him; they gave up their lives to protect the woman.

Thayya moved toward the doorway and slipped through it, closing and bolting the door behind her. Niall growled low in his throat, hurled himself even more savagely at the men who still faced him.

They went down before his blade until he was the only thing standing in the room. As the last man fell, Niall shook himself and lowered his sword. He moved toward the thick door that blocked the path deeper into the building. It was barred, bolted.

Niall shrugged. The woman was long gone. He turned and eyed the velvet bags that held the golden coins. He lifted one of the bags, hefted it. It was heavy with gold. He chuckled and twisted his fingers around the drawstrings.

This sack he would take with him, as reward for having overcome the ruffians Thayya had called up against him. He whistled as he moved out of the building doorway and set off down the street. The evening had turned out to be more exciting than he had thought it to be when he had left the palace.

He wondered again where the golden statue had come from, and what it might be.

As he turned into the small palace that was his home in Urgrik, he saw the gleam of candlelight in an upstairs window. When he had left earlier this evening, he had left no tapir lit. He drew his sword and moved up the stone staircase silently.

He came into his bedroom and saw a woman stretched out lazily on his bed, clad in rags that left her long, lovely legs bare, that hugged her body tightly at hip and breast.

Niall stood grinning in the doorway. "Lylthia!" he all but yelled as he moved toward her.

She scowled at him. "You would have gone with that tart, if she had proven more friendly!"

Niall laughed, sheathing Blood-drinker and moving toward the bed. "Would I, now? You know as well as I do that she offered herself to me and I denied her."

Lylthia sneered, but there was laughter in her voice as she said, "Ha! The only reason you denied her was that you were hoping for a fight."

His big hands reached for her and she fought him, but only halfheartedly. He kissed her soft mouth, crushing her in his arms, until after a time she returned his kisses and lay against him contentedly.

"We have no time to be making love," she murmured, stroking his jaw with soft fingertips.

"All the time in the world. I have nothing else to occupy me."

She pinched him. "Do you think I came here as Lylthia only to let you caress me? Korython has spoken to the gods, asking their help. That's the only reason I'm on your bed."

"Korython can wait. I can't."

Lylthia wriggled closer, stroking him, but she muttered, "We have to be away from Urgrik at once. No, stop that! I'm serious. The gods have sent me to help you."

Niall grinned. "And I thank the gods. Now the best way you can help me is...."

"You're impossible," she whispered, but she did not move away.

Long afterward, as they lay side by side, with Niall holding Lylthia close to him, she murmured, "We really should be on our way. Already the darkness has lessened."

"Mmmmm. Where are we going?"

"Northward, beyond the Uryllian Mountains."

Niall blinked. "There is nothing north of those mountains— except for the Dead Lands, that is."

"We are going to the Dead Lands, Niall. Once—many ages ago— those lands were alive and flourishing. Korython was worshiped in those lands. His shrine—what's left of it, that is—is there, and it is to that shrine we must go."

Niall kissed her soft lips. "Stay here. Be my love. It's a long ride northward of the Uryllian Mountains."

"That's why we must start now, without delay." She rose up to peer down into his eyes. "Or have you forgotten Thayya?"

He shrugged. "A mere woman. What can she do?"

"She serves Xollabar."

Niall scowled. "Another god? Pah! Can't you gods settle your own affairs without dragging us into your quarrels?"

Lylthia kissed him. "What would the gods be, without worshipers? Besides, if it weren't for the quarrels between the gods, you might not see me so often."

"There is that," he nodded. "But—"

Her lips silenced his. After a time, she murmured, "Are you ready to listen? I have a tale to tell you of a man named Sosalion, who lived when the Dead Lands were young, and who worshiped Korython with a great love.

"Sosalion was a poor man who made his living by making swords. He was a great sword-maker, the finest in the land. But others were not as fortunate as he. He knew many poor people, people who were in need. He begged Korython to help them—and one night as he prayed, Korython appeared to him.

"Korython would help him to aid those poor people by leaving a golden statue of himself. That statue would grant all the wishes which Sosalion would make to it."

Lylthia slid from the bed to pick up the leather pouch which Niall carried at his sword-belt She brought out the statue and placed it on a nearby table. Niall propped himself on an elbow and eyed it.

Lylthia said slowly, "If you make a wish to the god, your wish will be granted."

Niall grinned. "Come back to bed."

Lylthia stamped her foot. "Be serious! Can you imagine what might happen if this statue were to fall into the wrong hands?"

"The man—if he was a man—from whom I took this statue had been turned into dust. Possession of the statue didn't do him much good."

The girl sighed. "It was Xollabar,who turned Gruffon the priest into dust. Xollabar—whom Thayya serves. Xollabar wants that statue. With it in his possession, he can force Korython to serve him. And—Xollabar is evil. Evil!"

Niall sat on the edge of the bed. "All right. So Korython gave Sosalion this statue."

"And for the rest of his life, Sosalion used the power of the statue wisely. Always he asked favors for others, never for himself. And the god granted those requests.

"When Sosalion died, the statue disappeared. It was never seen again for thousands of years. And then Gruffon came upon it. How, I am not sure. But Gruffon used it selfishly, to acquire wealth and power for himself.

"He came at last into Urgrik, and here he intended to take power over the king, Lurlyr Manakor, to possess himself of his kingdom. It was then that Xollabar struck—wanting the statue for himself."

Niall sighed. "I found it instead of Thayya. And now Xollabar will be after me."

"Ah! Now you understand the need for haste, why we must return the statue to Korython.

Niall grumbled but rose to his feet, reaching for his clothing. He had learned that what Lylthia told him was always true. He began to dress, with Lylthia nodding her approval.

Chapter Two

Dawn was breaking in the east, beyond the Kalbarthian Mountains as they rode along the narrow road which twisted northward from Urgrik past the Malagon Forests. Niall sat the saddle of his big gray stallion while Lylthia moved easily to the cantering stride of a black mare.

Once or twice, Niall twisted to look behind him at the rooftops and towers of Urgrik. There was little to see, for in this early dawn hour, men and women were merely stirring from their beds. No one had seen them leave the city, there had been no lurker in the shadows to carry word to Thayya.

Behind them a brown stallion came at the canter, with wine-bags and food-sacks hastily assembled by Niall bouncing to its hoof-beats. Together with those necessary items the horse carried a powerful horn bow and a quiver filled with war-arrows. Niall meant to be well armed on this ride.

They went swiftly, easily along the dirt path. The dust they stirred up settled after them within moments, so that anyone watching from Urgrik would scarcely see it. Even with this, Niall was troubled.

"How can we hide from a god?" he asked Lylthia as they rode.

"We can't. But Xollabar has his limits, too, you know. He is not one of the Primary Gods, but rather one like Korython, with certain limited powers."

Niall grunted. "If I'm helping the gods, the gods ought to be helping me."

Lylthia smiled. "Are you sure they are not helping, Niall? We are riding toward the Dead Lands, and we are alive and well."

Niall sniffed deeply of the cool air blowing off the mountains far ahead. That air put new life into his veins; it exhilarated him. His hand touched his sword and he thought to himself that he might be ready for whatever it was Xollabar might choose to hurl at him.

All that day they rode, pausing only beside a little stream to eat their meat and bread and drink a little of the wine. Several times Niall would leave the stream to cross to a high hill from which to scan the land over which they had traveled. He saw nothing but the waving grasses and hard brown earth, and rocks.

"We seem to be safe enough," he grinned at Lylthia as they mounted up again.

To his surprise, she shook her head. "Not yet, my lover. Xollabar is searching for us. I can feel it. Ride on, faster!"

They galloped now, the horses running easily, seemingly without effort. This was a wild, almost uninhabited land through which they went. Far off the tracks of the caravans that moved from city to city, only a few wild men or hermits dwelt here. The sky overhead seemed bigger than it was in the city, it stretched from horizon to horizon.

Toward nightfall, they encamped on the slope of a low hill bordering a southern edge of the Uryllian Mountains. As he was about to lower himself from the saddle, Niall stood in the stirrups for a last glance backward.

Instantly he froze.

Lylthia noticed his tension and asked, "What is it?"

"Yonder, something black and cone-like comes!"

His arm swung her up so that she could put a foot in his stirrup and stare where he directed her. His arm that was about her sensed the rigidity of her muscles.

Niall could see the thing more clearly now as it swirled across the grasslands, coming closer. It was much like an ordinary dust-devil when the wind whips up dry dust and swirls it around and around, moving it across the ground. Yet this thing was of an ebony blackness and it exuded evil, an evil so intense Niall could feel his hairs ride up at the back of his neck.

It came on, but more slowly now, as though it were aware that it had been seen. It was cautious, was that moving darkness, yet still it advanced.

Niall growled, "Let me shoot an arrow at it."

Lylthia dropped to the ground as Niall lowered himself. He moved toward the brown stallion and lifted off his horn bow. Muscles bulged as he strung it; then he lifted an arrow from the quiver still tied to the stallion.

The bow bent. The arrow flew toward the oncoming blackness. It touched that blackness, flared upward, and fell to the earth as a heap of dust. The swirling darkness came on, faster now. Soon it would be upon them.

Lylthia smiled faintly and said, "Select another arrow."

As it came from the quiver, she leaned forward, put her fingers to the arrowhead, whispered softly. Niall saw the arrowhead glow whitely, then fade out to its normal color.

He put the arrow to the bowstring, drew back the great horn bow. Fast flew that arrow, so swiftly that it seemed almost to disappear. Then he saw it again, just as it drove deep into the darkness.

From far off, there was a high-pitched scream, a cry of mortal agony. Instantly the dust devil—or whatever it was, thought Niall —

disappeared, collapsing into nothingness.

Lylthia laughed softly. "Xollabar will not like that. It stung him badly. He will be more careful from now on."

Niall growled low in his throat. He did not like the gods—excepting always for Emelkartha who was also Lylthia—for he knew their ways were capricious, with little regard for human desires, and what the gods wanted, they took.

Still! As he looked around him now he saw nothing but open sky and great mountains, with a stretch of grassland below them reaching far away toward the distant river. The air was cool and clean, and it felt good to be alive. His eyes studied Lylthia as she bent above a little fire she had made. She was putting on steaks for their meal, humming softly to herself.

He enjoyed these interludes when he and the goddess in human form were together. He sighed. If he had to do battle with some god to have her come to him like this—why, then, he welcomed that fight.

He reached out and pulled her upward to him, putting his arms about her and holding her softness to his body. Her green eyes looked up at him, filled with sudden laughter.

"So, then. You think you have driven away Xollabar, do you? And that he will run back to his own worlds and leave you alone?"

"I care not for Xollabar. It's only you I care about."

Lylthia nestled against him, hugging him. This was a nice sentiment; she liked this devotion of Niall. Yet he must not become too complacent.

"There are other dangers ahead—"

He kissed her, interrupting her words, and Lylthia found that she did not care to warn him any longer. His kiss and his strong arms did things to her human body that she enjoyed very much. Pah! Time enough to worry about Xollabar when the evil god made his next attempt at them.

She even forgot about the cooking steaks.

Yet later, after they had eaten and were lying together on a thick blanket, she stirred in his arms and whispered, "There are dangerous days before us, Niall. This isn't the easy trip you seem to think it."

236

"We drove away Xollabar."

"But only for a little while. He will be back. Aye, and others from Urgrik."

Niall turned his head. "Others?"

"Have you forgotten Thayya and those men who serve her? They will be coming after us. Indeed, they may be ahead of us by now."

"Let them come. They are human, they can die by my sword's bite." He shook himself. "It's only the gods that worry me."

Lylthia shook her head. She was worried and vaguely troubled, for she knew the powers of Xollabar. But as Niall's arm tightened about her, she told herself to enjoy this moment. Time enough tomorrow and the next day to brood about the dangers that lay ahead.

An hour after the sun lifted above the Baklakanian Desert far to the east, they were on the way, picking a path along a boulder-strewn way that led upward, always upward, toward the heights of the Uryllian Mountains.

The higher they climbed, the colder grew the winds. Those winds swirled out of the far north, sweeping across fields of snow and ice and carrying the cold with them. Niall drew his fur parka tighter and saw to it that Lylthia wore the one he had brought for her.

Between slabs of granite and stone they made their way, seeking a path leading between huge boulders and jutting rocks, steadily riding higher. The wind howled now, whistling at times, and its fury grew so great that the horses and riders kept their heads low against its force.

It grew harder to breathe. The windy blasts whipped the air away from them; sometimes they had to turn their heads in order to gulp at air. Many times they stopped in the lee of some great rock to rest the horses, and occasionally Niall walked ahead to guide them over a narrow path, on one side of which the stone wall fell away to a drop of more than two thousand feet.

In time, they came to a narrow pass between two great rock outcroppings. They rode together into that pass and then drew rein. Before them was a valley of green grass and magnificent trees, through which little rivulets of water ran. It lay below them— primordial, as though it dated back to the very beginnings of their world.

"The glen of the gods," whispered Lylthia. "I thought it had died—along with the Dead Lands—ages ago."

Niall glanced at her. "The glen of the gods?"

"Here it was that the gods came to play and romp, long and long ago. It is a wild, sweet place, with air that has the bite of frost in it, yet with all the warmth of the summer sun. It is protected by the rocks and the high mountains so that heat gathers here and remains even in the coldest times of winter."

Niall grinned. "Then let's camp there awhile."

Lylthia frowned, glancing about her. "I'm not sure we ought. See the high hills on all sides? It is a natural hollow. We could be trapped down there."

He hooted. 'By whom? You worry overmuch, my love."

She shrugged, let him lead the way, following after. Yet her eyes went this way and that, very warily, as if she sought to learn whether any other living thing besides themselves were here in this remote spot.

They moved down a gentle incline. As Niall studied the valley, he told himself that he had never seen a fairer land. The lower he went toward its grasslands, the warmer the air became, so that he loosened the fur garment he wore.

His eyes saw the prints of animal feet here and there. This would be a good place for a man to come, to hunt and live for a time without caring about other men or their affairs. He turned in the saddle to say something of this to Lylthia and saw her shivering.

"Here there is everything a man needs," he told her.

Her green eyes slid toward him. "Here also is deadly danger. I can almost smell it." She shook herself. "Yet I am tired. It may be as you say. We shall rest a while."

Neither of them saw the cloud that came slowly across the skies. A small white cloud it was, yet it grew in size as it neared the hidden valley.

Niall was stripping the saddle off the horses when Lylthia cried out, pointing. He swung about, stared where her finger aimed. "A cloud, no more," he growled.

Yet he continued to eye it, as did the woman, and as he did, tiny prickles of worry ran down his spine. Ah, but it was only a cloud. Not a black storm cloud but a tiny one, all white and—yes! It seemed almost to glow. But that was probably because it was catching the rays of the sun.

"All-Father," Lylthia was whispering, "hear my plea! There is danger here, where we are, in the playground of the gods! Xollabar comes. I can feel it! Sense it!"

The white cloud grew in size even as it seemed to sweep down toward them. Niall felt his skin crawl. No normal cloud would act in such a way.

Pale white lightnings suddenly stabbed downward.

Lylthia screamed and threw herself flat. In an instant, Niall followed her example. All about them those pale white streaks of lightning were stabbing, stabbing. They sizzled as they drove ground-ward and he could smell ozone.

Everywhere those lightnings were stabbing, as though the cloud were blinded and could not see its target. Soon enough, those bolts would hit him or Lylthia. Frantically his eyes searched the grasslands.

There was nowhere to hide. Oh, there was a cave or two, here and there in the cliff walls, but to reach them one would have to run across the grass, and the lightnings would be sure to find anyone stupid enough to do that.

Yet, to remain here meant that they would die!

"And Xollabar will get the golden statue," he muttered.

"Great Father God, aid us! Hear my plea! Grant us the relief of your powers!" Lylthia begged.

Niall was staring upward, his teeth clenched, his body braced against the shock of a lightning bolt. It was he who saw the redness falling from far above.

"Look! High in the sky—above the cloud!" he called.

A sob tore its way from Lylthia's throat. "The All-Father has heard me. He grants my wish!"

Lightnings hit the ground a few feet from where he lay, and Niall growled. He rasped out an oath and sprang upward, lifting out his sword.

"Fool!" Lylthia screamed. "Drop the blade!"

He let go of it, but as it started to fall, a bolt of that pale golden energy hit it. Blood-drinker seemed bathed in an aureate splendor. For a few moments it hung there in the air, held by a great force. Then the golden lightnings fell away and the sword plummeted to the ground.

Lylthia lifted an arm, rising from the ground to join him. "See there, in the sky!"

The redness that Niall had seen was rain. He knew that now, as it fell upon the cloud. Vast hissings rose, just as hissings rise from white-hot iron plunged into water. The red rain was falling upon the white cloud and through it, covering it everywhere.

Faintly, from so far away that Niall could not be sure he heard correctly, came a great scream. That scream tore at his nerves, for in it was great anguish and desolation.

Beside him, Lylthia laughed softly. "Xollabar suffers! Aye, that red rain stings him! Perhaps now he will not attempt to stop us on our way into the Dead Lands."

Niall grunted. If he knew anything about gods, Xollabar would be even more angry. And Niall did not care to confront angry gods.

Chapter Three

For two days they remained in the glen of the gods, swimming in the tiny lake it boasted, feasting on the hares that Niall shot with his war-arrows. Gone was the cloud, gone was Xollabar. Warm was the breeze, pleasant was the sight of green grass and bluish water.

Even Lylthia lost a little of her worry and joined him in his swims, in his walks that explored all the corners of the valley. From time to time she would walk off by herself and stand, as though listening to something faint and far away. Niall never bothered her at those moments; he assumed she was communicating with the gods and goddesses she knew, or perhaps with the All-Father himself.

He was content to have her with him and to be alive.

"I suppose we ought to be moving on," he said one morning after they had eaten. He said it hopefully, almost asking that Lylthia would murmur that there was no hurry.

She disappointed him. "Xollabar is an angry god now, Niall. He has hidden himself away in his worlds and he plans your destruction." She sighed. "I wish I knew his thoughts."

"No need to worry about him any more. The All-Father has pulled his fangs."

Lylthia shook her head. "You don't know Xollabar. He is plotting something.... something. I wish I knew what it is. But we must be getting on toward the Dead Lands. Once we turn over his statue to Korython we will have defeated him. But until then...."

She shrugged. Niall did not have to look at her to know that she was badly worried.

They moved out of the glen of the gods by the middle of the day, climbing higher and higher into the mountains that surrounded it The winds blew with the chill of the polar regions in their every touch, and once again the riders wore their fur-lined robes.

The horses plodded on, heads down. Niall and Lylthia swayed in their saddles. The steady motion of their mounts, combined with the cold, rendered them only half-awake. They had no eyes for the path they traveled; they let their stallions pick it for them.

It was Niall who cried out first, straightening in the saddle and loosening his furred cape to stare around him at the flat, rocky landscape where they stood.

Gone were the mountains, gone was the cold. Instead, they were in a hazy, reddish world, where the air seemed thick to the nostrils, where there was no sun in the sky, no clouds, nothing but this pale redness.

"Where are we, in the All-Father's name?' Lylthia whispered, "It cannot be!"

Something in her voice made Niall look at her more closely, so that he saw something of the awe and terror within her. She was shaking, her hands trembling so much they could scarcely hold the reins of her mount.

"What is it? Where are we?" he demanded.

"How could it have happened?" she wailed. "How could I have slept and not been aware? The horses walked where they saw easier going—and Xollabar opened the way for them!"

She lifted her hands to move the fallen black hair from before her eyes. Her face was strained, a mask of disbelief and fear.

Niall growled and put his hand to his sword-hilt, but the girl shook her head. "Steel will not avail us here. Nothing will! Look around you. What do you see?"

"An empty land. Just rocks and pebbles."

"Aye! A lost world. A world belonging to Xollabar. He has trapped us neatly. And I slept!"

Niall growled, looking to left and right yet seeing nothing but this flat, dead land. "We have mistaken the path, that's all. We can find our way out as we found our way in."

"Look around you! Do you see mountains? Anything at all but rocks? No, no, Niall. We have crossed the voids between the worlds —aided by Xollabar. He has us now."

"What can he do?"

Laughter boomed from somewhere. It was all about them, echoing from the air, from the ground. Niall lifted out his sword, realizing as he did so how inadequate it was.

"Put down the statue," the new voice bellowed. "Put down the statue! Put it down and live. Keep it—and die!"

"We keep it," Niall snarled.

Silence descended around them, a silence so intense it seemed to hurt their ears. Niall looked at Lylthia, who stared around her as if seeking inspiration from the air. Twice her mouth opened, as though she would speak, but each time she frowned and shook her head.

"You are foolish, my Niall," she said suddenly. "Give Xollabar the golden statue. After all, what good is it to you? Besides, you were about to return it to Korython, anyhow."

"But—"

Lylthia smiled at him, a reassuring smile. But her eyes were not smiling: They were hard and cold. Even as he watched, she rose in her stirrups and bugled a call into the red-tinted air.

"A bargain, Xollabar! The statue—for our lives!"

There was a silence; then Niall heard a gigantic chuckle. "What care I for your lives? Take them, with my blessing. Only leave the statue!"

Lylthia nodded, smiling faintly. She stretched out her hand toward Niall. "Give me the statue, darling. I have traded it for our lives."

"But you are a goddess. Xollabar could not kill you."

"He could kill you. And I will not have that happen. No, don't argue. Let me have the statue."

Niall grumbled under his breath, but he took the statue out of his belt-pouch and handed it to Lylthia. He watched as the girl stepped out of her saddle to the ground. She knelt and put the statue on the pebbles.

"There, now. It is done." She lifted her head and called, "Xollabar! We have fulfilled our part of the bargain. Fulfill yours!"

Almost instantly, Niall found himself sitting astride his mount on the southerly slope of one of the Uryllian Mountains. The air was cold here, but not as cold as the air high up there on the peaks, past which he and Lylthia had come.

He turned in the saddle, seeing the other two horses—but no Lylthia. Fear touched him, freezing his heart. Had Xollabar betrayed them? Had he—kept the girl? Anger gripped Niall, made him groan and curse.

"Xollabar!" he bellowed. "If you harm her I shall follow you through all your hells and kill you!"

Be not alarmed, Niall. Carry on—as though I were with you!

His rage slowly faded. He did not know where Lylthia was, but it did not matter, now that the calmness of her thought-voice told him she was well. Niall straightened in the saddle, staring down at the distant Dead Lands that he could see faint and far away. It was several days' travel to those lands, but he would go there, if it was what Lylthia wanted.

"She knows better than I how to deal with gods," he growled.

With a lighter heart, he toed the stallion downward along the narrow path before him. It was still annoying him that he must go alone, but he knew that Lylthia—in her other-self role as Emelkartha—would be keeping an eye on him.

Niall rode easily, studying the far lands into which he was moving. Long and long ago, they had been fertile, those far reaches of barren ground. There had lived a race of men called the Granagors, reddish of skin and very warlike. The Granagors had worshiped Korython, and had built a magnificent temple to his name.

Sosalion, to whom Korython had given the statue, had been a Granagor.

Over the ages since the Granagors had flourished here, what had happened to that golden statue? Niall reflected on that as he swayed in the high-peaked saddle, as his eyes went back and forth along the path he rode. He scowled, telling himself as he rode that he would be wise to forget these quarrels between the gods.

Still, if he did that, he would not see so much of Lylthia.

Ha! Where was Lylthia now? She had left him, of course. She was watching over him, he knew that; yet it seemed to him, from what he knew of her as Emelkartha, that she would also be watching over that golden statue.

When he was almost down off the mountainside, he made out a dust trail off to the west. Riders were galloping there, moving swiftly, with loose reins and jabbing spurs. Niall scowled. Could there be others on their way to the ruined temple of Korython?

Ah, but—why?

He had been headed there to turn over his golden statue to the god. But Xollabar had stolen the statue. Xollabar would not be likely to take the statue to the old temple of his rival, surely! That made no sense.

Niall stiffened in the saddle.

Might Xollabar have some devilish scheme in mind that required the statue to be placed where the ancient temple once stood? Would that fact, in some manner of the gods, give him added power over Korython? Niall wondered what had put that idea into his head.

As he galloped his big stallion, he loosened his sword Blood-drinker in its scabbard. An inner feeling told him he was going to have to fight soon.

Niall grinned, as he always did when there was the prospect of a good fight ahead. Let the gods quarrel among themselves; he was always most at home when steel blades were clanging and blows were given and received.

There were a score of riders off to his left, he saw as their paths converged. One of them was smaller than the others. A woman? But what woman would ride with men such as those, who seemed to be the sweepings off some riverside dock?

Thayya! Of course. It had to be!

Niall grinned. She was a beauty, that girl. Was she also a priestess of the god Xollabar? Was it in answer to his call that she and those riders were racing so hard? She had tried to bribe him to give up that golden statue. Perhaps now she was here to see Xollabar triumph over Korython.

They came closer, closer.

They could see him, now. They were shouting, yanking out swords and waving them. Niall knew that the odds were too great, even for him, and yet he would not run from them.

Ha! Why not run—if he could make his running a weapon?

He angled his steed to one side so that it would appear that he was seeking to escape. They would understand that. Already he could hear their howls of exultation, and above them the shrill voice of Thayya.

"After him! Do not let him live! It is the order of the god Xollabar!"

They came for him as he knew they would, two men out in front, on the faster horses. The others were strung out behind those two, and racing hard.

Niall slowed his stallion just a little to let the two front-runners catch up with him. As they did, he brought out Blood-drinker, whirled the stallion and charged them. Those two men came on, shouting exultantly.

No man in all this land was the equal of Niall of the Far Travels with a sword in his big hand. He swung Blood-drinker once, again, and two headless corpses rolled from their saddles.

Niall wheeled and ran again, looking back over his shoulder. They were following after him, well strung out now. He held the big stallion back, to let some of them catch up to him. Let them overtake him. It was what he wanted.

He turned at last, swinging his great blade, knocking the swords of the others aside. His point drove into a chest, lopped off an arm, swung again to slash through a neck. As he fought, Niall bellowed out the war-cry of his native Norumbria. Few men in this comer of his world had ever heard that savage scream.

As though in echo to that cry, Thayya was shouting, "Kill him! Kill him! He must not be allowed to live!"

His stallion was tired. It had come far and it had run fast this day. Under him, Niall felt the great horse stumble as it sought to turn. Niall grinned coldly. They would overcome him, and there was no way one man—even as great a fighter as Niall of the Far Travels—could persevere against thirteen or fourteen men.

Yet he battled on. Emelkartha! How they would pay! They would die, as many as he could kill, and each of the others would bear his blade-mark until the day he died!

A sword hit his shoulder. Another slammed against the side of his head. Niall reeled in the saddle just as a sword stabbed at his chest....

Chapter Four

It was night. Niall lay almost lifeless on the hard rocks and felt life flow back into him, slowly. Vaguely, he knew that he was wounded. He was lying on his back, his eyes were open, and he was staring up at the blackness of the heavens.

He moved and groaned. There was dried blood all over him, and the pain of his wounds stabbed into him deeply. Under his breath he cursed softly, trying to move. It was useless. He could scarcely turn over.

He was thirsty, too. There was no water here in the Barren Lands. There had been water in the skins on his stallion, but the horse was gone, probably taken by the men who had been with Thayya.

Niall closed his eyes and slept.

He woke to the blaze of hot sunlight on him. He gritted his teeth and made it to his knees. Blinking, he looked around him at the empty plain. But, no! It was not empty. There was something moving out there.

It was coming closer.

Ah. Now he could make it out. It was his stallion, trotting toward him. Niall grinned. He was not dead yet. Maybe he was too badly wounded to walk, but there was a water-bag on his horse, and his horse could carry him.

He waited until the stallion came nosing at him, then he caught at a stirrup and using it as a crutch, got to his feet. The world swung around him dizzily then, and he had to grab and hold on.

It took him some time, but he finally managed to get a toe in the stirrup and claw his way upward to the saddle. He reached for the water-skin and drank deep. The water revived him a little, and he toed the horse, making it walk onward toward where the ruins of Korython's temple lay in the midst of the Barren Lands.

Where was Emelkartha? Where—Lylthia?

He was still very weak. Twice he fell asleep to the swaying motion of his stallion; once, he almost fell from the saddle. He grinned wryly, telling himself that he was not strong enough to fight, that if he came upon Thayya and her soldiers now, they would certainly kill him.

Of course, they thought him dead already. Still, there was life in him, to be nursed along until the time came when he might have to fight. He thought of the thousands of men in the army of Urgrik who would would gladly have followed him into these Barren Lands and grinned wryly. This task—whatever it was—was up to him alone.

Not alone, Niall! I am watching!

"I'm almost dead," he growled, yet he was thrilled to discover that Emelkartha had not deserted him.

It was as if he heard her gasp, then. He felt eyes upon him—eyes he could not see—and fancied that he heard a faint cry.

You are hurt! Almost unto death! Yet I knew not!

Terror was in that thought-voice—and raging fury!

The world shifted under Niall. He felt it slide away, tilt even more—and then it steadied. There was heat around him, awful heat, but there were soft voices crying out and girls running toward him, to help him from the saddle and half-carry him toward a couch.

Emelkartha was there, regal and proud, but there was pity in her eyes, and a great softness. She came toward Niall where he lay and knelt beside him, touching his forehead with her hand.

"Here you will mend, my darling. Here in this forecourt of one of my Eleven Hells, you can rest and be nursed back to health."

She clapped her hands and girls came running. Niall looked at them and grinned. They were all lovely, young, and their bodies took the breath away with their beauty.

Emelkartha saw his interest and frowned. "They are to bring you back to full health, Niall. Nothing more!"

He chuckled. "Beside you, my darling, they are pale shadows."

The goddess went on scowling for a moment, then laughed. "See that they remain only shadows!" But she leaned forward and kissed him, and Niall knew that he would live.

He never knew how long it was that he remained in that steaming room, with his wounds bandaged and with unguents applied to them. He slept and rested, and as he did, magical antidotes worked their cure. Always, the girls were on call to aid him.

He saw no more of Emelkartha; he reasoned that she was busy with her own problems. He waxed in strength, his wounds no longer troubled him, and now a restlessness began forming inside him. He would draw his sword and flex his muscles with it, and begin to wish for the more familiar world he knew.

What kept her? Why was Emelkartha not here with him? Niall began to chafe at his inactivity.

And then one time when he was asleep he woke to the touch of her lips on his. Her eyes laughed down at him. "Slug-a-bed," she breathed. "The time has come to send you on my mission."

"What mission is that?"

"Look—and know!"

The room in which he lay faded from view. He was staring down into ancient ruins. He saw the little golden god resting on an altar, before which was standing Thayya, her arms outstretched. Behind her were those hired killers he had fought. Niall grinned when he saw that each one of them was bandaged.

She calls to Korython and—Korython must answer!

Slowly, the god was forming. There at the altar, where he had been worshiped so long ago, he was rising into being. His outline was tenuous, but it was becoming stronger.

"Korython must obey—because he is present in the golden statue. He is helpless against the power of Xollabar as long as that condition exists!"

Niall frowned. "And I can help?"

He stared at the god Korython. It seemed that the god's outlines were fainter now. As he muttered something of this Emelkartha nodded.

"Korython plays for time, time in which the other gods and goddesses—myself included—can come to his aid. Alone, he would not be able to last too long, since Xollabar has power over that statue. But with our help—and yours..."

Her voice faded. Niall growled, "Aye! Now we come to it. What part do I play?"

Emelkartha nestled close, hugging him. "You fight those men of Thayya's—and Thayya herself, if need be. We will keep Xollabar busy."

The scene faded, and Niall shook himself. Emelkartha was nestled in his arms, but he was vaguely uncomfortable. He was used to Lylthia, not to the goddess herself.

"You would wish for my other self?" she whispered.

Niall chuckled. "I'd be more comfortable."

"Of course you would. You are used to grabbing Lylthia, pawing her, kissing her and bedding her as though she were some common wench."

"She never objected," Niall grinned.

Emelkartha sighed. "Here in my Eleven Hells I am adored and worshiped. It's fun sometimes to be in human guise, to be pawed and hugged and kissed."

She pushed away from him. "But we sit here while time grows short for Korython. It is time to be leaving."

Emelkartha stood, catching his hand, drawing him to his feet. Niall wore his chain-mail and his fur kaunake; his sword and dagger were belted at his side. Emelkartha put her hand to his forehead, and—

Niall stood on a rocky wasteland, aware that a wind was blowing and aware also that he could hear chanting by a female voice. The wind blew steadily, the chanting seemed to grow in strength. Niall saw broken columns and battered bits of what had once been temple walls.

A woman stood before what had been an altar, long and long ago. On that altar stood the golden statue of the god. Behind Thayya were her mercenaries, staring, watching what was about to take place.

Forward, Niall! Attack!

He grinned, remembering how those men before him had wounded him, left him for dead. He owed them for that! He raced forward, drawing out Blood-drinker and his Orravian dagger. His war-boots made hardly a sound on the rocky ground.

But they made enough sound to alert one or two of the hired swords who had ridden here with Thayya. They turned, those men, and their eyes went wide at sight of this man, whom they had thought to be lying dead many miles behind them.

One of them shouted hoarsely.

At his cry, the others turned, but Niall was upon them even as they swung about, and his blade licked out to slash through a man's neck. Even as he felt his steel bite deep, Niall yanked free his sword and drove it at a second man.

The odds against him were great, but at first his enemies thought they were dealing with a dead man raised to a mummery of life by some magic—so that in those first few moments Niall gained a great advantage.

One man fell, and then another. Niall was like a savage beast, springing here and there, his sword-point stabbing into a throat or its edge slashing downward across a shoulder or an arm. He growled as he slashed, and every once in a while he would snarl like an enraged tiger.

He became vaguely aware that the chanting had stopped, that Thayya had turned and was regarding him with wide eyes in which were mixed terror and superstitious horror.

Niall felt an anger beating down about him—gigantic fury that seemed to assault him with maddened rage. Yet something shielded him from that awful displeasure. Somehow, Emelkartha had thrown a corner of her cloak about him.

Thayya had turned now and was chanting with renewed power. It was almost as though the god Xollabar were entering into her, endowing her with his demoniac strength.

And in answer to that chanting—

Korython was appearing more fully, towering above the altar where stood the golden statue. It seemed to Niall—even as he fought—that Korython was also fighting, fighting to prevent himself from being drawn into this world, to be made the slave of Xollabar.

There were few mercenaries left now. One by one they had fallen to Niall who had fought as he had rarely fought before, and never against such human odds.

Only two men were left now.

Niall leaped, his sword flashed. One man dropped, the other turned to flee. Niall hurled his Orravian dagger, saw it sink to the pommel in the back of that last man.

Then the Far-Traveler leaped again.

Straight for Thayya he drove, his arms spread wide. The girl was in the middle of her chanting when he bowled into her, snapping off her words and carrying her to the ground. His fist hit her jaw and she slumped.

Kneeling above her, Niall felt the air grow hot. It was as though all the many hells had spilled out their glowing fires. Sweat oozed from his pores, and it grew hard to breathe. Within that almost fiery atmosphere, he sensed a titanic struggle taking place.

Dimly he could see Xollabar, dark and sinister, towering high above the dead floor of the once-great temple. His many eyes were boring downward—not at Niall, but at something beyond him.

It was Korython!

The god was writhing, twisting, seeking to avoid the tug of something that seemed far more powerful than itself. It was out of its abode by now, and seemingly helpless in this world. Niall saw that it sought vainly to avoid being drawn into the golden statue.

Now, Niall! Now!

He leaped from the fallen priestess toward the little statue. His great sword swung upward, glinting in the sunlight. Xollabar bellowed with utter fury.

Then the sword was cleaving downward, slashing at the golden statue. As it drove toward it, Niall saw his blade shine and glimmer as though with inward light. That light danced and sang along his steel—

His edge struck the statue! Cleaved through it! Xollabar screamed.

In that moment of his screaming, Korython leaped forth. No longer was the god fearful. Instead, it waxed even larger. Spread were its arms, or what served it for arms. Straight for Xollabar it drove.

Niall crouched on his knees beside that which had been the altar to Korython. On that altar lay the two fragments of the golden statue. Above him, the two great gods were doing battle, and the very air seemed almost to cry out at the fury of that assault.

Korython drove Xollabar back. Ever backward the evil god went, as though it sought to escape. But Korython pursued too relentlessly for that. Xollabar was caught and held, and though it fought savagely, it seemed to Niall that Xollabar was weakening swiftly.

And now Korython was dragging Xollabar toward the ancient stone altar. Xollabar struggled, but was too weak to oppose. To the altar Xollabar was drawn, then forced upon it.

Held on that altar! Helpless!

From above streamed a golden bolt, so vivid that Niall was momentarily blinded. He cried out, his arm going to shield his eyes. No need to fear, Niall. I protect you!

Then it was over. Whatever there was of Xollabar was gone. Devoured, in some strange fashion which Niall could not comprehend.

Silence lay across the old temple. Niall staggered to his feet, stared at the dead bodies, then at Thayya, who lay unconscious at his feet. The gods had come—and gone.

He shook himself. Well, he had done what they asked. He had fought and triumphed this day; he had stopped Thayya. Something assured him that he had eased the way for Korython by weakening Xollabar just enough.

Thayya stirred, opening her eyes. She looked up at Niall, sat up, stared about her. A gathering horror dawned in her eyes. No words

252

were needed to tell her what had happened. She could see the stained altar where Xollabar had writhed in its last moments.

Now she rose slowly to her feet, backing away from Niall. She turned and fled across the ground, toward and then between the corpses of the mercenaries who had come here with her. Past them she ran, then halted.

She bent over the body of the last man Niall had killed, lifting from his back the Orravian dagger. Niall shouted and ran to her, but he was too late.

Thayya drove that dagger to the hilt between her breasts. When Niall came up to her, she was dead.

A soft voice said, "It is better so. By her death, she has expiated her evil."

Lylthia came striding toward him, hips gracefully swinging. As he watched her approach, Niall growled, "I'm tired of these gods who fight among themselves—and drag me into their battles."

"Yet they are grateful to you. Xollabar sought to draw Korython into the golden statue completely. In that way he would have had dominion over him forever. You helped prevent it. Korython is grateful."

Niall eyed her suspiciously. "How grateful?"

Lylthia smiled teasingly. "He has filled the glen of the gods with gifts for you, with vessels of wine and hampers filled with good things to eat—so that we may go there and live for a little while." She hesitated. "Unless you'd rather not, of course."

He whooped and ran toward her. "Silly girl! Why are we standing here talking? Race you to our horses—and then to the glen of the gods!"

Lylthia tried to get to her horse, but Niall caught and kissed her before she could make it.

THE COMING OF THE SWORD

It has been recorded, in the lost scrolls of Caractos the Scribe, of which only fragments now exist, that... from the ice-world of Norumbria, many ages ago, there came a youth named Niall, son of Thorkon the Mighty, who was destined to roam the world as he knew it, and to whom was to be given the appellation, the Far-Traveler...

For many days he had trotted across the ice field, always straining his gaze ahead, ever seeking the figure of the man he hunted. He was close now, so close that he needed no longer to stare at the ground in search of footprints. For there ahead, revealed in the weak sunlight of this northernmost region, was the man, Gunthar.

Niall grinned wolfishly. Soon would Gunthar face the death he deserved for the attempted rape of lovely young Althia, who was sister to Niall and daughter of Thorkon the Mighty. In less than an hour, Niall would be up with him, would draw his sword and take the vengeance that was due his family.

Niall shifted the white bearskin which covered his side shoulders. Under that skin he wore a mail shirt, covered by a leather kaunake. Around his middle was a broad leather belt from which hung a dagger and a sword. Over his shoulder was his horn hunting bow and a quiver of long war arrows.

Niall disdained the arrows and the bow. He wanted Gunthar face to face, to know — before cold steel killed him — what it meant to assault the daughter of Thorkon the Mighty. Niall trotted faster; his long, thickly thewed legs ate up the ground that lay between him and the man he hunted.

Suddenly the ground under his boots shifted, rolled, began to rise and fall rhythmically, as might the waves of the Cold Sea. Niall staggered and grunted.

"May the gods grant I catch him in time," he muttered.

He ran faster, and yanked out his sword. As though the still-distant man heard that scrape of blade against scabbard, he looked back.

Gunthar had moved into a passage with no exit; to one side was the eternal ice of a mighty glacier, to the other a massive rock wall rising upward to an unscalable height.

It might be that Gunthar realized the futility of further flight, for now he stopped, turned and drew his own sword. Niall ran toward his quarry, shouting in exultation.

The ground still rolled and pitched, yet Niall ran across it swiftly, balancing himself. He was used to the plunging, churning deck of a longboat on the Cold Sea, and this motion of the ground was not unlike the roll of giant waves.

Gunthar waited, pale and somewhat grim. He knew Niall, knew the ferocity of his swordplay, understood that few men could stand against him — without luck. Gunthar prayed to Loki, god of mischief, hoping that the god would come to him in his moment of need.

Niall hurled himself forward, lips parting in a snarl of fury. His blade swept around, clanged against the weapon Gunthar lifted to parry its deadly sweep. Steel sang. Almost instantly, Niall was driving in again, beating back that sword which opposed him. He drove Gunthar back on his heels, making him give ground.

The earth shuddered beneath them. Ice cracked. There was a muted rumble off to one side. It was as if the very world shared his fury, Niall thought, as he beat down the sword which faced him.

"This is the day you die, Gunthar," he growled.

"I did no harm to Althia," the other panted. "She screamed, and others came to stop me. I fled..."

"You fled to your death! You know the law! To him who transgresses against a priestess of Freya, there is only one reply! Death!"

The ground rolled upward, cresting where they fought, pitching them toward the mouth of the pass and onto softer ground, where tall grasses grew. Niall bellowed his war cry and raised his sword.

"Death, Gunthar!" he roared.

His blade flashed downward. It made an arc of light where the sunlight caught it. It slanted into Gunthar's steel, brushed it aside, then continued downward into the man's neck, cleaving through flesh and bone. Gunthar's eyes rolled up into his head and he fell backward, mouth open in a soundless scream.

And in that very instant — the ground rose, pitching Niall forward, over the body of the man he had been fighting. There were the screams of tortured ice and grinding stone. The earth shook wildly.

Niall clung to the tall grasses into which he had been toppled. "Great Thor! Save me!" he breathed.

Yet the earth went on quaking and rolling. Behind him he heard stone crashing on stone, and he listened as great blocks of ice came free of the glacier and plummeted to the ground nearby.

Long he clung to the grasses, which held fast in the earth under them. Not until the last of the sounds had drifted away, until the ground had stilled, did he lift his eyes to stare about him.

Great Wodin," he gasped. The pass was no more. It was blocked now with crumbled, splintered masses of stone, with awesome slabs of glacial ice. No one could travel through that pass. It was closed forever. He would not be able to return to the stead of his parents — at least, not the way he had left it. He was excluded from the home he had known for all his seventeen years. The youth was an outcast, thrust into a strange land.

And yet it was not the tumbled mixture of rock and ice which caught and held Niall's attention. There was something else, something within the glacial ice itself. Niall growled low in his throat.

What was this thing he saw? Covered with ice, yet it had human form. He could see an arm, and the glint of sunlight revealed what seemed to be a golden bracelet adorning that pallid arm.

Niall took a few steps forward, his flesh crawling with wonder and readiness.

Could it be human, that which he was staring at? Now he could see golden hair, lighter even than his own, appearing white rather than yellow. There was pale flesh, covered in some way by a fur garment.

And — blue eyes, wide open! Staring at him!

Those eyes pleaded! They called to him, begging!

Niall shook himself. "I dream," he murmured to himself. "There is

256

no woman in that ice. And if there is — she must be dead! Long dead!"

Aye! How long ago must she have toppled into that ice? Or — been put there?

Was she a witch? A lamia?

No matter! For now he saw, as he moved closer to that ice barrier, that she was lovely, more beautiful than any woman he had ever seen before. Her eyes were blue, her mouth like a round, red fruit. Her body was full, her hips pleasantly rounded.

His hand lifted to touch the ice that held her.

Close were her eyes now, even more urgent the message they seemed to be sending. Free me! free me, man of the outer world! free me — and know my gratitude! It was as though her voice whispered in his mind.

Niall raised his sword and began hacking at the ice. Frozen chunks flew. Long he worked, and carefully, because he did not want to harm the white body that lay encased in this frozen sepulcher.

For hours he worked, stabbing with great care at the ice. After a time he could reach around the sides of the body, slashing with his dagger, using it as a pick. Slowly he freed the unknown woman.

Yet there was ice still close about her body. And now Niall paused, knowing that if he cut deeper into the ice, he might harm her. He turned and began cutting some of the tall grasses, arranging them in a pile about the icy statue.

He set fire to the grasses and watched as the yellow flames began to lick upward. Drops of water formed, glistened, ran down the ice. He cut more grass, piling it higher, growling as the water from the melting ice dripped and put out some of that fire.

When the fire had done its work, only a thin coating of ice remained.

The woman's body moved slightly. Some of the thin ice-crust cracked and fell away. Seeing this, Niall gripped the edge of another hunk of ice, tugged at it until it cracked and dropped.

And then the woman moved a leg. Both legs. Her arms lifted, freeing a hand on which a ring glinted. Niall worked faster, chipping away gently with his dagger so that more and more of the ice fell away.

First all of her body was free, and at last the ice fell away from around her head and shoulders.

Her blue eyes gazed upward into those of Niall. Her full mouth trembled, curved into a smile. "My thanks, stranger. Accept the gratitude of Clovia, who was once — many years ago — queen in Hellios."

Niall shook his head. "Hellios? I've never heard of it."

Clovia smiled wryly. "Is my fame so quick to fade? Once I was mistress of a mighty fleet, a great army. Kings and emperors paid me homage, until..."

Her lovely face darkened, her features twisted in anger. "Until a magician came out of the East and worked his magics in my city, and by them caused me to be borne away and imprisoned in that ice!"

She drew a deep breath, and her eyes roamed the grasslands. "Have you any idea what it was like, buried in cold and darkness — still alive! — for so many years? So many years!" Her eyes focused on him. "What is the year?"

Niall shrugged. "The year of the Boar, the month of the Ice Gods."

Clovia rubbed her hands up and down her arms. "That means nothing to me. Ah, well... This is a different world than the one I left, I know that. Even that magician is no longer alive. Dalvuus, his name was. Ha! If I could get my hands on him..."

She looked hard at Niall. "What about you? From whence came you?"

Niall explained how he had followed Gunthar, how he had killed him, how the earth had shuddered. His hand gestured at the fallen rocks and tumbled blocks of ice.

"I can go home no more. The way is closed. I must reach a seaport and find a ship to take me back to Norumbria."

Clovia eyed him musingly. "Stay with me, Niall. Be my guard, my warrior. Travel with me to Hellios, where I will make you rich."

Niall grinned. "Lady, your kingdom may no longer exist. You are an outcast, like myself." He hesitated, then said, "Still, I have a fancy to wander about this warmer world, to sip its ales and wines, to taste its foods. It might be that I will walk with you, take you to this Hellios."

Swiftly she twisted off the great emerald ring that graced her finger. To go with it, she took off a bracelet encrusted with diamonds. "Take these as first payment, warrior! They are but a small part of what Clovia will give you if you escort her safely to Hellios."

Niall chuckled, waving a hand, "Keep them, lady. They look better on you than they would in my pouch. Time enough for reward when I do what you ask — if I can."

He turned to stare out over the grasslands, which extended as far as he could see. Niall knew nothing about this corner of his world. He knew not which way to walk, did not know even what direction Clovia wanted to go. He turned to her and saw her frowning slightly as she, too, studied the vast prairie for a clue.

In almost inaudible words she was muttering, "This would be the region called Styglinia on the maps I have known. If that is so, then there will be a river running through it. But how far away?"

Niall grinned. "And when we come to this river, if we do, where will it take us?"

She turned to smile at him. "Eastward, toward the city Hellios. The river is named Thangara. It is long and winding, running across half the world. Could we but fashion a raft..."

Her words drifted off. Niall shrugged his muscular shoulders and said, "It isn't around here, so let's go find it."

He began to walk, and after a moment Clovia followed. They walked the sun out of the sky, pausing at last when the shadows lengthened and darkness began to creep across the grasses. They found refuge close by a rock formation.

Niall gathered sticks from the fallen branches of some trees that grew near that stone bulwark, set them together and made a fire, scraping a bit of flint against his dagger blade. From his pouch he took a bit of meat, some cheese, a little bread. Hunkered down, he offered half of what he had to Clovia.

They ate, and then they lay at arm's length, both within touching distance of the fire. Overhead the stars glinted in black space, and a cool wind roamed the grasses. Niall slept soon and soundly.

For three days they traveled south. The great bow and the arrows Niall carried were put into use, felling a deer and then a boar, so that the young man and the woman ate well. His companion was given to moody silences, or so it seemed to Niall. She brooded long and often, her blue eyes slightly veiled.

To Niall, it was a pleasant time. This was a new land, and there was much to see. The unchanging horizon extended as far as his eyes could reach — and he had excellent vision — but as the days went on, it became monotonous.

Something of this he said to Clovia, adding, "Even my north-land gives me a new view every so often. A bear might rush out at me, or a giant elk, or even a man who had been outlawed. But here..."

His huge shoulders lifted and fell, "...there is nothing to stem the boredom."

Clovia turned her head and smiled faintly. "Do not be too sure, Niall. Slowly, oh so slowly, I have been remembering. We are not far now from the river — and from the underwater lair of the sea serpent Xithalia."

"Sea serpent? I've heard of them. Some of them dwell in the Cold Sea. But I've never known any to swim about in rivers."

"The river Thangara is deep, very deep. It sweeps in from the ocean, and there are caverns inside its stone walls where Xithalia dwells."

Niall stiffened his shoulders. He did not like this talk of sea serpents. By Wodin! How could he fight off a sea serpent from the deck of a raft?

Three days later, they came in sight of a river. Its waters moved sluggishly between grassy banks rimmed with trees. As far as they could see, there were no habitations, neither the tents of prairie dwellers nor the mud huts of men who had been outlawed from the cities.

With his sword, Niall hacked down all the saplings he could find, trimmed them and then lashed them together with tough vines that grew nearby. With Clovia helping to twist the vines and saplings together, they built a serviceable raft, though Niall eyed it dubiously. It would have to do; they had no boat, nor any prospect of finding one in these remote regions.

They launched the raft, balanced themselves carefully on it, and pushed out into the river, Niall poling them along. The sun grew warmer as they made their way between high banks covered with wildflowers. Then they moved into an area where trees all but shut out the bright sky overhead.

Clovia sat quietly, seemingly lost in thought. Niall stared about him, his heart beating to the pace of this land where he was a stranger. How vast it was! He had never imagined that his world was so huge. All he had known until now were the cold sea waves and the little strand where his father had his steading. What wonders was he now to see?

All day they rode the river, landing at dusk to make a little fire and cook the fish Niall caught with a hook and some thin cord from the pouch on his belt.

When they were done eating, Niall asked, "How far do we have to travel to reach this city where you were queen?"

Clovia smiled grimly. "Many, many more days. We are now in a country where my people never went. Why should they? There is nothing here to tempt the merchants."

They had been traveling on the raft for four days when they saw the sailing ship. It was in the middle of the river, its sail billowed out, yet it did not move. Then Niall saw something wet and shiny moving slowly alongside the vessel. Thick and massive — and menacing — was that something.

Clovia cried out. "Xithalia! He has come from his rocky lair to feast on human flesh, to fill his belly and then retire to sleep."

Niall sought purchase for the pole, to make the raft move faster. As he did, Clovia turned a frightened face to him. "What are you doing? You're taking us toward that thing! Try to go around it. It may not see us."

"Those people aboard that ship may need help."

Clovia stared at him, her eyes wide. "What is that to us?"

The youth glared back at her. "It may be nothing to you, but I can't run away to let those folk face death."

He could see the head of the serpent now, as the beast moved out from behind the sail which had hidden it from his view. Vast was the head, wide its mouth. The creature slavered as it poised above the deck, where a group of terrified people stood huddled.

Niall reached for his bow. He knew arrows would be useless against such a creature, unless...

He pulled his bow, sent an arrow winging through the air. It hit the scaly hide of the serpent's neck and fell away. Niall grunted, lifted another arrow to the string. He took more time, studying the distant creature's movements, before he let fly again.

The arrow arced high, then as it began to descend it drove into the eye of the serpent. From its open throat came a scream of agony. Up reared Xithalia, its head turning one way and another as it sought out the cause of its pain.

Clovia hunched down upon the raft's deck. Her white hands were clenched into fists. To her continued amazement, Niall was poling feverishly, urging the raft toward that nightmare monster, and shouting as he worked.

"Have you gone mad?" Clovia yelled.

"No, no. Look — The beast is leaving the ship. It is starting to turn, to come toward us."

Niall moved to the edge of the raft, balancing himself carefully. He drew his sword and waited as Xithalia glided through the river toward him.

"What can you hope to do with that puny weapon?" Clovia panted. "He will open his mouth, gobble you up!"

Niall grinned. "That's what I hope he does."

The great head was over him now, its jaws wide apart. Long teeth glinted in the red cavern of a mouth. For a moment Xithalia paused, then its head darted downward.

Clovia screamed.

Niall sprang upward to meet the gaping jaw, his sword held up before him as if he meant to fend off that gaping mouth.

The jaw snapped almost shut — just as Niall fell sideways into the river. But before he fell, the thrust lodged his sword in the jaw of the sea serpent, with the point puncturing the roof of its mouth and the pommel lodged up against its bottom jaw. Even though impaled on the sword, those jaws gaped wide.

Xithalia bellowed. It thrashed its head and its vast body, straining to force the sword back out the way it came. When light caught the edge of the blade, it could be seen in the beast's throat cavity, lodged at an angle that made the serpent roar every time it moved its jaws up and down. Water foamed and flew about.

Niall swam to the raft and hoisted himself upon it. His booming laughter rang out. "Try now to swallow me, eater of men! Maybe now you'll starve to death."

He took up the pole, thrust it into the soft bottom of the river, and propelled the raft toward the ship which now sat sideways in the river, the people on it staring and crying out to him. Clovia rose to her knees, then to her feet, all the while eyeing the injured and enraged serpent, convulsing as it sought to free itself from that sword. Xithalia lost interest in its prey, and its thrashings carried it farther and farther away, until after a few moments it dipped beneath the surface of the water and was gone.

Almost in awe, Clovia shifted her gaze to stare at Niall. "You saved me, barbarian. You saved me."

"I saved myself," he grinned.

Ropes were flung from the ship's deck. Niall caught one, grabbed Clovia with his other arm, and leaped. His feet found the side of the boat, and willing hands grasped them and raised them upward until the deck planks were underfoot.

Sailors were running here and there, preparing to get the ship under way. The sail filled with wind, the hull turned about until it pointed into the current, and the river waters again began to glide past the hull as the vessel moved on with the raft in tow.

A man with a beard came toward them, smiling broadly. "My thanks to you," he happily growled at Niall, clasping the youth's hands. "You saved our lives and the vessel itself. I'll not be ungrateful."

Niall shrugged. "Just tell me where I can buy a little boat. I'm tired of pushing a raft along."

The captain chuckled. "You'll buy nothing. A boat shall be my gift to you." He hesitated. "But where do you plan to go upon the river Thangara?"

Niall glanced at Clovia, who said, "We travel to Hellios."

"Hellios? Where's that?"

Clovia stared. "Hellios is the most magnificent city in the world. From its docks, ships ply all the nine oceans. Its merchants eat from plates of gold."

The captain grinned. "Lady, I wish you only the best, but — Hellios? There is no such place. I know this river from the ocean to the mountains."

The captain walked away and Clovia stared at him, frowning.

Two days later the ship pulled into a wharf before a riverside city. Niall was at the railing, staring at the many rooftops, at the distant shine of sunlight on a golden dome. This was the first city he had ever seen. In his country there was no more than small steadings, or perhaps a gathering of steadings together with warehouses in which merchants stored their goods.

"You find it exciting?" Clovia asked from where she stood beside him.

"I've never seen anything like it," Niall told her, not taking his eyes off the scenes before him.

Her lips curved into a smile. "Wait until you glimpse Hellios. There is a city, a city that houses thousands upon thousands of people."

"The captain says there is no such place. I've spoken with him. He knows this river as he does his own home."

Clovia snapped, "The man is mad. I tell you, I know Hellios! I reigned there, as did my father and my forefathers."

Very gently, Niall murmured, "But that was a long time ago; Clovia. A very long time ago...." He put his arm about her. "How long were you inside that river of ice?"

"I — I don't know. But Hellios must still live. It must!"

"If it does, we'll find it."

Niall did not notice the sadness in her eyes, nor did he pay any attention to the manner in which she pulled her cloak about her. And though he sensed it when she shivered, he put that down to the cool wind blowing off the land.

They went with the captain, whose name was Dalamar, to his big stone house on a hillside north of the town. Clovia would have preferred to be alone with Niall, but the ship-master would not have stood for that. The two were to be his guests, to enjoy his hospitality.

They met his wife and children, they feasted at a huge table, they enjoyed the warmth of a great log burning in the huge fireplace. They shared bowls of rich wine, and when the children had been put to bed Dalamar brought out narrow wooden tubes which held maps.

These maps he unrolled on a table, and as Clovia and Niall bent over them, the captain's finger traced the route of the river Thangara from the mountains to the sea. On those parchment scrolls, there was no mark to point out the city Clovia called Hellios.

Her face grew paler as she examined the parchments. Her finger trembled as she pointed, "There is where Hellios should be. There!"

Dalamar's face wore a puzzled look as he stared at where she indicated. He drew a deep breath and said, "Lady, there is no city there. True, there are strange stones standing about — I've never put ashore to look at them closely — but only the wind roams between those stones. There are no people, there is no city. Believe me."

Clovia turned suddenly and walked across the room to stand at a window and stare out into the dark night. She stood there, motionless, for many minutes before she turned and came back to them.

"I have been gone far longer than I had believed," she whispered. "Far longer. When I was taken out of Hellios and put into that glacier by the magic of the wizard Dalvuus, Hellios was the greatest city in my world. Now it is dust and dead stone."

Dalamar cleared his throat. "But you still live, lady. There is much to be seen in this new world. You both must stay here with me and my family."

Clovia smiled and shook her head. "I thank you, but — no. I must look upon Hellios once again, or at least upon what remains of it."

Then she gazed at Niall. "Will you come with me? Or do you choose to stay here, or to wander elsewhere?"

"I agreed to see you safely to Hellios," the youth replied. "I will keep my word."

The next morning Niall went with Dalamar to the docks, where the captain pointed out a small boat with a mast. "It's a cock-boat I sometimes take with me when I sail out upon the ocean. It's fast, it moves well. I'll provision it for you, and give you a new sail."

"Accept my thanks, Dalamar," Niall said briskly and sincerely.

The captain chuckled. "If you hadn't come to fight the serpent, I wouldn't be here now. Speak no more of thanks."

Two days later Niall and Clovia pushed away from the wharf, with Dalamar seeing them off. The wind was brisk. It filled their sail and sent the craft speeding through the water. Niall waved once more to Dalamar, then set his face to the east and his big hand on the tiller.

Clovia sat in the prow, leaning forward, staring ahead of her as if she were trying to will the little craft to go even faster. She was huddled beneath her cloak, and every so often she shivered.

For five days they sailed, pausing only to sleep for a few hours each night along the deserted riverbank. Always, Clovia urged speed. It was as though something inside ate at her and would not be satisfied until she stood again in Hellios. They ate their meals in the boat as it scudded along; Clovia would not hear of stopping for a midday rest.

On the fifth afternoon she straightened suddenly, lifted her arm and pointed ahead. "See there, Niall! That tongue of rock jutting out into the river. My sailors called it Norban's Tongue, for the river god Norban whose tongue licks up the souls of dead sailors and carries them away to the worlds ruled by the gods. Hellios is not far now."

Niall merely grunted in acknowledgment. He was enjoying this trip. This was his chance to see more of this world into which he had been catapulted by the fates — though there was little to see, outside of the river and the plains and the forests through which they sailed.

He hoped Hellios would prove be interesting, though he suspected it would not. What was so interesting about a lot of ancient buildings? Yet he could understand why Clovia wanted to walk there, to set her eyes on those places she had known so long ago.

The little sloop seemed now to run faster through the waves. It left

Norban's Tongue far behind and approached a mass of tumbled blocks of stone along its banks.

Clovia stood and cried out, "This was the harbor!"

Niall moved the tiller delicately, and the boat crept between huge boulders jutting out of the river. His eyes scanned the land, saw here and there places where buildings might have stood in the distant past. Judging by the view from the river, which was obstructed by boulders and debris, no one would suspect that a mighty metropolis had once graced this shoreline.

He ran the cock-boat in against a big flat rock, tossed its anchor about a jutting piece of stone, then stepped up onto the rock and helped Clovia ashore.

Tears were in her eyes and running down her cheeks.

"Gone," she whispered, so softly that Niall could scarcely hear her. "All gone, all the ships, all the riches. Forgotten by the world. No more do the armies march, no more do the golden banners wave in the breezes. Dead. All dead!"

Niall did not speak. He looked out over the ruins which, from this vantage point, extended as far as he could see. From the river, a man could not glimpse the extent of what had been the glory of Hellios, but from atop this high rock the truth of Clovia's memories was plain to see.

The woman moved away, walking from the rock to the earth of the shore itself, striding slowly forward on what had been paving stones but which were now half-buried under dirt and grass. She went with bowed head, and Niall knew that she was weeping.

The youth shrugged. He might as well go along with her. Who knew? Perhaps he might find something here to take away with him: a bit of buried gold, or even a rare gem or two. He needed money to live, to eat and drink until he found service somewhere as a warrior or a laborer.

Clovia wandered along what might have been a great boulevard many years ago. From time to time she would pause to run her eyes this way and that way, and the wind blew her pale hair about her face as though to hide the tears that streaked her cheeks.

"There stood my palace," she said to Niall, pointing. "Its walls were high, its buildings the glory of our city."

The young Northumbrian muttered. "There must be some gold left, somewhere around here. You would know the location of the vaults. Take us there."

She shook her head slowly. "They would have taken all the gold, the jewels, when they abandoned Hellios. There will be nothing left."

"How can you know unless you look? You know nothing of what happened here. You were locked inside the ice,"

Clovia smiled abruptly, holding out her hands to him. "You are right, as always. I have been so sunk in my sorrow that I have forgotten I am alive, and that I will need gold to go on living — if I choose to do so, that is."

"Well, I choose to live," Niall grumbled.

Laughter rang out — the first time he had ever heard such a sound from her. "Yes, Niall. You are my warrior, my army. And it is the duty of a queen to care for her warriors. Come along!"

She took but one step, and then his hand shot out to catch and halt her. He lifted his other arm and pointed.

"I saw something, some sort of movement. There 'may be wild animals here, Clovia. Get behind me."

He drew the sword Dalamar had given him — his old blade, he suspected, was still caught in the serpent's jaws — and held the blade, out before him as he moved forward, with Clovia following close behind:

Suddenly a shrieking sound split the air from ahead of them. From behind the tumbled stones of the dead city rushed half a dozen men. They held clubs and rusted swords. They wore the barest of rags, and their feet were bare. They looked like less than a match for the burly young Niall, but they also looked determined and desperate.

Niall roared a battle cry and ran to confront them. He easily ducked under a thrown club, and a second later he was in the midst of them. His sword lifted and fell, sliced and thrust, and suddenly three of the ragged men were down, their blood staining the grass and stones.

As he struck and parried, Niall scanned these men, seeing something besides their rags and rusted weapons. Some of them had thick bracelets on their arms, one or two possessed rings, and all of the adornments seemed to be made of solid gold.

The three men still alive whirled and fled but Niall ran after them, bellowing in his battle-lust. Where two walls stood close together he cornered them and moved in with sword swinging.

The over-matched men fought grimly, savagely, but within moments they lie on the ground, dead or near death.

Niall stood over them as Clovia came running up.

"You killed them all," she accused. "They might have told us something!"

"What could such as these have told you? They're carrion eaters, and I would guess they eat human beings, too. Still, I think they have told us a little."

"What do you mean?"

He knelt, stripping golden rings and armbands from the dead men, and held them up to Clovia, who stared at them with incredulous eyes.

"Those were made in Hellios!" she said. "I know that workmanship." Her words tumbled over themselves as she sought to explain. "This ring was made by Frondag, who fashioned jewelry for me. Ah, and this armlet by Rogonor, whose artistry in gold has never been challenged. But how can this be? It was so long ago!"

"Gold doesn't die," Niall reminded her.

She shook her head impatiently. "No, no. I didn't mean that. Where did they find these things? That's what I want to know. If they stumbled on some lost hoard of gold, so can we!"

Niall grinned exultantly. "Now where would such a hoard be hidden?"

"In the palace, of course. And it is just over there."

They ran to where colored columns and tinted stone blocks lay in mad disarray. Clovia began to search with Niall at her side. They turned over stone blocks, #hey dug where she suggested, but the ruins were too heavy, and too much earth had blown into what once had been stairways.

Niall stood at last, scowling. "There is a different way into the cellars. There has to be. Those ragged men I killed would never do any digging. Besides, if they had, we'd see some sign of it."

Clovia sat on a fallen column. "Yes. There's a way in that is not blocked by rubble. All we have to do is find it."

They searched until hunger sent them back to the boat for the leathern sacks that held their food and drink. As the sun sank, Niall built a fire in the shelter of two standing walls, and there he cooked a meal.

While they were eating, Niall heard the beating of wings. Outlined against the darkening sky, he saw small flying things. He was about to put more meat in his mouth when he sprang to his feet instead.

"Those bats!" he shouted. "They can show us the way in!"

Clovia stared at him. "What?"

"Bats nest in caves — or an underground place like a treasure house. Or a corridor that will lead us beneath your palace."

Clovia licked her lips. "Then let's go find it."

"Not until the bats return," Niall responded. "Now, you sleep. I'll watch for them."

When the woman had rolled up in the cloak and fur wrap which Dalamar had given her, Niall sat back against a stone pillar and let his thoughts roam. He liked the excitement of this strange land into which he had come. Even more, he liked the idea of finding treasure. For hour upon hour he yielded to his dreamings, staying alert but preoccupied.

With golden coins, he could travel leisurely about this land, discover its deepest secrets, know its fairest women. There might be jewels too, and a mere handful of pearls or rubies or diamonds would make him a rich man.

Niall chuckled. As a rich man, he could return home to Norumbria, he thought, but then he scowled. Norumbria held no secrets from him; he knew it too well. Instead, he would roam this world into which he had been cast by the ground itself, and he would make a name for himself.

He was reflecting on this when he heard a stone roll across other stones. Instantly he was ready, rising quietly, lifting out his dagger. If death or danger came crawling forth in dawn-light, he would meet it.

Then it came, a nightmare-thing with five legs and three arms, hunched over so that it seemed to be a ball of black leather with red,

270

glowing eyes.

The thing moved in the direction of the sleeping Clovia, and Niall saw fangs glint in the dying firelight.

He rushed forward, putting his body between the leathery thing and Clovia. His shoulder hit the beasts body as he swung his dagger in a short, vicious arc.

The short blade bit deep. The beast-thing bellowed, lunged for Clovia and missed her by inches as Niall forced it to one side. They landed hard on stones and turf. Quickly Niall was back on his feet. Now he had time to yank out his sword, and he drove forward with it.

A clawed hand swiped at him. Niall ducked as he saw and felt his sword slash into a leathery shoulder. Then their bodies were twined together as he sought to free his steel from the beast-flesh where it was lodged.

The body of the thing he fought was hotter than a man's body, as if heated from within. Its breath was nauseating. Niall twisted, partially freeing himself of the grip of those mighty arms and taking scratches across his shoulders from the long, sharp claws.

Then his sword blade came free. Niall glanced at it and gasped. It looked as though acid had eaten at it. The flat of the blade was pocked with pits and holes. And its once-sharp edges were now dulled and eaten away.

"Wodin All-Father!" he gasped.

Niall dropped the sword, and in the same motion reached for a paving stone. He slammed the rock against the face of the awful being. Fierce was that blow, driven by all the power of his brawny arm, and flush against the forehead of the beast-thing it landed.

The creature bellowed. Its mouth gaped wide, showing fangs that threatened but could not penetrate Niall's defenses from such close range. Niall lifted the rock and hit with it again and again. He drove the creature backward with the rock-blows, never giving it a chance to steady itself for a counterattack.

"Water!" Clovia's voice cried from behind him. "It cannot stand the touch of water!"

Niall feinted another attack with the stone, then suddenly leaped toward the beast, his arms spread wide. He grabbed the leathery beast around the lower part of its torso, bore it backward, and rolled over and over on the ground with it. The river was not far away.

The young warrior snarled. He struggled to regain his feet and lift the thing off the ground. While straining to raise it, Niall began to move forward.

The monster's arms and claws raked at him, digging into his arms and shoulders. Niall grunted in response to the pain, but did not lose his grip. Now he was able to walk carrying the beast-thing. The river was closer... closer.

Within a few feet of the bank, Niall left his feet in a lunge. Still clinging to the leathery creature, he toppled into the water.

Immediately there was an awful hissing. A stench rose into the air. Niall choked and felt nausea all but overwhelm him. The thing he clung to was weakening quickly. Its struggles were not so savage, and in a moment it was all but inert in his grasp.

Niall felt the touch of hands from behind him, trying to help draw him upward out of the churning water. He released his grip on the beast's body and allowed himself to be dragged back onto solid ground.

He stood tottering at the river's edge. Clovia was beside him, gripping his arm tightly as she stared into the water.

The creature was disappearing — dissolving in the water! Fumes rose from the bubbling river, fumes that made Niall curse and draw Clovia away from the river bank.

He drew a breath. "How did you know that water would slay that thing?"

In a voice trying to be calm, Clovia replied, "It was a thordio, a thing that had come to my city from some forgotten world long ago. In my time it was only a legend. Something seems to have summoned it back now. But why?"

She stared at the ruins of the city and asked harshly, "What is there to protect here? What purpose would there be in summoning the thordia out of its own world to roam these ruins?"

To Niall, the answer came quickly. "Treasure."

"No. Something more important than gold or jewels," Clovia murmured, shaking her head. Her fingers tightened once again upon his arm. "Come! This has restored hope to me. There is something here, something waiting — sleeping, perhaps."

The big barbarian shrugged. "I care not for anything like that. What good would that do us?"

Clovia glanced at him slyly, smiling faintly. "Ah, but there will be treasure, young man. Treasure so great ten boats could not carry it. Are you interested?"

Niall grinned, putting his hand on her shoulder and squeezing it. "Lead on, lady. We'll forget about waiting for the bats."

Clovia walked forward, at times almost breaking into a run. It seemed as if her memory were coming back to her, as if in her mind's eye she could see Hellios as she had known it when she had walked its streets. Niall followed at a strolling pace, keeping up with her, fingering his again-empty scabbard. He felt partly naked without a sword at his side. Ever since he had been twelve years old —and a huge child for his age — he had walked with the weight of a sword dragging down his belt.

Clovia went between still-standing walls and broken columns, following an unseen path. Twice she hesitated, standing motionless and staring about her, frowning, before she resumed her stride.

At length she came to what must have been a big building. Between its walls she walked, on ornate paving stones half-hidden under grass and wildflowers Then she paused at a place where two walls met, and Niall could glimpse a larger paving stone set among the others.

"Lift this," she said, tapping the stone with a foot.

Niall knelt and slid his fingers beneath the bluish stone. Rising from his knees, he straightened his back until his arm and shoulder muscles bulged. Slowly, the stone came up. It was well over a minute later that he had raised it high enough to topple it, revealing a narrow stairway beneath where it had lain.

"Let me enter," Clovia said.

But Niall held her back, drawing his dagger. "There may be dangers down there, lady. Let me go first. You follow."

He put his feet to the stone of that ancient staircase, descending into almost total darkness. The sun's rays did not penetrate far, but they showed the barbarian the shape of a tunnel stretching out ahead of him.

Clovia was right behind him, fingertips touching his back. "Search along the walls. There ought to be torches thrust into iron holders."

By groping in the darkness, Niall discovered a length of resin-soaked wood. With flint and a bit of steel from his pouch, plus some tinder, he made a flame and ignited the torch. Holding it high, to cast the light as far as possible into the tunnel, he moved on.

It was dim in this tunnel, even with that torch, but there seemed to be nothing dangerous lurking within. At length they came to an oaken door, barred in iron and with a rusty lock.

Clovia said, "This is the treasure house of my people. Stand aside, Niall."

From her pouch she drew a small length of steel. At Niall's questioning look, she smiled wryly. "This I took with me — unknown to Dalvuus, naturally! — when they stole me from my palace."

She fitted the key into the lock, but could not turn it. Niall grasped her upper arms, moved her aside, put his hand to the key and, after grunting a bit from the exertion, turned it. His big hand pushed the door wide.

They looked in at a big room, fitted out with chests and coffers of varying sizes. As Niall strode forward, holding the torch before him, he saw what appeared to be a corpse lying atop one of the biggest chests. But it was not the sight of the body that his eyes rested on last.

Thor!" rumbled Niall. "What a sword!" It lay beside the corpse, its haft glittering from the torchlight, its scabbard revealing the jewels with which it was emblazoned. Its blade was partly out of the scabbard and shone brightly, unaffected by rust or decay.

Niall sprang to that sword, caught hold of the scabbard, yanked free the blade. He held it up, staring at its length. Never had he seen such a weapon as this; he had not believed that one could exist.

Clovia said softly, "That is the weapon called Blood-drinker. It belonged to my father, to his father, to all my male ancestors who were emperors and kings in Hellios."

"I claim this as my reward," Niall exulted. "Just this! With it I can gain all the gold I'll ever have need of!"

Clovia gasped, fell against Niall. "Niall! Look! By all the gods of Hellios — that thing is alive!"

A rustling drew his attention to the body on the chest. The hairs on the back of his neck rose up stiffly as he saw the thing stir, move, begin to sit up. Eyelids opened, and reddish eyes peered at them from under hairy brows.

"Who disturbs my slumbers? Who comes to the treasure room of long-dead Hellios?"

Clovia moved forward, eyes wide, her lovely mouth distorted in a mixture of horror and hate. "Dalvuus! You — still — live!"

"Slay him! Slay him!" Clovia screamed.

Niall lifted Blood-drinker, but in that moment — even as he tensed himself to leap forward — he found himself frozen. The reddish eyes of Dalvuus fastened on him, held him as helpless as any babe. He could not move a muscle.

Laughter shook the corpse-like being. Dust rose from the half-rotted garments that clothed it. "Foolish youth, foolish queen. Think you so easily to overcome Dalvuus the Mage? Pah!" He raised a hand. "I banish you both to oblivion! Begone, the two of you!"

Niall felt himself being lifted upward, then plunged into cottony clouds that pierced his flesh with cold. He was vaguely aware that Clovia was beside him, screaming with terror rioting in her veins, and he reached out through that cloudiness to grasp her arm, draw her closer to him.

Like that, they fell through nothingness...

Niall opened his eyes to stare upward at a yellow sky, a sky in which no sun glowed. He rose up on an elbow and saw Clovia lying beside him, unconscious but breathing normally. He lay upon ground that was brown, riven here and there by fume-roles from which steam rose into the air.

This world was hot, wherever it was. Already, Niall could feel sweat oozing from his pores. He lifted himself to his feet, realizing that his fist still held Blood-drinker.

He looked around. Everything was desolation here. Ruin, emptiness, There was no life, except for himself and the woman who had been queen in Hellios.

"Tartarus," breathed a voice at his feet.

Niall looked down at a haggard Clovia, then put out a hand to yank her to her feet. She shuddered and great tears rolled down her cheeks.

"The gods have abandoned us," she wept. "There is no hope now. We will die here, without food and water."

Niall scowled blackly. He was not one to admit defeat so easily. He had been put here, true. Yet where he had entered, he could leave.

"Think, woman!" he urged. "If you know of this place, you must know more about it. If there is any way out of here — any way at all! — it's up to you to remember what it is."

She stared up at him, eyes rimmed by tears. She shuddered, rubbing her hands on her arms. "No one has ever returned from here. No one!"

Niall growled, "That's no answer. What is this place? What do you know of it?"

"Tartarus is a magic region created by great wizardry. Only the mightiest magicians know the way to and from it." Her eyes widened. "From it... Yes, there is a way out, but I know it not. When I was queen in Hellios, I studied the history of many magics, as a pastime..."

She broke off, stood with bowed head, deep in thought. Niall eyed her for a moment, then took to studying his sword. It was a splendid blade, the finest he had ever seen. Its edges looked sharp enough to shave the hair from his head. He moved it back and forth, getting to know its feel.

Clovia said dreamily, "There is a guardian over this dead world, placed here eons ago by those who created this place. His name is... his name is... I cannot recall!"

"Try! If ever you would return to our own world, woman — think!"

Clovia looked up at him, eyes wet, tears running down her cheeks. She shook her head, her misery plain to see. "It's no use. I just can't remember. Dalvuus has won!"

Dalvuus?

It was a word from out of the very air. Niall grunted, lifted his sword and stared about him. Clovia gasped and clung to his side.

Who Is It who speaks of Dalvuus?

A vast green shape appeared high above them, seeming to grow in size even as it lowered itself to the bare brown ground where Niall stood with Clovia. The greenness was a vast cape or cloak, or appeared as such, with a hood beneath which was utter blackness.

What know you mere mortals of Dalvuus? Long and long ago did Dalvuus live!

Niall found his tongue. "He lives still, back in that land from which we came! He sent us here, to perish."

The darkness under the hood seemed almost to meditate. The cape which surrounded that darkness swirled as though blown about by mighty winds. From it stabbed an arm tipped by a dark hand.

Would you return to where it is Dalvuus lives? Would you slay Dalvuus?

"I would," Niall rasped, "if by his charms and incantations he gave me a chance to use this sword on him!"

Only I can send you back to that world. And only I have the power to draw you back here — should you fail in your quest!

The strange voice paused, as though the black being in the vast greenish cloak were thinking. Niall spoke into that silence.

"Return us and I'll kill Dalvuus for you!"

Eerie laughter rose from the seemingly empty hood.

Rash mortal! Dalvuus cannot die. Oh, yes — as you know death, he can. But should you slay him, his soul would come here to me, Tartarus. Ah!... I have waited long for that, to exact my vengeance!

Go then — back from whence you came! With my protection!

Niall felt the world shift about him, knew an instant of queasiness, and then he stood upright in the treasure chamber of the kings of Hellios, and beside him, her arm in the crook of his arm, was Clovia. His fingers tightened about the haft of Blood-drinker.

His eyes swept the chamber. All was as it had been when they had entered it, except that the magician had vanished. The woman shuddered.

"He's gone," she whispered.

"But not far," Niall bristled. "Come on!"

He ran along the corridor, touching the wall blindly, for Dalvuus had taken the torch. In utter blackness he ran, listening to Clovia crying out his name and stumbling after him far behind. Up ahead he saw faint light, and he ran as might the leopards of Poranga, so swiftly that his feet seemed scarcely to touch the stone floor.

Up the stairs he leaped, into daylight.

His booted feet slid to a halt. "Wodin," he breathed, and stared around him.

No longer were there ruins here. No! Upward around him rose the wails of a mighty palace. Great marble columns ran here and there, upholding a ceiling on which glinted gold leaf and brilliant paintings. There was a throne at the far end of this vast chamber, and at the other end, massive doors opened onto a sun-drenched street.

Clovia sobbed behind him, half in and half out of the stone stairway, "Hellios," she breathed, "as I remember it! What magic is this, Niall?"

He growled low in his throat. "Dalvuus is behind it. By some great spell, he has made that which was, now be again. But where is the swine?"

They heard the tramp of sandaled feet from outside the huge doors. Niall knew the tread of soldiers when he heard it. He swung about, lips lifted in a silent snarl, and he held Blood-drinker ready.

Ten men in mail shirts came marching into the throne room, and Niall viewed them with narrow eyes from a hidden vantage point. A man followed them inside. It was Dalvuus — but what a change there was in his appearance! No longer did he wear age-rotted garments, but now he strode along in an ankle-length garment of ebon blackness on which were sewn thaumaturgic symbols in silver thread. A golden cloak hung from his shoulders.

Niall bellowed and leaped out of hiding, placing himself between the guards and Clovia.

Instantly Dalvuus halted. His eyes went wide, his mouth fell open. Just for a moment he was paralyzed by amazement. Then his arm came up and he cried out orders to the marching guards.

"Slay that man! And the woman with him!"

But before any of them could react to his voice, Niall was upon those warriors. His blade darted once, twice, and two men dropped. Nor did he pause, but came on like a maddened elephant, his sword out before him, slashing, cutting.

"Abaddon," chanted Dalvuus. "Great Abaddon, hear me! Slay this man who kills my soldiers. Slay him and—"

Dalvuus paused for breath. Six of his men were down, and Niall was fast upon the others Like a Styrethian lion, he moved here and there, out of reach of the blades that sought to sap his life's blood, always slashing back in return and slicing through flesh and bone.

Dalvuus turned to flee, his robes flapping as he ran, and after him went Niall, blood dripping from his sword. Niall could run like a frightened deer, but there was speed in the magician, too. He fled up one hall and down another, never pausing to glance back.

Up to a blank wall Dalvuus ran. His hands went out to the cold stone — and where he touched, the stone slid back. Dalvuus leaped through the opening, and the stone wall closed just as Niall arrived. The warrior cursed silently as he heard faint, mocking laughter from inside the passage.

From behind him came the sound of sandals slapping the stone floor. He whirled, sword-point thrust up so that Clovia almost ran herself upon it. He let the blade drop and caught her in his arms.

"He's escaped me," he growled.

Clovia tried to catch her breath, shaking her head. At last she said, "No, no. Just a trick. A trick I know. Let me at the wall."

She reached to the wall, touched it with her fingertips as Dalvuus had done. "See? It operates in this fashion. Hidden valves force air into locks and — see! The stone turns."

Niall caught her up and leaped through the opening. Into a small antechamber he ran, still carrying the woman. Ahead was an oaken door, reinforced with iron. Setting Clovia down, Niall ran forward.

He leaped at the door, boots upraised, and slammed into it with all the fury his massive body could muster. He heard wood give way, heard and felt the screech of twisting metal... and the oak door burst open.

Niall stood in the open doorway, staring into a chamber fitted out with strange vials and alembics, with horn-books and palimpsests on racks and shelves. Standing before an altar of black stone, his back to the door and arms upraised, was Dalvuus.

"Great Abaddon, do not abandon me in my time of need! Heed my call, great lord of evil! Come to—"

"Foul slug," bellowed Niall, running forward. "Prepare to die — and to be welcomed into Tartarus by one who has waited a long time to get his hands on you."

Dalvuus swung about. Utter fear was etched on his face. His lips were drawn back, his eyes distended.

"Begone, creature of this world! Begone, into that world of Tartarus where once I sent you!"

The mage lifted his arms, made mesmeric passes with his hands. Yet still did Niall come for him.

Now Dalvuus screamed, sought to escape by dodging behind the altar. His hand lifted a vial of purplish liquid and hurled it at Niall.

Clovia screamed shrilly. Niall ducked under that hastily hurled glass tube, heard it fall and break on the floor behind him. Purple, searing flames leaped upward from the spot, and Niall knew that had that vial broken on his body, he would have been burned alive.

Dalvuus whirled and fled as soon as he threw the vial. His hands reached for a corner of the wall, and that wall also turned as he touched it, revealing a narrow passageway. Dalvuus leaped for the opening.

The magician was swift, but Niall was fast as lightning. No sooner had the magician entered the narrow opening than Niall was at his heels. Dalvuus stayed in the lead as the pair threw themselves up the narrow stairs leading to the top of the tower they were in.

Dalvuus ran into the topmost room of the tower and his hands went out toward a metal canister that stood upon a stone table.

His hands grasped that metal alembic, sought to tear away its cover. Niall did not know what power was in that thing, but he knew it would be deadly to him.

He caught the mage from behind, fastened his big hands on Dalvuus' wrists, and exerted just part of the strength of his mighty muscles,

Abruptly, Dalvuus' fingers were pulled from the metal top. Then Niall whirled Dalvuus' body around and drove his fist into his face.

The magician reeled back several steps, affected by the blow although he was apparently using some form of magical protection. Such a blow would ordinarily have crushed the skull of a man his size. He retreated until his back touched the cold wall of the tower-top. In a daze, he raised his hands.

"Bythagm noith juglasteros..." he began to recite.

Niall felt a coldness begin to form in the tiny room. His lips pulled back. He had had his fill of sorcery.

The young warrior drew Blood-drinker and thrust with it before the magician had time to finish his incantation. The weapon's full length went into the body of the magician. Dalvuus stiffened, his eyes went wide.

Still with that sword thrust into him from chest to back so that a foot of steel protruded from his spine, he staggered forward. Toward the canister his halting steps took him, hands outstretched.

Stop him, barbarian!

Niall leaped between the mage and the alembic he was after, intending only to forestall the magician until he must certainly succumb to the sword upon which he was impaled.

Dalvuus laid his hands on Niall, sought to push him aside. His eyes were wild, pleading. Niall did not know why, but that voice he had heard was warning enough. He stopped him: His big hands came up, caught Dalvuus, held him motionless — and in that instant, the magician collapsed and died. Niall's grip relaxed, and the magician's dead weight sifted through Niall's grasp and crumpled to the floor.

A blackness was now in the tower room, gathering slowly. Niall knew what that blackness was, and he shrank from it.

Yet that darkness held no menace for the big Northumbrian. It crept toward Dalvuus, slowly, and as though aware of its coming, the mouth of the dead magician opened as if to scream.

Then the blackness touched Dalvuus, embraced him.

And Dalvuus — or that essence which still lived within him — did scream. His body had dropped, yet some part of Dalvuus struggled as the blackness took over. Was this an act of Dalvuus' soul? Niall did not know, did not want to know.

Go, earthly being! Flee! And take with you my gratitude!

Niall yanked his sword from the cadaver that lay upon the stone floor, then ran. Swiftly had he run up those narrow stairs in pursuit of the mage. More swiftly still did he run down them, back into the room where he had left Clovia.

He said no word but snatched her up, still running. He bore her over his shoulder as he ran, with Clovia yelling questions, asking if he were mad.

Downward he ran, downward until he stood on the ground floor of what had been a palace thousands of years before, and was now again — at least for the time being. As Niall ran, he saw that the walls and floor, although still seeming solid, were shimmering and fading.

Just as he started to lower Clovia to the paving stones outside, the buildings disappeared, and they once again stood on the grass-infested debris of a ruined Hellios.

Slowly he lowered the terrified Clovia to the ground. Her eyes stared up at him, mutely questioning.

"What was it?" she quaked. "Why did you run so fast? What frightened you so?"

"The thing we saw in Tartarus. It — came for Dalvuus! It caught his soul — or something — in its grasp and carried him off."

Sweat was running down Niall's face. With a brawny arm he wiped it away, and then a grin rose on his face.

"He has what he wanted, that one. Now we shall take what we want."

Clovia asked, "And what is it you want, Niall?"

"Gold! Gold and jewels to see me on my way in this new world — new, at least, to me — into which I have been tossed." His arm went about her, hugging her. "Together, we can be rich, Clovia. We can hire a boat to take us to the south-land, into rich cities."

Clovia brooded. "I don't want to go."

Niall stared at her. "Not go? What will you do, then? Die here?"

Her shoulders lifted in a shrug. "It matters not to me. Hellios is dead. I might as well be dead, too."

"Nonsense. Come along! Feast your eyes on treasure and you'll change your mind."

He drew her unresisting toward the narrow stairway, relighted the torch Dalvuus had dropped, brought her with him back to the treasure chamber of the emperors and kings of Hellios. Clovia watched as Niall emptied out a section of the leather pouch he carried at his belt and began to fill it with the biggest gold coins, diamonds, rubies and pearls he could find, making his selections carefully. When his treasure pouch was full, he turned to the woman who had sat on a chest and watched him, vacantly smiling.

"Aren't you going to take anything?" he asked. "You'll need money in that world outside."

Slowly she shook her head. "I will remain here. You go, Niall — with my thanks. You helped destroy Dalvuus. You brought me here, to my birthplace. Here I shall stay, at least for a while."

He tried to argue, but she was adamant.

She walked with him to the cock-boat, watched as he tossed the anchor into the boat and then entered it himself. The wind had picked up; the sail filled rapidly.

"Come," begged Niall, making one last plea. "Come and see this world which will be new both to you and me."

Clovia only shook her head, and in that instant, Niall realized how very old she was, though her flesh was that of a mature woman only. She lifted a hand and waved it, and as she did, the breezes caught the cock-boat's sail and bore the craft out into the middle of the river.

Niall turned back once, as the wind whipped her garments about her body and she walked back to the ruins of what was mighty Hellios, long and long ago.

Niall could not see the glistening tears as they ran down her cheeks. Nor could he hear the silent sobs as they shook her body....

THE END

Thank you for purchasing Gardner Francis Fox's Sword & Sorcery classic: Niall of the Far Travels.

Find out more about Mr. Fox by visiting

GARDNERFFOX.com

Made in the
USA
Monee, IL